EVERY WICKEDNESS

CATHY VASAS-BROWN

DOUBLEDAY CANADA

Doubleday Canada and colophon are trademarks.

Canadian Cataloguing in Publication Data

Vasas-Brown, Cathy
Every wickedness

ISBN 0-385-25977-8

I. Title.

PS8593.A77E93 2001   C813'.6   C00-932795-9
PR9199.3.V37E93 2001

Jacket design by CS Richardson
Text design by Carla Kean
Printed and bound in Canada

Published in Canada by
Doubleday Canada, a division of
Random House of Canada Limited

Visit Random House of Canada Limited's website:
www.randomhouse.ca

FRI 10 9 8 7 6 5 4 3 2 1

To my wonderful husband, Al — you're simply the best.

ACKNOWLEDGEMENTS

DURING THE WRITING OF THIS book, I was bombarded with kindness. My deepest gratitude to those who helped me to realize my dream — thanks a million for being in my corner:

Lieutenant Judie Pursell, SFPD homicide, for patiently and graciously answering my many questions;

Eric Wright, mentor extraordinaire;

Nicki Bryant and David Landry, for sharing your medical expertise;

Magda Gold, Tim Simmons, Diane Kowalyshyn and Judy Malcolm, my comrades in ink;

John Pearce and Kendall Anderson, for your support, enthusiasm and encouragement;

Margaret Hart and Joe Kertes from the Humber School for Writers, for more of the same ...

... and from my soul, thank you Martin Smith, for always believing that this little engine could.

A belief in a supernatural source of evil is not necessary;
men alone are quite capable of every wickedness.

— JOSEPH CONRAD

1

THE GOODNIGHT DIED ON HER LIPS. Too quickly, the door closed with a cheap, hollow sound and she stood alone in the hallway, her Ferragamo shoes clashing with the beer-stained carpet. She inhaled musty air. Disgusted, she gave the finger to the creep on the other side of the door and hurried down the steps to the street.

A dense fog rolled along the sidewalk, curling around each lamppost and caressing her with the gentleness the schmuck upstairs hadn't bothered with. Her back ached. Her legs ached. Her crotch ached. She gulped in fresh air and looked at her watch. Shit. The last bus had already left.

The street was deserted. She turned abruptly and looked up. His light was already out. *Sleep tight, you bastard. Call me a cab? Please don't trouble yourself.* She reached into her shoulder bag for a Lucky Strike, lit it, and began to walk.

After two blocks, she weighed her choices. Walk around the park and be home at four. Go through the park and be in bed by three. Her head spun, the chemically induced fog as thick as the one rolling in from the bay.

The park it was.

Three cigarettes later, she gave the finger salute again, this time to a carload of teenage boys cruising along Martin Luther King Jr. Drive. A vagrant begged for change, and she swore at him, too.

She pitched her last cigarette butt into the dahlia bed and glanced ahead to where a wooden staircase cut its path through a cavern of dense trees and shrubbery. Not so bad, she thought, having jogged steeper than this in a daily ritual to keep her thighs and glutes bikini-perfect. She could do it.

Ignoring the tympani hammer of her heart, she began the ascent, privately cursing her high heels, her blind ambition, and her overindulgence. The autumn air had done little to clear her head. Her eyes were playing serious tricks on her, the steps weaving and pitching like some sadistic carnival ride. She stopped climbing, steadied herself against the rough bark of a tree and fought the wave of nausea rising from her stomach. Seconds or minutes later, the steps became still again, her stomach settled, and she resumed the climb.

There was a rustling, off to her left. She stopped. The rustling stopped, too. Four more cautious steps, and she heard the snapping of a twig. Any minute now there would be heavy breathing and high-pitched violins to complete the horror-movie cliché.

It's September, for chrissake. Twigs snap. Leaves rustle. It's their job description. Get a grip.

She tried to focus on the stairs ahead. Only a third of the way up. Go back? Carry on? Which? Her legs wobbled beneath her like a newborn giraffe's. Not much farther to go, she told herself, and was relieved to hear a group of late-night party animals carousing on Fulton Street. She'd be at the Arguello exit soon.

Then she tripped. Her knee hit the step, hard, and she swore aloud as she fell. Stunned, she knelt there, fingers clutching the step in front of her. She looked up. The trees overhead did a strange hula in the mist.

She blinked, ground her fists into her eyes, and the trees stopped dancing.

She felt like Dorothy in the haunted forest, as though at any moment some growly voice would bellow from one of the tree's black knotholes. But there was no voice, no pelting of apples, and judging from the quiet, the Fulton Street revelers had deserted her, too.

Her knee was tender and swollen and, for one miserable moment, she was tempted to just stay put, hunker down among the trees all night, and feel desperately sorry for herself.

Her decision was reversed by the uncanny feeling that she wasn't alone. The rustling was there again, like feet kicking dried leaves. And it was closer.

She forced herself to her feet and winced with pain. Where was the goddamn yellow brick road when you needed it?

Her mind chose the next best place to Oz. She imagined herself in Paris. On a runway. *Stand up. Shoulders back. Head high. Attitude. You're wearing Versace. You're tall. Gorgeous. Invincible. Now move, goddammit.*

Her heart jackhammered now, and she clutched her chest. She was having a heart attack — a cocaine heart attack, and she'd be found in the morning, stringy-haired, mascara-smudged, orifices full of semen, a grimace of agony frozen on her face. The final photo shoot.

She anticipated a sword of pain piercing her breast, but though she felt short of breath, there was no tightening across her chest, and as long as she could feel her heart pounding, she knew she was alive.

Cautiously, she took one step forward and planted her foot firmly on solid ground. Another step sent a shock of pain from her injured knee to her hip. Physical pain, she knew, was secondary now. She had to get out of here.

The park echoed with sound. Crackling, scraping, horrible noises, noises of shoes treading through the underbrush.

Fear drove her forward, though the more she ran the more she felt she was on one of those whirling playground contraptions, with the local bully spinning the thing too damn fast. Everything was out of control. She wanted off. Just one more careful step. The ground heaved again, and she felt herself falling. Instinctively, her hands stretched out in front. Her fingertips met cloth.

Smooth, cool cloth.

2

HE KNEW IT WAS ONLY a matter of time until she fell. She was clearly drunk, probably stoned, too, rumours being what they were, and it amused him to see her customarily confident strut reduced to a wino's shuffle.

She'd looked up at him, at first confused, then vaguely irritated, like he was some kind of buzzing insect that needed swatting. That look of hers made it easy for him to shake her groping fingers from his pant leg and kick her, just once, good and hard, in the head. She had let out a funny *oof* sound, and had been quiet since.

He'd never had to use force before. But she wasn't like the others. "I told you to get lost," she'd said once. "I don't need you."

Laughter gurgled up from his throat. As if any of this was about *her* needs.

Everything was set up. He repeated his list of things to do out loud, to make sure. Perfect.

He heard a moan from the next room. She was coming to. Let the games begin.

3

S HE WASN'T SURE WHAT HAD awakened her — the ferocious
headache about to explode inside her brain or the sound of footsteps
overhead.

There was a musty smell, not the odour of beer and marijuana this
time, but the foulness of wet earth, mildew, rot. She was indoors, but there
were no windows, and she was lying on something hard. A table? Her arms,
straight at her sides, were bound at the wrists. Her feet, too, were tied
together. Heavy tape sealed her mouth. And where were her clothes?

Christ. As if he hadn't done enough already, now he was planning
something kinky. She'd be lucky if she ever walked again. Where the hell
had he brought her? She remembered being in his apartment, but hadn't she
left? She was too strung out to recall.

That'll teach her for believing what that damn agent said. She'd fallen
for the oldest line in the book. Plum role on a new nighttime soap. Sure.
The crummy dump he lived in should have told her he had no major con-
nections to anyone in the entertainment industry.

Her mouth wiggled under the tape, and she prodded the gluey adhe-
sive with her tongue. When she got the tape off, she'd scream every loath-
some word she could think of to bring the bastard out of his hiding place.

When she realized the tape wouldn't budge, she gave up and turned her
head sideways and cast her glance toward the murky, windowless walls on

5

either side. She knew then that she wasn't strung out anymore. This was real.

Beside her was a gallery of horror, the walls adorned with unspeakable images too vivid for any nightmare. She strained against the ropes that held her, not caring if she broke her wrists trying, not caring about anything anymore except escape.

When the shadow appeared in the doorway, she began to pray, searching her memory for words from childhood, words that had no meaning then and eluded her now. She was left with incoherent ramblings that even an omniscient god wouldn't be able to decipher.

The shadow moved forward, and the face was partially illuminated in the halo of an overhead bulb. It wasn't the face she expected.

But it was a face she knew. It wore a curious smile. Iceberg eyes stared through her. When he stepped fully into the light, she saw the glint of the bulb illuminating the smooth white edge of the object he held, and suddenly the walls made sense. Dreadful, unbearable sense.

4

THE LAST TIME BETH WELLS had been inside the Fairmont was for a wedding Ginny Rizzuto had dragged her to. It seemed eerie being in the same hotel ballroom where she'd once got her feet trod on by an inept dancer, to now hear her friend Lieutenant Jim Kearns speak about death. Then, the room had been filled with Ginny's relatives dancing the tarantella — now, the rows of seats were occupied by people too frightened to venture out at night, people who wondered if they could trust their neighbours, their friends, their family.

Beth glanced at the podium. Kearns stood before a projector screen, on which were emblazoned the words:

Oro en Paz

Fierro en Guerra

Gold in peace. Iron in war. The motto of the San Francisco Police Department. The lieutenant looked as though he might not survive this particular battle. It wasn't that long ago that Kearns resembled a bouncer in a dive bar — big shoulders, big hands, big feet, and a dangerous, don't-mess-with-me face. Tonight, his pants hung low and loose. His entire body seemed to have shrunk, and his expression, instead of being darkly threatening, was somehow resigned, the facial muscles flaccid. Even his orangey-red hair seemed faded. Clearly, the Spiderman investigation was taking its toll. Public pressure to catch the killer was heavy in the air. The battalion of television cameras and microphones didn't help. From where Beth sat, Kearns appeared impaled by media technology.

The recent discovery of model Natalie Gorman, arrogantly displayed in a fountain in Levi's Plaza had made the city of San Francisco erupt with such fury that the police were holding a public forum to allay fears. Beth recalled the dozens of times she'd sat in the solarium at Il Fornaio on Battery Street, sipping a latté and gazing out at the fountain now made infamous by Natalie Gorman. The site had become a gruesome magnet, attracting scores of onlookers fascinated by the macabre, some even going so far as to step into the fountain, pants rolled up to their knees while cooperative companions took snapshots. Some of those spooky types were probably sitting nearby, hoping not for information on personal safety but more gory details of the crime.

Kearns wasn't providing any. He wasn't stupid, not by a long shot. The information he was giving to the crowd would have reached thousands more had he chosen to appear on "Devereaux Direct," but instead Kearns and some representatives from his task force were here, proving the police were accessible to the public, that they understood everyone's concerns and shared their fears.

Beth, like many in the predominantly female audience, was here to learn more about self-protection, but, though she hated to admit it, even to herself, she was intensely curious about the killer the media had christened the Spiderman.

"It's like he lures women into his web," television personality Sondra Devereaux had said after the third victim had been discovered. "A real predator."

Spiderman, Beth thought. What a clever journalistic invention. Perhaps Devereaux could still get a rebate on her college tuition. Thankfully, Jim Kearns made no mention of the silly moniker when he addressed the crowd. He maintained a professional stance and business-like tone, trying to counteract the hysteria generated by the media. He spoke calmly about pepper spray, mace, eardrum-splitting alarms, and warned about the false confidence of self-defence classes. Some women were taking notes.

Someone in the audience asked about the killer.

"He will have experienced some form of abuse during childhood," Kearns explained, "either physical, sexual, or emotional. Too, there is the homicidal triangle — arson, cruelty to animals, bed-wetting. There's frequently evidence of one or more of these in a killer's childhood. Teachers may have noticed a loner or a bully, someone who delighted in damaging someone else's possessions ..."

"Shit," whispered someone behind Beth. "I'm a teacher. He's describing half my class!"

"... some form of sexual deviance, too, a possible arrest for voyeurism, exhibitionism ..."

A sixtyish woman seated beside Beth nudged her. "A pervert in San Francisco? There's a narrow field."

Beth managed a polite smile.

"... charming, convincing," Kearns continued. "Generally, his victims went willingly. No defence wounds, indicating the killer either elicited their trust, or they were already acquainted."

Who was he, Anne? Why did you go with him?

"How old do you think this bastard is?"

Beth craned her neck to catch sight of the speaker, a husky-voiced woman seated in the second row.

"At least twenty-five," Kearns responded, adjusting the microphone slightly, "but more than likely in his thirties. He's becoming more accomplished with each crime. We think he's been fantasizing for quite a few years. Also, he seems comfortable with the city, judging by where he's left the victims' bodies."

"He dumps them like yesterday's trash," the woman beside Beth whispered.

She was right, Beth thought. That's exactly what he's doing.

The first victim, Carole Van Horne, a dancer well known to local theatre-goers, had been discovered by a hiker at the base of a steep incline on Route 1 just north of the city. Beth recalled the hiker's unfortunate quote. "Didn't know what it was at first," the newspapers had printed. "Thought it might be a pig."

Esthetician Monica Turner, the killer's second victim, was found at the bottom of the Lyon/Broadway steps in Pacific Heights. The Spiderman had gone to a lot of trouble to position the body so that it would tumble down dozens of steps.

A shaken tourist located what was left of the third victim, salesgirl Lydia Price, when he'd paid his quarter to look through the high-powered Bausch and Lomb binoculars in the circular parking lot at Coit Tower. Swivelling the viewer from the Angel Island setting to scan the flower gardens snaking up Lombard Street, he'd lost his grip, and the binoculars tilted straight down the hill to where Lydia lay, blockaded from street traffic below by a chain link fence.

And the fourth victim, Anne Spalding. How many times had that vision haunted Beth's sleep? She couldn't think about Anne now. She had to focus on the present.

"He doesn't appear to mind driving with the bodies in his vehicle," Kearns was saying, "searching for what he considers a suitable place for the bodies to be found. In fact, this particular type of killer loves to travel. He'll roam the city, frequenting places where women go, trolling for his next victim."

Beth looked around the room, in itself a great place to troll. A roomful of potential victims, women of all shapes and sizes, their palpable fear an aphrodisiac for a killer. Was he here now, enjoying his publicity, laughing at the police? She had to stop this. Lately, she was seeing the bogeyman in every parked car, behind every bush.

That was the problem, of course. With the Spiderman having achieved cult status, he seemed to be everywhere, and everyone was reporting having seen him, too. The phone at the Night Investigations Unit must be ringing off the hook.

Beth quelled a shudder, thinking of all the evening walks that she used to take, alone, to rid herself of everyday stress. It was the end of September now, her favourite time of year, but her last nighttime walk was almost a month ago. Anne's death had changed everything.

"This city will not mourn another victim," Kearns promised the audience. "We will all be more aware, be on the lookout for anything that strikes us as unusual. The person who keeps odd hours. The acquaintance who has a stash of sadistic pornography, the boyfriend who —"

"Boyfriend?" The husky-voiced woman spoke again, her tone raised to near soprano. "You mean this guy could be dating somebody?"

Kearns nodded. "It's a possibility. And he'll go to work, just like you and me, but all the while, he's a dormant Vesuvius. Then, after the explosion, he experiences a period of intense depression, when he realizes the murder he has committed can't measure up to his fantasies."

Beth shivered again. Someone right now could be having a glass of Chablis with this man. Maybe someone was picking out the perfect birthday card, telling him a dirty joke, hiring him for a job. No one existed in a vacuum. Someone must know, must sense something. Maybe even someone here. No one could be such a monster without it showing.

Beth had to believe that the Spiderman wasn't human. For what sort of human being could stand by while his victims slowly bled to death?

5

THERE WAS A SMELL IN the room he liked, a mixture of perspiration, urine, and blood, that when blended, equalled fear. He wondered if anyone else detected the scent, then thought not. He had always been acutely sensitive.

It was a singularly stupid crowd for the most part, plain people asking plainly stupid questions.

"When will the killer strike again?"

"Is the FBI involved in the investigation?"

"Do you have any leads?"

"How can we protect ourselves?"

He resisted laughing. Didn't they know there was nothing they could do? He would strike when he needed to, when he was ready, and he'd fool them all over again.

"Watch the ones you know," Kearns replied.

It was amusing, listening to the profile of the killer. Organized. That word cropped up frequently during Kearns's presentation. He liked the sound of that, because that's exactly what he was. An organized, calculating machine — well oiled, smooth running, long lasting. A real Duracell man. And, contrary to what was being said, he'd never pissed the bed in his life.

Kearns and his henchmen would be prepared, of course. They got enough of it right to predict he would be sitting here tonight, basking in his glory. He didn't bother hiding from the cameras, knowing that the jeans, T-shirt, Giants cap, and four day-old stubble altered his looks without resembling a disguise. He'd even pressed a little dirt under his fingernails. Over the next few days, when the police viewed the videotapes and analyzed the male faces in the crowd, they'd come up with nothing. No VICAP match, no adult arrest record. He'd even chosen his seat carefully — there was a single woman on his right to whom he spoke from time to time, a couple holding hands on his left. On the tape, they would look like a foursome, just two married couples who'd probably slip out for a few beers after.

He leaned toward the single woman. "My dad would say it's time to bring back the lash. Guy like this should suffer."

That was good. A little folksy, but good.

The woman nodded in agreement.

"Tell ya," he said, "this makes me wanna rush right home and hug my wife."

The woman leaned toward him. He could smell her perfume. "This makes me want to catch a plane for anywhere," she said.

"No kiddin'."

Amazing. In spite of everything they'd been told tonight, women still talked to strangers, still persisted in being friendly and polite. This one had no idea who she was dealing with.

He looked up at the podium. Kearns was dishing out more advice. "Band together. Phone someone. Let someone know you've arrived safely at your destination. The same streetproofing tips you've taught your kids will help your loved ones sleep more easily."

Then the presentation was over. Kearns looked bagged. The audience seemed to organize itself into protective clusters — those going to underground parking lots assembled in one corner, those taking the Powell cable car behind the hotel congregated at another exit, and on it went, until everyone seemed to have a partner or ten to escort them from the hotel.

Be smart. What a joke.

It made no difference. Too bad that clown Kearns couldn't understand that. It was already too late.

6

FOR SOME TIME, MANY NATIVE San Franciscans had begun to think of their city as seedy, equating its decline to the arrival of the hordes of transients seeking warmer climates and generous social assistance programs. In spite of the growing number of homeless, San Francisco was, to Beth, a transplant from Eureka Springs, Arkansas, still the most beautiful city in the world. The sight of the Golden Gate Bridge cloaked in mist still thrilled her, as it had the day she'd arrived, eight years ago.

Tonight, driving home from the Fairmont, Beth was struck by the sensation that indeed, something had changed. On Lombard, the city's motel row, the sidewalks were empty. Friday evening, and not a tourist in sight. Reflexively, she checked that her car doors were locked, then realized she'd already done so. Twice. When Beth steered onto Chestnut Street, with its generally thriving village atmosphere, she spotted a bit more life. Still, the cafés, boutiques, and two Art Deco cinemas didn't burst with the usual TGIF crowd. The deli, where Beth stopped to have a salad, was nearly empty.

It wasn't until she reached her own street in the Marina district that Beth relaxed her grip on the wheel. Her shoulders sunk back into place. The Marina was a safe neighbourhood, not like the areas south of Market that the cabbies warned the tourists away from. "Respectable," her parents had said when they'd come out for their first visit.

Beth's automatic exterior lights were on, as was a table lamp in her living room window. The alarm system, installed scarcely a month ago, provided a measure of security, though there were still the last few steps to climb at the top of the tunnel entrance that rendered Beth's front door invisible from the street. Anyone could be lurking there, waiting for her. A sub-zero shiver skimmed her spine.

She dismissed the fear with a furious shake of her head, ashamed at the hysterical thoughts she'd been having lately. Sondra Devereaux had done her job well.

Seeing her pale yellow Mediterranean house with its clay-tiled roof usually cheered her, but now the view of the blackened second-storey windows filled her with dread. Just a few short months ago she'd joked with Ginny about how ideal it was having a flight attendant for a roommate. Anne was hardly ever home.

Anne Spalding had come to San Francisco to begin a new life. She had fled from an abusive ex-husband and hoped, once the dust settled, to explore the city like a tourist. Months after her arrival, Anne was found in one of the most touristy areas, Golden Gate Park, her body having been hoisted over a railing near the Academy of Sciences, then dropped onto a path about twelve feet below. The bitter irony made Beth want to scream. Anne, who wanted to fade into the woodwork, made the front page of the *Chronicle*. FLIGHT ATTENDANT SPIDERMAN'S FOURTH VICTIM. Beth felt a lump lodge in her throat.

Anne had occupied Beth's furnished guestroom and was thrilled with it. She had brought few possessions. Her clothes, which had barely filled the closet, had been donated to charity. Beth kept the half-dozen paperback novels Anne had owned. Within days, the few tangible traces of Anne Spalding had disappeared. Beth swallowed hard, shut off the ignition, and stepped out of the car.

The wind had picked up. She had always loved the wind, preferring it and the West Coast climate to the blistering heat that rose relentlessly from Manhattan's miles of pavement. But tonight the wind whistled mournfully, adding an eerie melody to the preternatural quiet. It was as if some alien craft had descended and plucked the street's inhabitants, their radios, and televisions, from their roosts, all vanishing without a trace.

"Idiot," she said aloud, her voice sounding oddly disembodied as it was swallowed by the wind.

Everyone was inside. Everyone except Tim O'Malley. As Beth approached her front steps, Tim emerged from the house next door. Thirty-four years old, Tim was always on the go, but he still managed to find time to prune the shrubs on his lush rooftop garden. Tim moved toward his fresh-ly waxed white van, his company name, "Wearing of the Green," proudly displayed on the side. The landscape architect's well-respected name was attached to several of the city's loveliest gardens, and many overseas as well.

"Big night tonight, Tim?" Beth called out across the grassy median sep-arating her home from his.

He grinned when he saw her. "Thought I'd grab some dinner, maybe hit a few clubs later. Usual Friday night stuff. How 'bout you?"

"Something tamer. I'm exhausted."

"I watered your evergreens," he said, pointing to the pair of conical boxwoods in large terra cotta pots that flanked the entrance to her home. "Hope you don't mind. They dry out pretty fast in those containers. Oh yeah, your heartthrob's been by on his skateboard."

"Bobby? What did he want?"

Bobby Chandler was Beth's paperboy, a fourteen-year-old with a huge crush on Beth, which Tim apparently found amusing. "Probably wanted to wash your car again. Maybe walk your cat."

"Poor Bobby," Beth said. "I'm old enough to be his ... older sister. I hope you didn't tease him." Beth sized up Tim's muscular build, bright smile, and sandy blonde hair. Was it her imagination or was Tim sizing her up, too?

"Nah, but I can't figure out why you're so nice to him," Tim said. "You might be giving him ideas."

Beth shook her head. "Bobby's just lonely." Loneliness was something Tim O'Malley, with his *GQ* good looks, would probably never understand. Even back in Eureka Springs, a fourteen-year-old who still had a paper route was a geek. Beth felt sorry for Bobby, though she had to admit he'd been hanging around more often than she wanted lately.

"Speaking of lonely," Tim said, "look over there."

In-line skating his way along the sidewalk was Bobby Chandler.

7

"HEY GUYS!" BOBBY CHANDLER CALLED out as he approached. At the foot of Beth's driveway, he attempted a quick stop but failed, narrowly avoiding a collision with a NO PARKING sign.

"Bobby, when are you going to get shin guards?" Beth asked when Bobby regained equilibrium. Judging from the condition of his knees, this wasn't Bobby's first mishap.

"And a helmet," Tim O'Malley added.

Bobby ignored Tim, keeping his gaze riveted on Beth. "That equipment's for wimps. Besides, I'll have my stops down pat in a few days. Just takes practise." He flashed Beth a toothy grin. "Soon, I'll be as good on these as I am on my skateboard." Many of Bobby's weekends were spent practising skateboard stunts on the flat pavement at the Embarcadero Centre with dozens of other young teenagers who had nothing better to do.

"Hey, Beth," Bobby said, "where you been tonight?"

"Way to go, Ace," Tim muttered. "Subtle as a brick through a window."

"I was just asking," Bobby continued, his voice taking on a petulant whine, "because Beth's not usually late on Fridays. I was worried."

"That's sweet, Bobby," Beth said and meant it, though she hoped he interpreted the word "sweet" the way she'd intended it. "I was downtown, at that police information night."

"The Spiderman thing," Tim said. "I was there too, for awhile. Funny we didn't spot each other. Whole city's gone crazy. Some of my customers are buying German Shepherds. The client I called on this morning has an arsenal in every purse. Mace, beepers, nail files, you name it. Guess you must have the same stuff, Beth, after what happened to Anne."

Beth nodded. "I feel like I'm living in Fort Knox. An armed guard can't be too far off."

That was all the encouragement Bobby Chandler needed. "Don't you worry, Beth," he told her. "Soon I'll be able to chase anybody on these things." He looked at his skates again. "If that guy shows his face around here, he'll have to deal with me." Bobby teetered, then regained his balance.

"Say, Sport," Tim O'Malley said, "why don't you wheel yourself home and change modes of transportation? The Spiderman could show up at any time. Wouldn't want to see you hurt yourself."

Bobby's face went crimson. "Tim," Beth cut in quickly, "didn't you say something about a late dinner?" She knew Tim was trying to be helpful, but she couldn't conspire so obviously against Bobby. There was no crime in being lonely.

"Yeah, you're right. Can I talk you into joining me?"

Beth caught Bobby's frown. She shook her head. "I can barely make it up these stairs. You enjoy yourself."

"Always do." Tim unlocked the door to his van, climbed in, checked his appearance in the rear-view mirror, then he rolled down the window. "Remember, Beth, there's such a thing as too friendly."

"I get the message. Have fun."

"What was that about?" Bobby asked once Tim had driven away.

"Oh, Tim just wants me to be cautious," Beth lied. "We were talking about the Spiderman before you came."

Bobby skated up Beth's driveway and stood beside her. "Boy, you sure get a lotta mail."

Beth's brass mailbox was crammed, the lid wedged open with the overflow. "Bills mostly." Beth glanced through the pile, again wishing Bobby wouldn't feel quite so comfortable on her property. "Here's a coupon for Dino's pizza. Half price. Maybe you could take a girlfriend."

Bobby took the coupon. "You like pizza, Beth?"

She shook her head. "Bad for my waistline. It's been a long day, Bobby —"

"Hey Beth," Bobby cut in, "you think Tim O'Malley's good lookin'?"

The question caught her off guard, but Bobby's wide-eyed gaze made it clear he expected an answer.

"I haven't thought too much about it, but yes, I suppose. Tim is an attractive man. Now I really should —"

"If he's so good lookin', seems he should be spending more time with a girlfriend, that's all."

"How Tim spends his time is none of our business. I'm going in now, Bobby," she said firmly. "Talk to you soon, okay?"

"I'll just wait here until you're safe inside," Bobby said behind her.

Beth mounted the steps to her front door, punched in the number code, and hurried indoors. Oddly, she was glad of Bobby's presence on the driveway, though how he would have climbed the steps on roller-feet to thwart a potential intruder she didn't know.

Since Anne's death, Beth's arrival-home ritual had changed. Before, she would drop everything in the entry hall, scoop up her ginger tabby, Samson, and murmur endearments while she opened a can of kitty stew in the kitchen. Now, she kept everything in hand — purse, mail, car keys — and re-activated the alarm, peeked around the kitchen corner, opened the pantry door, checked all closets upstairs and down before returning to the kitchen where a disgruntled cat posed expectantly by his food dish. Jim Kearns had reassured her that such behaviour was normal, but he didn't tell her how long she would need this obsessive routine. Beth hoped her panic attacks would subside soon before she turned into a complete nutcase.

It was only when Beth set her stack of mail on the desk in the living room and glanced out the window that she noticed Bobby Chandler was still standing on her driveway. His unexpected appearance startled her for a moment, then she realized why Bobby hadn't left. She gave a thumbs-up signal, mouthed the words "I'm okay," waited for another toothy grin, then waved as Bobby skated off down the street toward home.

My fourteen-year-old guardian angel, Beth thought, as she drew the louvered shutters across the bottom half of her windows. Lucky me.

8

THE SIGHT OF CLEMENT STREET brought a smile to Jim Kearns's face, the first genuine smile he'd exercised in weeks. He could almost feel the burden of lives-too-abruptly-ended leave him. For what seemed like ages, he had been operating in two gears — Automatic Pilot and Pissed Off. Robotically, he had already followed up on hundreds of leads, screened calls, and chased down criminals skulking in bushes, only to turn up a string of false alarms and one very frightened skunk.

The victims' relatives, co-workers, and friends had also been interrogated, to no avail. Lydia Price's ex-boyfriends all had alibis up the wazoo; her co-workers adored her. And so it went with Carole Van Horne. No backstage jealousies, no string of broken-hearted lovers, just a nice lady who loved to sing and dance. Monica Turner's client list revealed nothing to Kearns other than, in his opinion, there were far too many men in the city who enjoyed pedicures. The scuzzball agent who screwed Natalie Gorman the night she disappeared was guilty of many things, among them possession of enough cocaine to render a football team senseless. Still, though he managed to deposit his semen in Natalie and feed her a few empty promises, he could not be connected to her murder. Anne Spalding's ex-husband, while stooping low enough to beat the shit out of the flight attendant, wouldn't, it seemed, sink to the level of killer. So the dead were of no help to Kearns. That pissed him off.

The known perverts — peepers, flashers, gropers — had been rounded up and brought in for questioning. A few, harbouring grandiose delusions, claimed to be the Spiderman, cashing in on the killer's cult status for their fifteen minutes of fame. Kearns and Manuel Fuentes fetched and carried like bellboys at the Mark Hopkins. The low-lifes got gum, water, diet soda, whatever they wanted. Short of serving caviar and Dom Perignon, the police catered to the scum, because the scum had rights. When the killer was caught, he'd be screaming about his rights, too. Another piss-off.

Plainclothes cops patrolled the killer's dumpsites, expecting him to appear like magic to reminisce about his handiwork. Gawking locals and tourists alike appeared instead, armed with cameras, wanting their pictures taken on the spot where one of the victims had been left. Serve them right if Kearns made them watch one of the autopsies. They'd puke their guts out, have nightmares for weeks. Maybe then the public wouldn't be so fascinated.

Rumours were rampant about the condition of the victims' bodies. The less-scrupulous journalists reported savage mutilations, assuming that the police force's reluctance to divulge details meant something ghastly had occurred.

And it had, but there was nothing Jack the Ripperish about it. Each victim was found fully clothed. There was no evidence of sexual penetration, no saliva, no fingerprints. But each woman's right wrist bore the killer's signature, a two-inch long testimony to the horror that had taken place.

Truth be known, his boss was pissing him off too. Until this week, Kearns thought flaring nostrils occurred only in novels, but this morning he'd seen the real thing up close and ugly, and Elliott Lloyd, the Captain of Inspectors, was cranking up the heat. Through the left side of a perpetually crooked mouth, he said, "Five women dead, Kearns."

As if he didn't know.

"Two squads working this thing. Fourteen of our best, hand-picked by you."

As if he couldn't count.

"Your annual salary is how much again?"

Not enough, Kearns thought bitterly.

Whether Lloyd had spent his youth compensating for his physical puniness, Kearns didn't know, but somewhere along the way the captain had practised the art of intimidation and had perfected a stare so icy it could freeze the devil in hell.

The Spiderman wasn't a conventional criminal, Kearns wanted to say, and no amount of conventional investigating would smoke this snake from his hole. But Lloyd was levelling another stare at him, so Kearns had remained mute.

Kearns shook off the residue of his job, parked his Crown Victoria, and made his way along the sidewalk toward his one-bedroom apartment above the Russian bakery.

Here was where real people lived. The aroma of Asian cuisine assailed his nostrils mingling with a rich tomato-basil odour from an Italian bistretto. The German deli where he bought his favourite knackwurst on a bun was closed, but the Irish pub, where he used to quaff a Harp lager (or seven), was still going strong. It paid for a cop to live in this kind of neighbourhood where he could kibitz with shop owners and customers of all kinds and colours. It helped him understand both the perpetrators as well as the victims of crime.

"Hullo, Jimmy!" Ahead, Henry Ng appeared on the sidewalk, a soiled apron around his waist. In his hand was a decapitated duck. "Graduating night school next week. You come for supper. English pretty good, yes?"

Kearns smiled. "You're a regular Richard Burton, Henry."

"I know. Focking amazing, heh? You catch spider yet?"

"Only a few under my sink, Henry," Kearns said, then crossed over to the other side of the street.

Henry hollered after him. "You catch bastard, Jimmy. I make him like this!" Henry waved the headless duck in the air.

Kearns nodded, and the crush of responsibility returned. It didn't matter that the fourteen officers on his task force were immersed in the Spiderman, inhaling the minutiae of the case files until they were crosseyed; as long as the madman was loose, it was Kearns's ass on the line.

He remembered his earlier promise that the public would have no more deaths to mourn. Yet he knew, deep down, that for him to catch the lunatic's scent, another murder was exactly what he needed.

Inside his apartment, he called out, "I'm home, Mary," and untied his shoes, leaving them, as always, heels to the baseboard, in the hallway. It had always been one of the things they chuckled about — why he would insist on lining his shoes up like twin soldiers, when there was a perfectly decent closet not two feet away.

He wiggled his toes, sure his swollen feet would never fit inside shoes again. The TV came on next, as always. He didn't care much what was on. The company of human voices, no matter how inane the chatter, dissipated the funereal quiet of the apartment.

He checked his voice mail. His therapist had been playing phone tag with him all week, and this was her third attempt to get him an appointment. He erased her message and shuddered to think what would happen if his visits to a shrink became known by his squad. For all his pontificating about coming clean with feelings and encouraging his men to communicate, Kearns knew he couldn't do the same. He was a bald-faced hypocrite, plain and simple, but a cop who took antidepressants and participated in therapy sessions also became a full-fledged member of the Rubber Gun Squad, complete with accompanying whispers and a quiet desk job. Until Kearns's superiors got in step with the times, he was safer locking his blues in the closet.

Kearns got organized — bottle of ginger ale, remote control, and a bag of pretzels on the end table beside his chair, his daily dose of Paxil from the bathroom, the video taken at the Fairmont popped into the VCR. Once he sunk into his favourite chair, he knew it would be game over. Probably fall asleep there, like most nights, fully clothed. Mary had been gone five years now, and it was still a toss-up as to what was worse — sleeping alone or eating breakfast alone.

Exhaustion had burrowed through to his bones, that awful whacked-out, rag-doll feeling brought on by his medication and the depression that crouched in wait for him.

The naugahyde recliner squeaked when he settled into it. The ginger ale didn't fizz. The video made him more miserable, with its sea of anonymous faces staring at him, counting on him to bring in the killer. And was he among those faces, the lunatic who preyed on the vulnerable? If he was, Kearns couldn't tell. The video camera wasn't likely to catch a fleeting glimpse of some Manson lookalike, with a big red X on his forehead.

He wanted others to stop calling the killer a monster, stop making him larger than life. Kearns loathed the name Devereaux had invented. Spiderman, to Kearns, endowed the killer with animal powers, a super-human ability to entice prey, mutilate, then skitter away. Devereaux wasn't the only one who had christened the killer. A journalist from the *San Francisco Independent* referred to him as a homicide machine, citing the coldly mechanical way in which he entrapped his victims, subjected them to days of terror, then tossed them away like a used Q-Tip.

Kearns was adamant that no special title be bestowed upon the killer. He rejected the beast/machine analogies and ordered his task force never to use the name "Spiderman" in conversation or in print. People still wanted, even needed, to trust one another. This desire to believe in the goodness of other humans had once spawned the birth of vampire and werewolf legends. To savage a body for the sheer pleasure of it could not be the work of an ordinary mortal.

But this killer was human. Nothing more. He stood in line at the Safeway, paid his hydro bill, got holes in his socks just like everybody else. He probably owned a microwave. His shit stank. He looked like your brother, your nephew, your uncle. Because he was a human being, he could be caught by a human being. It wouldn't take a superhero to cut him down. Kearns, a member of his task force, or some blue-haired lady from Fresno would be in the right place at the right time and *adios, araña*.

Kearns clung hard to that belief. As long as the killer was on equal footing with Kearns and his team, there was hope. Without that belief, all the Paxil in the world wouldn't be able to pull Kearns from the murky pit that beckoned to him.

He was rewinding the tape, intending to watch it again to see if he'd missed anything, when the phone rang.

"Jim? Can you come? I've got another one."

9

ONE COUPON OFFERED FREE LEG waxing with the purchase of a
facial, pedicure, and manicure. Another advertised a one-time-only
deal on cleaning broadloom — three rooms for $59.99. A dubious envi-
ronmental group begged for donations. It was innocuous junk mail, yet
when Jim Kearns rifled through the stack, he felt as though he'd just discovered Beth Wells's underwear drawer. At the bottom of the pile was the
plain white envelope — no return address, just her name typewritten on
the front. Inside, the message was simple, direct.

I'M WATCHING YOU BITCH.

Beneath it was a crude drawing of a spider.

Kearns set the pile on Beth's kitchen counter. "I know what you're
thinking," he said. "That the killer wrote this."

"Can you blame me, Jim? Once, I can pass off as a practical joke, but
twice? This isn't funny."

"No. You're right."

Together, they carried a coffeepot, a pair of mugs, and a plate of oat-
meal cookies into the living room. Kearns sunk into the downy cushions of
a chintz-covered loveseat and surveyed the room. Every lamp glowed. Even
a small accent lamp on the antique desk in the corner contributed its forty
watts' worth, as did a pair of brass sconces flanking a painting over the
mantel. This woman didn't want any shadows in the corners.

At one o'clock in the morning, without makeup, Beth Wells still looked gorgeous. In any light. Her long dark hair, still damp from the shower, was clasped in an upsweep. Tiny tendrils framed her face. She sat beside him, poured decaf, then tucked her feet under her.

Her first letter had come a week ago, exactly one month after Anne's body had been discovered. THE KISS OF THE SPIDERMAN, it had read. Kearns had understood her concern, made note of the incident, but reassured Beth by saying it was some crackpot looking for a quick bit of excitement. Still, it had shaken her up, and when he gave her his home phone number, she seemed to feel better. "Watch the ones you know," he had told her at the time. It was the same advice he'd given to his audience at the Fairmont earlier this evening.

Beth Wells was right. Twice wasn't funny, and he knew the minute he'd received her call he had to come over. The night he'd told her Anne Spalding's body had been found was, perversely, the night he and Beth had somehow become friends. She had wanted to help, had searched her memory for any worthwhile scrap of information about Anne, but in the end, there was nothing. She felt guilty for not knowing her roommate better. And she was afraid. Now here, in her own home, she was scared shitless all over again, but in spite of that, she was still acting the part of hostess. She nudged the plate of cookies toward him.

"Tell me about the evening, how you came across the note," Kearns said, helping himself to a cookie.

"I'd been at the Fairmont," she began. "You were great, by the way. Came home, talked to the neighbours, grabbed the mail, and came inside. I didn't think about the mail again until half an hour ago."

"What made you remember?"

"The usual. I couldn't sleep, so I figured a good thick book might do the trick. That's when I thought about the mail. I belong to a book club and thought the new listings might have arrived." She sipped her coffee. "Jim, I really hesitated calling. I saw how exhausted you looked earlier. But I was ready to jump out of my skin."

Jim Kearns noticed the tremor in Beth's hands as she gripped her ironstone mug. "Once you read the note, what did you do?"

She flushed. "What any hysterical female would do. Turned on all the lights, checked under the bed. Tried to pretend the note didn't matter. I looked out at the street too, through the slats in the shutters. There wasn't anyone there, of course — no scar-faced villain standing under the lamp-post — yet I felt I was being watched."

"Just what the bastard wants you to feel." Kearns gulped the coffee, allowed Beth to refill his mug, and wished for a snifter of Napoleon brandy. "It's not the killer, Beth."

"How can you be so sure? The spiders —"

Kearns shook his head. "The other victims didn't receive notes. Our man charms 'em, he doesn't scare 'em off. He'd want to savour the fear first-hand. It's part of the ritual high. If he was writing letters, he'd want to see you open the envelope."

"Maybe he's changed strategies to throw you off."

Kearns smiled. The glut of fiction about serial killers made everyone an armchair detective. Beth's pained expression made him lose his grin. He didn't want her to think he was laughing at her. The last thing she needed now was a patronizing cop.

"I'd say the killer's current strategy is working just fine. We're no closer to the bastard than we were months ago."

"I thought you said you were working on several leads."

"Sure. All five thousand of them. All dead ends. Let's see, there was Carl from Cucamonga who has a friend whose cousin has a collection of dead spiders mounted on pins in a trophy case. There was Peter from South Pisspot who, neighbours say, has a penchant for women's shoes. And I can't forget Glen from Gonadsville, Bob from Barfdom, Damian from Dick City ... you get the picture?"

Beth nodded. "I guess if we all started looking around, we'd discover a lot of weirdos."

"And if we started locking 'em up, there wouldn't be a soul left walking around. Myself included. This case is making me as nutty as everybody else."

"Still, Jim, all the drudgery has to be paying off. Look at all the people you can cross off your list of suspects."

"Nice try, Beth, and it's not that I don't appreciate your enthusiasm, but this wouldn't be the first time a suspect got crossed off when he should have stayed on. For all we know, our man could be Peter from Cucamonga."

"Pisspot."

"Huh?"

"Pisspot. Peter was from Pisspot. South, I believe. Carl was from Cucamonga." She smiled.

"No one can fault your listening skills, that's for sure." He helped himself to another cookie. "But these stranger crimes are a bitch. We feel like we're running in circles. Just once, I'd like to pull my tail out from between my legs so I can see it better when I chase it."

He was glad she was gracious enough not to laugh.

"Jim, I'm sorry. This must be terrible for you. The pressure, I mean."

A faint trace of her shampoo, a sweet apricot scent, drifted toward him. He inhaled deeply.

"Yeah," he sighed, "between the crap in the papers, my boss, and the mayor on my back, I'm skewered. And don't even talk to me about that bitch, Sondra Devereaux. She wants my balls for shish kebab." Kearns cleared his throat. "Pardon me."

"Any idea why she's being so hard on you?"

He shrugged. "At first I thought it was all about ratings. Now, I think Devereaux's got some kind of hate-on for the police. Everybody needs somebody to talk to, I wonder who Devereaux tells her troubles to? And by the way, when did this turn into my therapy session?"

"You just said everyone needs someone to talk to, Jim. And you're entitled to feel a little sorry for yourself."

"Whenever I do too much of that, I think of the victims, their families, what that madman has put them through. With Devereaux perpetuating the Spiderman mystique, giving the guy the identity he craves — well, it pisses me right off. Under Devereaux's hornet's nest of a hairdo lurks the brain of a flea." He drained his second mug of coffee, then grinned. "We were supposed to be discussing your letters. Put your fear aside for moment and forget about the Spiderman signature. Someone sends you anonymous notes. What kind of person comes to mind? You meet all sorts of people in your line of work. Think."

Beth pressed an index finger to her lips and Kearns waited.
Finally she spoke. "A coward. An immature coward."
"Exactly."

10

PERSONAL TOUCH INTERIORS ON SACRAMENTO was immediately recognizable by its crisp green-and-white striped awning. Brain-weary though she was this morning, Beth still felt a rush of pride at the sight of her shop. During the seven years Beth had been open for business, Personal Touch had been transformed from quaint and casual to citified chic. Now, the affluent clientele streamed in steadily, and Beth's reputation as one of the area's most innovative designers was sealed. Thankful for her good fortune, Beth turned the key in the lock and stepped inside.

As she did so, she heard a crunch. Looking down, she saw a white envelope, the front of it now marred by her dirty shoeprint. For a moment, her stomach knotted, and she remembered the last white envelope she had opened not so long ago. Then she relaxed. The word LANDLORD was scrawled across the front.

Rex McKenna, the insurance agent who leased the office upstairs, had come through with October's rent. And on time for a change. Beth stooped, retrieved the envelope, then closed the shop door behind her.

She scrutinized the cheque's date, the signature, the amount. It wouldn't be the first time Rex had fouled something up, forcing her to chase him down. Satisfied that everything was in order, Beth put the cheque in her purse and resolved to deposit it in a bank machine before meeting Ginny for supper.

In less than an hour, customers would begin their Saturday browsing routine along the stretch between Spruce and Divisadero, and Beth would be ready. Quickly, she grabbed a watering can from the storage area at the rear of her shop, filled it, then returned to the front sidewalk. She gave the brilliant red geraniums blooming in huge cast-iron urns a good soaking and pinched off the dead flowers. When she looked up, she was surprised to see Rex McKenna making his way along the sidewalk.

"Working on Saturday, Rex?" she called out in her friendliest tone. She didn't like the man but still believed in the sugar-versus-vinegar philosophy.

"Hardly," he grunted, brushing by her. "Just came for a few papers."

Usually, Rex wore one of two checked suits, but today he was clad in lime green slacks, a plaid shirt, orange windbreaker, white belt, and shoes. Beth blinked as Rex made his way up the stairs to his office. Too soon, he was back, as surly as ever. "See you haven't fixed that ceiling fan yet. Gets hotter 'n hell up there. Seems for what I pay in rent —"

"You're right, Rex," Beth said quickly. "I'll have someone come out early next week."

A rusty Honda Civic pulled alongside the curb. "For chrissakes, Rex! Hurry the hell up. We tee off in twenty minutes. Maybe you can charm your landlord some other time, huh, Tarzan?"

Ida McKenna tapped on the steering wheel. Permed blonde hair sprouted from beneath a fuchsia sun visor. If ever two people deserved each other, Beth thought. Her father would say that at least they weren't spoiling two marriages.

Meekly, Rex approached the car, and Beth detected a slight limp as he walked. Rex would need an electric cart if he hoped to play a full eighteen today, she thought, and returned inside.

Beth frowned inwardly at the arrival of her first customer, Horace Furwell, who had a specific design project in mind. He wanted his condominium to be transformed into a replica of a bordello he'd frequented in France during the war, complete with red velvet bedcovers, black fringed lamps, and gilt-framed mirrors. Beth had politely turned down the project before and would be firmer in her refusal this time. Though she was able to efficiently eject Furwell from her showroom, the image of the

31

grandfatherly type with the St. Nicholas face stayed with her long after he'd gone. Hardly the sort Beth would have guessed to have such bacchanalian tastes, but then, most people had secrets.

The rest of Beth's day passed quickly. In fact she was too busy to realize just how tired she was, but at five thirty when she tallied up her sales — one inlaid butler's table, a pair of porcelain lamps, two fireside chairs, and two sofas on order — she realized there wasn't a muscle group in her body that didn't ache.

She longed to cancel her dinner plans with Ginny but knew there was no way to reach her by phone. Ginny had been giving violin lessons all day, and right now was seated amid the congregation of Saints Peter and Paul attending 5:30 Mass.

Beth tried to look on the bright side, imagined thirty blissful minutes alone sipping a mineral water in the North Beach, then she remembered Rex's ceiling fan. Not wanting to face another complaint on Tuesday morning, Beth locked her shop and trudged miserably up the stairs to Rex's office.

When she opened the door, she didn't know whether to scream or throw something. Even in the fading light, Beth knew she had entered Rod Serling territory, a place vaguely familiar yet unshakably surreal. The office, which she'd painstakingly decorated, was a dump.

In spite of her rising anger, she flicked on the light switch. Overhead, the ceiling fan remained still, though had it whirred on full blast, it wouldn't have made any difference. Cigar smoke clung to everything. Ashtrays overflowed with stubby butts. The micro blinds Beth had installed were a mess, some of the slats bent, others missing altogether. The hard-wearing wool carpet would need replacing, the blue tweed mottled with stains and burns.

Bastard, Beth muttered. She was damned if she would replace the carpet only to have Rex burn holes in a new one. His lease was up in nine months, and then she'd kick him out, rip up the carpet, sand the hardwood floors underneath, and turn the office into her sample room. She no longer needed Rex's rent to stay afloat. And when he showed up for work next week, she'd tell him to buy an oscillating fan. The ceiling fixture would remain broken.

If he showed up for work. Beth hadn't seen much of Rex this past week, and the few times he'd passed through their common front entrance, he hadn't stayed the whole day. No wonder. With the office looking the way it did, it was impossible to imagine even the most loyal client sitting across from Rex, allowing himself to be bamboozled into buying more insurance. Client? Beth hadn't seen many of those lately either. If new clients weren't signing on, how long before U.S.S. *McKenna* sank? Along with the stench of cigars, Beth smelled bankruptcy.

Nine months. Beth was reminded of women in their final stages of pregnancy — simply wanting the ordeal over with. Nine more months with Rex. Beth contemplated abortion. The sooner she could kick Rex's polyester ass down the stairs, the better.

Beth moved to the casement windows, unlatched each, and lifted them open. Fresh air entered the office for what must have been the first time in weeks. Already she planned how she would divide the space when she moved her samples upstairs — fabrics hanging from chrome hooks along the wall to her right, carpet squares to her left, wallpaper books arranged in a divided Arborite counter beneath the windows, a coffee maker on top. In the centre of the room, four comfortable chairs and a large table where her clients could browse through suppliers' catalogues ...

Her daydream was interrupted by an insistent drip from the adjoining two-piece bathroom. A leaky faucet. Rex would complain about that next, she knew, so Beth moved toward the sound. If the appearance of the front office was a shock, it did little to prepare Beth for the sight in Rex's bathroom.

Every square inch of wall, from floor to ceiling, was papered with pictorial layouts of women. All were nude or semi-nude, but the pictures went beyond erotica. The women's poses were contorted, painful to behold, backs arched, necks twisted. Many were bound — to trees, flagpoles, railway tracks. Several were gagged, mouths held shut with every imaginable ligature. One woman's scream was silenced by a golf ball wedged between her teeth.

And there were hundreds of them, on the wall behind the toilet, above and below the sink, covering the tiny window facing the rear parking lot.

Rex even had one taped to the shaving mirror. The photograph showed a supine woman, clothing strategically torn. Pressing down on her throat was a man's steel-toed boot. Was this Rex's favourite? Did the mirror serve as a changeable display space, like a Baskin-Robbins flavour of the month?

Sickened, Beth yanked the picture from the mirror, crumpled it, threw it into the garbage can and left, the faucet still dripping.

11

SENIOR INSPECTOR MANUEL FUENTES WALKED into Jim Kearns's office and closed the door. Kearns recognized when Manny was trying to pussyfoot around, and this was one of those times. There was a cushiony quality to his walk, and a tentativeness when he poked his head into Kearns's doorway, the caution of a man who'd been shot at too many times. Kearns set a half-eaten salami sandwich on top of his in-basket.

"Juicy Fruit?" Fuentes asked. "Hey, weren't you supposed to have today off?"

Kearns declined the gum offer. "Spiders on the brain," Kearns replied. "Thought I'd paddle through the quagmire awhile."

The truth of it was that Kearns spent every day and quite a few nights at his desk, finding solace in work, which had become his replacement for alcohol. Away from his apartment, he couldn't notice the infernal silence, the empty echo of his footsteps on the linoleum. Fuentes knew it too, and Kearns appreciated the discretion his trusted friend used in not saying so.

The surface of Kearns's desk was invisible, papers strewn everywhere. Files were stacked on the floor, miniature leaning towers of folders that a good sneeze would topple. Fuentes dragged a moulded plastic chair across a clear path and sat down. Kearns waited for him to adopt his usual posture, feet up on Kearns's desk, but instead Fuentes kept his feet planted on the floor.

"What's that?" Kearns asked, pointing to a video cassette in Fuentes's hand. "Dirty movie for you and the wife?"

"Yeah, real filth. You making a dent in this stuff?"

"Uh-uh. Just pushing it around. What's the film?"

"I told you. One hot dame on here," Fuentes said, holding up the video. "Bushy blonde hair, nails scratch your back like a rake —"

"Say it isn't so," Kearns groaned. "Devereaux?"

"This morning's broadcast. Wanna watch some TV?"

"Why not? I've got no appetite anyway." Kearns tossed the remains of his sandwich in the wastepaper basket, then he rose and followed Fuentes to the outer office, a noisy, spiritless space crammed with desks of various sizes, some metal, some wood. Every other desk had a laptop connected to the main computer. A few of the inspectors hadn't bothered trying to personalize their workspace, but other desks were laden with framed photos of family members and assorted dogs, cats, and ferrets. Small reminders that there was indeed life outside this windowless place.

In the far corner, a television and VCR rested on a rolling cart. Kearns nudged a "Fabulous at Forty" coffee mug out of the way with his rear end, then he perched on the edge of an unoccupied desk. Fuentes popped the video into the VCR.

Moments later, the discordant jazz theme to "Devereaux Direct" whined through the speakers of an eighteen-inch TV.

"Needs a new song, right Jimmy?"

"New face, more like it."

"Save some of that anger for the end of the show. You're gonna need a hole in your head to let the steam out."

Devereaux, on camera now, looked ready for battle. Her eyes, heavy under the weight of eyeliner, still managed to bore into Kearns. "Wimps!" she shrieked, then plunked herself into a tub chair. "A murderer has been running loose in the city for months and women are supposed to play nice, travel in pairs, and treat our loved ones like suspects until this lunatic is caught? The police are twiddling their thumbs while women get carved up."

"Shit," Kearns moaned.

"Hey, she could have said we've got our thumbs up our asses."

"I gave that up years ago."

"Listen. It gets better." Fuentes cranked up the volume.

Devereaux went on to interview three women, each confessing their fear of going out at night.

"My social life is ruined," complained one.

"I've gone right off men," said another.

"Damn," Kearns said. "And she was my type too."

"Why aren't the cops patrolling the streets?" ventured the third television guest, a fortyish woman with salon-streaked hair.

Kearns shook his head. Papering an area blue didn't work. When uniformed officers walked the beat, the crime simply moved to another location.

"You're right, ladies," Devereaux said. "Give us the streets, walk the beat," she chanted, pointing a taloned finger. "Don't be slobs, do your jobs."

"Who's she calling a slob?" Kearns scoffed, patting a firm stomach. "Why doesn't the Spiderman do us all a favour? The only good Devereaux is a dead Devereaux. We don't need that overstuffed sausage casing adding more coal to the furnace."

"Yeah, who do you want to be? Shadrach, Meshach or Abednego?"

"Groucho," Kearns responded. "Oops. Different trio."

Fuentes nodded. "Every vigilante will be on her high horse. The gun shops will love this."

Devereaux was wound up now. The three women had served their purpose and were thanked perfunctorily for their time, then escorted from the stage. Devereaux would solo.

"The Spiderman's victims have all been hard-working, respectable women," Devereaux stated. "That, at least, should give this manhunt some impetus. This city doesn't need some religious version of the Zodiac Killer —"

"What the hell?" Kearns shouted. "Where'd she get that?"

"Thought that would get you," Fuentes said.

The Zodiac Killer had murdered several people in the San Francisco area during the late sixties. He taunted the authorities with cryptic letters and used a cross within a circle as his trademark. After a few months, the murders abruptly ceased, and no one was apprehended. Police, Kearns recalled, suspected the killer had been caught for another unrelated crime and incarcerated, or had been confined to a mental institution. Kearns found neither explanation acceptable. He hoped the bastard had killed himself.

The public was aware that the Spiderman bled his victims to death. The process had been helped along by massive doses of blood thinners administered to the victims during their captivity. The fact that he performed ritual carvings, though, had been a carefully guarded secret until now. But only Kearns and his task force knew that, like the Zodiac Killer, the Spiderman had adopted his own symbol: a Christogram, an elongated printed P with an X through the stem. The stem, the killer's first cut, was the fatal one. It ran vertically along the radial artery, sending blood pulsing from the victim's body with every remaining heartbeat. By the time the mutilation was complete, the killer would have been bathed in blood, the murder scene a scarlet swimming pool.

Fuentes, a devout Catholic, had explained the Christogram to Kearns after the first victim had been discovered. Christograms, he said, were symbols composed of two or more letters, often interwoven with other symbols like laurel wreaths. They were intended to represent God or the Trinity. The ☧, or Chi Rho monogram, combined the first two letters of the Greek word for Christ; together they resembled a cross. Others interpreted the P and X as a shortened form of the Latin word "pax" meaning "peace." Whatever the killer intended by carving the Christogram on his victims' wrists, peace had nothing to do with it. The killer had some knowledge of organized religion, could even be an ex-priest or seminarian.

And somehow Devereaux knew it too.

"Wonder who Devereaux slept with to acquire that hot tip?" Kearns said. "Someone's gonna fry for this."

Devereaux went on to say that the people of San Francisco could not afford to wait for some damning piece of lint to show up linking the serial killer to his victims, then mercifully, the jazz theme played, and Fuentes began to rewind tape.

Right now, Kearns thought, he would be grateful for a piece of lint.

Lint, with some incriminating hair and fibre, had been enough to capture Atlanta child killer Wayne Williams. But Kearns and crew had squat. No fingerprints, no saliva, no metal shavings from whatever the women were cut with. His task force swarmed the knife shops; a few keeners researched the history of whaling and told Kearns about the bone knives used by the Inuit. A knife expert from the San Juan Islands was flown in. Now Kearns had information galore about knives, their blades, and which edge produced which cut. All well and good, if only the killer's hand were at the other end.

Serial killer, Kearns thought, hating the phrase that had become a cliché. He and his task force had tried in vain to conceal the probability that a serial murderer was what they were dealing with, knowing there was a fine line between caution and panic, but moments after the killer's second victim had been found, the press flew to their word processors. The Spiderman had left his signature and demanded serial-killer notoriety, which the press gave him. In the years to come, women would mail him their underwear, propose marriage, and the inevitable books would be written. Spiderman history. His brain would be x-rayed, his childhood examined. Schoolmates would be interviewed, teachers probed for their recollections. No one would remember the names of the victims — Carole Van Horne, Monica Turner, Lydia Price, Anne Spalding, Natalie Gorman. Devereaux hadn't mentioned them once during her television show. No one could compensate the families, understand the torture they endured when journalists invaded the bedrooms where the victims had once played with dolls, written in diaries, dreamed about their futures.

Kearns knew that the profile they'd put together on the Spiderman applied to every deviant walking. The information he had recited at the Fairmont was nothing more than Serial Killer 101. Anyone who read current crime fiction or watched TV docudramas already knew the profile. Besides, profiles had been wrong before. There'd been that case up in Canada, where the FBI had concluded that the murderer of two teenagers was a manual labourer. Son of a bitch turned out to be an accountant. Couldn't be more far off than that.

An astrologer from Mill Valley postulated the Spiderman to be a

Capricorn, a hyper-organizer with a strong need for control, a man not crippled by fear; he would lack buoyancy but struggle to project a normal facade. He could be compensating for an absentee father.

A psychologist specializing in Adlerian birth order professed the killer to be the oldest in a family, dethroned from his favoured position by the birth of siblings, admiring power and striving to regain it.

They could both be right. Or nuts. Either way, the field was still too broad, and they weren't even within sniffing range. Neither the press nor the public would let up.

The click of the VCR brought Kearns back to reality. He turned to Fuentes. "We need a suspect."

"We need the Spiderman," Fuentes emphasized, then realized his slip in using the name.

"Oh, sure. Be greedy. Until this creature decides to walk in here on cloven hoof, a suspect will do nicely. At least it might keep the bloodhounds off our backs."

Back in his office, Kearns retrieved the salami sandwich from his wastebasket, blew some pencil shavings off the kaiser roll, and polished off the remains in three bites.

12

THE TWIN SPIRES OF SAINTS Peter and Paul impaled the sky over North Beach. As Beth passed in front of the Romanesque church, she took in the details of the architecture. She had been inside once, nearly a year ago with Ginny, and remembered the ornate altar inlaid with mosaic and framed in white Carrara marble. The peacefulness she had expected from a place of worship had been conspicuously absent as parishioners crammed the pews, greeting each other in Italian or Chinese. Tourists had stood at the back of the church, coming and going as they pleased, according as much reverence to the Mass as an excursion to Disneyland. A visiting missionary delivered a twenty-five-minute homily about the evils of materialistic society, and concluded with a plea for generous donations to his outreach program. Beth hadn't returned to Saints Peter and Paul or any other church.

She paused before one of the newsstands on Washington Square, paid for a *Chronicle* and *New York Times*, then pushed open the lower half of the Dutch door to Mama's Girl and went inside. From her table by the window, she could watch a cluster of Italian men playing *bocce* in the park across the street as a handful of Asians practised Tai Chi nearby. From this vantage point too, Beth could flag down Ginny coming out of Mass — Saints Peter and Paul was right next door.

She ordered an Evian and unfolded the *Chronicle*. Pictures of the

Spiderman's victims were plastered on the front page beneath the headline SPIDERMAN SNARES MODEL. Sardonically, Beth supposed Devereaux ought to be congratulated for her journalist coup. Everyone was using the arachnid metaphor. Everyone except Jim Kearns. Beth understood Kearns's feelings about Devereaux and shared them. The woman's job title was tough to pin down — not quite journalist, nor solely a morning-show host but a curious combination of both. Beth supposed Devereaux would be pleased with being labelled a Media Personality. Her television show, "Devereaux Direct," aired each morning; she wrote a weekly newspaper column bearing the same title, and occasionally, her strident voice could be heard from some local radio station, shrieking about some Important Issue. These days, it didn't seem to matter what switch you flipped or what page you turned to — there was Devereaux. Beth couldn't understand why San Franciscans even cared what the woman had to say.

But they did care. That was the problem. And right now, Devereaux had more credibility than the police.

Today's editorial slammed Kearns's forum, citing it as a feeble attempt to appease frightened citizens while telling them nothing new. By the third paragraph, Beth had the gist of the piece, and she flipped back to the front page.

With a mixture of fascination and revulsion, Beth read the *Chronicle*'s latest instalment about the killer and his victims. Natalie Gorman's photo was, to Beth's mind, inappropriate and sensationalistic: in it, Natalie wore a black lace bustier, her claim to fame as a Victoria's Secret lingerie model. The news article included a map of the city, with bright green arrows pointing to the locations where each victim had been found. Anne Spalding, like the others, had been reduced to a jumble of words and a diagram. Beth read and reread the article, hoping to learn more about the woman that she hadn't taken the time to know.

Beth became so engrossed in the summary of the murders and the lives of the victims that she was unaware of the passage of time. Her rumbling stomach and the appearance of the waiter offering another mineral water brought her back to reality. It was six-thirty. Beth accepted the drink, thinking Ginny should be along any second.

A few people meandered along the sidewalk, Ginny not among them.

Beth wasn't particularly surprised — Ginny was frequently late. In the past, she'd run the gamut of excuses.

"There was this great vintage clothing shop on the Haight, Beth. Had to stop."

"Mama needed help rolling lasagna dough. How could I turn down my mother?"

"I just started my period. No lectures about being late, okay?"

Beth had heard them all, some of them twice, so she was certain Ginny would concoct some intriguing tale this time. Perhaps she'd been overcome by a need to make her confession and was whispering a list of venial sins to a priest right this moment. Quickly, she dismissed this notion. It was far more likely that Ginny was grilling the priest about his single male relatives. Though Beth's friend might be infuriating, she was never dull.

At six forty-five, Beth ordered a fruit salad. By 7:10, she was worried enough to consider going next door to explore the church, pew by pew.

Just then she spotted her, a flurry of colour carrying a violin case across Washington Square. Ginny's diminutive height didn't get her noticed in a crowd, so she made damn sure she got herself noticed. She clad herself in anything that was a direct assault on symphony black and white. Today's ensemble was a caftan, its spectrum of colour reminding Beth of a jungle parrot. She breezed into the restaurant, then plunked onto the bleached wooden chair opposite Beth.

"Oh-oh," Ginny said, adjusting her tie-dyed outfit. "You're not happy. You know tardiness is part of my appeal, Beth." An oversized raffia shoulder bag and the violin case thudded onto the floor. Ginny, resembling a reincarnation of Mama Cass, propped her granny glasses on top of her head.

"And you're in too good a mood," Beth countered, "so it's obviously not your period this time. For God's sake, where were you?"

"Confession?"

"Try again. I saw you running across the square."

"Okay, there was this really cute guy sitting beside me at Mass — the Saturday night Masses get all the single people — so after the recessional hymn, I followed him."

"You what?" Beth had long since gotten used to Ginny's unpredictability, but this bordered on lunacy.

"All the way down to Duds and Suds on Columbus." Duds and Suds was a combination café cum laundromat where singles congregated. "I have to strike while my iron's still plugged in. Ya gotta love a guy who comes for a dose of religion between loads of wash."

"Irresistible. Let me see if I've got this straight. You kept me waiting here for over half an hour while you chased some stranger through North Beach?"

"Not an ordinary stranger, Beth. He could have been The One."

"Ginny," Beth sighed, "to you, any man who owns a Gillette razor could be The One. What happened?"

"His roommate was already folding the whites by the time I got there. Why are all the cute ones gay? Oh, well. Did you eat?"

Beth nodded. "Fruit salad."

"That all?" Ginny signalled the waiter, flashed him a wide smile, then ordered the black bean soup and the pasta of the day.

"Why the violin?" Beth asked when Ginny had finished ordering.

"Practising with Dieter tonight. You remember, the cellist I played the duet with in the West Marin Festival? Maybe later he'll pluck my strings."

The waiter set a basket of bread on the table. Ginny tore into a slice.

"Ginny, you've got to be careful," Beth cautioned.

"Why? These pesky extra pounds are here to stay."

"No. I mean, you can't go following strange men, especially now. And what about this Dieter?"

"Hey, why not? Nice Catholic boy, a musician. He could be a contenda."

Beth thrust the *Chronicle* in front of Ginny. "Virginia Rizzuto, get serious. Look."

"You flatter me, Beth. Those women are gorgeous."

"Those women are *dead*. I don't relish the thought of seeing your photograph in the *Chronicle* alongside theirs, Gin."

Ginny glanced at the photos, her gaze lingering on Natalie Gorman. "Well, I wouldn't be in my underwear, that's for sure. Mama would have a stroke."

"Gin —"

"Come on, Beth. Lighten up." The waiter returned with Ginny's soup and set it on the table. "This city's always been home to society's fringe

groups. The Symbionese Liberation Army, Jim Jones's People's Temple —
now we've got the Spiderman."

"You're minimizing the danger, Gin."

"And you're exaggerating it because of Anne," Ginny said, raising her
voice. "Beth, we've had this conversation before. I'm not about to change
my lifestyle because of the Spiderman. I know about bad people doing bad
things. I'm sorry about Anne, and I'm sorry about Natalie Gorman, too,
but face it, she was stupid to cross that park at night. Any tourist guide will
advise you to stick to the main roads. But the odds of the Spiderman
harming me are slim."

"Still, Gin, you don't have to go tipping the scale by following
some stranger."

"The Spiderman won't get me, Beth. I'm not his type. You, on the
other hand ..."

"What do you mean?"

Ginny chomped the pointed end of a crusty roll. "Sometimes," she
said between chews, "you're too polite for your own good. Guy stands on
your doorstep with a set of ten-year-old encyclopedias, and you'd let him
in because it's cold outside."

"I would not."

"Beg your pardon? How many times has that McKenna character
screwed you around with the rent?" Ginny paused, and when Beth didn't
answer, she said, "See? What did I tell you? Good manners are for family
and close friends."

"Thanks, Ginny. I feel much better."

"Listen, just take some of your own advice. Be careful."

"Anne was careful. He got her anyway."

"I know," Ginny's voice softened, "but she wasn't abducted from anywhere near your house, and she wasn't killed there, either. You've got to let
it go, Beth. Don't give this stranger so much power over you."

Beth nodded, not so much in agreement, but more to signal the end of
the conversation. She let Ginny eat her soup in peace.

Had she been obsessing about this killer? Since Anne Spalding's
death, Beth had thought of little else. She wondered where Anne had

met the killer, and why, after fleeing from a husband who had beaten her senseless, she would trust another man so soon, and so completely. Was Anne that hungry for male companionship? Or was the Spiderman so damnably slick?

Since Anne's death, during many sleepless nights, Beth imagined footsteps padding across her spare room carpet. One night she sat up in bed, certain she saw Anne sitting on the upholstered chaise in Beth's bedroom. Once, she even heard her speak. "I can't go to my room, Beth. *He's* there."

So many times, Beth remembered Anne coming down to the kitchen for a late-night snack while Beth sat at the living room desk, buried under her accounting ledgers. She had hardly looked up when Anne had passed by, so concerned was she with maintaining her privacy. She had provided Anne with a place to stay and wanted no involvement. No responsibility. If only she'd been more sympathetic, more open, perhaps Anne would have confided in her, told her something about herself. Maybe then Beth would have information to share with Jim.

"Mmm, that was good." Ginny's soup bowl was whisked away, replaced by a steaming plate of fusilli. "Banzai!" Ginny said and buried her fork in the pasta. Pomodoro sauce spattered across Natalie Gorman's picture. Mouth full, Ginny gurgled, "Enough about murders and such. Tell me what's new with you."

"I got another anonymous note yesterday."

"Oh, hell. More bad news? No wonder you're paranoid. What'd this one say?"

Beth explained, then told Ginny about Kearns's reaction.

"He's right," Ginny said, wiping her mouth. "It's not the Spiderman's style. The guy writing those notes isn't some fang-toothed stalker. I'd stake my life on it. More likely someone who's already in your face, gauging your reaction to his literary creativity."

In your face. Beth thought of Bobby Chandler, who certainly had been in her face, in her yard, in her life lately. Was Bobby capable of such maliciousness? The mental image of the skateboarder with the lopsided grin didn't jibe with the steely coldness of the two notes. Still, Bobby was fourteen, and weren't all teenagers equipped with enough angst to baffle

Freud? The memory of her own adolescence made her wince. Thank goodness for the advance of years.

The pomodoro sauce dried a rusty brown on the newsprint. The slain model's face appeared spackled with blood.

"You must come across the occasional kook in your store, Beth. What about one of your customers?"

"Like Horace Furwell?"

"Is that the pervert you were telling me about?"

Beth nodded. "Not to hear him tell it, though. He thinks his bordello project will catapult me onto the pages of *Architectural Digest*."

"Like you need his help getting there. Listen, Beth, any guy who wants a designer of your calibre to turn his bedroom into a replica of a whorehouse has more than a screw loose. We're talking the whole toolbox. I'd steer clear of that bozo. Next subject. When do you see your new man again?"

"Monday night," Beth replied, feeling her mood lighten. "I can't wait."

"That good in the sack, huh?"

"Don't know yet."

"Head over heels after only a few weeks? That's not like the sensible Beth I know." Ginny wagged a finger and grinned.

"Maybe a little of the Rizzuto impulsiveness has rubbed off on me."

Ginny's smile faded as quickly as it had come.

Beth said, "What's up? Indigestion?"

"I was just thinking." Ginny swallowed the last noodle, and mopped up sauce with the bread, "— you got your first letter a week ago...."

"That's right. So?"

"So, how well do you know this Jordan Bailey?"

13

WESTMINSTER CHIMES SOUNDED THROUGH THE corridors of
the mansion on Russian Hill. Nora Prescott's hand-sewn shoes
trod delicately across the Bokhara rug.

By the time she smoothed her chignon and checked her lipstick in the
hallway mirror, whoever had rung the doorbell was gone. On the front
veranda, wedged against a concrete urn brimming with azalea blooms, was
an exquisitely decorated parcel.

Nora resisted a squeal. Her birthday was three weeks away, but obviously Phillip couldn't wait to spring a little surprise on her. She would be
fifty-five soon, but hard work and meticulous care made her look ten years
younger. Nora glanced right and left along the street, scanning for signs of
a delivery truck or perhaps Phillip's Lexus turning the corner. Then, seeing
nothing, she picked up the box and went inside.

Inside the package, Nora found another box, then a third. Even during
childhood, Nora had hated this foolish game, knowing the final gift never
matched the expectation. This one, though, wasn't bad. It was a brooch, in
the shape of an N, encrusted with pearls. Nora didn't care for initialled
jewellery; it reminded her of days-of-the-week underwear from a catalogue.
Still, this brooch, while not worth a sultan's ransom, was an antique, and
the pearls seemed to be good. She would find out just how good when she
got the jewellery appraised.

Looking in the mirror, Nora affixed the brooch to the jacket of her Armani suit. It didn't do justice to the ensemble, but she left it there, curious to see Phillip's reaction when he arrived home.

There'd been no reaction from him when she'd worn the watch, nor the diamond earrings. The Delft urn she received now graced the stark mantel of their all-white living room. No comment.

Had that been part of this whole charade? Phillip, sending her gifts, waiting to assess her response? Of course, by saying nothing, Nora was leading him to believe there might be another admirer, maybe two.

She supposed she should dash into Phillip's arms later, coo her delight at the gifts and scold him for being a naughty boy, teasing her this way.

But, if it wasn't Phillip....

One of the exasperating things about her fiancé was his practicality. The house Phillip had purchased because it was "solid," his Lexus because it was dependable. His wristwatch was a Timex, which he'd owned for the past eight years, he often boasted. Expensive jewellery, to Phillip's way of thinking, was frivolous, and Phillip Rossner was too stodgy to indulge in frivolity. Well, perhaps her faithful hound had learned some new tricks.

In the silk-papered powder room, Nora applied a fresh misting of perfume and continued to puzzle over the gifts. The manicure set she had been sent was tasteless, dimestore stuff, its black vinyl case decorated with ersatz embroidery. The Delft urn, too, was an oddity. Nora had never been to the Netherlands, and her background was Scottish, so the meaning behind the Dutch pottery was lost to her. The Andrew Lloyd Webber CD might be considered romantic to some, but it was a far cry from the Cartier watch. The sender, be it Phillip or someone else, certainly had eclectic taste.

At first, she had been tempted to pitch the gifts in the garbage, then she realized she was being toyed with and decided to play along. She didn't understand the game yet, but she couldn't deny its intrigue. Besides, the Cartier was definitely a keeper.

For a split second, she again debated confronting Phillip about the gifts. Then she decided to shut up. Either Phillip, in frustration, would eventually pout about her being ungrateful for his trinkets, or another suitor, perhaps with a fatter wallet, would reveal himself and the significance of the gifts, soon.

49

14

M ONDAYS WERE SACRED. ON HER day off, Beth usually allowed
herself an extra half hour in bed, but this morning she was up and
dressed by six. She power walked up to Chestnut Street, constantly alert to
cars parked curbside, but there were no bogeymen waiting to jump out at
her. In her favourite coffee haunt, she perched on a stool facing the street
and tried to read the morning paper, but her concentration constantly jos-
tled between scanning the café for suspicious-looking strangers and reliv-
ing her last conversation with Ginny. Beth still found herself stewing over
her friend's insensitive remark about Jordan. Every time Ginny experienced
a dating drought, she would take it upon herself to ruin everyone else's fun.
Criticizing Beth's male friends was part of her surly face-saving, and occasionally, Ginny's assessments had been accurate. But Ginny's implication
that Jordan might be the one behind Beth's hate mail was eroding what
remained of Beth's compassion and patience.

Beth understood Ginny's insecurity and used every technique she knew
to bolster her friend's self-image. It couldn't have been easy for Ginny,
growing up as the youngest of five Rizzuto children. Ginny's four brothers
were members of a dance band that played all the local European wed-
dings. It wasn't enough for Ginny to be lumped in with "those Rizzutos,"
so she sought to outshine them and by her twentieth birthday, she thought
she had, by securing a first-violinist position with the San Francisco

Symphony. But Beth knew that Mr. and Mrs. Rizzuto saw Ginny's music as a hobby, something Ginny could occupy herself with until she found a husband. When her own musical gift still brought no recognition, Ginny took pains to stand out in other areas, not the least of which was the development of a personality that would intimidate Don Rickles. She became a self-professed expert on everything, especially men.

"He sounds too good to be true," Ginny had said when Beth first told her about Jordan. "A pilot? You'll never get him to settle down. Those guys want their freedom."

I'll find out for myself, if it's all the same to you, Gin.

She was seeing Jordan tonight and tried desperately to think more positively, but she knew she would have to take a stand with Ginny, and soon. If Ginny wanted to compete with her brothers, fine, but Beth wasn't going to be part of any contest that involved allowing Ginny to insult her. Maybe if she said exactly that to Ginny, she would back off.

And Sondra Devereaux would bake Jim Kearns a carrot cake.

Beth's coffee was coated with a filmy skin. She shoved the mug aside and returned her attention to the newspaper.

At home, Beth's foul mood was reinforced by a call from her bank manager telling her that Rex McKenna's rent cheque had bounced. She slammed the receiver onto its cradle and swore. She tried to phone Rex at his office, but there was no answer. He had been limping when Beth last saw him. Maybe he was at home, recuperating with a box of cigars and some girlie magazines. It was worth a try.

"What the hell?" Ida McKenna hollered into the phone. "You mean that dumb-ass isn't at work? I'll broil his balls for dinner!" Ida couldn't have stood more than four foot nine. Where she storing that operatic shriek?

"He's probably out on a call, Mrs. McKenna," Beth said gently.

"My ass," Ida replied, then hung up.

By six o'clock, Beth had housecleaned and exercised away her anger. She indulged in a bubbly soak, styled her hair, and applied the finishing touches to her makeup. She wriggled into sheer black hose. She slipped her red crêpe suit on, fastened the row of buttons, added a gold bracelet and earrings, then stepped into suede pumps.

"What do you think, Samson? Do I look businesslike but sexy? I'm shooting for both."

Samson, who had been mesmerized by the goings-on, yawned, stretched, then jumped from the top of Beth's armoire and headed downstairs to the kitchen. Beth followed the tabby, opened him can of something revolting, then locked up her house and headed toward her Audi.

Beth judged Van Ness to be the quickest route to Jordan's house in Noe Valley, but by the time she reached the O'Farrell Street intersection, traffic was hopelessly entangled, and a uniformed police officer was waving traffic east to avoid an accident ahead.

The convoy of vehicles crawled along O'Farrell, giving Beth the opportunity to read a painted mural outside one of the city's porn palaces. *Admission is limited to adults who will not be offended should they observe any type of sexual activity.*

Reflexively, Beth pushed the button for her automatic door locks. As she did so, she noticed movement in the doorway under the theatre's marquee. A man emerged from the shadows. He wore a pale green checked leisure suit, beige straw fedora. Though the hat was angled oddly over the man's face, Beth had no difficulty recognizing Rex McKenna.

Her first impulse was to hunch behind the wheel so Rex wouldn't see her. Their next meeting would be uncomfortable enough, with only one item on the agenda: the NSF cheque. But Rex's gaze remained fixed on the sidewalk.

What Rex McKenna did in his spare time was none of her business. Still, if he poured his cash into establishments like the one she'd just driven by, and if he wasn't attracting new clients or doing anything to keep the old ones, she just might have her sample room sooner than she thought.

15

MANUEL FUENTES PROPPED HIS FEET on Jim Kearns's desk. His Senior Inspector status allowed him that privilege. Too, he and Kearns had once been partners, in the early days, before Kearns had cut the determined swath through to lieutenant. "Still can't smell him, can you, Jimmy?" Fuentes's black eyes were dull, all the usual spark gone.

"Not a whiff. You?"

Fuentes shook his head.

Kearns was doodling on a pad of yellow paper. He had been in his thinking posture for close to an hour, fingers laced behind his neck, gaze focused on the ceiling. When his neck began to stiffen, he switched to doodling. Now, he took a good hard look at Fuentes who was rolling a wad of gum between his index finger and thumb. "That bitch Devereaux is right, Manny. This guy scares me."

"Why should you be immune? We're all scared. Don't let Devereaux get to you." He shot the gum into the garbage can.

"You mean she's still alive? Damn."

Though it had been two days since Kearns had watched Devereaux's video, he was still plagued by strobe-like images of the woman, shrieking her opinions at the masses. It hadn't taken long for other members of the media to follow Devereaux's lead and jump on the barbecue-the-cops bandwagon. This afternoon's *Examiner* had published "Dispirited Police

Seek Public Understanding" on its front page. Kearns had been quoted: "The police always make the news when the public perceives us to be unresponsive, and when the public's afraid. Now, more than ever, we require the support of our citizens. The force is working round the clock, pursuing every lead, following up dozens of phone calls, to catch this criminal."

In the article, the reporter cited several recent instances where police were being held accountable for their vices. One inspector was currently doing community service and spending several weekends in jail after hitting her live-in lover over the head with a full jug of Almaden. Another, who worked in the Juvenile Bureau educating kids about alcohol and drugs, had been arrested for drunk driving.

"There have been mistakes made," Kearns acknowledged to the press. "The police force is constantly held up to scrutiny. The best of us can fall from the pedestal. I assure the public that corrective measures as well as preventive ones are being taken to provide the best law enforcement possible."

Kearns had assumed the article would generate empathy and support from the public. Instead, it merely served to make the police look inept and weak. Now, with frustrations at epidemic high and morale at rock bottom, that traditional back-patting, shoulder-punching camaraderie among fellow cops, though superficial, was nearly non-existent. If the public's desire for a macho, fearless police force was strong, the determination to maintain this image was trebled within the task force itself. Kearns's team would compensate for this latest attack on their infallibility and puff their chests with adolescent bravado.

Everything Kearns had worked so hard to change had come undone with the press's coverage of the murders. At all costs, Kearns had to continue to conceal his depression, his use of Paxil, and his visits to a therapist.

Fuentes shook his head. "I don't know how much more of this cop-slamming any of us can take."

Too often, Kearns was overhearing complaints from his team. The VICAP forms were too long, took forever to fill out. No one wanted to be bothered, and what was the use anyway? Kearns praised his task force when he could, and gave them shit when he had to, though recently, the latter was more the norm. If he had to offer them chocolate cake, then stab them with the fork, well, that was an inconsistency they would have to live with. Kearns was determined there would be no repeat of the Green River Killer fiasco, the Seattle madman who eluded capture because of monstrous egos and law enforcement's refusal to share information between jurisdictions. All the cracks would be sealed, and if it took a rainforest of paperwork and thousands of telephone calls, that was a price worth paying.

Kearns stared at the sheet of yellow paper he'd been doodling on. The page was covered with drawings of spiders.

"Your artwork's improving, Jimmy, but it's getting us nowhere," Fuentes said.

Fuentes, along with everyone else, was fed up with the investigation's inertia. Kearns saw the stress building daily, and now Fuentes was in it up to his eyeballs, with much of his frustration directed at Kearns. "Let's go over what we've got and see if anything fresh surfaces," he said, the futility of the suggestion clear in his voice.

Kearns resisted a groan, yawned instead, then forced himself to sit up straight. Time for the Kearns-Fuentes tango, where each would take turns reciting what they knew, hoping that, hearing a phrase reworded, a fact presented from a different voice, something important might be triggered. Kearns hoped that with a positive attitude, the exercise in tedium might yield more than a yawn and the desire for a Johnny Walker's. He stifled a second yawn.

"Five victims," Fuentes began. "All with WASP names. Two blondes, two brunettes, one redhead."

"Esthetician, flight attendant, model, salesgirl, dancer," Kearns chanted, trying to muster enthusiasm. Fuentes had chosen the victimology route, hoping that the women's profiles would somehow create a link to the killer's psyche.

"Occupations requiring some level of physical attractiveness —"

"They were lookers, all right. But they didn't know any of the same people, none had steady boyfriends — God, it feels so good every time I bang my head against a wall."

"They were more than just pretty, Jimmy. They worked hard to enhance their femaleness."

"What?"

"Each of them presented her best face and body to the public. They were all in excellent physical shape, they had great skin —"

"Where's this going, Manny?"

"Remember Lydia Price? Salesgirl's wages. Not big bucks. What did her older brother tell us she liked to spend money on?"

Kearns scratched his head and tried to conjure an image of Price's brother, sort his face out from among the hundreds of friends and relatives he had interviewed. "Got it," he said. "Clothes. Simple, classic jewellery — bought a Stairmaster the week before she died."

"See? Not just attractive. Worked at it."

"So we're after a killer who hates women because they treat themselves to a few niceties? Come on." As soon as he'd uttered the statement, Kearns realized where Fuentes was going.

"Maybe the killer sees these women as selfish."

Kearns let the idea settle, then nodded. "Could be something there."

"Abducted on different days of the week," Fuentes continued, "on average once a month since April. It's like some bizarre menstrual cycle. 'Cept he missed his period in May."

Kearns nodded. It was thought that some serial killers operated on a kind of hormonal timetable. "Kept the women alive for three to eight days. And no one anywhere reported hearing any screams."

"Not yet, anyway. The women bled to death either in silence or in isolation. Where's he getting the anticoagulants?"

"We've been through that," Kearns said, frustrated. "No report of theft from any of the hospitals or pharmacies."

"He could have access — he could be a doc. Or work in a drugstore."

"Or, like you and me, visits his local hardware store for a supply of water-soluble rat poison." Kearns changed tack. "Why were victims' bodies dropped or made to roll downhill?" This was a new twist, something neither had thought of. "Natalie Gorman was *displayed* in a fountain. Ironic, considering her profession. The only body not toppled from some height.

But what if the killer hadn't intended to leave her there? Maybe he planned to drop her down the Filbert Street steps."

"Or the Greenwich Street steps." Fuentes's eyes lit up. Both sets of stairs led from the Coit Tower parking lot. The Spiderman had been successful in dumping Lydia Price on the opposite side.

"But something went wrong."

"The Filbert steps are narrow," offered Fuentes. "Body wouldn't roll far without getting stuck. Not the effect he'd be going for."

"Too many houses near the Greenwich stairs. Lots of picture windows," Kearns recalled, having scouted the area after Price's death. "He'd be seen. So he drives around to the bottom of the hill and leaves her in Levi Plaza."

Fuentes's index fingers tapped rhythmically at his temples. "What would that do to you, Jimmy," he said, clearly agitated, "if you were a killer, a stylist with a plan, a vision, and you had to settle for something less than your best …"

"I'd be pissed off," Kearns said simply. "I'd plan the next one better, cruise around for a perfect spot, make sure the act, from beginning to end, fulfilled my fantasy."

"Right. And if this guy's sticking to schedule, we better get our shit together. It's already October. Can't afford to let his homicidal PMS kick in again."

"Time to get back to the phones and follow up on our countless leads, you know, the ones we keep telling everyone we have." He heard the bitterness in his own voice. Kearns didn't relish another chunk of time spent calling crackpots, but he was fresh out of creative alternatives. He felt the energy drain from him, fatigue settling on him like a wet shroud. "Like we're not busy enough," he added, "now I find out there's another nut on the loose."

"Yeah? Where?"

"Someone's writing nasty letters to Beth Wells. Signs 'em 'the Spiderman.'"

"And?"

"So I had to check it out."

"Personally? Why not send one of the plebes?"

"She's a nice lady, Manny. A ... friend. And she was freaked out."

Fuentes removed his feet from Kearns's desk, his expression full of concern.

"What's that look?" Kearns asked.

"Listen," Fuentes began, "don't take my head off. One, the Spiderman's huge news. Two, you're the big cheese at the centre of the investigation, a local celebrity. Three, Beth Wells wouldn't be the first woman to fall for a big, strong heroic type like you."

"What's your point, Manny?"

"My point is, maybe the lovely Beth Wells is writing the letters to herself."

16

ONCE BETH EXTRICATED HERSELF FROM the snarl of downtown traffic, she put the sleazy vision of Rex McKenna behind her and thought about Jordan Bailey.

It amazed her how vividly his image came to her, even in the middle of a working day with customers all around. Jordan was tall, with brown hair cropped short, which only made his eyes all the more noticeable, eyes that drew her in, mesmerized her past the point of caring. They'd had only two dates, once for lunch, the next for dinner, both to discuss decorating Jordan's house. They'd talked about everything but. Finally, it was agreed Beth should come and see his place, and now she hoped they could get the business part over with quickly.

Ginny was right. Beth usually resisted beginning relationships, often refusing second dates from perfectly decent men because they failed to captivate her instantly. "Can't you date a few Mr. In-Betweens while you wait for Mr. Right?" Ginny would wail.

No, it seemed, she couldn't. But when Jordan walked into Personal Touch Interiors, after Beth had spotted him pacing the sidewalk outside on three separate occasions, she was ready to strap him into a chair so he wouldn't leave. He had been getting up the nerve to come inside, he'd said.

Now, two weeks later, she was paying a house call, and she was nervous, too. As she steered the Audi through the steep streets of Upper Noe, she wondered about the home that Jordan had described as a fixer-upper. She was not ready for what she found.

The house, painted Wedgwood blue, was a classic example of San Francisco Stick architecture. Tones of plum, greyish-turquoise, and cream accented the ornate trim. A milk glass lantern hung from a brass chain, illuminating the front porch, its delicate archway resembling a crown of pearls. No detail had been overlooked; even the discs that flanked a bay window had been painted in gold leaf, like a collection of coins.

Beth lingered in her car, drinking in the facade. It was warm, inviting, and knowing what she did about houses and their owners, Beth assumed this place reflected something about Jordan. From the outside, the fixer-upper was a showpiece. Maybe the inside needed gutting. She shut off the engine and got out of the car.

Jordan, wearing snug faded jeans and a white cotton shirt, greeted her from the doorway with a broad smile. As she passed him, she caught a trace of musky cologne and turned toward him. His feathery kiss brushed her forehead, and she had to remind herself that this was primarily a business meeting.

"Nice to see you again." Quickly, he closed the door and ushered her inside.

It was the kind of house you could sink into when the fog wrapped itself around the city. Standing in the warmly lit foyer, with a partial view into the front parlour, Beth thought Jordan had gone a long way to creating the sanctuary he claimed to crave.

Each room on the ground floor was as lovely as the next. A gas fireplace burned brightly in the living room. The dining room displayed a magnificent lincrusta wallcovering at the cornice, producing an elegant frieze effect. The kitchen was a chef's dream. Even Jordan's furniture, an eclectic mix of Empire, Eastlake, and Mission oak pieces, suited the house perfectly.

A bottle of white wine stood on the central island in the kitchen, chilling in a ceramic cooler. "Like to see the upstairs?"

She preceded him up the front staircase, his hand holding her elbow as they climbed the narrow steps. The rich wooden banister felt cool and smooth. Jordan's closeness was overwhelming, and when they reached the top of the stairs, he didn't move away, but kept a strong hand on the small of her back as he guided her from room to room.

Beth expected to see at least one room torn apart, plaster removed to the bare struts. Two of the bedrooms were small, one converted into a study. Each had been recently redone. She recognized the wallcoverings from a brand-new collection.

The upstairs bath had an authentic clawfoot tub raised on a platform in the centre of the room. Beth's attempts to remain professionally detached evaporated. She was overpowered by a vision of sharing a soak in the tub with Jordan, candles lit.

"A bit unconventional, I suppose."

"What?" Beth asked.

"The tub. In the middle of the room like that. But when you're in it, you feel like you're on an island. A great stress-buster. Come on, one more room to go."

Jordan's master bedroom was spacious. Facing the rear yard was a large bay window; in its recess, a wood and brass telescope was mounted on a tripod.

"Go ahead," he urged. "The view is spectacular."

Beth went over to the telescope and peered through. Several neighbouring houses came sharply into view. "Ever see anything kinky with this thing?" Instantly, she regretted the question. Ginny was beginning to rub off on her.

Jordan laughed. "Women in hair curlers, mostly."

"Disappointing."

"Not to me," he answered, his voice suddenly close to her ear. "Hair curlers turn me on."

Beth moved toward the carved cherry posts of Jordan's antique bed, wondering how she was ever going to get out of this room without flinging herself at him, when the doorbell rang.

"You haven't eaten, have you?" he asked her.

She shook her head.

"Then dinner is served. This way."

She followed him back down the stairs, staring a moment longer than was proper at the way his jeans fit, the pale denim clinging to muscular thighs. Very businesslike, she told herself. Who was she kidding?

Minutes later, a bottle of wine was uncorked, and a meal was set out picnic-style on the carpet before the fireplace.

"Salmon teriyaki, *nikuyasai, tonkatsu*," Jordan said, pointing at each dish. "Okay?"

"If you say so," Beth replied, lowering herself onto the carpet and tucking her legs under her. She opened her packet of chopsticks. "As long as you don't tell me afterward there are snails in here. I won't eat anything that has to carry its own house."

"You'd probably want to decorate it," he teased. He settled in cross-legged, opposite her.

"Speaking of decoration, exactly which room did you want my advice on, the hall closet?"

"What do you mean?"

"Your home is beautiful just the way it is."

"Maybe I needed a professional to reassure me," he said, levelling his gaze at her.

"Know what I think? I think you got me here under false pretenses. Strolled by my store, pretended to need a decorator, lured me here ..."

"Now I'm plying you with liquor and Japanese food, lowering your guard." He smiled.

Ginny's words came to Beth whisper-soft. *How well do you know this Jordan Bailey?*

Beth took a polite sip of wine, then pushed the goblet away and looked around the room. "Jordan," she said, "I can't get over how lovely your home is. Did you have help decorating it? Sister? Mother? Ex-wife?"

He grinned. "Fishing expedition?"

She felt warmth creep up her neck, but she pressed on. "I know the kind of food you like to eat, your taste in music, your favourite places to travel, but that's all." That said, Beth didn't know whether to be relieved or embarrassed. Perhaps Jordan only wanted a superficial relationship. Had she jumped the gun?

"I'm an only child," Jordan said. "Born right here in San Francisco. I haven't spoken to my mother in years, nor do I plan to in this lifetime. My father must be a wonderful guy — look how great I turned out — but I haven't got a clue who he is."

"I didn't mean to dredge up something unpleasant. I —"

He put a finger to her lips. "Don't worry about it. I'm realistic about my past. Plenty are worse off. My life right now is good. I love my job, I've made a few good friends, and I've enjoyed working on my house. It really was a fixer-upper when I bought it. An acid rock band owned it in the sixties, then it was rented out for years. That wall over there," he pointed toward the dining room, "had slogans spray-painted on it."

"Hard to believe."

"'Let your love shine down,' 'speed kills,' you name it. The basement was a recording studio."

"What's down there now?"

"Sawdust. Chemical strippers. On my days off, I like to refinish furniture. I spared you the ten-cent tour."

"Are you working on anything now?"

"There's an oak pressback rocker ready to be sanded, but it's taking forever. I'd much rather spend my time with interior designers."

The heat rose to her cheeks. "So you did get me here under false pretenses."

"You better believe it. Now eat, before you realize you're alone with a virtual stranger." He smiled.

She cleared her throat, looked at her wineglass, nearly full, and wished for Evian. She watched Jordan deftly manoeuvre his chopsticks and lift tiny kernels of rice to his mouth. He was faring much better than she, her hands suddenly feeling like they had ten thumbs.

"I can see why the Japanese stay so slim," Beth said. "Half my food is on the rug," She made a hopeless gesture with her chopsticks.

"Their carpet beetles are enormous, though. Wipe an entire village right off the map." He smiled again. "Allow me."

Skillfully, Jordan wedged a tender piece of salmon between the chopsticks and raised the morsel to her lips. She chewed slowly, knowing she was blushing, and hoping, in the semi-darkness of the room, he couldn't tell.

"There," he said softly. "Good?"

She nodded.

His face was close to hers. "Now your turn."

Beth took the chopsticks from his hands, their fingertips brushing. "Maybe yours are lucky."

She managed to trap a piece of salmon and was about to lower her mouth to the food when Jordan said, "No. Here." He pointed to his mouth. She watched as his tongue flicked out to receive the food.

They went on that way for awhile, eating some, dropping some, Beth readjusting her grip on the chopsticks between fits of nervous laughter. "Much better," Jordan said when they'd had enough. "See? Practice helps."

"That holds true for a lot of things," Beth said, then bit her lip. "Sorry. That sounded coy and silly. Must have been the wine talking."

"No, it wasn't." Jordan picked up a chopstick. "You've hardly had any." He traced a line down the deep V of her dress.

She shivered. "How did you know about me, Jordan? What brought you to my store?"

"More questions?"

"This is it. I promise."

"You're not going to like the answer."

"Try me."

"I saw you eating breakfast in the café down the street from your shop."

"Beyond Expectations?"

He nodded. "I was having coffee, saw you, rehearsed a thousand lines in my head, but they all sounded ridiculous. Just when I'd decided to ask you if you were finished with the newspaper, you got up and left. So," he hesitated, "I followed you."

"You what?" Was it only the other day Ginny tried the same thing with a stranger? "What would you have done if I'd gotten into a car and driven off?"

He shrugged. "Probably would have chased your car, hollered that I thought you were gorgeous, something like that. Look, I don't do the bar scene. I'm not smooth. I saw you, liked what I saw, wanted to find out more. So I followed you. Spent the next couple of days gathering up the courage to speak to you. Then what was I supposed to say? 'Excuse me, but I've been following you and I really want to take you out?'"

"Dating seemed easier when I was younger. I find it awkward now, too."

"You're just saying that to make me feel better. You have a right to be angry." He moved a little closer, brushed a stray wisp of hair from her face. His touch grazed her cheek. "Are you?"

"You've obviously misrepresented yourself, Jordan," Beth said, her tone serious. "You don't need a decorator. You've admitted to following me, pacing in front of the store, now you've enticed me here, poured some fine wine ... this situation could be dangerous."

"Only as dangerous as you want it to be," he said, his voice low.

"I'm in trouble, aren't I."

"Deep."

"Good," she murmured, tilting her face upward. "I was afraid I was misreading your signals."

He kissed her then, a deep lingering kiss, and he wasn't shy any more. Beth felt his arms around her, the powerful strength of his body against hers as he pulled her to her feet. She didn't think she could kiss him deeply enough, long enough, hold him tight enough, and when he whispered, "Come upstairs," she wasn't sure she'd make it.

It wasn't like in the movies. It never is. Their clothes didn't mysteriously melt away. In truth, their clothing didn't cooperate at all. Jordan's shirttail caught in his zipper; his watchband snagged Beth's stockings. They took turns muttering "damn," "sorry," and "I don't believe this." When one of Beth's earrings became entangled in her hair, they decided slowing down might be the answer. But they couldn't, and it was only after they'd climbed into the antique four-poster that Beth realized Jordan still had his socks on. And then there was no way, and no time, to do anything about it. Their coupling was feverish, frenzied, and over too soon.

Lying in each other's arms, they laughed about Jordan's lack of restraint, which made everything wonderful.

"Talk about warp speed," he murmured against her neck. "Next time, I'll go so slow you'll beg for release. Honest. It will be excruciating."

She felt his lips tickle the hollow of her throat. "Are you planning to torture me anytime soon?"

"Insatiable, aren't you." His tongue traced a path between her breasts.

"I am now. Especially with a man who makes love with his eyes open. Hypnotic."

At once, Beth felt him pull away.

"What's that noise?" Jordan asked.

"What noise?"

"That clicking."

"It's my heartbeat," Beth said.

"Come on, I'm serious."

"So am I, Jordan. It's an artificial valve." She explained her condition, mitral valve prolapse. "My case was more debilitating than most. The simplest activity left me short of breath. So, I became the lucky owner of a manufactured valve. A little noisy sometimes, but it works." She held out her wrist. "Hence, the medic alert bracelet, the abstinence from alcohol, and —"she stroked an area on her breastbone, " — this scar."

Jordan ran his lips over the fine white line. "And here I thought I was making your heart race."

She laughed. "Feel free to take some of the credit."

"Do you have to be careful? I mean, your heart —"

"Relax, Jordan. Please. I won't drop dead from making love. At least, not unless you've got some unusual proclivities. I don't see a chandelier —"

"Don't joke around, Beth. I'm concerned."

"No need. I take my medication faithfully, get regular checkups, use a soft-bristled toothbrush, and an electric razor."

"Why?"

"I can't afford to cut myself. Now please, no more. You're ruining my afterglow."

Nestled in the crook of Jordan's arm, Beth stroked his chest. For the first time, she noticed a gold serpentine chain, from which hung an ornate medallion, a blood-red stone in its centre.

"A leftover from my school days," Jordan explained, his hand closing over hers.

"Parochial school?"

He nodded. "I'm a Good Shepherd boy. It's down the coast a bit. Sheltered youth, incense ..."

"I've corrupted you, then," Beth said, rolling over on top of him.

"No," he murmured, looking up at her, "but I'd love it if you tried."

This time, they moved slowly, purposefully, and Beth learned the art of sock removal. The awkwardness of their first experience was gone. The worries of being too fast, too slow, too loud, too passive, were replaced by arms-and-legs-flailing, roll-around rollicking sex. "You're driving me crazy," Beth managed to gasp, as his hands, his lips, his tongue, brought her repeatedly to the dizzying edge of ecstasy.

Again, when it was over, they joked about their desire. "You're under arrest, Pilot Bailey," she whispered in his ear. "Flying out of control. A turbulent ride. Definitely under the influence."

"I love being under your influence," he responded. "You have to admit, the landing was smooth. But please," he warned, "no jokes about pulling up on my throttle."

17

It was 7:30 a.m. when Beth pulled into the driveway, time enough to grab a quick shower, throw a muffin in the microwave, then head to work.

"Play hooky today," Jordan had begged, and more than once she was tempted, especially since, in bed, Jordan's powers of persuasion were off the seismograph. Ultimately, she chose business over pleasure, knowing there would be many more nights like the last one. Jordan didn't have a flight until next week, and during the night, while she slept, he'd pencilled his name in her datebook. For every night.

Beth fed Samson, donned a navy suit, activated her security system, then headed back to her car. Tim O'Malley, bleary-eyed and yawning, emerged barefoot from the house next door, his button-down shirt and khakis freshly pressed. Even at his worst, Tim looked good.

"Tough night, Tim?"

"Nothing I can't handle." He smoothed his already neat hair.

"I don't know how you do it," Beth said, "maintaining such a hectic schedule. I would think your work would be winding down now that summer's over."

Tim shrugged. "I've always been a high-energy kind of guy. You're right, though. Things are starting to settle down, and I can't say as I mind." He shot her a wide smile, then quickly cleared his throat. "See your heartthrob delivered your paper right to your mailbox. Must be nice." Tim bent to retrieve his *Chronicle* from the middle of a rosebush.

Reaching for her own paper along with yesterday's mail, Beth said, "If I carry any clout with Bobby, I'll coax him to aim for your porch." After wishing Tim a good day, she got into her car and drove off.

At Personal Touch, she found Ginny pacing the sidewalk with two Styrofoam cups of coffee. Ginny's outfit was slightly less garish than the last one Beth had seen her in — today, Ginny teamed rainbow-striped palazzo pants with an oversized crocheted sweater. A slouchy velvet hat with a huge flower attached to it completed the look.

"What brings you by?" Beth asked after she parked her car.

"Practice session with Dieter. You remember the cellist? He lives in Laurel Village, so I thought I'd kill a little time here first."

Beth unlocked the front door, and Ginny followed her inside. They sat down on a leather sectional toward the rear of the showroom, setting the coffee and Beth's mail on a reproduction steamer trunk. "You've seen this Dieter a few times since your duet at the Marin Festival, haven't you?"

"Strictly in the musical sense," Ginny replied, "although if he plays women as well as he does his cello, then I definitely want a piece of the action. Maybe today's the day. I just know he wants my body."

As did the last four men Ginny had dated. Or so she said.

"I'm sure things will work out as they should," Beth said noncommittally. "But if things don't go your way, maybe I can help. You're invited to a party."

"Yeah? Where?"

"Some friend of Jordan's, a squash partner, I think he said. The Saturday after next. Interested?"

"Of course I'm interested. Do I have to bring a date?"

"You're not supposed to. Everyone has to come in threes."

"Great! For once, being the third party could be beneficial."

"I think that's the idea behind it. Interesting way to meet new people."

"Plus I get to check out Mr. Perfect. Make sure his intentions are honourable."

Beth smiled.

"Oh-oh. Did you do something dishonourable last night, my friend?"

"I wouldn't exactly put it that way."

"Yes, I do see a difference. A glow, a radiance. I'd know that AFO look anywhere."

"Pardon?"

"All fucked out."

"Thanks for the coffee," Beth said. "Very thoughtful."

"Quick study that I am, I recognize you're changing the subject." Ginny glanced at the stack of envelopes on the table.

"I'm actually nervous to go through my own mail these days." Beth sifted through the pile. "Oh no. This is why."

It was a white envelope, like the others, with nothing but BETHANY WELLS typed on the front.

"I take it that's no love note," Ginny said. "Let's see what the jerk came up with this time."

"Here, Ginny," Beth said, handing her the envelope. "You open it."

Ginny grabbed a pewter letter opener from the display of masculine bric-à-brac on a sofa table behind her, slit the envelope and looked inside. "What the hell? Beth, it's all bits of paper. Look." Ginny dumped the contents of the envelope onto the table. Some of the pieces had small print on them; others were varying shades of grey. "Wait. If I turn these bits over ..." Ginny placed the printed side down. "Now we have something." She fiddled with the mess, working it like a jigsaw puzzle. "I think it's a picture."

Even before Ginny had finished, Beth said, "It's me." Her voice, quivery and soft, sounded alien to her.

"What? Hey, you're right," Ginny said, fitting the remaining pieces together. "Where'd it come from?"

"I don't know who sent it, but the picture was from the *Chronicle*. Remember the feature the paper did on the Designer Showcase?"

"Yeah," Ginny nodded, "you and the store got a great write-up."

The Designer Showcase had gathered the Bay area's best decorators, given them each a room in a dilapidated mansion to restore to its former grandeur, the money from tickets sold going to the Pediatric AIDS

Foundation. Beth's rendition of a conservatory, complete with a Bosendorfer grand piano, won rave reviews, and her picture had made the newspaper.

"But Beth," Ginny said, her voice rising, "that showcase was over a year ago."

"I know. What kind of person do you suppose would save my picture for that length of time?"

Long after Ginny had gone, Beth tried to make sense of the letters and the picture. She put it in a desk drawer and, during a lull in business, tried to call Jim Kearns, who was out of the office. Did she want to leave a message? "Just tell him 'Beth got another letter.'" When she was asked to repeat the message, a warm flush rose to her cheeks. Embarrassed, she hung up.

She remembered Tim O'Malley saying Bobby Chandler had personally put her newspaper in her mailbox. He could have slipped the letter in then, too. Was Bobby just lonely, or was he really disturbed? She tried to imagine Bobby, sitting alone in his bedroom, a cache of newspaper clippings hidden between pages of an overdue library book. Suddenly she was tired of watching the ones she knew and wished Jim Kearns hadn't given such advice to the crowd at the Fairmont. Beth's caution was giving way to paranoia. Picturing freckled Bobby Chandler hunched over her photograph, slicing it to ribbons was laughable. Almost. In future, she would follow Tim's advice and not be so invitational. If Bobby needed someone to talk to, it certainly didn't have to be her.

The appearance of Ida McKenna around noon made Beth wonder what else could possibly go wrong.

"Rex won't be in to work today, so I brought this by. Your rent cheque," the woman said. Ida's voice was decibels softer than the last time Beth heard it, the volume trapped behind clenched teeth. "I assume that's why you phoned yesterday. The other one was made of rubber, am I right?"

"I'm afraid so."

"That's what he told me when I finally dragged it out of him. Never can tell when a man's lyin', can you? Sorry for the inconvenience. Business has been a little slow."

"These are tough times," Beth agreed.

"You seem to be doin' okay." Ida turned over the price tag on a Sheraton sideboard.

"There are good and bad days," Beth said, trying to defuse the potential bomb.

Ida took another look around, grunted, then turned tail and left. With a sigh of relief, Beth watched the woman cross the street, get into the beat-up Civic, and drive away.

18

ON TUESDAY MORNING, JIM KEARNS woke up with a bugger of a headache. After meeting with his task force, he felt worse. The Chief of Police had played racquetball with the mayor, and after drinks in the fitness club's lounge, the question naturally arose, So how many days until the Spiderman's behind bars? Kearns was sure when they smashed that little ball around the court, it was really his head they were vicariously pounding. The stink was all over him, and since he believed in sharing, Kearns deflected some of the smell onto the task force. The gathering had been ugly, accusatory, demoralizing. Tonight, at least one cop would pick a fight with a spouse or spank a kid. And so went the cycle in this, the house that the Spiderman had built.

By 10:00 a.m. Kearns had already popped a smorgasbord of pain relievers, and even forced himself to grab a decent breakfast, but the pounding persisted. The sky seemed to have sunk lower with the weight of the grey clouds, and the change in air pressure turned his head into a bowling ball.

No wonder he was sick. Now he hated reading the papers, too. The proponents of capital punishment were out in full force, demanding the killer's blood. Kearns, like his psych colleagues, didn't advocate frying the bastard, preferring instead to keep the son of a bitch alive to study him. Besides, death would be too quick. The editorial columns were devoted almost exclusively to people's views on what should be done with the Spiderman, as well as what should be done with the police. Kearns wondered whose carcass the jackals wanted more.

Another hysteric wanted more involvement by the FBI. Kearns laughed when he read that, amazed that the general public still thought a bunch of guys in trench coats would start combing the streets and somehow save the day. The FBI assessed crime scenes, worked up profiles of killers, offered advice, and the agents wore some pretty snappy suits. The real fun — the tracking and apprehending — they left to the cops.

The true lunatic fringe, the psychologists, were having a field day too, contributing their two cents' worth about the killer's troubled childhood and making generalizations about abuse. If Kearns heard one more word about dysfunctional families and neglected youth, he'd upchuck on some shrink's shoes. Hell, his childhood was no fairy tale, but he never thought carving up some defenceless woman would make him feel better.

Disgusted, he pitched the papers in the garbage. Bottom line, there were a whole lot of people out there who thought they could do Kearns's job better than he could. Well, shit. They could have it.

He stared at the array of headache medicine on his desk. There might be enough in each of the plastic bottles to cure his headache, but his stomach would probably disintegrate first.

The Deputy Chief of Investigations was on the blower almost daily now, seeking updates on the task force's progress. His bureau captain rode his back like a cowboy. And Devereaux was still being Devereaux. Kearns had so many people grabbing him by the short hairs, it was no wonder he couldn't get it up anymore.

On a whim, he headed to Ghirardelli Square.

One of the upscale stores located in the renovated chocolate factory had an interesting collection of gadgets designed to rid the body of tension. For the budget conscious, there was a hard plastic ball covered with nubby spikes that you could roll all over yourself. At the other extreme was a reclining leather massage chair that Kearns wouldn't have minded trying out, exorbitant price tag be damned. He could almost hear Mary laughing at his foolishness and imagined what such a chair would look like in his dinky apartment with the rest of the twenty-year-old furniture. But it looked like he wasn't going to get the chance to even see how the rich relaxed. A tourist, with dirty bratwurst toes and a stomach too full of sourdough, wouldn't get out of the damn chair.

In the end, he seriously considered a hand-held, battery-operated contraption with a nozzle end that vibrated against one's aches and pains. At ninety-nine dollars, Kearns thought it was worth it. The thing felt great on his neck, and he could keep it in his desk.

It was when he was reaching for his wallet that he saw it: the store's glass-enclosed knife display. He would have passed right by it, except one knife in particular drew Kearns closer to the rack — a nine-inch slicer with a pure white blade.

"Excuse me," Kearns said to a passing clerk. "The blade on this knife. What's it made of?"

The salesclerk, a walking Ralph Lauren ad, seemed pleased to share his knowledge. "Ceramic blade, sir."

"Many people buy it?"

"I couldn't say, sir. But it's quite a piece. That blade will never rust."

Or produce metal shavings for the fibre boys, Kearns thought. Aloud, he asked, "How much?"

"Only $69.95, sir."

Kearns bought it. "If I pay cash, there's no way this knife can be traced to me, is there."

"No, sir," the young man replied. A frown line appeared on his forehead.

"Relax, kid. I'm not Jack the Ripper."

Kearns's reassurance had little effect. The clerk completed the transaction quickly, though Kearns suspected the guy was memorizing every detail of his face.

"Save you the trouble, kid. Forty-eight years old, five ten, two hundred pounds. Police officer." The clerk's frown line disappeared. "Good job, too," Kearns said reassuringly. "We need more people watching. Just one thing though," he said, producing his badge and showing it, "don't believe someone's a police officer just because they tell you." He grinned, took the package and left.

The killer's weapon. This could be it. With all the researching, interviewing, and investigating his team had done, it was Kearns who, because of a stinking headache, might have stumbled onto it, here, in of all places, a yuppie store. Naturally, the Spiderman would have paid cash. But just in case he was a little stupider than he seemed, Kearns would assign someone to get the store's credit-card receipts for knife #ID050 anyway. He'd put the push on to match the blade with the wounds to the victims' wrists too. It wasn't much, but it was more than he had an hour ago.

What he needed now, more than an electronic or medicinal cure to ease the pressure, was an arrest.

19

HE ALWAYS LOVED HIS VODKA, preferring it from a very young age to any other alcohol, though in those days, he couldn't be as discriminating. He drank whatever he or the older boys could steal. Now, it was Stolichnaya or nothing. He filled a tumbler with ice, then poured the Stoli to within an inch of the rim.

He had started drinking early to fit in, like most kids. He didn't worry about that now. He knew he was different. There were two ways to look at it — you could either consider yourself weird or special. He knew what he was. Though he often felt removed from the mainstream, he had read dozens of biographies of notable people who had felt the same way.

Geniuses.

He smiled and took a long drink. To think he used to be punished for being different. Now he was famous for it.

He loved the complete sensuousness of the ritual, the feel of the blade penetrating skin, the most superficial slice sending explosions of blood coursing from the radial artery. He could never understand the hurried butchery of many of his predecessors, couldn't imagine why a Ted Bundy or an Andrei Chikatilo would want such a sublime experience to be over so quickly. Art, like grand cuisine or vintage wine, was meant to be savoured, to be left lingering on the palate. When blood streamed from the women, it spattered everywhere, much of it on him, covering him with the warmth of a womb.

The smells, at first, he couldn't appreciate. He tried to mask the odour of blood, urine, and feces with scented candles, incense, aerosol deodourizers. Now, those smells were with him all the time. Disguising them would be artificial.

The sound of his victims, like sacrificial lambs bleating, had a music of its own.

He raised his glass and toasted the pair of priests who had taught him about the richness of symbolism, the beauty of agony. They taught him how to *feel*, at least some of the time. He'd shake their gnarled hands in gratitude this minute if he could. If they were alive.

Though he didn't appreciate their efforts at the time, he now gave the two old bastards credit for giving him a routine he could depend on.

Not like her.

The woman changed her hair colour as often as she changed underwear. Apartments, men — there was always something better around the next corner.

Naturally, he wouldn't be getting a thank-you call for the gifts. She was still likely flattering herself, thinking some lovestruck millionaire was trying to win her affections.

The next gift wouldn't be quite so subtle. He had toyed with her long enough. It was time to turn up the heat, get *her* to feel something for a change.

He drained the last of the vodka and checked his watch. Time to get a move on.

It was Patricia Mowatt's day off, and ninety minutes from now, true to form, she'd be jogging along the Marina Green. She would act surprised to see him, though he knew she'd secretly be thrilled he had showed up. Women were so transparent.

He laced up his Nikes and headed for the Marina.

20

"GODDAMN," KEARNS MUTTERED LOOKING FOR a place to spit. "Another homicide. Manny, you sure know how to murder a cup of coffee." With a dramatic grimace, Kearns swallowed the bitter mouthful, then thumped the nearly full mug onto his desk. Brown liquid sloshed onto a stack of files.

"Sorry I'm no Wolfgang Puck," Fuentes countered. "You want gourmet, go see your girlfriend."

"Knock it off, Manny. Beth's not my girlfriend." Kearns thought back to last week's visit, regretting having mentioned it to Fuentes who had been razzing him ever since. "She can have any guy she wants. Dating some pilot now, as a matter of fact."

"So she says. How do you feel about that?"

"Save the Gestalt. I've got no designs on the lady."

"No one would blame you, you know. Mary's been gone a long time. A man can get lonely on a cool autumn night."

"Loneliness can happen any time of day, in any season," Kearns said then quickly added, "but Manny, you're forgetting. I've got you." He puckered his lips and blew a kiss across the desk. "And my faithful soldiers. Just look."

Fuentes turned back to look to where Kearns pointed. The squad was earning its salary. A few had already hit the street to check out the latest string of Spiderman sightings. Ted Weems was on the telephone nodding patiently to whoever was at the other end. Sharon Anscombe, who apparently didn't mind Fuentes's coffee, was sipping her third cup as she thumbed through a text on religious symbols, researching the significance of the Christogram. Beside the text, Anscombe had amassed several church bulletins, as well as a listing of religious bookstores and seminaries in the Bay area, hoping that the killer's insignia would jump off one of the pages as someone's logo. As yet, it hadn't.

Erik Bauer, at the desk furthest away, had removed his corduroy sports jacket and loosened his tie. He was hunched over a slew of file folders. With his small hands busily shuffling credit card stubs, Bauer reminded Kearns of a nervous insect. The medical examiner had matched the ceramic knife's blade to the Christograms on the victims' wrists; one of Kearns's lousy headaches had yielded a minor miracle and now Bauer was trying to link one of the yuppie store's customers to the murder weapon.

"Isn't that a beautiful sight? What more could a guy want?"

Kearns tried to stifle a yawn, but it was no use.

"Maybe you oughta go home. Take a day off."

Damn Paxil, Kearns thought. If it wasn't the yawning and insomnia, it was the trots. Aloud he said, "I'm *fine.*"

"You seem tired," Fuentes persisted.

"And you seem nosy. I told you I'm fine," he repeated, his voice sounding more edgy than he'd intended.

Fuentes shot him a look, part curious, part accusatory. He opened his mouth, but he was interrupted by a knock on the door.

She was a frail young thing, with eyes that seemed to fill her face. Her lips, devoid of makeup, were naturally red, as though she'd spent the day crying. The girl's gaunt frame was swallowed up by a scoop-necked madras cotton dress. Her collarbone protruded almost painfully, barely covered by pale, translucent skin. Even her strawberry blonde hair was thin. Kearns thought fifteen pounds and a good hairdresser could make this girl a knockout.

Ted Weems, who Kearns thought of as "the Kid," ushered the girl into Kearns's office. With his quarterback's neck and broad square shoulders, the young cop made the girl appear that much more fragile. "L.T.? This is Stefanie Gorman. Natalie's sister."

Fuentes and Kearns simultaneously rose to their feet. Fuentes beckoned her inside and offered his chair. "Sit down, Ms. Gorman. Please."

"I don't want to interrupt —"

"Not at all," Fuentes said, holding his chair for her. He leaned against a metal filing cabinet. Weems retreated from the office.

Kearns shook the girl's hand and said, "Miss Gorman, may I say how truly sorry we —"

"I know," she cut in. This girl had heard it all before. "The police have been very kind." Her voice had the life squeezed from it. Her posture though, suggested desperation, a need to speak while she could still find words. She perched on the edge of the chair, head and shoulders forward, fingers laced tightly in her lap.

Kearns returned to his seat, grateful to hide part of his own bulk behind the huge metal desk. The girl's fragility made him feel like a lumbering Kodiak. "How can I help you, Ms. Gorman?" he asked, keeping his voice carefully modulated.

"My sister — there's something missing. I've been cleaning her room, going through her things …"

Her voice broke, and Kearns let her sob, listening to the soft gasps for air. The Gorman family would be in the worst of it now, leafing through photo albums, packing clothes, calling charities to see who needed what. The funeral had come and gone, the donated casseroles were eaten, and friends and relatives would continue with their lives while Natalie's parents and this young girl were left to deal with their grief.

Kearns, remembering last spring's allergy attacks, opened his bottom desk drawer, and set a box of facial tissue near the girl. She could be eighteen, twenty at the most. Older sister Natalie must have been her idol.

"Something's missing?" he coaxed, when he decided she could begin again.

She nodded, then dabbed her eyes with a tissue. "A brooch. An initial N, with pearls. A gift from our grandma Nettie."

"How do you know it wasn't lost?" Fuentes asked.

The girl shook her head furiously, as though anyone who had ever owned anything of sentimental value ought to realize this wasn't possible. "Natalie would have been devastated," she replied. "If she lost the brooch, the whole family would have known. She'd have torn the house apart, called friends, put an ad in the paper." Stefanie Gorman struggled to maintain composure. She seemed frustrated that the police didn't know Natalie as well as she.

Kearns was frustrated for the same reason. "So this was a special piece to your sister."

"Yes," she nodded again. "When Natalie wasn't wearing the brooch, she kept it on a little satin pin cushion on her dresser. It's not there, so she must have been wearing it, but it didn't turn up when the funeral parlour...."

Closed the lid on the casket, Kearns thought.

Their meeting ended awkwardly. Stefanie Gorman had said what she'd come to say, refused Kearns's offer of coffee, yet she continued to sit across from him. He filled the silence with mumbled phrases of reassurance, his voice sounding to his own ears more like a tape-recorded message. When the clichés exhausted themselves, Kearns stood and noisily pushed his chair away from his desk. Stefanie rose too, though her perplexed expression revealed she wasn't sure where to go next. Kearns felt like he was abandoning a puppy in the country. He knew the minute Stefanie Gorman hit the sidewalk, she would dissolve into tears, yet he was careful to keep his physical distance as he escorted her to the door. He'd had plenty of women collapse in his arms over the years, had done more than his share of comforting, but this time, with this girl, he didn't think he could take it. Fuentes followed her out.

Long after Stefanie Gorman had gone, Kearns was still haunted by her face. The girl's sense of desolation was contagious, and it brought back his own misery with full force. The emptiness he still felt over losing Mary left a gaping wound where his soul used to be, but at least he'd been able to say goodbye. The killer hadn't given the Gorman family that chance. Stefanie would walk around in that pathetic daze until the guy was caught. Only then could she replace her disbelief with hatred.

A piece of jewellery was missing. Kearns would get Bauer to call the slimeball who had screwed Natalie the night she was abducted, but he was sure the bastard wouldn't have the damn brooch.

It looked as if the Spiderman was taking trophies.

Kearns knew this wasn't uncommon, yet none of the other victims' families had reported anything missing. Of course, they might not know what they were looking for. Now the task force would have to double back and coax the families to check again. He couldn't expect each of the victims to have someone like Stefanie Gorman in their corner, bursting in with news of some article missing from a kitchen cupboard or purse. It wasn't realistic.

Kearns was sick to death of reality.

Later that night, reality kicked him squarely in the crotch. He was already battling a four-Advil headache when the phone rang. Ellen Sims, a student at the Art Institute, had called to report that her roommate, Patricia Mowatt, an aerobics instructor at a downtown fitness club, hadn't returned from her jog.

21

IN THE YEARS SINCE HIS wife had gone, Kearns exhausted all the remedies for loneliness. Weekends were the worst, when missing Mary went from a quiet, dull ache to a pain deeper, sharper, and more difficult to banish than his frequent headaches. In the beginning, there had been caring friends who'd taken the time to listen. Eventually, he caught their heavy sighs and pursed lips, signalling that enough was enough. Life had to go on, those friends had told him. Drinking at the "Plough and Stars" had anesthetized him for a few years, until of course, that cure became part of the problem. The convivial atmosphere of the pub and the welcome bitter taste of imported beer Kearns eventually replaced with communion wafers and the hushed quiet of daily Mass at Saint Dominics. A convert to Catholicism after his marriage, Kearns tried to keep the spiritual side of himself intact while the rest of him disintegrated. Though he attended church less often these days, he still committed himself to the ritual every Sunday. Somehow, he hoped Mary would be pleased.

Now, work was his drug, both amphetamine and sedative, and he knew he'd need it tonight. Patricia Mowatt was still missing, and though the task force had spent the entire day interviewing family members and fitness club employees, they were no closer to learning where Mowatt might be. When darkness fell and Kearns was still at his desk, he caught

Fuentes's disapproving stare. Manny had his coat on and was heading off for a night of pizza and cards with Rosalie's parents. He tossed Kearns his jacket, and Kearns obliged him by putting it on and heading home. He could work in his apartment just as easily.

Kearns did some rough arithmetic, concluding that this would be his 250th dateless weekend in a row. Favourite chair, big-screen TV, and a bowl of beer nuts — it wasn't so bad. Kearns poured himself a soda water, and in his mind's eye, he flipped a coin. When it came up heads, he opted for purgatory over hell and swallowed his Paxil. He imagined his therapist nodding her approval. He had no use for an erection anyway.

Friday. The thirteenth. A perfect night for some horror flicks. Kearns reached for a short stack of videotapes, each one carefully labelled, and popped the one with Lydia Price's name on it into his VCR. Neither Monica Turner's nor Carole Van Horne's funerals were on tape — the police weren't yet fully aware what sort of killer they were dealing with. After Lydia Price died, the Spiderman legend had been born.

Lydia's funeral, a large gathering, had been held at the First Congregational Church of San Francisco on Mason Street. The native San Franciscan had drawn a crowd of relatives, high school acquaintances, and even a score of strangers, coming to gawk at the killer's third victim. The closed casket, Kearns thought cynically, must have been a disappointment. Friend, relative, or stranger — all visitors were requested to sign the elaborately bound guest book, supervised by two plainclothes officers masquerading as funeral officials.

The list, when compared to the guest books provided by the Turner and Van Horne families, produced nothing. No two names were alike.

He could have used an alias, Kearns thought. He may not have signed the other books. He may not have attended all the funerals.

He may be smarter than you, you dumb shit.

Repeatedly Kearns asked himself what the point was in viewing and reviewing the tapes. He was only becoming more depressed, the sight of so many mourners and their sorrow gnawing at his soul.

He forced himself to think about Patricia Mowatt, still missing, and imagined the anguish of her parents, her friends, and the roommate who had called the station in a panic.

Mowatt had no steady boyfriend, though there were several interested admirers at the fitness club where she taught aerobics. The young cops, itchy for any kind of physical activity, were out shaking down Mowatt's potential suitors. The task force seemed to prefer dead ends to sitting down and thinking, the youngest of the bunch still yearning for the kind of excitement seen only on a movie screen. Kearns knew the killer would be caught by sheer brainpower. Still, if the greenhorns wanted to wear out their shoe leather on a quest for a Hollywood rush, well, it was one less thing Kearns had to do.

Ellen Sims, Patricia's roommate, had already assured members of Kearns's task force that Patricia wasn't shacked up with some guy in Mendocino or Napa. The roommates faithfully reported their whereabouts to each other, even before the Spiderman had rendered the city captive.

The bastard had her. In less than a week, Patricia Mowatt's body would turn up somewhere. While the tape of the Price funeral rewound, Kearns opened a city map and flattened it on the coffee table. Where would the son of a bitch dump her? It could be anywhere. San Francisco had more green space than any other American city, so he could choose another park. Griffith Park? The Palace of Fine Arts?

How the hell could Kearns follow his own dogma of being preventive rather than reactive when he couldn't begin to predict the movements of the lunatic? In one angry gesture, he swept the map off the table. He'd already written off Patricia Mowatt as another statistic, searching for her resting place, when what he needed to do was get inside the killer's head.

He ejected the Price cassette and popped in the funeral of Natalie Gorman.

Natalie had been baptized Roman Catholic, though the bulk of the congregation who had come to say their goodbyes had likely never seen the inside of a church. The tape revealed an attractive crowd, models, actors, and a few local celebrities. Several attempted to imitate the more faithful parishioners by awkwardly genuflecting in the aisle and making haphazard signs of the cross. Most though, didn't bother, slouching in the pews instead, looking bored.

The Spalding tape was saddest of all. The pretty flight attendant had no living relatives, and, being new to the area, had made few friends. Her ex-husband, the picture of grief, was among the handful of mourners, mostly flight attendants and pilots who scarcely filled three rows of the Calvary Presbyterian Church in Pacific Heights. Beth Wells hadn't even been able to attend. She had gone to England to scout for antiques with a client.

Beth had felt guilty about that too, Kearns knew. Anne Spalding's life these past years had been the shits, having to uproot herself to find a meas-ure of peace in a new city, but things, according to Beth, had taken a turn for the better. Anne loved her job with the airline, and there was even a new boyfriend. Kearns studied the video. Maybe it was one of these guys. Could be that airline types were like cops, sticking to their own kind.

His cop's nose began to twitch, and Kearns knew himself well enough to pay attention. He rewound the Spalding tape and played it again. Something about the killer's profile nagged at him.

Outwardly functioning as normally as most. Often able to play-act at some sort of relationship. Mobile. Warped time clock.

Whose circadian rhythms could be more askew than a pilot's?

Kearns catapulted from his easy chair and paced the length of the tiny living room. He debated calling Fuentes, then nixed the idea, aware of Rosalie's reaction the last time Kearns had picked Manny's brains on a weekend. Kearns shoved the videos into a grocery bag and drove to the Hall of Justice on Bryant Street.

In his office, Kearns unlocked his filing cabinet and yanked the folder labelled "Spalding." A photocopied page of the guest book listed less than thirty names. A computer check surrendered ages, occupations, addresses.

Five pilots had paid their respects to Anne Spalding on Friday, August 19 — Brent Turnbull, Peter Samuelson, Linc Gaudette, Martin DiMascio, and Jordan Bailey.

22

BETH FELT HER JAW TENSE. She took a deep breath and tried to quell the anxiety bubbling inside her. For nearly twenty minutes, she rooted in her closet for an appropriate outfit. She shoved hangers aside, dismissing a black cocktail dress as too formal, a yellow sundress as too summery. Her green wool suit was too serious.

If only she knew more about what kind of party Jordan was taking her to. Though Beth dealt with dozens of people every day, and had been raised with strangers coming and going at her parents' inn, she was uncomfortable in socially contrived situations, and this trio party spelled mix and mingle with two capital Ms. After a long week at work, she would have preferred to spend a quiet evening at home, or better yet, in Jordan's bed.

Jordan had seen her dressed up, dressed down, and undressed every night since their first time together, and had told her she'd look sensational wearing a garment bag; still, she wanted to look perfect. Tomorrow, he was flying overseas, so she wouldn't see him for days.

Finally, she settled on an ivory shantung double-breasted blazer and matching slacks, and just as her doorbell rang, she clasped a four-strand faux pearl choker around her neck. If everyone else went in jeans, she'd be in trouble.

When Beth opened the door, she was relieved to see Jordan wearing a black linen sports jacket and tan slacks, and when he took her in his arms, she wondered why they were going to the party at all.

"Come here, you," he said, opening his arms. "It's been a helluva day." He pulled her close.

"What's wrong?"

"Nothing now," he murmured, burying his face in her hair.

"Are you sure? You sound exhausted."

"I'm fine," he insisted. "Really."

"Do we have to go out?" she asked, snuggling closer. "I'm not much of a party person."

"Me either, but you're forgetting Ginny. She'll never forgive us if we back out. Didn't you tell me she's been talking about nothing else?"

"A man with a conscience can be such a pain," Beth groaned. "Okay, have it your way. I'll go, under protest, but I can't guarantee libidinal control. If during the party, I haul you into a closet, don't be surprised."

"Surprised?" He traced a line of feathery kisses down her throat. "I'd be delighted. Now, come on. The sooner we get there, the sooner we can leave."

Ginny was waiting for them curbside when Jordan pulled his Mazda before her low-rise building in the North Beach. Her usual psychedelic garb had been traded in for Greenwich Village beatnik — black turtleneck, suede boots, and black jeans that hugged her chunky calves. While Ginny's clothing selection was subdued, her exuberance was not. She'd scarcely clambered into the back seat when she started in on Jordan.

"What's the scariest thing that's happened on one of your flights? Is there really a mile-high club? Is it true most pilots are gay?"

To Beth's relief, Jordan appeared amused by Ginny's candour. He responded to her interrogation with the patience of a kindergarten teacher. Beth had prepared Jordan for Ginny's lack of subtlety en route to her friend's apartment.

As they crossed the Golden Gate Bridge, Ginny said, "Since Beth's parents aren't here, I'll ask on their behalf: What designs do you have on my designer friend?"

"Ginny," Beth said, "we've been in the car ten minutes, and the only thing you haven't asked Jordan is whether or not he has a prison record. A little small talk would be refreshing."

"It's okay," Jordan said, reaching for her hand and giving it a squeeze.

He half-turned to address Ginny over his right shoulder. "Ginny, Beth's lucky to have someone like you looking out for her. As for my intentions, well, all I want is for Beth to fall in love with me, then I plan to work like hell to keep her that way. And no, I don't have a prison record."

Ginny laughed. "That's good enough for me. You're in, Jordan."

Beth turned to him. "I think I'm already in love with you," she said, hoping he heard her above the radio.

He smiled.

A cool mist fell as they headed north along Route 1. Beth hoped they weren't going all the way to Stinson Beach. The hairpin turns and the hour-long drive always made her carsick. One of Beth's clients resided on Seadrift Road, an exclusive residential enclave with its own private lagoon; invariably, Beth would show up green around the gills. She warned Jordan.

"We're just going as far as Muir Beach," he said. "Will you be all right? Roll down your window a little."

After too many sleepless nights, the intermittent thwacking of the windshield wipers lulled Beth into a semi-trance. She leaned toward Jordan and rested her head comfortably on his shoulder. Ginny, too, was quiet, and the radio was playing mellow tunes. Jordan drove carefully, conscious of the dangerous road. The fog rolled in thickly now, and Beth hoped there were no deer wandering anywhere near the road.

The road narrowed, and minutes later a white flat-roofed house came into view. It was brightly lit, and rock music thumped from within. Knocking on the door or ringing the bell would have been pointless, so the three went directly inside, where the party was in full swing.

"Holy shit," Ginny said.

Beth nodded. There were easily forty people in the living room, yet there was still a feeling of spaciousness. Beth absorbed the details of the room, though there weren't many. The host had chosen a contemporary minimalist look, perfect for the house — no clutter to mar the view of nature from the top of the hill. Everything was sleek, low, and smooth. There was an L-shaped white leather sectional, a black marble cocktail table, black and white floor tiles, a massive black acrylic wall unit. The only real texture came from a zebra-print throw rug, sprawled before a white brick fireplace. The loud music bounced off the hard surfaces.

"Whoever this guy is, I hate him," Ginny wailed.

"For heaven's sake," Beth said. "Why? We don't even know which one he is."

"Look at this place. It's spotless." Ginny ran her hand along a Plexiglas sofa table. "Not a speck of dust. And the food!" The dining room table was covered with platters of Dungeness crab, spring rolls, and smoked salmon. Garlicky shrimp simmered in a silver chafing dish. Not a rubbery cheese puff on the table, Beth noted, her curiosity about their host matching Ginny's.

"So much for winning your friend over with my cooking, Jordan," Ginny said. "Guess I'll have to wow him in the boudoir. What does this guy do for a living?"

"Whatever it is," Beth said, "he must be good at it. This place is worth a fortune."

"Come on," Jordan said. "Let's look around." Jordan led Beth and Ginny down a wide corridor to the right of the entryway. The walls here, as everywhere, were stark white, illuminated with pot lights. A collection of photographs spanned the length of the hall. The black and white essays were framed in chrome and clustered according to theme. One grouping appeared to deal with aging — withered faces, dried leaves, eroded mountainsides, crumbling gargoyles. Another, Beth guessed, focused on innocence, with photographs of frolicking children, a bride, and a parade of nuns, in full white habit, carrying candles to vespers. There were scenes depicting poverty, natural disasters; there was even a collection of bridges. Beth recognized the Pont Alexandre III in Paris and London's Tower Bridge. There was a wonderful shot, taken at night, of a wooden drawbridge, with thousands of lights reflected in the waters of the Amstel.

"Brad took these?"

Jordan shrugged his shoulders. "I couldn't tell you, but they sure are good."

"Enough already," Ginny moaned. "The suspense is killing me. The guy's rich. Is he cute? Is he single? Is he in here somewhere?" Ginny craned her neck for a better view.

"Over there," Jordan pointed toward a set of sliding doors leading from the dining room onto a deck. "But Ginny, I should warn you. Brad's engaged."

Ginny gasped again. "That's your friend? I don't care if he's married with ten kids. See ya later. I'll make my own introductions."

Cute was a ridiculous word, Beth realized, as the host of the party came into full view. He wasn't nearly as tall as Jordan, but he was hard to miss. Brad Petersen was drop-dead gorgeous, with a smile that, in Beth's father's phrase, could charm the ass end off a snake. Brad looked like he'd just returned from heli-skiing the New Zealand glaciers or surfing the Banzai Pipeline. His skin was deeply tanned, his hair white-blond. Now Ginny stood near him and helped to transfer ice cubes from a plastic bag into a large crystal punch bowl.

"Didn't take her long," Jordan said.

"Poor Brad. He doesn't know what he's in for." Beth turned to face Jordan. "I must say you came through Ginny's inquisition unscathed. You can't say I didn't warn you."

"Don't think I didn't appreciate it. Ginny's something else, all right. Though," he said, pointing to where Brad and Ginny were standing, "Brad doesn't appear to mind." Jordan's friend was grinning widely at Ginny, who looked ready to melt.

"I'm sure Brad can take care of himself," Beth said, "but let's try to rescue him from the Italian barracuda anyway."

They made their way through a crowd of dancers and headed toward the European-style kitchen where Brad was mixing Ginny a drink.

"Jordan!" Brad called out. "Glad you could make it." He clapped him on the back. "And you must be Beth." He flashed a megawatt smile. "Jordan's squash game's been way off ever since he met you. Can't say I blame him for not being able to concentrate."

She glanced at Ginny, who didn't look happy that Brad's attention had focused on someone else. Quickly, she said, "I see you've met my friend, Ginny, champion violinist and lasagna maker."

"Sure have," Brad said, looking down at her. "Now do you see why I love parties? I get to meet such interesting people."

Ginny beamed.

"How about introducing us to that fiancée of yours?" Jordan said.

"Ingrid? She's not here. Off in Europe on a photo assignment. She called last night. Won't be back until Tuesday."

"Are those her photographs in the front hall?" Beth asked. "They're fabulous."

Brad nodded, obviously proud. Ginny's disappointment deepened. "Tell me," Brad said, draping his arm across Ginny's shoulders, "do classical musicians like heavy metal?"

"Do Italians make the best lovers?"

"Rumour has it. First things first. Come on, let's dance." Brad faced Jordan and Beth once more. "Excuse us, won't you? And Jordan, excellent taste, as always." He flashed Beth another smile, then led Ginny through a set of sliding doors and onto a redwood deck where several couples were pounding out the rhythm of a Bon Jovi song.

"Well," Beth said, "it looks like Ginny's geared up for a great evening."

Jordan slipped an arm around her waist. "Chin up," he said. "Ours is just beginning. Let's get some appetizers, then we can talk about all the things we'll be doing to each other later."

23

THREE MEMBERS OF THE SPIDERMAN task force stood in a semi-circle in front of Kearns's desk. Kearns pointed at Weems, the youngest and most nervous of the bunch. When stressed out, it was easy for Kearns to pick on the junior cop, whose smooth pink face always looked like it had just received its first shave.

"Anything come of your discussions with Mowatt's admirers?"

Weems shook his head. "Seems lots of the guys at the fitness club had a thing for Mowatt. That includes one or two of the instructors, not just the members. But they all said the same thing, L.T. Mowatt was energetic, friendly, and helpful, but she never encouraged so much as a coffee date with any of 'em. One of the guys got the impression she was already seeing somebody."

"Or so she said to brush him off. Of course, you asked each member of Mowatt's fan club where he was on the twelfth."

"Checked 'em all, L.T.," Weems answered, his glance darting around Kearns's office. "It's all there in the notes." His gaze came to rest on the file folder he'd set before Kearns. "They're clean."

"That's not what I wanted to hear," Kearns said, sending a disgusted look across the desk.

Erik Bauer, a glob of dried mustard still stuck to the corner of his mouth, looked apprehensive. "Mowatt's roommate gave me a list of places where she likes to hang out. I've shown her picture at Starbucks, at the place where she buys her workout gear — I've even stopped a few joggers along Mowatt's running route. No one's seen her, L.T. Not her hairdresser, her doctor, her dry-cleaner. Nobody."

"Well, Bauer," Kearns said, fixing a stare at the cop whose wavy black hair needed cutting, "you tried. I just hope to hell when you spoke with Ellen Sims and all the others who knew and cared for Patricia Mowatt, you weren't still wearing your supper on your face."

"No, L.T." The serviette Bauer scanned the room for didn't appear, forcing him to improvise with a saliva-dampened fingertip.

True to form, Anscombe stepped in to mediate. "We want to find Patricia as badly as you, L.T. And we want the bastard who's got her. But Mowatt's roommate and her parents are in shock. We've got to respect their right to come to grips with what's happening. We can't very well camp out in their living rooms. Some of the other families, especially the Van Hornes, are starting to hate the sight of us. They need time to heal, to grieve in private. They need a *break*, L.T."

"I'm sure they do," Kearns replied, "and if our killer promised to leave everybody alone, I'd say let's all take a break. But I don't think that's gonna happen. So unfortunately we're back to the redundant, nasty business that's called good police work. And if that means we have to camp out in someone's living room to keep the trail hot, then that's what we'll do. Got it?"

Anscombe nodded. Bauer still seemed to think there was something on his face and continued to rub the corner of his mouth. Weems checked his fingernails, then looked at his shoes.

"And don't ever imagine I'm not thinking about what the Mowatts or any of the others are going through," Kearns added. "You oughta know better."

He could have slapped their hands a little longer, but Anscombe muttered something about having to arrange a time to interview Carole Van Horne's choreographer, and her awkward exit opened the door for Weems and Bauer to make their excuses and leave.

Good, Kearns thought. Message received.

Alone in his office, Kearns realized he'd been nitpicky, bugged not so much by his task force's whining but by the interviews he'd conducted with the pilots earlier. The five who had attended Anne Spalding's funeral had been brought back in for questioning. Although Anscombe had done so after Spalding's death in August, Kearns wanted to talk to each one personally.

Brent Turnbull was happily married with three kids and living in a nice Tudor house in St. Francis Wood. Peter Samuelson was a newlywed, and Linc Gaudette lived in the Castro with a male partner. Martin DiMascio had been divorced for nine years and had dated nearly every flight attendant he'd come into contact with. Except Anne Spalding. Unremarkable biographies, Kearns thought, recalling the information he had accumulated. With a few case studies, some jargon and a little imagination, any psychologist could turn one of these guys into a slavering killer. But you couldn't argue with airtight alibis, and each of the pilots had one. Kearns tried to shoot holes in the pilots' stories; in the end, with some crosschecking and verification of their flight schedules, the four held up to scrutiny. They were off the hook.

The last pilot he interviewed, however, turned Kearns's litmus paper the wrong colour. Jordan Bailey not only intrigued Kearns but also disturbed him.

Bailey quickly admitted he was in San Francisco when each of the Spiderman's victims was killed. His flight schedule confirmed this. No, he couldn't remember what he was doing on most of those days, but on the night Anne Spalding was reported missing, Bailey was celebrating his birthday with a few friends at a restaurant downtown. The place didn't take reservations, nor did it accept credit cards, but Bailey's four friends, also pilots, vouched for his being there. He'd already given this information to Inspector Anscombe, he said, but he didn't mind repeating it. Anything to help catch Anne's killer. Bailey also had no problem telling Kearns he'd dated Spalding a few times, but that their relationship fizzled before they'd so much as held hands. The night that Anne died, Bailey was home entertaining some friends. He remembered them talking about Spalding, how they hoped she'd turn up safe. Bailey's dinner guests backed him up, one going so far as to rave about the *coq au vin*.

Although Kearns reluctantly sent the pilot on his way, he couldn't get him out of his head. Something about Bailey nagged his cop brain and wouldn't let go. A few phone calls of his own and some old-fashioned leg-work revealed enough about the man to set Kearns into high gear.

Bailey, according to the school officials Kearns had contacted, had lived with his single mother, Rita, a waitress, until he was nine years old. Rita managed to provide her son with a decent but simple life. They'd lived in a two bedroom no-frills apartment in Potrero Hill, a working-class area with the most agreeable climate in the city. Several cottages in the area still had Russian steambaths, or *banyas*, in the backyards. There were worse places to raise a child. The young Bailey achieved above-average grades in school, then, shortly after his ninth birthday, he was sent to a parochial school hundreds of miles away.

This banishment struck a chord. Kearns, after a lengthy phone conversation with the school's retired principal, reported that Bailey had never been a behaviour problem, nor was there any record of him having seen the counsellor to discuss difficulties in his home life. Bailey's relationship with his mother was solid; there were always letters and phone calls.

Until he turned thirteen. Then the letters stopped, and Jordan Bailey cut off all ties with his mother. Adolescence could be difficult for anyone, Kearns knew, especially for a boy growing up with only priests as role models. How many times had his own mother said she wished she'd given birth to all girls?

A little more digging revealed that Rita Bailey had changed her name to Sally Monroe, then Leigh Childs and that she was well known to the vice crew. Though she was in her fifties, the pilot's estranged mother could still command a good buck as one of the city's more experienced call girls. Prominent businessmen and habitual conventioneers appreciated Rita's aristocratic looks, her articulate companionship at restaurants, not to mention her sexual expertise. At some point, Rita must have figured there'd be more money in turning tricks than waiting tables. When had Bailey discovered the truth about his mother? Could it have been around the time he turned thirteen?

Kearns's information about the pilot was coming together like the ingredients in a dimestore cologne, and Jordan Bailey was beginning to stink.

He dated Anne Spalding. And now, Anne Spalding was dead.

But the fact that made Kearns's alarm bells ring loudest was this: Jordan Bailey's alma mater was a strict parochial school, a school whose emblem was a Christogram, the Chi Rho symbol identical to the carvings made by the Spiderman on his victims' wrists.

24

BETH REPLENISHED HER DRINK AND reminded herself to never attend another party. She disliked inane banter, didn't appreciate strangers petitioning her for free decorating advice, and she was tired of explaining why her glass contained 7-UP and nothing stronger. People, it seemed, were interested neither in her artificial heart valve nor the hazards of mixing too much alcohol with her daily doses of warfarin. A lurid tale about being a recovering alcoholic would be a more gripping icebreaker. Jordan was apparently faring better on the chitchat circuit. For someone who had originally struck Beth as shy, Jordan was having no difficulty keeping three very attractive women riveted to him. Behind him, a line-dancing lesson was in progress on the deck. Beth sipped her drink and scanned the room.

"Read your palm?"

Beth turned and looked over her shoulder. A scrawny blonde wearing an ankle-length cotton skirt and beaded suede vest smiled at her.

"I beg your pardon?"

"It's what I do," the blonde said. "Read palms. No charge tonight."

Beth wondered about the odd assemblage of guests at the party and whether Brad had any idea how many kooks were under his roof. "Sure," she decided. "All in fun, right?"

The blonde, who introduced herself as Peggy from Mill Valley, seemed miffed. "Palmistry is a science," she said with a trace of a pout. She led Beth to a relatively quiet seating area near the living room window. "If fingerprints reveal one's individuality, just imagine what the lines on your hand indicate. Did you know people with Down's Syndrome have only one horizontal line on their palm? Two horizontal lines of equal length might mean you're predisposed to leukemia. Even serial killers have quite distinctive hands."

"Covered in blood would be an obvious tipoff," Beth said.

Peggy's lower lip made another appearance, and Beth decided it was time for damage control. "Yours must be an interesting profession," she said.

Peggy appeared pacified. "I have doctors and lawyers as clients. Even a few police officers."

Peggy's credentials established, Beth turned her palm upward. "What does my palm tell you about me?"

There was the usual jargon about the heart line, the life line, then Peggy looked up and frowned. "You've been hurt by a man, haven't you?"

"Haven't we all?"

"You've never gotten over his betrayal."

Beth gulped, but said nothing.

"You trust people too easily."

"I've been told that before." Beth recalled Ginny's admonishments about being too polite.

"You should be more cautious," Peggy added. "You're emotionally vulnerable right now." She traced a line on Beth's palm. "I see some health concerns too."

Suddenly, Jordan hovered over them. "What does the future hold for us, Beth?"

Peggy smiled and excused herself.

"Nothing," Beth replied, "unless you take me out of here. I'm afraid I'm not much for parties."

Jordan nodded and looked at his watch. "Me, either. I'll make our excuses to Brad, round up Ginny, and we're gone."

"Let's synchronize our watches," Beth whispered conspiratorially. "Ten minutes and we meet at the front door. Right now, I'm in search of the powder room."

There were two washrooms beyond Brad's corridor of photographs — the main one, with four women lined up and waiting, and another adjoining Brad's bedroom where the line was shorter by one. Beth took her place behind Peggy and two of the women who had been speaking to Jordan earlier.

"I shoulda peed on the beach," said a redhead standing in front of Peggy. She tapped her foot. "This is ridiculous."

Beth looked around. So this was Brad Petersen's bedroom, she thought, wondering what the walls would say if given the chance. A king-size bed dominated the room. It was piled high with trench coats, windbreakers, and umbrellas. A framed photograph of a stunning brunette graced the bedside table. The talented Ingrid, Beth thought. An absolute knockout.

A lacquered entertainment unit was angled into the corner nearest Beth, housing a large-screen television, VCR, and a sizeable collection of videos. Beth could make out a few of the titles: *Gentlemen Prefer Blondes, Top Hat, Around the World in Eighty Days.* Hardly the film library Beth expected him to have.

The bathroom door opened, and the line moved ahead. "Thank Christ," the redhead moaned.

The pile of coats on the bed moved, just a little. The redhead noticed it, too. "Honestly, can't they wait until they get home?"

Peggy rolled her eyes.

The redhead spoke. "I tell you, if I was in that bed, I'd want Brad Petersen in it with me. What a hunk. I'd go for him in a second."

"He's engaged, I hear," Peggy said.

"Well, there's engaged, and then there's engaged, know what I mean?" The redhead turned and faced Beth. "You're here with Jordan, aren't you?"

"Yes," Beth replied.

"He's a hunk too. Nice to see him back in circulation."

The bathroom door opened again, and the redhead disappeared. Peggy seemed reluctant to talk, and Beth preferred it that way. She glanced at her watch. Five more minutes and she would be buckling her seat belt.

To Beth's consternation, when she finally gained entry to the coveted washroom, there was no toilet paper and no extra roll on the back of the tank. Slacks bunched around her ankles, Beth searched the vanity under Brad's sink and discovered not only toilet paper, but also a box of condoms, some aftershave, several economy-sized bottles of Pepto-Bismol, some sedatives, and a bottle of aspirin.

Brad Petersen, a Type-A worrywart? With his Colgate smile and wholesome good looks, Beth would have assumed Brad never had anything to worry about.

When Beth emerged from the bathroom, she noticed the pile of coats had stopped moving. The bedroom was empty.

At once, Brad appeared in the doorway. "I'm sorry you're not feeling well, Beth. Migraines can be a bitch."

"Migraine?"

Brad grinned. "Yeah, that's the excuse Jordan made up for the two of you ducking out so soon. Your boyfriend's a lousy liar. Listen, before you go, how's this for a business proposition? My condo in St. Croix needs some refurbishing. Maybe we could put together some ideas, and you and Jordan can join Ingrid and me for a week in the sun."

"If you can wait until November, you're on. October's almost booked solid."

"November it is," Brad smiled.

Beth fished in her purse for her datebook.

"Pencil me in. Here looks good," he pointed. "We'll get together, toss a few ideas around, and the four of us can ring in the New Year on the island."

New Year's Eve with Jordan. On St. Croix. What was there to think about? Beth nodded as she scribbled Brad's name. "My part-time help is a whiz. She'll love having me out of her hair after the Christmas rush."

"Good. And Beth, you're working wonders on Jordan. It's nice to see him happy again."

"Happy again? Why? Was he sad before?"

"Anne's death shook him up pretty badly."

"Anne?"

"Spalding. Maybe you don't remember her name, but she was one of the women killed by the Spiderman. Anne was a flight attendant. Jordan dated her."

A chill swept over her. Even the pristine whiteness of the walls threatened to close in on her.

"Beth? Are you all right? Relax. Don't let any green-eyed monster come between you two. Anne's death was tragic, but it's part of the past. When Jordan looks at you, it's the real thing. Anyone can see that."

From the kitchen came a loud crash, followed by an "oh, shit."

Brad's smile vanished. "Excuse me while I inspect the damages. We'll talk condo soon, okay?"

When Brad released her, Beth felt sure she'd fall over. Jordan had known Anne. This fact alone shouldn't have disturbed her. Jordan and Anne worked for the same airline. She should have put that together before.

But Anne had spoken about a new boyfriend, someone she thought she could really care about. And now Anne was dead. Had Jordan been that special person?

A whirlwind of information assaulted her. Jordan had seen her, followed her from the café to her store. His childhood had been unpleasant, so ugly he refused to discuss it in detail.

She remembered Kearns's profile of the Spiderman, a madman who stalked his victims, mutilated their bodies . . .

No! It wasn't possible. She couldn't be so far wrong.

In spite of what Ginny said, Beth knew Jordan, knew him as well as she knew herself. The science of palmistry be damned, too. Trusting people was a positive quality, wasn't it? Hadn't she been raised to believe people were inherently good? Besides, if Jordan had wanted to harm her, he could have done so — he had had many opportunities.

She made her way back to the kitchen. Brad was on his knees, whisk broom and dustpan in hand, sweeping up the remains of a crystal goblet.

Strong arms gripped her waist from behind. "Good news," Jordan whispered in her ear. "Ginny's having too good a time to leave. Told me she'll hitch back to the city later. So it's just you and me."

25

MANUEL FUENTES DID NOT APPRECIATE the jangling of the telephone in his ear at 12:30 a.m. Beside him Rosalie rolled over and groaned. They both knew who it was.

"Make it good, Jimmy," Fuentes whispered harshly into the receiver.

"Is that any way to talk to your best friend?"

"At this hour, I treat you like any obscene caller."

Rosalie groaned again.

"Hang on," Fuentes said. "I'm going to the downstairs phone." He handed the receiver to his wife.

Rosalie cupped her hand over the mouthpiece and hissed through the darkness. "Has that man forgotten you have a family? Luisa has figure skating at six, and it's *your* turn to drive."

"Shh, he'll hear you," Fuentes said. He groped in the dark for a T-shirt. He didn't dare turn the light on.

"I don't give a good goddamn. Maybe he oughta get a life."

Fuentes found the T-shirt and pulled it over his head. "I know," he mumbled. The T-shirt was inside out.

Rosalie wasn't ready to give up. "Calling at this time of night? Somebody better be dead."

Fuentes grabbed the receiver and shoved it under his pillow. "Rosa, what kind of thing is that to say?"

"I mean it. If your crazy friend has called just to cry the blues, I'll give him something to be unhappy about."

"He doesn't need your help with that. This case is practically killing him, and he has no understanding wife to turn to." Fuentes tried to caress his wife's cheek, but she moved out of reach. Wearily he said, "He's lonely."

"Lonely?" Rosa's whisper split the air between them. "How lonely can he be? Mary Kearns only lives five blocks away."

Rosa was right. Since Mary had left him, Jim had forgotten what it was like to have a wife sleeping beside you and two kids down the hall who had to be chauffeured everywhere. Kearns assumed Fuentes, his friend for over fifteen years, would adapt to his divorcé lifestyle, not needing sleep, never having sex, available at the drop of a hat. Fuentes knew what Rosalie was thinking: When was Kearns going to snap out of it? Mary had been gone five year this December, but Jimmy was still acting like it was yesterday. And behaving like a widower.

Fuentes bent over to kiss Rosalie's forehead, his lips landing instead on one of her eyelids. He murmured a hasty apology, then padded barefoot downstairs to the kitchen.

"I got it, Rosa," he said and heard the abrupt click at the other end. He sat in the dark, on the sturdiest of four vinyl swivel chairs and hoisted his cold feet onto the Arborite table. "Jimmy, you better have the Spiderman behind bars or Rosalie will have my ass."

"I haven't got him," Kearns replied, "but I can smell him."

"You get me out of bed because of a smell? Son of a bitch."

"Manny, you disappoint me. You usually show my bloodhound schnozz more respect."

"At this hour, I'd blaspheme the pope. Go ahead, if it makes you feel better. I'm listening."

Kearns reminded Fuentes about interviewing the pilots who'd attended Anne Spalding's funeral, and, in particular, his suspicions about Jordan Bailey.

"Let me get this straight," Fuentes said when Kearns was done. "One very mobile guy, single, late thirties. Whore for a mother equals troubled childhood, right? Spiderman's mutilations match the symbol of the parochial school this guy attended. And he dated Spalding."

"You got it."

"Well, Jimmy, that's something. Anything else?"

"Try this on for size. Bailey lives in Noe Valley." He told Fuentes the address. "Think back to your days in Narcotics. Ring a bell?"

Fuentes thought for a moment, then it came to him. "Son of a bitch," he said again. "Not that house. I know it inside out." Fuentes remembered countless drug busts in the late seventies and early eighties. "Bailey lives in that dump?"

"Yeah. What do you remember about the basement?"

"Stepping over sleeping bags full of wasted would-be musicians."

"Recording studio, remember?"

"Uh-huh." Fuentes knew he was being nudged, but the lateness of the hour had made his mind fuzzy.

"Soundproof," Kearns said. "So, if you had someone down there, and by some miracle, she broke free from her restraints, no one could possibly hear her screaming or pounding on the door ..."

"I'll admit there's quite a stink here, but need I remind you a cop's worst enemy —"

"Yeah, I know. Tunnel vision."

"You got it. We can't be so narrow-minded we zero in on this Bailey and ignore everything else."

"Come on, Manny. Get on board. First thing tomorrow, I'm sending someone to check out the Bay Club on Greenwich. Patricia Mowatt, one of the club's aerobics instructors, is still missing, and maybe our man Bailey has a membership at the club."

Fuentes knew there would be no stopping Kearns now that he thought he was onto something, but a part of him was still worried. Bailey might fit the profile, but so did thousands of others. But the police and especially Kearns were being lambasted daily from all directions. Just this afternoon, the captain and the deputy chief had ridden Kearns to the stockade and back. He still claimed to have the spur marks in his side.

Maybe Kearns was right. Bailey was the only thing they had, and there was enough smell there to pick up a trail. Cases had been solved on hunches more far-fetched than this.

"Let's go for it, Jimmy," he said. "We can't just wait for Mowatt to turn up. Right now, though, I'm going back upstairs, grab onto my wife, and make sure she doesn't get away. If she's still speaking to me, we may put the time to good use."

"Say sorry to Rosalie," Kearns said, a trace of sadness in his voice.

"One more thing," Fuentes cut in. He was wide awake now, and a startling thought struck him. "Your friend Beth Wells."

"What about her?"

"Her new boyfriend. Didn't you say he was a pilot?"

26

THE FOG WAS VELVET THICK, settling on the car like a suffocating pillow. Beth squinted, her eyes straining to find the road's centre white line, but ahead there was only grey, and more grey. She was certain that any minute now the Mazda would hit the loose gravel shoulder and spin into a ditch or off a cliff.

Although he drove slowly, Jordan appeared at ease, unfazed by the hazardous conditions. He steered left-handed, using his free hand to scan for an easy-listening radio station. That done, he reached across the console for Beth's hand.

"Loosen up, Beth," he said, unknotting her fingers. "I've flown 747s in worse than this. Haven't lost a passenger yet."

"Still, maybe you should keep your hands on the wheel," she cautioned. "It's not your driving I'm worried about. It's the other guy's."

Jordan did as he was told, but his face registered disappointment. For a while, neither spoke. Occasionally, Jordan hummed along with the radio. Beth looked out her side of the car, blinking rapidly to resist the hypnotic effect of the fog.

Jordan's hand brushed her knee. She gasped in surprise. He pulled his hand away.

"My God, Beth, what's wrong?"

"Nothing," she replied, too quickly. "It's the fog, I guess. I don't like it. Pretty dumb for someone living in San Francisco, isn't it?" She mustered a half laugh.

"Try to relax," Jordan said.

"I'd feel better if Ginny'd come back with us. I don't like the thought of her catching a ride with some stranger."

"Ginny's a big girl. Besides, Brad'll probably drive her home and Ginny would never forgive you for horning in on that golden opportunity."

"But Brad's engaged. Why would I want my friend getting in the middle of that?"

"I'm sure you don't, but it's Ginny's choice. Hers and Brad's."

"I guess you're right. Still ..."

"Ginny will be fine," Jordan said firmly.

The fog seemed to ease, but Beth's anxiety did not. The atmosphere inside the car was strained, with Jordan trying to fill in the stretches of silence with light-hearted chatter about some of Brad's guests. Several were squash and tennis players, and a debate had ensued about whose turn it was to host the next party. She vaguely heard Jordan say something about being glad he'd already taken his turn, but she could barely concentrate, and her responses were monosyllabic and lame.

Jordan and Anne.

"Beth," Jordan said at length, "this conversation is bizarre. We sound like two people trying to be polite after a bad blind date. Tell me what's bothering you."

"Nothing. Really."

"You're lying," Jordan said tightly, his gaze riveted on the road.

She tried to still the shudder rippling up her back. A slight tremor shook her shoulders. She gulped. "Pardon?"

"You're lying," he repeated and glanced at her, his face stern. "Something happened at the party tonight. Did Brad make a pass at you?"

The question took Beth by surprise. "Why would you think that?"

"Come on, Beth. Brad's a good-looking guy, he's gregarious, athletic. If something happened between you two —"

"Nothing happened. Brad was a gracious host. A perfect gentleman."

"If it isn't Brad, then ... ah." He snapped his fingers. "Let me spare you the speech. 'Jordan, it's not you. It's me. This is moving too fast. I need more time, more space. Maybe in a month or two —'"

"I wasn't going to say that! Nothing like it."

"Let's have it then, the reason for the deep freeze."

Beth paused, tried to collect her thoughts between deep breaths. Her heart beat rapidly. She envisioned her little mechanical valve working overtime.

"Come on, Beth," Jordan said, his impatience growing. "Don't bother choosing your words. I'm already offended."

They were still miles from the Golden Gate Bridge, too far from home. She had to think of something. "Green-eyed monster," she blurted out, echoing Brad's words. "I admit it, and I'm embarrassed."

Shit. Could she pull this off? She had no choice.

"Someone at the party mentioned how nice it was to see you back in circulation," she said, realizing how stupid and incomplete that sounded.

"So?"

Exactly. "So," she continued, "is this some kind of rebound relationship?"

"I don't believe it," Jordan said, shaking his head. "You think you're some kind of replacement, that I'm carrying the proverbial torch for the woman who got away?"

"It's been known to happen."

"I suppose it has, but not in this case. Have I made you feel like a replacement?"

"No, of course not. It's just that — well, what was she like?"

"Nothing like you, Beth. She was a frightened rabbit. No confidence. Full of secrets. Her lid was screwed on pretty tight."

At this moment, Beth thought, Anne sounds exactly like me.

"Then what attracted you to her?"

He gave her a weak smile. "I guess every guy wants a chance to be a rescuer of damsels, at least once in his life. She certainly brought that out in me. My instinct to protect. Over the long haul, I'd have probably grown tired of her weakness."

"Is that why the relationship ended?"

He shook his head. "It was hardly a relationship. Nothing more than a few drinks and a movie or two. Then she met someone else."

"And now she's happy?"

Jordan paused and shrugged.

"What was her name?"

"What difference does that make?" His voice filled the car's interior. "Enough interrogation, Beth. We've gone through all the precautionary dating rituals. We've discussed our sexual histories, bought condoms together. I've been open about my experiences. I'm HIV negative. You're HIV negative. That's it. Names of women I've dated I do not owe you."

"But Jordan —"

"Drop it, would you please? You've been acting strangely ever since we left Brad's. Any explanation for that?" He waited, then said, "No. Didn't think so."

He increased the volume on the radio. Stevie Wonder's bouncy "Part-Time Lover" echoed through the car.

Finally, they crossed the Golden Gate Bridge, fingers of fog playing along the six lanes of pavement. The nozzle shape of Coit Tower loomed atop Telegraph Hill. The Transamerica obelisk, the lights of Fisherman's Wharf, all familiar landmarks of the city's skyline, yet Beth felt as though she'd been transported to some alien world.

Why hadn't Jordan told her Anne's name? Because it was none of her damn business or because Jordan knew dating two roommates, one of whom was now dead, was too much of a coincidence for anyone to believe? She'd never know. She wouldn't be seeing Jordan again.

Her need to have all cards on the table and his need not to reveal his hand had come between them. Beth had played poker and she'd come away empty.

Beth glanced at Jordan. His right hand rested loosely on top of the steering wheel, as though he couldn't be bothered with the effort of driving. If Beth didn't know better, she would swear he was bored. But it was his face that betrayed his true feelings.

His jaw appeared locked into position. He was furious.

Minutes later, Jordan pulled into Beth's driveway, but instead of shutting off the engine, he let the car idle and stared up at Beth's darkened bedroom windows.

He wouldn't be inviting himself in, and she wouldn't ask him. Yet in spite of her nagging suspicions, her raging paranoia, she was reluctant to leave the car. Something didn't feel right.

"Jordan, I —"

"Goodnight, Beth," he said, still staring at Beth's upstairs window.

"Please. I didn't mean —"

"Goodnight, Beth."

She hadn't even reached her garage door — ten walking steps ahead — and the car was already disappearing up Scott.

Fumbling in her purse for house keys, Beth knew it would be another sleepless night. She would wash up, find her cosiest nightgown, and curl up in bed. The television would provide background noise while she wrestled to discover who was to blame for this disaster — Jordan, with his obsessive need for privacy, the Spiderman, who was making every woman imagine ogres under her bed, or worst of all, and probably closest to the truth, herself.

27

Beth's reflection in the bathroom mirror at 8:00 a.m. on Sunday told her she couldn't afford another night with less than two hours' sleep. Her eyes were ringed with black, her complexion pasty. She stumbled back to bed for whatever extra minutes she could get, but Tim O'Malley, who it seemed never slept, had already started up some electrical tool next door.

After a shower, she didn't feel much better, and her skin still looked rotten. She ran a comb through her hair, grateful there were still no signs of thinning, one of the hazards of anticoagulant use. By noon, she had already reached for the phone three times, the temptation to talk to Jordan overwhelming. She'd been an idiot, a suspicious paranoiac, and she wanted to tell him exactly that. There were reasons for her behaviour, though the more she thought about it, the less sense those reasons made.

Jordan's dating Anne didn't make him a killer. The look in his eyes when he'd said goodnight had nearly ripped her heart out. With a long lonely Sunday stretching ahead of her, she would do the sensible thing — curl up on the chaise in her bedroom and figure some way out of this miserable mess.

Beth pulled on leggings and an oversized football jersey, then applied a pinkish face mask, hoping to rejuvenate her tired skin. Samson, bemused at the sight, stared for a moment, then scooted under the bed.

The ring of the phone beside her made her jump. If it was Jordan, what would she say? She took a deep breath and forced herself to calm down. After the fourth ring, she still hadn't gathered enough courage and decided to let voice mail get it.

When the red flashing light came on, Beth punched in her code and listened to her message. Ginny's voice pealed from the other end. "S'me, Beth. Call me when you emerge from between the sheets. Any time before midnight, 'kay?"

Beth speed-dialed Ginny's number.

"Hiya, kid!" Ginny's voice was shrill at the other end. "Surprised to find you at home, though I bet you're not alone."

"Actually, Ginny, I am." Samson crawled out from beneath the dust ruffle, reappraised Beth's face, then jumped onto the chaise and curled up at her feet.

"Just called to thank you for taking me to the party last night. I had a blast."

Well, Beth thought, that makes one of us. "Glad to hear it," she replied. "Obviously you got home okay. I didn't like the idea of leaving you there."

"Are you kidding? Best idea I've ever engineered. *Brad* drove me home."

Beth heard the innuendo loud and clear. "Is there a story here?"

"Well, I don't want to brag, but ..."

"You and Brad?" Beth felt her face mask crack. She raised a fingertip to her forehead. "Ginny, you hardly know him."

Ginny hesitated, then said, "I do now. Besides, look who's talking about whirlwind romances. You and Jordan are into what — your third week? When something's right, it's right. I could tell Brad wanted my body the second he laid eyes on me."

Beth said, trying to muster some enthusiasm. "Are you seeing him again?"

"Probably not," Ginny replied casually.

"What do you mean, 'probably not?'"

"Hey, Beth, there's lots of fish out there, as they say. Why shouldn't La Rizzuto have some? Sure, Brad was great, a real stud, and a gentleman, too. Offered to take me to lunch next week, but I played it cool."

Beth's mask cracked along her left cheek. In Ginny's school of suitors, Brad would be a big fish. She couldn't believe Ginny would allow Brad to swim away without even a shot at getting her hooks in. Maybe Brad had pulled a caveman routine on Ginny — some flattery, a little food and drink, some slow dancing — the standard courtship ritual before dragging her by the hair into bed. What if Ginny's phone number was already a crumpled ball in Brad's car ashtray? Beth didn't want Ginny to get hurt. "Ginny, are you okay?"

"Okay? Never better. Why?"

"I don't know. I guess I expected more pomp and circumstance."

"Shame on you, Beth, wanting all the details. You're getting more like me every day. Brad Petersen was just the way you would expect him to be in bed. Couldn't ask for better. But he is engaged, after all."

Beth recalled the redhead's words. *There's engaged, and then there's engaged.* Obviously Brad's definition of engaged included a quick fling with a more than willing female. Beth wondered if Ingrid was prepared for Brad's interpretation of commitment, and less kindly, she wondered why Brad, with a gorgeous, talented fiancée, would be interested in a romp with Ginny. Again, she questioned her ability to assess people.

"And speaking of happily ever after, your Jordan Bailey is one helluva guy. I retract my suspicions. He's crazy about you, too."

At least he used to be, Beth thought, as she closed the conversation with Ginny. The front of her jersey was covered with dried pink flakes. In the bathroom, the mask took more than a gentle rinse to remove. Now she resembled a tired lobster.

For much of the afternoon, Beth plodded through a romance novel, eventually making her way to the riveting climax promised by the cover blurb. She closed the paperback just as her phone rang for the second time.

It was Jim Kearns. "Any more word from your phantom correspondent?"

"Not since the shredded-picture episode, Jim. Maybe the jerk is tired of the game." Beth certainly hoped so and knew Jim Kearns had more important things to do than chase down some practical joker. Beth didn't want to minimize the seriousness of the letters, or how each one made her feel. Still, she hadn't received one lately, and compared to last night's fiasco with Jordan, the letters didn't seem worthy of her attention.

"Yeah, you're probably right. Still, let me know if anything else turns up. Bastards like this deserve a good scare. Exactly what *are* you doing home on such a fine day? Hope there's no trouble in Shangri-La."

"Jordan's flying to Europe tonight," she answered, hearing the defensiveness in her own voice, "so he's got a full day ahead of him." She couldn't admit, to either Kearns or herself, that her relationship with Jordan might be over before it had started.

"Has he got a last name, this Jordan?

"Bailey. Why?"

"You know me," he answered. "A stickler for details."

"Speaking of which, how's the investigation going?"

"One potential suspect crawling out of the woodwork," Kearns said. "It's more than we had last week."

Kearns launched into his Spiderman profile again and ended with his credo, *Watch the ones you know.* Beth worried about Jim, knowing the pressure he was under. Still, long after he'd hung up, she wondered why he'd gone on at such length about the Spiderman. Indeed, she wondered why Kearns had phoned her in the first place.

Beth could hardly sit still. She filled in time by cleaning her bathroom, reorganizing her closet — even Samson's litter box got a good scrub. A glance at her kitchen clock told her only an hour had passed.

In spite of everything, she missed Jordan already, and half hoped he would call. She could easily fall in love with him. Already she loved what she knew about him, but what about all those things he wouldn't talk about? There had to be some way she could find out more, but if Jordan wouldn't tell her, then who?

Late in the day, Beth was hosing down her car in the driveway when Bobby Chandler shuffled by. He wasn't his usual bubbly self. Instead, he regarded Beth with a quizzical stare.

"Sunday and no skateboard, Bobby?" she said, releasing the trigger on the hose's nozzle. "It doesn't seem natural."

"Didn't feel like it much," he replied, still staring at her with a confused expression.

Beth dipped a soft mitt into a bucket of soapy water and began suds-
ing the car. "Everything okay?" She had to ask, in spite of Tim O'Malley's
warning about being too friendly. If Bobby was her mystery correspondent,
perhaps he was feeling guilty, and if she proceeded gently, he might show
his hand.

"Sure. Everything's fine. You got a boyfriend, Beth?"

The abruptness of the question startled her. "Yes, Bobby, I have a
boyfriend."

"Guess you like older guys, huh?"

How would she answer this without hurting his feelings? Or making
him angry? She stalled for time and gazed upward. Tim O'Malley was
observing them both from a second story window. When Beth looked up,
he disappeared back into the room. Beth focused again on Bobby and chose
her words carefully. "I like men who have similar interests to mine, Bobby."
She hoped that answer would suffice and that Bobby would pick up on the
word "men" and cast his misguided affections in another direction.
"Halloween's just around the corner," she said, changing to a more comfortable subject. "Is there a dance at school?"

"Yeah, but I'm not going. Halloween's for kids. Costumes are silly."

"When I was your age, I still enjoyed dressing up. My mother and
father would have the inn decorated, and we'd greet trick-or-treaters
dressed as the Three Musketeers."

Beth was relieved to hear the faint ringing of her telephone; the conversation with Bobby was growing more difficult by the minute.

"Go ahead and get that," Bobby said. "I'll finish doing your car."

"Jordan?" she breathed into the wall phone in the kitchen.

It was Rex McKenna. "Had to call you at home. Won't be coming in
for a few days. Wonder if you could see your way to loosening up the dead-
line for November's rent."

The first of the month was still two weeks away, and Rex already
knew he couldn't make the payment. Beth sighed. "How much time do you
need, Rex?"

"I'll double up in December, I swear. Things are a little slow right now,
that's all."

Beth could almost hear Ginny's voice admonishing her for being a pushover, especially since Rex's last cheque had bounced. "Rex, the best I can do is to give you an extra seven days. I'm sure you'll agree that's more than fair."

She heard him mumble something, but she couldn't make it out. Then he hung up.

At least Rex was behaving predictably, Beth thought, and wondered why her conversations with Jim Kearns, Ginny, and Bobby Chandler had left her feeling confused. Had everyone changed, or were they reacting to changes they'd noticed in her? She shook her head. Exhaustion hadn't done her brain any favours.

By the time she got outside again, Bobby Chandler had finished rinsing her car and had disappeared.

For the remainder of the day, Beth's phone didn't ring.

On Thursday evening of that week, Beth knew Jordan was back from Europe.

On Friday, Patricia Mowatt's body was found in a crumpled heap at the bottom of the children's slide in Alta Plaza.

28

YELLOW TAPE SECTIONED OFF THE four square blocks of Alta Plaza, a place where nannies frequently wheeled young charges from the mansions of Pacific Heights. Sunbathers sometimes gathered on a treeless section near the Jackson and Scott corner, glancing up occasionally to look at Twin Peaks off in the distance. Now, until the investigation was complete, the only people frequenting the park would be Jim Kearns, Manuel Fuentes, and a crew of investigators toting tweezers and plastic bags. Kearns ducked under the tape at the Steiner entrance to the park and climbed the curved steps two at a time.

In the centre of Alta Plaza was a children's playground. Patricia Mowatt had been found here, apparently set at the top of the slide, then pushed down, like so much trash down a chute. She was clad in a white tank top, shocking pink nylon track pants, gym socks and Reeboks. Her streaked hair was fashionably cut, though now it was littered with clumps of dirt and debris. In life, Kearns supposed Mowatt might have been described as perky. Or pert. She was a small woman, but not scrawny, as Kearns could see from lean but well-defined biceps. Her right wrist bore the Chi Rho monogram.

Kearns squatted beside the body, drinking in Patricia Mowatt as she was now, before the medical examiner took the Stryker saw to her. By tomorrow, a Y incision would reduce her to an organless mass of tissue and statistics. Her fingernails were perfect ovals, polished a pale pink. There were sooty blue smudges below her eyes. Her mascara had run with her tears. She wore tiny pearl studs. With a gloved hand, Kearns gingerly spread the elasticized cuff of one pant leg and noticed the three pink stripes of her socks matched her track pants perfectly.

"You liked being a woman, didn't you, Patricia? You looked after yourself. Took that extra time, made an effort, even if you were only going jogging."

Those who had examined crime scenes with Kearns before were used to his dialogue with the dead and gave him room. He heard their murmurs in the background, the occasional intelligible word revealing they were talking about everything but the murder. He heard muffled laughter. Kearns recognized the others' need for detachment, knew how gallows humour could help shut out the horrors his squad faced.

Coping strategies were so personal. Nothing right or wrong here. Still, he left his task force to theirs, and they would wait until Kearns was through with his. The measuring, plucking, and pawing in the dirt could wait a few minutes, and so could the Crime Scenes Inspector. Death, Kearns reminded himself, wasn't about numbers. It was about people.

Kearns's practice of keeping the victims human hurt like hell, but he had to feel their pain. He needed that incentive, that motivation. His therapist warned him about it, saying that Kearns wasn't allowing his medication to reach its full effect. The antidepressant, while keeping him from breaking into tears or flying into a rage, still wasn't leveling him out the way it should. His body, rubbery with fatigue, was often at odds with his mind, which still raced from thought to unconnected thought.

He bent over Patricia Mowatt's body and closed his eyes. He imagined her, lacing up sneakers, fluffing her hair with her fingers and checking her appearance in a mirror before venturing out on her run. In Kearns's mind, Patricia was rosy-cheeked, wholesome.

"You were running, Patricia," he whispered. "Were you getting tired, out of breath? Were you cold? Wet? Is that why you went with him?"

Kearns opened his eyes and cast a quick glance to where the ambulance crew, the woman from the photo lab, the two patrol officers, and their supervising sergeant still stood. No one was looking at him. Junior Inspectors Bauer and Weems kept a respectful distance, too. Most had grown accustomed to Kearns's methods, and if anyone thought him odd, they'd never say. He leaned closer to Mowatt. "Your roommate told us you were smart, that you'd never go off with a stranger. You knew the guy, right? Trusted him. Where did you meet?"

Patricia Mowatt had no answer for Kearns.

Gently, he took hold of Patricia Mowatt's hand, pressing the flesh through the plastic bag covering it. Not long ago, he had thought another death would yield more information. "I didn't mean for it to be you," he whispered to her. "I didn't mean for it to be anybody." He released her hand and stood up.

Even in wide-open spaces, there was a stink to death. To Vicks or not to Vicks. Each investigator had his preference. Kearns thought about the Spiderman's first victim, Carole Van Horne. With the passage of too much time and the buildup of gases, Carole's body had bloated and split open. He'd needed a gas mask for that one. Olfactory senses were supposed to be rendered numb after a few minutes in the company of a rotten stench, but Kearns knew once you smelled a popper, there was no going back. Tonight, Kearns would shower, rinse his hair with vinegar, and go to Henry Ng's for Szechwan food. With any luck, by morning, the smell would be gone.

The ME, Janos Horvath, stout from too many servings of chicken paprikash, checked Mowatt's body for usable evidence. Eventually, he shook his head, muttered something in Hungarian, then retreated from the body. Kearns could hear him setting up a golf date with one of the ambulance drivers.

The area around Mowatt's body was free of blood, though there must have been buckets of it flowing when she died. Kearns was sure once Horvath put Mowatt on the slab, he would discover fixed lividity, the deep purple settling of blood on Mowatt's dorsal side, not the front. Mowatt, some kid's future gym teacher, had been killed while lying face up, then moved. The killer wanted to see her face, to watch her as she died. There would be bruising too, neither from the fall nor from a physical confrontation with the killer, but from internal hemorrhaging brought on by

megadoses of an anticoagulant. Kearns could predict Horvath's report —
jaundice, enlarged liver — death due to massive bleeding. He didn't envy
Horvath his job, staring into those cloudy, flattened eyes, x-raying, dis-
secting, recording every scar, mole, and filled tooth. At least Kearns could
return to the land of the living. Horvath didn't have that luxury.

Kearns gazed at the homes surrounding the park, quaint Victorians
that were now being invaded by Kearns's investigators, searching for potential witnesses. Someone must have seen something. The killer was becoming increasingly brazen. Surely he couldn't lug the body up the curved steps
at the Steiner Street entrance without being seen, nor would any of the
other accesses afford him the shelter of treed cover. Dammit. Kearns
refused to believe Patricia Mowatt had died in vain. They had to learn
something this time.

"Quite a challenge you've got, Jim," Janos Horvath said, clapping him
on the back.

"In a crossword puzzle, I appreciate a challenge, *öreg ember*," Kearns
replied, using his limited knowledge of Hungarian. "This I can do without. When did she die?" He knew Horvath couldn't be specific — that
happened only on television, but a ballpark figure was all Kearns needed.
The ME would have already checked the body's temperature, noted the
onset or the absence of rigor, assessed the parade of insects.

"Killed last night. Sometime between the six o'clock news and
Leno. Dumped here long after the neighbours over there were tucked in
their beds."

Enough time for the scene to become contaminated, Kearns thought.

A car door slammed, and Kearns saw Fuentes emerge from a black
Taurus parked on Clay Street. He could hear his friend report to a patrol
officer who was recording his name in a Crime Scenes log.

Then Fuentes was beside him. Instinctively, both men jammed their
hands in their pockets for the initial walk-through, aware that cops could
contaminate a scene as inadvertently as anybody. Kearns knew others
would be in Mowatt's company for the better part of the day, bagging evidence, measuring, taking pictures. Another downside? It looked like rain.

He took another look at Mowatt's body, knowing the kabuki pallor of her skin would haunt him tonight. "Manny? This girl disappeared on October 12."

"Right. Her roomie Ellen Sims said she went out after supper, remember? Never came back."

"Did she have a regular jogging route?"

Fuentes nodded. "Usually made her way from their apartment on Russian Hill down to the bay, then she'd either cut east and hook up with the Embarcadero or go west along Marina Green and into the Presidio."

"Ambitious girl," Kearns remarked, wondering why anyone in her right mind would run anywhere if she didn't have to. "Pretty breezy down by the bay on an autumn evening. Seems to me, if I remember that night correctly, it rained."

"She's wearing weather-resistant pants."

He stared at the bright pink pants, mottled with muddy splash marks, then at Mowatt's muscular bare arms. "So ... where's the jacket?"

29

INSPECTOR BAUER'S VISIT TO ELLEN Sims's apartment on Leavenworth near the Art Institute confirmed what Kearns had already surmised — Patricia Mowatt did indeed own a pink water-resistant running suit. Though she couldn't swear to it, Ellen was fairly certain Patricia had worn the jacket jogging the night she'd disappeared. Ellen remembered the drizzle that had fallen around the supper hour — she had just recovered from a cold herself and had intended to take a walk, but the rain made her change her mind. Patricia though, craved her evening run and would most likely have worn the pink jacket with the hood up. There was no sign of the jacket anywhere in the apartment, in Mowatt's car, or at her parents' place in Sausalito.

Natalie Gorman's missing brooch was no fluke. It, along with Patricia Mowatt's jacket, belonged to the Spiderman museum collection, the killer's own Academy Award for outstanding performance in a role. To Kearns, though, the taking of trophies signalled the opposite. This guy was ordinary, not the first killer to remove possessions from the victim and not the last.

Perfect. This was his excuse for making a lunch date with Beth Wells. He could question her about Anne Spalding's possessions, not that she'd be able to tell him anything, but the conversation would segue nicely to Kearns's real agenda.

When he'd last spoken to Beth on the phone, he suspected she was still too infatuated to hear him clearly. His reciting the killer's profile had left her bored rather than wary. This time, he wouldn't be quite so circumspect. Regardless of how she felt about him at the end of the conversation, Kearns had to let Beth know that the man she'd fallen for might be a murderer.

Ten days before Halloween, Nora Prescott turned fifty-five. So she wasn't surprised when the Westminster chimes announced the arrival of an enormous bouquet of Stargazer lilies at noon. The flowers were accompanied by a card from Phillip, instructing her to remain home for the day; at one o'clock, a cashmere sweater in her favourite colour arrived, followed at two by a bottle of Cristal champagne. The three o'clock gift was her trademark perfume and a box of Godiva chocolates. So unlike Phillip to be this extravagant or this imaginative, then she remembered the creative session she'd treated him to in bed last night. Men were so grateful for sexual favours, and Phillip was endowed with as many brain cells between his legs as any other male. Later, she'd protest his spending so much money, then spank him for it.

When the doorbell rang again at four o'clock, she sprang from the sofa. At the front door she paused, wondering what the next package contained. She had seen a lovely antique silver dresser set last week. Perhaps Phillip had remembered her talking about it.

She flung open the front door. On the front verandah lay a parcel, beautifully wrapped in gold embossed paper with an elaborate red bow. Nora looked left and right along the street, searching for signs of a delivery truck or van, but there was none. Some fool had just kissed a substantial tip goodbye.

The box was too large to contain jewellery, too small for an evening gown or fur. She shook it. Lingerie?

She lifted the lid. It was some sort of windbreaker, the shiny material making Nora's skin crawl. The colour, too, was a horrendous fluorescent pink, a shade she had never worn and never would. What could Phillip be thinking? Perhaps he wanted her to take up golf, wear one of those silly little plaid visors and horrible saddle shoes. Was he taking her somewhere for a golf vacation? Bermuda? Or perhaps the Caymans? She rummaged in the pockets for plane tickets.

On closer inspection, Nora saw that the jacket was used. There was a ballpoint pen mark near the right slash pocket, and when she lifted the garment to her face, she smelled perspiration and stale cologne.

She knew Phillip could be frugal, but not even he would stoop so low as to present Nora with a piece of used clothing. Suddenly the presence of the ugly jacket in their beautiful living room filled her with revulsion.

When Phillip's key turned in the lock, Nora hastily stuffed the jacket back into its box, crumpled the wrapping paper into a ball, and shoved everything under the skirted chesterfield.

"Darling!" Phillip trilled, sailing into the living room. "Miss me?"

It amazed her how this shrewd businessman, with his tremendous physical size and *basso profundo* voice could walk in the door, look at her, and metamorphose into a pussycat. An annoying pussycat.

She rose to her feet and opened her arms. "Of course I missed you, dearest," she cooed as she glided toward him. She planted a kiss on his cheek. "And the lovely gifts, Phillip. Really, it's too much." She oohed and ahhed over them, displayed like priceless statues on the Hepplewhite sideboard. She didn't mention the pink jacket. "You've made my birthday so special, darling. Now, enough about me. Make yourself comfortable on the sofa, I'll pour you a sherry, and you can tell me about your day."

And for a solid half hour, he did. Nora had long since mastered the art of appearing to hang on every word. She knew just when to nod, when to mutter "oh, dear, how dreadful — or wonderful or shocking —" and when to forsake the adjectives in favour of more physical cures for stress.

"My goodness," he said finally, "I've been prattling."

"Not at all, sweetheart." Another cool cheek kiss.

"Nasty business at Alta Plaza. Did you see it on the news?"

Nora pursed her lips, allowed a small furrow to appear on her forehead. "You know I don't watch the news, dear. Too depressing."

"The police found that missing Mowatt girl. Remember the jogger? Didn't live too far from here."

"Oh dear. How dreadful."

"Yes. Gave Warwick at the bank quite a turn. Thought at first it might be his daughter. Went white as a sheet when the news came over the radio."

Nora remained focused on Phillip's face and wondered why someone born and bred in San Francisco would pepper his vocabulary with British-isms.

"Seems Warwick's daughter, a free-spirited type, had gone to Carmel to study art. She hadn't called for a few weeks, so naturally Warwick was worried."

Nora refilled Phillip's sherry goblet and poured herself a generous Scotch. "Why would Warwick think the dead girl was his daughter?"

"It was the pink jogging pants," Phillip explained. "Warwick's girl had a pink jogging suit, so of course, when the body was discovered in ..."

There was more, but Nora didn't catch it. More important things commanded her attention — a cassette of Lloyd Webber show tunes and a manicure set. She'd read something a while ago about a dancer, gone missing after a rehearsal and an esthetician, a young girl who removed hair with hot wax, gave facials, and applied nail polish for a living. There had been other girls, and other gifts. Suddenly, she knew the identity of her gift giver, and the realization wormed through her with a creeping dread.

Her mind was a maelstrom of activity. She'd have to dispose of the jacket immediately. Perhaps, in bed later tonight, if she was very good, she might convince Phillip to move up the wedding date, tell him how she'd been dreaming of a world cruise and could they leave immediately? She had not come this far, to this mansion and this life, to lose it all. Not for the sake of a goddamn jacket. And Phillip, with his influential friends and his spotless image, must never know.

"Darling!" Phillip's voice boomed.

"Yes, dear?" Nora felt an embarrassed flush creep up her neck.

"You seemed so far away. And that outfit."

Nora glanced down at her lounging ensemble, a navy raw silk tunic and matching slacks. "I thought you liked this outfit, darling."

"You've forgotten, haven't you?" Phillip's expression reminded her of a child who was being denied an extra cookie. She had the urge to slap him.

Then she knew why Phillip was sulking. "Our engagement photograph. It's tonight, isn't it? What outfit had we decided on?"

"Your turquoise suit, dear. Does wonders for your eyes," he said, looking deeply into them. "Quick like a bunny upstairs to change. That photographer chap won't be here for another half hour."

As she planted another kiss on Phillip's cheek, she gave the package under the chesterfield a reassuring nudge with the heel of her shoe. Tonight, she would smile for the birdie, then give the performance of a lifetime in the bedroom. Within a week, Mr. and Mrs. Phillip Rossner would set sail, and any future packages could pile up on the front verandah until they rotted, for all she cared.

Nora went upstairs, and so did the bottle of scotch.

30

BY THE TIME KEARNS ENTERED Beyond Expectations, it was 12:20. He'd circled Laurel Village twice before snagging a parking spot six blocks away from the café. Beth Wells, punctual to a fault, would be waiting.

Kearns grabbed an iced tea from the cooler at the front of the cafe and sidled by a ponytailed man leafing through a copy of *Poetry Flash*. As Kearns muttered "excuse me," he wondered why anyone would consent to having one's nose pierced not once, but twice. He paid for his drink at the counter and threaded his way to the rear of the café where Beth sat, drinking a cappuccino and reading *San Francisco Weekly*.

"Sorry I'm late," Kearns said and pulled out the woven chair with chrome supports. "Breur's chair, right?"

Beth smiled. "I'll make a designer out of you yet, Jim. Maybe once this lunatic is caught, you'll be ready for a career change." When he sat down, she looked him straight in the eye. "I read about Patricia Mowatt. How awful for you."

"Never mind me," Kearns shrugged. "I'll survive." Still, he appreciated the empathy.

"Makes my horrid little letters seem ridiculous by comparison."

"Not ridiculous, Beth. Just ... different. You didn't get another one, I hope?"

"No, thank heaven. I'm starting to believe in our theory — more immature than ominous. I think Bobby's finally recognized the foolishness of his fantasy. Anyway, no more letters, and no Bobby hanging around lately either."

"Still, you may have something there. More often than not, the people who do us the most harm are the ones right under our noses."

Beth agreed. "It's like what you said about the Spiderman. He's somebody's son, somebody's neighbour —"

"Somebody's boyfriend, for all we know. What better cover than to hide in a relationship? Trouble is, this guy's not gonna have too many outward signs pointing to his deviance. Most of us can't recognize a murderer until he pulls out a machete and chops our heads off. Oops, sorry."

Beth shifted in her seat. "Jim, on the phone you said you needed my help. What is it?"

He took a long gulp of iced tea and cleared his throat. "It's about Anne Spalding."

"Oh, Jim," Beth sighed, "there's nothing more to tell. I knew next to nothing about Anne. Lousy as that sounds, it's true."

"Look, Beth, I'm not here to push your guilt buttons. Seems you do enough of that on your own. But sometimes, if enough time passes, memories surface. Think."

He waited, but though he could read her expression and knew she was trying her best, nothing came.

"It's no good, Jim," Beth replied, sounding as frustrated as he felt. "Anne and I weren't close. I know you think just because two women shared a house, we should have been having pajama parties, setting each other's hair, and talking about men and sex until the wee hours, but we didn't. I'm sorry."

"Anne was a good-looking lady," Kearns prodded. "She must have had some kind of social life. There had to have been a boyfriend. Surely some small talk, a casual comment —"

He caught it then, that look — the field mouse had spotted the hawk, but too late. Her eyes gave her away.

"I — I told you, Jim. Anne was very private. We both preferred it that way. No, that's a lie. *I* preferred it that way."

"No men coming to the house? Dates picking her up?"

Beth shook her head. "Nothing like that. Not even a phone call. When Anne was around, she watched television, read romance novels."

Kearns took a small spiral notepad from his inside jacket pocket. "Listen, when Anne's belongings were removed from your guestroom, did you notice anything missing?"

"Missing? She had so little to begin with. When I say Anne was running from an abusive husband, I mean that literally. She jumped off the plane, appeared on my doorstep clutching a copy of the newspaper with my ad for a roommate circled. All she had was her flight bag, some toiletries, a change of underwear. During the six months she stayed with me, she'd bought some casual outfits, two pairs of shoes. She didn't own a dress, and her only jewellery was a Bulova wristwatch."

Kearns remembered Inspector Anscombe's list of Anne's things. It had included the watch.

"My guest room is small," Beth continued. "You remember. But Anne's possessions weren't cramming the drawers or closets. Not by a long shot."

"Sounds sad."

"It was. *She* was. I should have gotten to know her."

Kearns heard the regret in her voice for about the hundredth time.

"Why do you ask if anything's missing?"

"It seems, true to the organized killer's profile, our perp is taking trophies. Wondered what he might have of Anne's." Kearns levelled a gaze at Beth. "You realize this is privileged info. If Devereaux were to get wind of this, I'd have to kill you." He smiled, but Beth didn't. Her expression was pained, tense with forced recollection. She wanted so badly to help, yet Kearns knew chances were slim to none that Beth would remember if anything had been taken. The Spalding trophy would turn up, with the remaining treasures, on the killer's premises, when and if they caught him.

Something must be missing, but Kearns didn't know what it was, and Beth couldn't help him. He was pleased to see Beth concentrating so hard, and knew he'd done a good job setting up the trophy issue as the reason for their meeting. Now he could really get down to business.

He glanced at his watch. "I know you've got to be getting back soon. Let's talk about more pleasant things. How's the boyfriend?"

Beth frowned. "Mad at me."

"Oh-oh. Trouble in Dodge. Is that why you're not sleeping?"

"Something like that. You know, Jim, I'd make a good textbook chapter for a shrink. Anne Spalding lived in my house, and I treated her like a stranger. Rex McKenna, whom I loathe, gets treated with kid gloves, and he walks all over me. Ginny drives me crazy with her insecurity, but do I sit her down and tell her? No. And just when I think I finally find someone I might want to share my life with, I drive him away. I'm thirty-five, for God's sake. When am I going to get it right?"

"That's how we learn, Beth. By our mistakes," Kearns said and meant it, knowing he didn't have enough fingers and toes to count the number of times he'd screwed up. "So you and the pilot are kaput?"

"I don't know. I hope not. But Jordan hasn't returned any of my calls, and I haven't seen him since Saturday night —"

"Cheer up, Beth. Plenty more where he came from. Nothing since Saturday, you say?"

She shook her head. "It may not sound like a big deal, but you have to understand, Jordan and I spent most of our evenings together since the day we met. We'd been to a party last Saturday and I — well, I'm not proud of how I behaved."

"I can't imagine you doing anything so wrong that some guy would just stop speaking to you. Want to talk about it?"

"I'd rather not. Jordan dropped me off curbside. I went my way. He went his."

Yeah. Straight home to check on his latest victim.

Kearns avoided Beth's gaze, not wanting her to see what had to be a glimmer in his eye. He doodled on his notepad. "Pilot, huh?" He looked up. "Those guys must have a tough time staying on the ground once they've experience the wild blue yonder. Probably not lasting-relationship material." He watched her face. That comment struck a nerve. "Beth, it hurts now, I know. But you were moving kind of fast with this guy. Maybe this is a good thing in disguise."

She frowned again. "It sure doesn't feel like it."

Kearns knew he was walking that fine line now, where he had to pretend his questions were nothing more than friendly concern, when in truth, he was a full-fledged cop on duty. He had to know how Bailey drew her in. "What did you think was so special about this guy?"

To Kearns's relief, Beth's frown softened, and her eyes took on a faraway look. She was ready to talk all right.

"He made me realize that I needed balance in my life. That everything doesn't need to be about work. A simple lesson, I know, Jim. But until Jordan came along, I was moving too fast to learn it."

"He encouraged you to open up, is that it?"

She nodded. "About things that really count. My conversations with Ginny and my clients are so superficial. In the context of those relationships, that's fine. But Jordan gave me something more. I really connected with him."

"What about *him*, though? He reveal anything about himself?"

He caught it again, that look. *He hid things from you, didn't he, Beth. Like what?*

"You don't learn a person's life story in a few weeks," she said.

Touché, Kearns thought. "Well, you know what they say about 'if it was meant to be.' You never told me how you two met."

She told him, and he knew his expression concealed nothing. "Lower those eyebrows, Jim, and stop being a cop for a second. Jordan is shy. Following me from this café to my store is kind of sweet, really. Romantic. If he'd plied me with liquor in some singles bar, would that have seemed normal to you?"

"You're right, Beth. Everyone's mating ritual is different." Again, he avoided her gaze, his pencil scratching across the paper.

Jordan Bailey custom fit the profile. Kearns didn't like the way Bailey and Beth had met — what Beth had called sweet sounded a lot like stalking to Kearns. As far as he was concerned, the pilot could stay the hell away from her. He punctuated his drawing with a series of exclamation marks.

"Jim," Beth said suddenly, "that does it. I'm definitely signing you on as an apprentice. Drafting board, unlimited supply of pencils, enough to satisfy the frustrated artist in you. What exactly are you drawing?"

He managed a sheepish grin. "You should rescind your offer. I'm no Picasso."

He turned the notepad toward Beth. Her pupils fully dilated. A small gasp escaped before she could compose herself to feign nonchalance. "I give up," she said. "What are those?"

The sheet was covered in Chi Rho monograms of varying sizes, thicknesses, some adorned with ornate serifs, wreaths of olive branches.

"Privileged information, part two," Kearns whispered, leaning across the small Arborite table. "The killer carves this symbol on the victims' bodies."

So the way she muttered a hurried "my gosh, look at the time" and bolted from the restaurant confirmed Kearns's suspicions.

He steepled his fingers together, took a deep breath, and glanced around the café. Framed children's drawings from the Monart School of the Arts decorated the walls. The noon-hour crowd still sipped lattés, munched on salads, and appeared as bright and cheery as the artwork surrounding him. At once, the clanking of silverware against clear glass plates made Kearns ravenous. This wasn't the sort of place to satisfy a truck driver's appetite, nor a cop hungry for an arrest, but Kearns went to the counter and ordered a hot pastrami and Swiss anyway.

Back at the table, with no female to observe his table manners, Kearns wolfed the sandwich. His brain raced alongside his metabolism.

He flipped the page of his notepad and wrote.

1. mentioned Anne's boyfriend — Beth nervous? What does she know?
2. fight with pilot; SATURDAY — Bailey left for Europe on Sunday.
3. In town for Mowatt's death. Mowatt kept alive/starving while pilot overseas? Possible?

Kearns knew he had thrown Beth off balance, which was exactly what he'd set out to do. She wouldn't be seeing the pilot again, that was for sure, not after all the doubts Kearns had so carefully planted. The Christograms, though, had done the real trick. Kearns had played out a spur-of-the-moment hunch, not knowing if his doodlings would lead anywhere, but the look in Beth's eyes, the panic he'd seen there, told him one thing — she recognized the symbol.

31

B ETH LOCKED THE DOOR TO Personal Touch, relieved to be finished for the day. Though the afternoon had been slack, Beth bustled around the showroom, dusting furniture, rearranging accessories, and straightening piles of invoices and fabric swatches on her desk.

At home she found her mind still racing. Samson was clearly annoyed that his owner wasn't ready to settle into the bedroom chaise for their nightly cuddle. The cat raised its head in a haughty display of disgust and padded from the bedroom in search of serenity. Though Beth had performed her usual ritual — face scrubbed clean of makeup, long hair tied back, work clothes swapped for leggings and a sweatshirt — she still couldn't relax. Her lunch meeting with Jim Kearns had left her on edge.

Beth set her mug of tea on the English tray table beside her chaise. The tea was stone cold anyway. With determined steps, she walked across the hall to the guest bedroom.

The room appeared exactly as it had when Anne occupied it. A large Nova Scotia pine dresser stood against one wall, a Bull's Eye coal oil lamp on top of it. Cherry Windsor chair against another wall. Round skirted table beside the pullout loveseat. Inside the armoire, a 24" Toshiba television, VCR, a CD player. All Beth's. Well, what did she expect? The killer wouldn't have marched in here to claim a trophy. If one of Anne's possessions were missing, the Spiderman would have removed it from her purse. Or her body.

Beth struggled to recall her last brief conversation with Anne. What had they talked about? Anne was leaving for Amsterdam, a city Beth loved. They spoke of canals and bridges, flower markets, the Van Gogh Museum. Antique shops in the Singel. And diamonds. Anne planned to tour a diamond factory, and Beth had given her a blank cheque. "If you have time," she'd said, "I'd love a pair of diamond earrings." Anne had agreed.

She didn't want to think about Anne anymore. She needed a break from Jim Kearns, too. His obsession with the Spiderman was quickly becoming her obsession, fuelling her already turbo-charged anxiety. She hadn't received any more creepy letters either, so there was no need to be in such close contact with Jim. Too, she didn't like the direction their conversation had taken today.

He'd asked her about Anne's boyfriends before, of course. She'd answered truthfully — she hadn't known of any. Now, with the full knowledge that Jordan had dated Anne, Beth kept this information from Kearns. Why? What difference would it make telling Jim, after all? Jordan and Anne's relationship had been brief, not even a relationship at all, really. Then Anne had met someone else.

How would that have made Jordan feel, a shy man who found dating so awkward, so difficult. Dejected? Jealous? Betrayed?

Consumed with rage?

As if sensing Beth required a response, Samson opened one eye and meowed.

"You're absolutely right, Samson," Beth said, scooping up the cat. "I'm being ridiculous. And I've got to relax before I drive us both crazy."

In her bathroom, Beth placed Samson on his usual perch, the toilet seat. She filled her whirlpool bath, lit some candles, then sunk into the steamy water, hot jets pummeling the tight muscles in her neck.

She thought about Jim's profile of the killer. Mobile. Charming. Kearns was no dummy. He knew Beth had attended his presentation at the Fairmont. Why repeat the speech?

And why did he want to know so much about Jordan, even to the point of asking how she and Jordan had met? He seemed oddly pleased that they had quarrelled and weren't seeing each other.

Had that been Jim's real intent, to quiz her about Jordan?

Patricia Mowatt's body had been found on Friday.

And Jordan had arrived home from Europe on Thursday night.

The longer she stayed in the water, the worse her tension became. Now her shoulders ached, and she felt her scalp tighten. The overture of a monstrous headache.

The Christograms had done the damage — Kearns's absurd little drawings on his omnipresent notepad, symbols that looked exactly like the one on the medallion Jordan wore around his neck. Towelling herself dry, Beth realized Jim's doodling had been quite deliberate, meant to elicit some kind of reaction from her, and she'd sure given him one, vaulting from the café like a launched rocket.

How much did Jim know about Jordan and the parochial school?

What *was* there to know?

Right now, she had no answers, only more questions.

In her bedroom, Beth slipped into paisley silk pajamas, curled up in her chaise, and draped a mohair throw over her bare feet. She reached for her remote and clicked on the television, which Samson took as his cue to come aboard. In seconds, the cat had nestled snugly in Beth's lap and was purring contentedly.

As a sedative, the television proved no more effective than the bathtub, and soon Beth realized her hyperactivity had been nothing more than a frenzied attempt to prevent her from thinking. A press of the volume button rendered the bedroom silent, save for Samson's purr and the ticking of the old-fashioned brass alarm clock on the bedside table.

Ten forty-five. Beth was wide awake. Jim needed a killer, wanted an arrest so badly anyone would do. What better way to get Devereaux and her brood off his back than to announce he had someone in custody?

Jordan. The sacrificial lamb. Beth was certain that Kearns did suspect him. Jim had tried everything short of voodoo to steer her away from any kind of relationship with Jordan, hardly the behaviour one would expect from a friend.

What was it Kearns had said at the Fairmont? *This particular type of killer loves to travel. A possible arrest for voyeurism.* Jordan. A pilot. With a telescope in his bedroom.

She needed to know what Kearns knew. Then she could make up her own mind about Jordan, whether to fight for the survival of their relationship, or stay as far away from him as possible.

By the time Letterman delivered a mute monologue, Beth knew what she had to do.

32

Inspector Anscombe poked her head into Kearns's office. Fuentes, seated across from Kearns's desk, swivelled to look.

"Okay, Anscombe," Kearns said, "let's have it. The good news. Am I gonna get some sleep tonight?"

Sharon Anscombe shot Fuentes a quick look then took a step further into the room and leaned against the doorframe. "Bailey has a membership at the Bay Club."

"Yes!" Kearns shouted, his fist raised in triumph. "I knew it!"

"But L.T., I've marched all over that club, talked to a good dozen of the staff, and no one can recall ever seeing Bailey with Mowatt."

"Just because they didn't see it doesn't mean it didn't happen. What else did you get?"

"Talked to the club's squash pro. Says Bailey's a real stand-up guy. Good squash player. Good sport. Does a little weight training once in a while. But Mowatt taught step aerobics and a Pilates class. Mostly women. Squash pro says he can't picture Bailey at one of those sessions."

"Not even if the instructor was attractive?"

Anscombe shrugged and shot another look in Fuentes's direction. "I suppose it's possible, L.T. Quite a few guys wanted some action with Mowatt. Why should Bailey be immune?"

"No reason I can think of."

"I've still got some people to talk to, L.T.," Anscombe said, producing a notepad from the pocket of her navy slacks. "Couple of Bailey's squash buddies have a game booked for 4:30. I figure I can catch them when they come off the court."

Kearns knew Anscombe would be thorough, and if there was anything to get on Bailey, she'd find it. But her tone of voice told Kearns she just wasn't into it, and when he spotted her parting glance at Fuentes, he knew she was going through the motions to appease him.

When she left, Fuentes swivelled back toward Kearns and said, "Good cop, that Anscombe."

"First rate," Kearns replied.

Fuentes polished off the last of a stuffed pepper from his brown-bag lunch and wiped his mouth with a quilted paper towel. Stray grains of rice littered Kearns's desk. Kearns aimed and shot each one, crokinole style, in the direction of Fuentes's lap.

Fuentes swept them onto the floor. "Your nose is really twitching for Bailey, huh?"

"You better believe it. He's made to order."

"I'll agree, he's got a few pieces that fit quite nicely —"

"A few pieces? The list is as long as a gorilla's arm. To add to it, Bailey got back from Europe on Thursday but didn't see Beth. Translation? Maybe no alibi for Mowatt."

"I was in town that night too, but that doesn't mean I killed Mowatt."

"I know. But Bailey and Beth haven't spoken since Mowatt was killed. Why? Depressive phase. Mowatt's death didn't live up to Bailey's fantasy. Nothing can. So he starts retreating into his own dark corner where he can plan his next kill."

"Maybe Beth and Bailey just need some cooling-off time," Fuentes said uncertainly. "Rosalie and I do, after we've had a whopper of a fight."

"Manny, trust me. This isn't tunnel vision. Bailey's all wrong." Kearns picked up a pencil and started tapping.

"But he was otherwise occupied the night Anne Spalding disappeared, remember?"

"So his friends say. Could be that pilots, like cops, protect their own.

I repeat, Bailey's all wrong."

"Sure he is. He's taller than you, makes more money than you, and he's got the girl you want."

"Knock it off, Manny. But listen, there are a coupla things bothering me about our killer's time clock."

"Shoot."

"Carole Van Horne was killed in April, Monica Turner in June, Lydia Price in July."

"And Anne Spalding in August, Natalie Gorman in September —"

"Now we've got Patricia Mowatt, our man's Miss October."

"Point being?"

"Why no murder in May?"

"Van Horne was his first, so he was able to live off that fantasy for two months."

"Or?"

"Or he was fighting his urge to kill again. Or he got the flu. Or relatives were visiting from out of town."

"No other ideas?"

"Maybe this asshole's like the rest of us. Needs a holiday once in awhile."

Kearns nodded. "I hear Amsterdam's nice in the spring. All those colourful tulips."

"Amsterdam?"

"Bailey flew the San Francisco to Amsterdam run in May. I'm waiting for a call from the head of Amsterdam's homicide unit. Worth checking to see if some poor Dutch girl has met our man."

"Well, Jimmy, you're making good sense."

For a brief moment, Kearns thought he and Fuentes were thinking in tandem the way they used to, then he took a look at his friend's expression. "Now what's going on in that fine Latino head of yours?"

"Something you said. The killer's depressive phase. Funny you should mention that."

"Why? Nothing new there."

"No, I mean it's funny coming from you." Fuentes got up and shut the door then sat back down and nailed him with a steady stare.

Kearns heaved a sigh. "How long have you known?"

"Forever."

"Guess I haven't always been easy to get along with. Us depressed folks are good at driving people away."

"You've been a shit. Been treating me like some lackey."

"Hey, wait a minute, *amigo.* Cut me some slack."

"Be glad to, if you'll promise to cut the Spanish bullshit."

"I didn't mean —"

"It's annoying as hell."

Kearns felt his face go hot. He could count on the fingers of one hand the number of arguments he and Fuentes had had over the years. They communicated better than most married couples, knew each other better, too. Or at least they used to.

"I deserve better, that's all," Fuentes said.

Kearns waited, allowing the sentence to hang in the air like a bad smell. He couldn't pinpoint the exact day he and Fuentes had stopped being a team, when their thoughts, instead of meshing, had driven them in opposite directions. They had become like the Kilkenny cats. The Irish rhyme came to him from some faraway place.

There once were two cats of Kilkenny,
Each thought there was one cat too many,
So they fought and they fit,
And they scratched and they bit,
Till, excepting their nails,
And the tips of their tails,
Instead of two cats, there weren't any.

All couples need a cooling-off period. He and Fuentes clearly needed one now, the air thick with animosity.

Fuentes seemed to sense it, too. He stood and headed toward the coffee machine, an aging Norelco that another cop had nabbed as part of his divorce settlement.

Kearns was dimly aware of the bustle around him. There were phones ringing and file drawers slamming, yet it was as though someone had placed a glass cube over him — he could observe, he could listen, but he couldn't participate. The numbness was familiar. He and Mary had countless cooling-off periods during the final years of their marriage. In the end, there had been only ice.

Fuentes returned with two cups of coffee, an improvised peace offering. He sat down again.

Kearns spoke. "Bailey's no damn good, and we're gonna prove it. I'm going to learn everything I can about our parochial school alumnus, so that by the time we bring him in, I'll know him better than he knows himself."

"I'll talk to Bailey's pilot friends again," Fuentes offered. "See if his alibi for Spalding still holds up. But I'll have my kid gloves on. If Bailey turns out to be the doer, the last thing we need is for him to vamoose because we're breathing down his neck."

Fuentes stood, then paused. "You said there were two things bothering you about the Spiderman's time clock. What was the second one?"

"It's almost Halloween, Manny. Hormones being what they are, our man is already planning his November murder, trolling for another victim. I don't want to unroll any more yellow tape. Time to get our asses in gear."

33

E L CAMINO REAL, LITERALLY The Royal Road, was California's first freeway. It parallels the coastline for some 650 miles, connecting the twenty-one Franciscan missions erected in the eighteenth and nineteenth centuries. The Mexican secularization of the missions resulted in the historic buildings falling into decay. It wasn't until the end of the nineteenth century that a group of dedicated preservationists moved to save the crumbling edifices from destruction. The Church of the Good Shepherd, with its accompanying school, was built at the beginning of the twentieth century, a modern tribute to its historical counterparts.

Beth had done some reading on the plane, trying to get a feel for the area. By the time she landed in L.A., picked up a rental car, and made the drive to Ventura, she was more than a little curious about the place where Jordan had spent his childhood.

She had scheduled an appointment with a Father Daniel Fortescue for three o'clock, and though the priest had been pleasant on the phone and agreeable to their meeting, Beth detected a note of what — amusement? in the man's voice. How must this look to an outsider? Here she was, on her day off, jumping on a plane solely for the purpose of checking into Jordan's past, a past he had been reluctant to discuss. She pictured a kindly white-haired cleric who would listen patiently, then perhaps provide her with generalities about Jordan, information that could apply to any of thousands of students who had passed through the parochial system. Still, foolish though the excursion appeared, it was too late to cancel. The digital clock by the car radio read 2:45. She had to do this. Jordan had secrets, and Beth had nowhere else to turn.

You were moving kind of fast with this guy. Kearns's words. And true enough. Even Ginny had been surprised at how hard Beth had fallen. Beth thought about her feelings for Jordan. Away from the intimate dinners and dizzying sex, Beth wondered what truly drove her into the relationship.

She was intrigued by the mystery of Jordan, wanted to know everything about him. There was something about him that reminded Beth of a wounded animal, one who needed nurturing.

But there was so much more. Jordan brought out the best in her.

So why was she here?

Because women were dying.

Because Kearns was a good cop.

And something wasn't right.

The Church of the Good Shepherd was barely visible from the main highway. A rustic carved wooden sign and two white crosses at the foot of a long gravel drive were the only indicators that any building lay beyond the grove of immense redwoods. When the church finally came into view, Beth gasped. It was beautiful, remarkable in its simplicity — stark white stucco, with a red tiled roof. There was a scalloped gable and a three-tiered *campanario*, or bell tower. Beth imagined squeaky wooden kneelers, the cloying aroma of incense, votive candles flickering in the narthex. As if out of respect for the place, Beth shut off the car radio and slowed her speed. Drawing nearer, she noticed the single contrast to the church's simple architecture — a pair of massive Moorish doors with huge iron ring handles.

A crushed stone pathway snaked in front and bisected a garden full of yuccas and lilies. The façade of the church had just received a fresh coat of paint. The scaffolding was still assembled at the northwest corner, but there wasn't a painter in sight. In fact, there wasn't a soul about anywhere, and almost immediately, the peaceful hush that Beth had found soothing became disturbing.

The school, when it came into view, wasn't quite as white as the church, but it bore the same red-tiled roof. It stood three storeys tall, fronted by a magnificent garden of more yucca, cacti, and fronds of palm.

Beth recalled her own school days in Arkansas — children shrieking outdoors, the ones in the younger grades scrambling for swings and teeter-totters, sprinting for the baseball diamond as they grew older. The truly sophisticated ones, the eighth-graders, clustered around the doorways, exchanging gossip and phone numbers. But there was no one on these school grounds, and Beth doubted that she'd find any playground equipment behind the building.

Beth stepped out of the car and stretched, again overwhelmed by the stifling quiet of the place. What time did classes dismiss? At this moment, Beth would have been grateful for a rush of young bodies pouring out of doorways, racing each other toward some more cheerful destination. She tried to imagine Jordan, or any child, spending time in such an antiseptic place, and half-expected to see another calligraphied sign: No Frolicking Allowed. Vowing to adopt a more positive attitude by the time she met Father Daniel, Beth reached for her purse, locked the car, and made her way toward the school.

Inside, to Beth's left was a glassed-in reception area. As she approached, a small window slid open. A dour-faced matron ruled the kingdom on the other side. Beth resisted the impulse to request a cheeseburger and an order of fries; the woman's raised eyebrow told Beth she was all business.

"May I help you?" the woman asked, her voice cracker dry.

"I'm here to speak with Father Daniel Fortescue. My name is Beth Wells."

The woman raised slightly off her swivel chair to get a better look and didn't bother to disguise her disapproval of Beth's above-the-knee skirt.

"He's expecting me," Beth added firmly. "Could you tell me where I might find him?"

"His room is at the top of the stairs. Name's on the door." With that, the woman closed the glass partition and sat back down. Beth wondered whether the glass was to keep the woman in or other people out.

Ahead was a large open concourse and, against the far wall, a statue of

Jesus, a flock of sheep at His feet. An inscription above the tableau read: *And the lost shall return to the fold.*

Beth recalled the parable of the prodigal son, a story she had learned so many years ago. Was this reflective of the philosophy of the school, to shepherd those whom others had led astray? A formidable task. Beth wondered how the teaching priests kept the black sheep in line, then quickly dismissed the thought. One stern-faced secretary and the eerie quiet did not a prison make.

Dividing the foyer were two open staircases, one to the right, the other to the left. Great. Father Daniel's office is at the top of the stairs, the charming hostess had said. Of which flight? A quick scan of the empty lobby told Beth she was on her own. There was no one to ask, and she wouldn't be caught dead going back to the receptionist for clarification. Appropriately, she remembered some basic Latin — *sinister* meant left, so accordingly, Beth went to the right and proceeded up the stairs.

Rounding the landing to the second floor, Beth was nearly trampled by two youths, fifteen years old, she guessed. One mumbled an apology, then they both continued their descent, two stairs at a time, before Beth had a chance to ask for directions. From the flight below, Beth heard a wolf whistle. At least this was normal.

At the top of the stairs, Beth faced another dilemma. She could turn right or left — straight ahead would send her back down the opposite staircase. Either corridor was a Pavlovian nightmare — a warren of doors, archways, and ramps. Some sadistic architect had fooled the casual observer by designing a building, symmetrical on the outside, a circus funhouse within. Again, lacking a coin to toss, Beth turned to the right.

Her shoes resounded on the tiles. The initial feeling of peace she'd experienced upon seeing the church was completely gone now. The interior of the school was as dismal as the receptionist had been. Everything was in tones of brown — reddish brown tile, sienna-coloured brick walls, wooden baseboards, and doors stained burnt umber. The lone bulletin board was bare, its natural cork adding another brown to the palette. The absence of students' artwork made Beth wonder again what Jordan's childhood must have been like.

Three doors up on the left, a man poked his head into the corridor. "Beth Wells?" he said. "I'm Daniel Fortescue."

Well, she thought, here goes nothing.

34

STANDING BEFORE THE WHITE STUCCO building, the place where so many dreams had taken shape, he marvelled at how sharp his mind was, how after so many years, the sounds, smells, and impressions of those earlier times remained so clearly in focus. He sat beneath a huge sycamore tree, barely aware of the coldness of the earth, his sense of the present overshadowed by the vividness of the past.

He remembered the night the two priests stood in his room, their stern, wrinkle-ravaged faces glowering. The older one, Father Francis Xavier, held a bottle of Russian Prince vodka in one hand, his Bible in the other. Father Anthony Bennedetto, only slightly less wrinkled than Father Francis, stared over his bifocals, first at the boy, then at the stack of magazines lying open on the bed.

"You have much to atone for, young man," said Father Francis.

The boy gave them his best wide-eyed expression. "But you don't understand! Those aren't mine!"

"Lying will only make it worse," the old priest said. "You must repent."

"Ask the other boys, why don't you?"

"Now is not the time for cowardice."

"What about that kid at the end of the hall? The goody-goody. He could have set me up."

Father Anthony remained mute. His bifocals had slipped farther down his nose.

"The Eighth Commandment," Father Francis said. "Recite."

"But —"

"Recite!" A large purple vein bulged at the priest's temple.

"Thou shalt not bear false witness against thy neighbour," the boy mumbled hurriedly.

"Again!"

The boy spoke louder this time, carefully modulating his voice to mimic sincerity.

The old priest appeared satisfied. "Come with us, son. And make no sound."

Father Francis threw the vodka bottle onto the bed. It landed beside a semi-nude centrefold. The three left the room and moved in silence down the corridor. They reached a stairwell at the far end of the hall. Father Francis pushed the door open and stepped onto the landing. With Father Francis leading the way, they descended the concrete steps single file, each gripping the banister for support. The boy heard the stairwell door overhead clunk shut.

The old priest was wheezing now, an asthmatic whistle coming from somewhere deep within his chest. The boy pictured a pair of shrivelled, frail lungs crumpling to grey dust like a scorched butterfly's wings. He smiled a little at the image, knowing the priests couldn't see his face. Another image broadened his smile — that of Father Francis tumbling head over feet down the concrete steps. This, the boy found caricature-funny, the black cassock flailing about, billowing above the priest's head, bony hands reaching out to grab at anything along the way. Maybe there would even be a glimpse of some very unpriestly boxer shorts. The boy bit his lip.

He wondered what the sound would be like — Father Francis's head hitting the concrete. Would it be a thud, like dropping a melon on pavement, or a sharp crack like splitting a log with an ax? And how many times would it hit? Just once, and break wide open, or would the body gain momentum and somersault all the way to the next landing just like in the cartoons?

The boy's hand stretched toward the old priest.

Just in time, he remembered Father Anthony. The boy glanced over his right shoulder. The second priest was still silent and peering over his bifocals, which the boy was certain were worn for authoritative effect. The boy's hand returned to his pocket.

Where were they going? Father Francis continued to shuffle downward in the semi-darkness, moving past the doorway for the second floor. The boy was surprised, for this was where the classrooms were. There had been marathon recitations of scripture in the deserted study hall until his voice was hoarse and his eyes burned with fatigue.

At the main floor, too, Father Francis ignored the door and continued still downward. So they weren't going to the priest's office either. Or the cafeteria. Mentally, the boy ticked off the punishments — scrubbing the cafeteria floor, cleaning the priests' toilet, dusting each page of the leather-bound volumes in the priests' study, all seven thousand books. Any one of these he expected, but as the silent group continued its descent, he knew the priests had come up with something new.

He was, for a moment, flattered they were going to so much trouble, that for him, they'd exercised some creativity. Whatever they had planned excited him. There would be a great story to tell tomorrow, and when he told his schoolmates how the old farts hadn't gotten to him, there would be nothing they wouldn't do for him. Yes, tonight he would climb another rung on the ladder.

As Father Francis reached a double set of doors at the bottom of the stairs, his breath came in short bursts, the flute-like whistle constant now.

They entered the gymnasium.

Even in the darkness, his mind could picture the blue concrete block walls, the wooden bleachers along the west wall, six basketball hoops, one of them still bent forward from when he'd swung on it. Ten cracks with a ruler and no gym for a week after that little stunt.

He predicted they would make him run laps, do one hundred pushups or perform some other feat of muscular endurance until his body collapsed. In his weakened, defeated state, they would make him pray the rosary and expect him to make a good confession. He would have to complete some duty in public, too, as an example to the other boys that such behaviour at the School of the Good Shepherd was not to be tolerated. He prepared himself mentally for the exertion to come, knew just how to shut off enough of his mind so he wouldn't really notice what was happening. He imagined himself physically strong, unbeatable, and listened to Father Francis's laboured breathing. No contest. He could outlast these two relics.

The hardwood floor creaked as the three walked across the gym. The boy pressed his sneakered feet against the floorboards and twisted, each step producing a high-pitched squeal. Ahead of him, there was a flash of white collar as Father Francis turned around, his glare slicing through the darkness like a scythe. The boy, suppressing a grin, resumed his normal gait.

The gymnasium reeked of stale sweat and damp socks, and the odour seemed to intensify as they moved deeper into the room. As they neared the lighting panel at the far end the boy paused, waiting for one of the priests to throw the switch that would bathe the gym in pale, cheerless light. But the click that came from the panel left the gym in darkness. Instead, there was a faint glow ahead of them, visible through the separation between another set of double doors.

The change rooms. Father Francis still led the way, holding one of the doors open for the boy, who squinted as his eyes adjusted to the light. Hurrying after the old priest, the boy released his tentative hold on the door, allowing it to slam on Father Anthony.

In the change room, the stale body odour was strong and mingled with spray deodourant and foot powder. The block walls were painted the same industrial blue as the gym. Blue for the heaven to which they were to aspire, and red for the blood of sacrifice and the sacred heart of Jesus. The school colours.

There was a long bench against each wall in the change room, which was otherwise an empty square. Tarnished hooks jutted from varnished pieces of plywood screw-nailed into the concrete. Many of the hooks were broken off. Others dangled from loose screws.

The oppressive presence of Father Anthony behind the boy's shoulder was unnerving. The priest had yet to utter a single word, but somehow, his role in the drama raised the small hairs on the boy's back.

Father Francis beckoned them onward, and they passed through an archway into the next room. Here, the boy nearly laughed aloud. Sinks and showers. They were going to wash his mouth out with soap.

Honest, Father. I'll never sin again, he could hear himself say. *I just wanted the others to like me.* Yeah, that would work. The question was, when should he start apologizing? When they produced the soap, or should he let them get in a few sudsings first?

Eight grimy sinks lined the wall to the right, with rubber stoppers suspended from chrome beaded chains. Vertical paths of rust stained all eight basins.

The sinks weren't the intended destination. Instead, Father Francis moved toward the shower stalls at the back of the room. Finally he stood in front of the last stall on the left.

Suddenly there was a tightness in the boy's throat, and he thought of making a run for it. But Father Anthony was too close and seemed to sense his thoughts, for at that moment, he grabbed the boy's right forearm.

Father Francis seemed to be examining the shower stall. It was curtainless. The ceramic tiles were dull and mildew-stained, the grout black. Several tiles were missing, leaving gaping green-black squares that made one wall resemble a grinning skull. Two push brooms leaned near the stall entrance.

From the folds of his cassock, the old priest produced a small bottle of oil. He uncapped it, then poured the contents onto the floor of the shower stall. This small effort seemed to expend what little energy the priest had, his wheezing now accompanied by a rattle.

The boy stared transfixed as the last drop of oil left the bottle. Like lightning, Father Anthony's grip shifted, both arms locking around his waist.

"No!" the boy yelled. He kicked out at Father Francis, landing the shot at the old priest's shin. Doubling over, the priest swore, and the boy kicked again, this one catching the priest in the chin. There was a crack, and Father Francis howled. When he stood up, blood trickled from the corner of his mouth. He had bitten his tongue.

The boy winced in preparation for a blow, but there was none. Instead, Father Anthony wrapped a leg around the boy's legs from behind, preventing another kick. With equal efficiency, Father Francis began stripping him, tearing the clothes from his body. The priest's breath quickened.

They shoved him into the stall and stood as a barricade across the entrance.

"You must take care not to move quickly," Father Francis instructed, his voice barely audible. "The floor is very slippery, and you may do yourself an injury."

Father Anthony turned on the tap. Jets of cold spray flew from the nozzle. Embarrassed by his nakedness, the boy turned his face to the corner, away from the water and the gleaming, greedy eyes of the priests. The water was freezing now, like daggers of ice piercing his back.

He began his monologue. "Please, Father Francis. Father Anthony. I'm sorry for what I've done. Those magazines were mine. The alcohol too. Please forgive me."

Although the cold water was bad enough, the boy was more put off by the fact that the two old geezers were seeing him naked. Probably liking it too. He kept his front pressed into the corner.

There was something else, too. Something that he couldn't quite figure out but gave him the creeps anyway.

The brooms.

He begged some more, pleaded, but his penance fell on deaf ears, for the priests had begun a litany of their own.

"Repent and find peace."

"Through punishment find salvation."

"Suffering shall set you free."

"Let the water purify you."

He shouted, "I said I was sorry! Christ Almighty!"

The water stopped.

For seconds, it was deadly quiet. Over.

His toes were slick with oil, his scalp numb, his penis shrunken. His entire body shook.

Behind him, he heard the faucet.

He screamed.

The water, scalding hot, pelted against his bare flesh like millions of fiery needles. He turned to reach for the faucet, shielding his face, his genitals. Father Anthony anticipated the move and picked up one of the brooms. Above the sound of the rushing water was a hard crack, as the handle of the broom came down on the boy's groping hand.

The boy lunged at the priests, slipped, and fell hard onto his knees. He cursed aloud. The stall quickly filled with steam as he slid around the oily floor, trying to escape through the priests' legs. They both had brooms now and were shoving at him, the harsh bristles razing his tortured skin. They forced him into the corner, one broom at his neck, the other at his back. He covered his head with his arms and made himself as small as he could, but still the water burned, searing his exposed flesh like raw meat. He was sure he was bleeding, that every blood vessel in his body had exploded, and he was slowly dying.

The water went cold again, ice-cold, and he waited for the heart attack that he was certain would accompany the shock. From some faraway place, he could hear the priests chanting, fragments of their sadistic benediction rising above the torrent of water.

35

THE WITHERED, HUNCHED-OVER CLERIC Beth had expected didn't appear. Father Daniel stood straight and tall and was clad in navy sweats and red sneakers. His long hair, greying only slightly at the temples, was tied back in a ponytail. Beth judged him to be in his mid-fifties, though it was difficult to be certain. This man probably always looked younger than his true age.

After a friendly handshake, Father Daniel beckoned Beth to follow him into what she assumed was his classroom. The space was anything but traditional and bore none of the depressing beigeness of the corridor. Desks were arranged in groups of six, the teacher's desk in the centre of the room. The walls were alive with history, art, music. Every square inch was filled with posters — Paul Revere, Benjamin Franklin, Susan B. Anthony — all drawn by students. A clothesline strung across the width of the room. From it hung the class's projects, replicas of explorers' logbooks, the pages artificially aged with brushed-on coffee. Clay pots of philodendron, English ivy, and sanseveria flourished on a ledge by the window.

The priest led the way into his office, another space that revealed much about the man. One glance around told Beth this teacher was truly beloved, that he'd established a rapport with his students that made him more friend than teacher. Mementos from former pupils were everywhere — plaques, photographs, paperweights. Coffee mugs with witty sentiments lined up on a shelf.

"You know you're getting old when former students come in with pictures of their own children," Father Daniel said as he filled the kettle.

A guitar rested in one corner. Beth sat on a leatherette divan next to it. She and Father Daniel exchanged niceties for a while, their conversation filled with observations about architecture, how kids have changed, the demands of the teaching profession and the priesthood. It was easy for Beth to understand why students felt so drawn to this man. He had a broad knowledge base but, more importantly, he was a good listener.

The priest poured strong tea into two stoneware mugs, handed one to Beth, and sat in an oak armchair across from her. "I hope Earl Grey is all right? Miss Wells, how do you think I can help you?"

Beth felt the flush of embarrassment warm her cheeks. "I'm not sure you can, Father Daniel. To be honest, the longer I sit here, the more I wonder why I came. I already feel guilty for taking up your time. You must have other business to attend to."

He dismissed this with a wave of his hand. "*People* are my business. Besides, guilt is good for the soul."

"Really?"

"Nah. I just made it up." He smiled. "But when a priest says something, people take it as gospel. Now Miss Wells, you haven't come all this way on a whim. Anyone can see something is troubling you, and *my* guilt won't allow me to send you away without at least your plane fare's worth." He smiled again. "On the phone you said you have some questions about a former student?" Father Daniel prompted. "Jordan Bailey, wasn't it?"

Beth nodded. "Father," she began, then paused. "This is so awkward —"

"I've been leafing through these old yearbooks and school records to jog my memory," he cut in. "Jordan Bailey was a diligent student. Quite a few Bs and As on his report card. He was the kind of kid who threw himself full tilt into everything — schoolwork, athletics, the Church."

"Was he very religious?"

"Not fanatically so, but he was a good altar boy. I think he found some kind of peace through his faith. He had a very grown-up understanding of the world. He realized how faith can be an anchor when the waters get choppy."

"He needed that anchor, Father?"

"I think so, yes. Particularly during adolescence. While most begin to question their faith during those years, Jordan became a more devout Catholic."

"Why was that?"

"He stopped going home for weekends. Stopped going home to see his mother completely, in fact. The Church became a kind of security, something he could count on."

"Did you discover why he wasn't going home?"

Daniel took a sip of tea and shook his head. "Jordan never confided in me. Though we had a good relationship, I suppose some things are just too painful to discuss."

"Something dreadful must have happened."

"For that information, you'll just have to ask Jordan yourself."

"Did his mother care about him?"

"In her way. Sometimes people have too much of their own baggage to be effective and loving parents. I think Jordan's mother may have been one of those, but it doesn't mean she didn't want to see him grow up to be a fine man. She seemed quite concerned about him."

"Were you?"

Father Daniel looked at her, almost through her. "What you're really wondering is whether Jordan sustained some kind of damage, whether something in his past caused him to become ... unhinged, is that it?"

Beth was shocked. "I was going to put it more subtly."

"When you've come all this way and your time is limited, it's more expedient to dispense with the b.s., don't you think?"

"I suppose you're right. Father Daniel, what else can you tell me about Jordan?"

"Miss Wells, all I can relate are some vague recollections about Jordan as a schoolboy. People change. Don't you think you already know him better than I?"

"But it's his past I want to learn about, Father. Jordan won't tell me much, and frankly, a few things have me climbing the walls."

"And until you have all the pieces, you think Jordan might be the killer the police are looking for?"

Beth opened her mouth to speak, but the priest held up his hand.

"I understand everyone is paranoid about this Spiderman I've been hearing about. In fact, you just missed Lieutenant Kearns. He was here this morning."

Naturally, Beth thought, relieved at least that she hadn't run smack into Jim in the hallway. How would she have explained that?

"Why don't you tell me why you think Jordan fits the description?"

Beth listed her suspicions. "And he won't talk to me about his past —"

"Haven't you ever concealed information about yourself, something you felt was so awful or embarrassing that you thought no one would understand it?"

Of course she had. "It's just that the police cautioned us to watch who we know, saying someone may be unwittingly shielding the Spiderman, and I thought —"

"You didn't want to stick your head in the sand. Listen, Miss Wells, I've read what the police have put together about the Spiderman. Still pretty general. For all anyone knows, *I* could be the killer."

"But you didn't date Anne Spalding, Father. You didn't follow me for weeks."

"Look, all I can say is that I remember Jordan Bailey as a pretty good student. A few adolescent pranks, just like any other kid, in my opinion. Over the years, teachers learn a lot about the kids they teach. Any educator worth his paycheque can spot the ones who haven't got a hope in hell of making it. If there's a kid with a screw loose, we generally know who he is. I never placed Jordan in that pigeonhole, and I pretty much told Lieutenant Kearns the same thing," he paused, then managed a sheepish grin, "though I've often been accused of being naïve."

"In other words, you can't reassure me."

Father Daniel leaned forward, rested his elbows on his knees and gazed at her intently. "Let me ask you something. Your relationship with Jordan, is it serious?"

"It was."

"Yet instead of staying in San Francisco trying to rebuild whatever has fallen apart, you're here, talking to a complete stranger about someone he knew twenty-five years ago. I can't give you some magic phrase that will make your suspicion of Jordan disappear."

"I don't know why I thought it would be that simple." Beth was about to thank the priest for seeing her, wanting nothing more than to exit gracefully, but Father Daniel was pouring more tea.

"Listen, since I've gone to all this trouble to clean this office for your visit, why don't you take a look at a younger version of the man you've been dating."

Father Daniel nudged three yearbooks across the coffee table toward Beth, the appropriate pages marked with yellow Post-it Notes. Beth smiled at Jordan's seventies' hairstyle, a heavy lock of dark brown hair swooping across his forehead. Even then, she would have considered him a hunk, would have followed him from class to class and scribbled his name on her binder. Another photo showed Jordan, third from the left in the back row, in basketball uniform with his teammates. There was Jordan the altar server, Jordan working in the library, Jordan boxing food for the poor.

"Well, what do you think?" Father Daniel asked.

"I don't know. Father, you must think I'm crazy."

The priest smiled, his expression full of compassion. "These are difficult times. A little suspicion is understandable."

Beth closed the yearbook. On the front cover was a gold Chi Rho monogram. She traced the symbol with her finger. "The killer's signature," she said.

"The Chi Rho is a commonly used symbol, Miss Wells," the priest said, again sensing her concern. "Since Lieutenant Kearns made me aware of the killer's mutilations, the Christogram angle has bothered me. While it's not necessarily a link to the school, I understand why Kearns is pursuing the religious aspect of the murders. And hey, parochial schools are no different from any other with regard to the cross-section of kids we get. Like I said, every classroom has a requisite number of oddballs, and once in a while, a teacher comes across a student who exhibits all the signs of psychosis. Still, I could hardly give the lieutenant a list of those names. What a wild goose chase that would be."

"What about you, Father? Have you ever taught someone you thought was psychotic?"

The priest leaned forward again, placed his mug on the table, and seemed to struggle with a memory. Then he smiled again. "No," he said, his voice hesitant. "No, of course not."

The question was on the tip of her tongue, but it went unasked. She looked at her watch and knew she'd have to hurry to make her plane.

At that moment, Father Daniel was rising to his feet, and he appeared relieved to see she was doing the same. "Let me walk you to your car," he said.

36

He couldn't remember how long he'd been trapped in the stall, cowering in the wretched, mildewed place, being alternately burned and frozen. He decided he must have passed out, for when he looked up, the water was off, and he was alone. He tested his environment, rising tentatively to a crouch, then pushing up with his hands until he was semi-upright. There was a sudden jab of pain from the small of his back, and he knew what had happened. He could feel the watery centre of what must have been a huge broken blister oozing its way between his buttocks.

He didn't dare look at his body, certain the sight would cause him to faint again. Instead he focused on the tiles around him and forced himself to count to 500 before he peered around the partition to ensure that he was indeed alone.

Cautiously, he ventured from the stall, catching himself as he began to slide, half-expecting the priests to jump out from the change room and brutalize him all over again. But the change room, too, was empty.

They'd taken his clothes.

The final humiliation was the journey across the gymnasium floor and up the stairs, naked, to his room. Racked with pain, he moved as quickly as he dared, hoping he wouldn't be seen. On the second floor landing, he stopped. There was a sound of slippered feet in the hallway. A shadow passed in front of the window in the stairwell door.

It must be Father Simon, sleepwalking again.

When the shadow passed, the boy continued until he reached his own corridor. The doors were still closed, and the hall was chilly. Though the floorboards creaked with each agonizing step, he made it to his room undetected. The magazines and the vodka were gone.

Once in his room, he couldn't bear to lie down, though his body cried out for rest. The notion of anything touching his skin brought sour bile to his throat. He choked it down and remained standing, naked, in the centre of his room. In the darkness, he felt his left hand. Swollen. He wiggled his fingers. Nothing broken.

He thought that at some point during the night, his skin would surrender the fight and split wide open, that somehow his fragile outside shell would crack and leave nothing but a humped mass of muscle and organs. He would wind up looking like one of those drawings he'd seen in a gruesome fantasy comic book.

At last, he was ready to look at himself, to examine what the priests had done, but he didn't dare turn on the light. Lights-out policy was strictly enforced, and he couldn't risk waking one of the priests. He could wait until morning to assess the damage. Both knees were most certainly bruised, but he thought his face had probably survived any blistering or scraping.

When dawn broke, he went to the window. The sun was rising, a brilliant orange ball peeking just above the silhouette of the Church of the Good Shepherd. In spite of his physical pain, he felt a curious peace, not in any way related to the glory of the sunrise or the venerable sight of the Spanish-style church. His peace came from the simple knowledge that he had survived. The ordeal by water, the agonizing prodding with the brooms, the priests' incessant mumbo-jumbo were mere flirtations of what he could rise above. It was morning, and his skin hadn't split. He was still in one piece, the same person as always. Hell, better. He'd shown was kind of cloth he was cut from.

Now, sitting on the ground looking up at the *campanario*, he delighted in the knowledge that others, too, had since discovered the kind of person he was.

Movement in the parking lot interrupted his reverie. She was getting into her car.

One thing his childhood had taught him was the importance of discipline, that waiting could be so sweet. Comedians knew timing was everything. He knew it too, and this knowledge helped him through the periods when he would sink into a vortex of desolation so great that only a new project could relieve it.

Maybe this time, he could come closer to perfection.

He had big plans for Beth Wells. She would be the best yet. He knew it from the moment he'd met her. She was stunning, her shoulder-length hair the colour of rich sable, her eyes an intriguing blue-green, able to swallow him like the depths of the sea. Her perfume, a heady mixture of jasmine and musk, the full sensuous lips, all there to ensnare him. For him, time slowed to a crawl as he found himself lost in her. The force of their first touch jolted him. There had been no turning back.

He had always been a planner and loved to imagine scene and sequel much as a writer would. The two priests had served as adequate opening acts, though both their deaths had not come about exactly as designed. Still, Francis did croak eventually, and so did Anthony.

He hadn't had the privilege of seeing Francis die, but Anthony had done him the courtesy of showing him exactly what it sounded like when a human head came into contact with pavement. That had been an unexpected bonus. Pretty much everything since had gone his way.

Soon it would be time for his next project, and to keep the game from getting dull, he had given himself a little mental challenge. He recorded the series of medical symptoms of anticoagulant overdose as they occurred, then he would predict the time each victim would die. He had nailed down the jogger's death to within five minutes.

The women's scripts were getting to be a drag, though. They were always saying the same things, begging him not to hurt them, offering him anything. Most annoying was when they told him why they wanted to live. They wanted to travel, get into movies, start their own business. He could yawn.

They made feeble attempts to say what they thought he wanted to hear. They called him master, king, stud, god. When he heard all he could take, he cut them.

Maybe this one would be different. He knew why she was here, of course, and her intrusion into the environment where he'd grown up evoked in him an irony that made him smile. He wondered what she knew, then realized it didn't matter. He could have her any time.

Following her had been easy. Since he had first seen her, he'd gotten to know her routine pretty well. Today though, she was less predictable. Today was an adventure. Tailing her to the airport, grabbing a last-minute flight to LAX, his taxi pursuing her rental car at a discreet distance, just added to the thrill of the quest. His wig, unshaven face and baggy clothing rendered him nearly unrecognizable. As an added precaution, he'd popped in tinted contact lenses and applied a different aftershave. In retrospect, he needn't have bothered. On the plane, she was absorbed in some book or other and hadn't even looked up as he sidled by.

An image formed in his mind. The Peace Pagoda in Japantown. No, he thought, ashamed of himself. Too complicated. Even if he could successfully get his cargo to the top, he would be too far away to hear the force of the impact. Then there would be his escape from the top of the tower, an impossibility if curious onlookers began gathering below.

The Golden Gate Bridge was a cliché; too many others had fallen from it. He thought a moment about Pier 39 and imagined a dozen fat, blubbery sea lions around her dead body. A possibility.

The image that stayed with him, grew and festered until he actually saw it in colour, was the sight of her perfect body tumbling down Lombard Street, the crookedest street in the world. Would she ricochet off each concrete barrier when she rolled? Not likely. Regardless of the steep slope, the shape of the human body prevented it from gaining the necessary velocity. Still, the notion amused him.

Bethany Wells. Human pinball.

37

"No action is in itself good or bad, but only such according to convention." Beneath the black silhouette that replaced his grad photo in the yearbook, the boy had quoted Somerset Maugham.

Father Daniel hadn't thought about him in years. Now, the boy was on his mind constantly. And in his prayers.

Monday's visit from Lieutenant Kearns had stirred up memories, recollections that, over time and with steely discipline, Daniel had managed to bury. Still, he believed there was a reason for everything. Eventually, perhaps with a small mental nudge, he would learn why his stomach roiled relentlessly and why he hadn't kept food down since Kearns had called.

Beth Wells, too, with her particular brand of desperation, confusion, and nagging doubts, would contribute to Daniel's sleepless nights, sweat-drenched hours of tossing and turning, flailing legs shackled by soaked sheets. With as much motivation and determination as he could muster, Daniel finished preparing the next day's history lesson. He hoped the class wouldn't rehash today's discussion of the Spanish Inquisition. Young people were fascinated by the ghoulish nowadays, it seemed. Or had they always been?

When he was young his family had vacationed one summer in Niagara Falls. They crossed the border into Canada, Daniel's only visit to another country, and had scoured every souvenir shop and T-shirt place on Clifton Hill. A visit to Madame Tussaud's wax museum was a required tourist attraction, but the chamber of horrors, with its instruments of torture, gave Daniel nightmares for weeks. He usually revelled in a good horror story, his collection of H.P. Lovecraft his most prized possession. But Lovecraft wrote fiction. The Inquisition and all the atrocities committed upon humans in the wars, before and since, were fact.

So was the Spiderman.

Daniel steadfastly ignored any news printed about the killer, his only information gleaned from the hallway chatter of his students. By avoiding immersing himself in suffering, he felt he could deliver a more positive gospel message. Now he wondered if all the years of guitar playing, basketball games, and zealous camaraderie meant not that he was a good priest, but instead one who skated across life because it was easier. He knew how to be a pal, but could he be a friend?

Daniel was as guilty of abusing the boy as the priests who beat him and his mother who ignored him. He'd done nothing to show the boy right from wrong, his inaction sending yet another unclear signal about life and how it should be lived. Instead, he swept the boy's illness into a corner and played one-on-one with the kid to work off all that energy.

He closed his binder, rose from his desk, and walked over to the classroom window. The church's white *campanario* was floodlit, its contrast to the surrounding black a symbol to Daniel that goodness, purity, the awesome power of God, could triumph over the dark forces. He had never questioned his vocation, knowing deep in his soul he was meant to teach and to serve. He loved clamour in his classroom, cheers in the gymnasium, a full congregation of voices raised in song. This evening, he would forsake his acoustic guitar for the electric one. A little noise, for the love of God. Tonight, Daniel found the infernal quiet that enshrouded the place after lights-out to be disturbing.

It had begun with the dog, a Heinz variety of no fixed address that regularly wandered onto the grounds in search of food scraps and companionship. The dog had become a kind of mascot for the boys, who took turns feeding and grooming it. When its body had been discovered hanging in Father Francis's confessional, a puerile vigilante squad was formed. Father Anthony quickly quashed the idea of vengeance. So long ago, yet sometimes Daniel still felt the stiffness of the pathetic creature's carcass, rigid in his arms as he'd cut it down. He led a burial ceremony in the garden behind the school.

A week or so after the dog had been killed, a fire broke out in the office adjacent to Father Francis's study. Someone had set all the priests' vestments ablaze. Father Francis, as was his habit, had consumed his evening sherry and was snoozing in a leather chair. He had awakened, groggy and disoriented, to find the office and adjoining study thick with smoke. The priest groped his way to the door leading to the corridor, only to find the heavy oak portal jammed shut. The casement window on the opposite side of the study wouldn't budge either, and the elderly priest's feeble shouts received no response. Everyone else was in the gymnasium, watching an exhibition basketball game. Francis's last desperate act before succumbing to smoke inhalation was to hurl an armchair through the casement window and propel himself after it.

The combination of the priest's age, his angina, and his panic brought on the heart attack that kept Father Francis hospitalized for well over a month. Father Daniel, though only a recent addition to the Good Shepherd staff, had gone to visit Francis, hoping to offer some comfort. Francis, however, could not be comforted. The police had said his sherry had been spiked with Seconal, the study door pennied shut, the casement window nailed down to prevent the priest's escape. Attempted murder. A sick practical joke gone horribly wrong.

In a matter of days, Father Francis appeared to decay before Daniel's eyes. The old priest's gnarled hands lay clasped together on top of a lightly woven hospital blanket. His wrinkled cheeks were concave, as though the element that had once given them shape had been vacuumed away. His complexion was sallow, his eyes sunken in their sockets, eyeballs covered with film, their usual darting motion halted by the realization that he would never leave the hospital.

"Watch him, Daniel," he'd gasped on a rush of exhaled air. "You must watch the boy."

Daniel had tried to pacify him, urged him to get rest and allow the police to gather the necessary proof.

"Proof!" Francis hissed. "They'll never prove he did it. You *know*. The boy is beyond clever. He's evil. He must be stopped."

Three dagger spikes blipped across the heart monitor's screen. Daniel remembered patting the priest's hand, wishing he would exhaust himself and fall asleep.

The film across the old priest's eyes seemed to disappear, his gaze widening in agitation. His scrawny hands groped for Daniel's black shirt. "In the name of all that is holy, the boy hung that dog in my confessional. I was meant to find it, to have this heart attack then. He knew about my angina."

Gently, Father Daniel tried to remove the priest's fingers from his shirt, uncurling them individually until Francis's hands rested underneath his own. "With all due respect, Father Francis," he'd said, "everyone knows about your angina. You're never without your pills, and all the boys have seen you pop a nitroglycerin under your tongue. It could have been any one of them."

"Why do you close your eyes to what he is?"

"I know how you feel about the boy —"

"He's evil," Francis repeated, his voice growing faint from fatigue, "and don't tell me you haven't seen it. You know him better than anyone."

"I know he's had some problems, that his mother —"

"Spare me the armchair psychology, Daniel." The old priest's bony fingers moved under his, making weak fists. "I know you're young. Seminarian idealism. Evil exists, Daniel, and it lives in that boy."

"Then it's my — our — job to save him."

"It's our job to *control* him. It's too late for salvation. He spits in the eye of God." The notion that the boy blasphemed appeared to upset Father Francis more than the attempt on his life. For a moment, he looked about to say more, but both men's thoughts were interrupted by a hacking, ragged cough. The old priest covered his mouth, but a moment too late. A spray of spittle dotted the blanket and the front of Daniel's shirt. Father Francis jackknifed upright, his cough robbing the rhythm from his breathing. His face reddened, then went purple. Daniel reached for the nurse's buzzer, but Father Francis waved his hand in protest.

When his cough subsided, he spoke again, his voice a mere rasp. "Stop him, Daniel. Please."

Daniel bit his lip and nodded, but Francis had already closed his eyes. His flushed face returned to its previous pallor.

Daniel remained at the ailing priest's bedside for another forty minutes, wanting to reassure himself that the old priest was resting peacefully. The corridor was quiet, the evening hush broken only by Father Francis Xavier's frail lungs whistling as they laboured for air.

Finally, the obnoxious caw of a crow on the ledge outside the hospital window roused Daniel from his chair. The sound filled him with dread. Dreams of birds, in traditional folk wisdom, signified death.

Like that night years ago, a gentle drizzle was now falling, and it pattered against Daniel's classroom window, coaxing him into the present and blurring his vision of the *campanario*. He moved away from the window, grabbed his windbreaker from the back of his chair, shut off the lights, and rushed outside. The rain was cool, and he turned his face upward.

In the distance, Daniel heard the roll of thunder, like a giant's growling stomach. He turned up his jacket collar and headed for the church. Minutes later, he stood before the huge double doors, the pair of ringed handles like two vacant eyes staring at him. If he concentrated, he could almost hear the strains of the opening hymn as it had been sung that night.

Seven o'clock mass had begun, and he remembered slipping quietly into the church, sidling into a pew directly behind the boy. Father Anthony was bellowing the liturgy, as though volume was some kind of measuring stick for devotion. Daniel had been unable to concentrate on the scripture, his gaze so focused on the boy.

He couldn't believe how much the boy had changed in the few months he'd known him. His shoulders had broadened, his unblemished face now in profile, so hard and chiselled like a man's. When he turned to face Daniel for the sign of peace, there was a trace of a grin at the corner of his mouth. Their handshake was robust and friendly.

Evil. You must stop him.

After communion, Father Anthony appeared visibly shaken. Even from where he sat, Daniel noticed the priest's hesitant steps, the teetering as he moved from altar to tabernacle to chair. Drunk? Daniel dismissed the thought. Priests drank, of course. Lots of them. It was a lonely life, but Daniel had never seen Anthony have more than the occasional glass of wine. There was a bad flu going around. The church was three-quarters empty; many of the boys were sick, so Anthony had likely picked up a bug. He didn't even sing the recessional hymn as he came down the aisle, and by the time Daniel chatted with a few of the regular parishioners and exited the church, Father Anthony was nowhere in sight.

Some of the boys had started a game of British bulldog on the grounds below the *campanario*. It was pouring rain now, but Daniel left them to it, issuing a light-hearted warning about tracking mud into the residence. Several gave him a friendly wave, and he was just about to move on when one of the boys hollered, "Look! Up there! The tower!"

Daniel turned to face the *campanario*. Standing in the rounded archway of the bell tower was Father Anthony, his vestments rippling in the wind. With the *campanario* illuminated, the priest appeared messianic, his arms outstretched in some mock crucifixion. Daniel called up to Father Anthony, but if the priest heard, he gave no indication. He stared straight ahead, at some mysterious focal point in the pitch black, a vortex of nothingness, then he hurled himself toward it.

It could only have been seconds, but for Daniel, time froze. Even now when he remembered the scene, he pictured Anthony's body not plummeting, but drifting downward, like a stray tissue waiting to be caught.

Much of what came afterward was less clear, obscured by the flurry of commotion, the boys' piercing screams, and the passing of too many years. Daniel had tried to quell the panic. He urged the boys to turn away from the sight of Father Anthony, who lay spread-eagled on the brick sidewalk, a relentless pool of blood forming beneath his head.

But one detail stood out Venus-bright in Daniel's mind, in spite of countless hours questioning his own vivid imagination and the effects of Father Francis's chilling words. The boy appeared inured to the grisliness of the scene as well as his peers' shock. In spite of Daniel's repeated requests to step back, the boy remained at the front of the crowd, his head tilting from side to side, as he examined Father Anthony like some lab specimen. He glanced up at the *campanario* too, then again at the priest's remains, seemingly transfixed by the aerodynamics of what had just taken place.

A massive dose of LSD was discovered in the dregs of the Communion wine, the police said. Since it was cold and flu season, many parishioners, out of consideration for one another's health, declined drinking from the chalice. Father Anthony had to drain the contents. Fifteen minutes later, he was convinced he could fly.

In the days and weeks following the tragedy the police narrowed their list of suspects, but the boy didn't make the cut, and in the end, even those who had endured countless rounds of questions were exonerated. Eventually, the death of Father Anthony became one of the spooky stories the students told on camping trips.

The iron rings on the church doors seemed to wink at Daniel, jarring him back to reality. Quickly he glanced around, wondering if any witness had been privy to his nocturnal wanderings, the lunacy of a priest standing in the pouring rain, staring at the ghosts that continued to haunt him.

As Daniel hurried across the front lawn, he gazed up at the lighted windows of the residence. Mercifully, no one was looking out, and he reached his room unobserved. A warm shower did little to remove the chill that permeated his marrow, and for a solid hour, he sat in his easy chair, willing his muddled thoughts to align themselves in some logical order.

He still had Jim Kearns's number tucked into a corner of his desk blotter at school. In a few days, once he had gathered his information and rehearsed how to present it without sounding like a blood-and-guts-fascinated loony, he'd call the lieutenant. He would need to gather his courage, too.

There was a chance the call would amount to nothing, and Daniel would join the ranks of other armchair profilers with overactive imaginations.

So why bother?

Because the past was beginning to gnaw at him like some flesh-eating virus and it was time to exorcise his demons.

Time to stop making jolly, strumming his way into people's hearts, and glossing over their pain. He used his enthusiasm as a tool to convince others that life on this Earth was akin to heaven, if only one had a positive outlook.

Bullshit.

Evil did exist, and he'd known it all along.

38

THOUGH HER VISIT TO FATHER Daniel yielded little information to relieve her suspicions about Jordan, Beth found herself overcome by guilt at having chosen subterfuge over confrontation. During the days since her trip to Ventura, she reminisced about evenings spent with Jordan, discussions where the past never intruded, where only the present and the future mattered. She struggled with her fears, but it wasn't long before her heart triumphed over her head, and she knew she had to see him. She left messages on Jordan's answering machine, imploring him to return her calls. He didn't.

Finally, on a desperate Thursday evening, Beth jumped into her car and drove to Noe Valley. There was a cool mist falling, and the autumn air was chilly enough to warrant her turning on the heater. As she turned onto Jordan's street, Beth saw his Mazda pulling into the driveway. The sight of Jordan emerging from his car, athletic bag in one hand, car keys and squash racquet in the other, reminded Beth of how she'd missed him. He looked great, hair still damp from the shower.

Jordan was already climbing the steps to the front porch when Beth parked her car behind his, and when he turned, she noted the puzzled expression on his face. She shut off her ignition and bounded up the driveway after him like a crazed fan chasing a rock star. It was all she could do to keep from wrapping him in a wrestling hold. Two things stopped her —

her own nervousness and the look on his face. He wasn't thrilled to see her.

"You wouldn't send away a woman who's driven clear across town, would you?"

Clear across town? She sounded like Minnie Pearl.

"Beth." He didn't smile. His voice was toneless. "This is an unexpected — quite a surprise."

She guessed the phrases "unexpected pleasure" and "nice surprise" were too much to hope for. Still, he wasn't beating a hasty retreat.

Her words tumbled out. "If you'll let me explain, Jordan, and you still don't like the reasons why I've been a complete fool, you can call me every vile name in the book, throw me out on my behind, and I'll promise never to bother you again. Deal?"

"This is awkward, Beth —"

"Oh," she cut him off, saving them both the embarrassment, "you're expecting someone, aren't you? There's another woman."

Great. Now she was into soap-opera dialogue.

"No," he replied quickly. He turned his key in the lock. "It's not that. I'd invite you in only —"

"Only what?"

"Only, I'm not in the mood for the third degree tonight." His gaze bore through her.

"I guess I deserved that," she said, moving past him through the door.

Inside, Jordan's manner was stiffly formal. He didn't offer her coffee, didn't help her with her trench coat nor motion her toward a chair. Clearly he did not expect her to be staying long. This was all business, her idea, and he had the home-court advantage. He waited until Beth settled at one end of the sofa before he sat in a tapestry wing chair opposite, a huge square coffee table between them.

"Been working out?" she asked, gesturing at his grey sweats. *Idiot.*

"Squash game with Brad," he answered politely. "He cleaned my clock."

In one swift breath Beth said, "Jordan, I've got some explaining to do. If you'll let me."

"This should be good," Jordan said. "It's not every day someone tells me why I'm being interrogated like I'm some kind of criminal."

Beth inhaled deeply and wished for a glass of wine, whisky, turpentine. On the bright side, she told herself, their relationship couldn't get much worse.

"I loved growing up in Eureka Springs," she began, feeling ridiculous. "I had an idyllic childhood, the whole routine. But you know what happens to teenagers, full of questions. You begin to imagine what life has in store for you beyond the boundaries of your home town."

Jordan sat, immobile, straight-backed, hands resting on his thighs. Even in his sweats and well-worn sneakers, he looked uncomfortable.

"I feel as though I'm on *This is Your Life*," she said.

"Beth, you've come here for a reason. Let's have it."

She took another deep breath and tried to ignore the sting of his indifference. "Because my parents owned an inn, they knew everyone in town. I dated local boys, sons of my parents' friends, and it was assumed I'd go to college in Little Rock and eventually settle down nearby."

"Doesn't sound that bad," Jordan said.

"No, it doesn't. But the inn was a real tie. We could never travel, never had a real family vacation, and the only time we closed down was when we were renovating. As beautiful as the town is, I wanted to see more. I was always good in art. I helped my mother select furniture, wallpaper, drapes for the inn, so naturally interior design beckoned, and so did the bright lights of New York. It seemed so exotic, so unlike what I'd known. I became determined to live my dream."

"Which you did."

She nodded. "But not before I shared my grand idea with Robert Clay."

"One of the locals?"

"No. Robert was a guest at our inn. He was gorgeous. Long sandy hair, the bluest eyes, flashing bright smile. He was twenty-four, drove a Mustang — all pretty cool to a seventeen-year-old."

"Let me guess," Jordan said. "He got you pregnant."

Beth shook her head. "He didn't stick around long enough. But I harboured the usual adolescent fantasies. I imagined Robert whisking me off with him — he was travelling across the country before beginning a new job with a brokerage firm in, of all places, New York City. He'd propose to me, relieve me of my virginity, and I'd go to school while he worked. Great plan."

"He wasn't interested?"

"He never knew, thank God. I was so captivated by his glamour, the stories he told about New York — restaurants in Greenwich Village, off-Broadway theatres, carriage rides in Central Park. It was enough to listen to him talk. Plus there was the perk of being seen about town with him, riding in *his* Mustang. Me, Bethany Wells from Eureka Springs cruising around with a handsome older man. In two days, I was head over heels."

"So, to quote someone's maiden aunt, Robert Clay was quite a catch."

"Robert Clay wasn't Robert Clay."

Jordan raised an eyebrow, the first indication of more than polite interest in her story. "What do you mean?"

She repeated. "Robert Clay was a work of fiction. The name I'd stupidly scribbled on pads of paper along with my own — Mrs. Bethany Clay — didn't exist. Robert Clay was really Adam Scott. He was from Pacifica, not too far from here, and his Mustang wasn't *his* Mustang. It belonged to some poor guy in Berkeley. Then there was a Corvette in Sacramento, an MG in Reno, a Thunderbird in Denver. I may have the cars and cities mixed up, but you get the idea."

"Ah, Beth," Jordan said, his facial features softening as he thought he gained understanding. "You fell for a thief. But you were seventeen. Being starry-eyed isn't a crime. Still, what does this have to do w —"

"Starry-eyed is an understatement," Beth's voice escalated. "I was stupid, plain and simple. I followed my heart while my head took a holiday. Yes, Adam Scott was a thief. And Adam Scott was a very nearly a murderer. And everything that happened was my fault."

39

IN THAT MOMENT, BETH GLIMPSED the return of the Jordan she'd come to care so deeply about. His face registered shock, sympathy, and concern that went beyond courtesy. He felt something — she knew it. Whether it was love or not remained to be seen, and for the briefest time, it appeared that he might rise up, rush to her side, and put his arms around her.

Then it was Jordan's turn to inhale deeply. He remained where he was, took another moment to digest what she'd said, then spoke. "What do you mean it was your fault?"

She closed her eyes, trying to will away the hideous memory, but she knew Jordan was waiting for, and deserved, an explanation. After several deep breaths she still couldn't meet his gaze.

"It was one of those perfect nights," she began, staring at the ceiling. "Gentle breeze, plenty of stars — we were drinking lemonade on the front porch. How hokey it all must have seemed to him. But he played it for all it was worth ..."

Beth paused again, sighed, then braced herself to continue. "The next afternoon, I came home from school, later than usual, to find my mother unconscious."

"Jesus. This Scott guy?"

She nodded. "He'd hit her with the metal box full of money he was stealing." She looked at Jordan then, his expression still not understanding the whole truth. "And who do you suppose let slip where we kept our money?"

Jordan seemed about to react then thought better of it.

"I was such an ass," she said and hung her head. "I also told him that mom was going to meet with her garden club and would be gone for the better part of the day. The only way it would have been easier is if I'd just handed him the money outright. And the blood, Jordan — so much of it. I thought my mother was dead."

Her voice caught, and she found it difficult to swallow. Jordan remained silent, giving her time to wrestle with the murky shadows of her past, memories of a fantasy gone horribly wrong. Eventually he asked, "What was this creep doing in your bed and breakfast? The whole image is ridiculous."

"Would you go looking for a killer at a quaint Victorian establishment? Adam Scott was practised at the art of the unpredictable. He didn't appear to be on the run. He planned to stay in Eureka Springs for a few days, take in some of the sights. In reality, he was scouting around for license plates to steal, or another car. Those few times I was with him, I never suspected that anyone might be in danger. All I could see was a dazzling smile, a hot car, the smooth charm —"

"Don't torture yourself, Beth. You were all of seventeen. You were attracted to the things most young people go for. But why, so many years later, are you suspicious of me? Do I remind you of this guy? You seemed willing enough to trust me earlier."

She nodded, feeling herself warm slightly at the thought of how quickly she'd jumped into bed with Jordan, how badly she wanted to be there right now. "I told myself never to follow my heart again, that during times of vulnerability, one's heart as a guide is hopelessly inaccurate. So I became a champion workaholic. Queen of the Two-Date Quickstep. No involvement, no hurt feelings."

"And?"

"Then I met you and all my sensible advice flew out the window. Everything felt so right."

The soap-opera diva was back.

Jordan leaned forward. "Then why the turnaround?"

She paused, knowing no amount of diplomacy or subtlety would make what she had to say easy to hear.

He seemed to sense this. "Go ahead, Beth. You've come this far."

"Part of it is the hysteria surrounding the Spiderman," she admitted. "Jim Kearns, who is in charge of the investigation, is a friend of mine."

Jordan looked surprised.

Beth nodded. "He kept reminding me about this lunatic at large. His obsession became my obsession. The Spiderman was jumping out from behind every bush, and some of the characteristics of the killer could have belonged to you."

"Wait a minute. So all the questions weren't really about my so-called mysterious past? You actually thought I could be some psycho killer?" He shook his head in disbelief. "Beth, the Spiderman's profile could fit almost any guy between the ages of twenty and forty-five."

"I know, but those letters I've been getting have me spooked, and Ginny casually pointed out that they first appeared shortly after I met you."

"And here I thought she liked me."

"You were so reluctant to discuss your past ..."

"You didn't tell me about Adam Scott. Doesn't that qualify as part of your secret past? Look how what he did affected the way you see people. Everybody has a skeleton or two they feel should stay locked up."

"You have to understand how Jim Kearns rattled my chain. He asked me loads of questions about you, and constantly reminded me of the Spiderman's profile. So many things fit. The way we met — Jim made it sound like you'd been stalking me. The medallion you wear — the same symbol is connected to the killer. Then when I learned you'd dated Anne Spalding —"

He seemed genuinely confused. "How did you know I knew Anne?"

"Come on, Jordan."

"You've lost me."

She stared at him. If he lied to her now, would she recognize it? "Anne lived with me."

"What?"

"She rented my spare bedroom. Brad told me you dated her. Your being with Anne was too much of a coincidence."

"Suddenly, I feel the need for a drink. Be right back." He got out of the chair and went into the kitchen, returning minutes later with a bottle of Sauvignon Blanc, some Evian, and two glasses. The action of uncorking the wine, filling the glasses, and pausing between sips relaxed the atmosphere and slowed the momentum of the conversation.

At length, he said, "I never knew."

"Jordan, how is that possible? You two dated, you must have picked her up at my place, dropped her off —"

"Never. You see, Anne and I met for drinks after a flight, usually at a bar near the airport. We never went beyond that, and it was clear she guarded her privacy. I didn't know where she lived. None of us did. She always insisted on taking a taxi home, and because I knew about her husband's violent bent, I let Anne call the shots. She apparently didn't want to entertain the possibility of her address leaking out somehow and getting back to her ex. She was petrified."

It made sense. Anne would be cautious, and Jordan would respect that. "Then whoever killed her must have worked overtime to gain her trust. Poor Anne. And poor you. Jordan, I'm more sorry than I can ever tell you. Since I'm already in the confessional booth, I may as well tell you my ultimate sin."

She explained her visit to Father Daniel Fortescue, how she pumped the priest for information about Jordan, thinking this would nail the coffin shut on their relationship permanently. Oddly, Jordan seemed neither surprised nor angry.

"I guess with the emotional climate of the city right now, everyone seems guilty until proven innocent. If it makes you feel any better, the police questioned me about Anne, and they seem satisfied that I'm on the up and up. In fact, your buddy Kearns spoke to me the morning of Brad's party."

Beth remembered how exhausted Jordan had been. Her interrogation, on top of Kearns's, had understandably angered him. "Oh Jordan, I've been just awful. Hell, you should be bouncing me out of here after what I've done. Can you forgive me?"

"Forgiving isn't a problem, Beth. Forgetting will take a little time, but I'll work on it."

"Can I make a toast?" Beth held up her goblet. "To keeping a balance between head and heart."

He stood, glass in hand, stepped around the table and sat beside her on the couch. "To new beginnings." They clinked glasses.

Beth knew then that things would get better. Not only did her honesty feel liberating, but voicing her story about Adam acted like a kind of catharsis, too.

"You never said, Beth. Whatever happened to Scott?"

She shrugged. "Adam Scott is probably on his twentieth alias somewhere, duping some other poor fool. If I could erase one thing from my past —"

"But you can't. And neither can I. But since you've gone to so much trouble to learn about my past, I may as well tell you."

Jordan refilled his wineglass, took a deep breath and began. "I was thirteen. I had this brilliant idea to jump on a bus and surprise my mother for her birthday. We hadn't seen each other in awhile, so I thought she'd get a kick out of it."

He paused, his voice tinged with bitterness. Beth waited in silence while Jordan wrestled with a memory. He took several gulps of wine before he could continue.

"The long bus ride left me bagged, but I was so excited I almost forgot how tired I was. I ran the last three blocks home, flowers in one hand and a birthday card in the other. I could already imagine how happy my mother would be when I raced in hollering 'surprise!' But of course it didn't go like that.

"I stood in her bedroom doorway like a prize idiot, holding a bouquet of wilted daisies while some fat, naked creep lay on top of her, pounding away."

His face was frozen in anger, his mouth a tight straight line.

"It seems there was a long list of naked creeps willing to pay significant sums of money for the pleasure of mother's company."

At once, the wineglass shattered in his hand, the contents forming a dark circle on the rug. Jordan stared, transfixed by a rivulet of blood running between his thumb and index finger.

"Oh, Jordan, I'm sorry." Beth reached across to examine his injured hand, but Jordan dismissed the gesture. He gazed a moment longer at the blood before pressing the cut to his lips. "Are you all right?" she asked.

"I'm fine," he replied, his eyes focused on the stain on the carpet.

"I can't tell you how sorry I am," she repeated, hoping he could somehow forgive her. "I never should have pried."

"Nothing to be sorry for. Besides, the past doesn't matter. It's the future that counts. See? The bleeding's stopped." He showed her his hand, then stood up and beckoned to her. "Follow me," he said. "I've got something for you."

He led her, not upstairs to the bedroom, but into the kitchen and toward a narrow door to the left of the refrigerator.

She laced her fingers through his, loved the feel of his hand, the strength of his grasp. "Where are we going?" she asked.

"A project I've been working on," he said with a smile. "I want you to see it. It's in the basement."

Jordan clicked the light switch, but the stairway remained dark. "Damn," he said. "Must have blown a bulb. Don't worry. There's another light on a pull chain down there. Just be careful."

Beth let him lead the way. She put one hand on his shoulder. Her other hand clutched at a wooden railing. They descended the steps to the cellar, and behind Beth, the narrow door closed, enshrouding them in darkness.

40

SONDRA DEVEREAUX SAT OPPOSITE KEARNS, the media maven's dressing room at the cable station little more than a walk-in closet with two chairs, a cluttered table, and a mirror. There was space on the pink walls for one piece of framed art — a botanical poster in a mélange of candy colours that made Kearns think of Smarties. Devereaux wore a tailored royal-blue suit. A boldly-patterned scarf was tucked into the round neckline. Kearns thought the woman had good skin, underneath the pancake makeup, though the crow's feet were cracking through the layers. As for her teeth, he couldn't tell. Devereaux wasn't smiling.

"You look like you're sizing me up for a ribbon at the county fair," she said. "But I'm sure that's not what brings you by."

"You don't like me much, do you, Ms. Devereaux?" Kearns asked.

She laughed from deep in her belly. "You're kidding! Instead of catching killers, you're here because your feelings are hurt? Oh, that's rich."

"We're working our tails off on this case."

"Yeah, yeah. I know. 'Pursuing countless leads,' isn't that what you keep telling everybody? Spare me. You and your Keystone Kops have got diddly. What are people supposed to say — thanks for trying, guys? No matter what cop jargon you try to shovel, it still translates to six dead women, doesn't it?"

"No one knows that more than I do, Ms. Devereaux. You think a little piece of us doesn't die too when we visit a crime scene?" Kearns bit his lip. This wasn't going as planned. He was exhausted, edgy, and re-entering the realm of the perennially pissed off. Devereaux was getting to him.

He took a long breath and forced himself to relax in the stiff chair. "We need the public's support," he said. "Someone out there knows something, and we want them to feel they can approach the police. You, Ms. Devereaux, are turning people against us."

"So it's co-operation you want, is it?" the media queen huffed. "Well, let me tell you a little story about what happens when people cooperate, Lieutenant Kearns. And after you're done listening, if you still want to whine about no one wanting to play in your sandbox, then you're not the man I want in charge of this investigation."

Devereaux crossed her legs, and Kearns tried to avoid staring at her shapely calves. She leaned back in her chair and propped her elbows on the table behind her.

"It was July," Devereaux began. "1992. I had a lunch date and had just unlocked my car door when this goon comes charging out of nowhere, shoves me onto the seat, holds a knife to my throat, and tells me to drive. I don't need to spell out what happened next, do I? Or how many times?"

Kearns shook his head.

"As if what he did to me weren't bad enough, I got victimized all over again at the hospital. Cop number one asks me what the guy looked like, what he wore, what he said. Cop two takes my underwear. Cop three asks me the same questions as cop one. It was a freak show. Come see the victim! Seventy-five cents!"

Devereaux uncrossed her legs, leaned forward, and stared hard at Kearns. "So you see, Lieutenant Kearns? I co-operated. And guess where it got me. Fucking nowhere."

Manuel Fuentes gobbled the remains of a spicy capicollo on a kaiser. His current food craze was deli meats, which suited Jim Kearns just fine since that was his own lunch of preference. He had previously observed Manny's fibre phase, where lunches alternated between multi-grain bagels and spinach salads. Then there'd been the fruit phase, the protein phase, and the no-mixing-carbos-with-protein phase. Fuentes fervently embraced each new dietary quirk inspired by the latest article Rosa would find in a woman's magazine, aware that a week or two hence, he'd be off on some other food detour. Kearns knew too, that Manny could be on a mastadon-and-whipped-cream diet and still fit into the tux he wore at his wedding.

Kearns caught Fuentes's glance at his rare roast beef sandwich, only two bites missing.

"Diet?" Fuentes asked him.

"No thanks. I like it the colour it is," Kearns answered, smoothing a hand through his red hair.

"That line's as old as you. No appetite?"

"Not much." He shoved the sandwich toward Fuentes. "Go ahead. Be my guest."

Fuentes hesitated, as if he suspected Kearns might regain his appetite in a half an hour or so, then reconsidered and took the sandwich.

"Does it taste funny to you?"

"Nothing wrong that I can tell." He swallowed loudly.

He watched Fuentes devour his sandwich. Kearns never needed to diet. Bouts of chronic depression melted the weight off him like a rubber straightjacket. There was a rhythm to the illness that Kearns could count on. Whenever his pants started fitting snugly, some event, something his therapist called part of his "toxic environment" would emerge, then close in and suffocate. Neither Kearns nor Fuentes spoke about their recent argument, though today, Kearns noticed that their voices were more sub-dued, almost wary, as if any change in the volume or tone might upset the equilibrium both were trying to regain.

"Never thought I'd say this, but I'm starting to understand where Sondra Devereaux is coming from. She's got her own issues to work through." Kearns chuckled at his own psychobabble, then explained the meeting he'd had with the prima donna of the cable set.

"Did they ever catch the guy?"

"Nope. Any wonder she hates us all? We couldn't do our job then, and we can't do it now. I tell you, crazy as that woman makes me, I do feel sorry for her."

Fuentes took a final bite and followed the mouthful of horseradish with a gulp of Diet Orange Crush. "Wasn't that long ago you wanted her dead."

"Now I only want to murder her evil twin, you know, the persona Devereaux's created."

"I guess you never really know someone, huh? Wonder what we'll learn about our arachnid friend when we catch him?"

"Same crap we learned about other serial killers. That, in spite of wanting to be special, they're ordinary, boring sons of bitches. Physical or emotional abuse — hell, my mother was no saint, but — hey, speaking of background info, what did Bailey's pilot friends have to say?"

"Thought you'd never ask. Jordan Bailey is a fine, upstanding citizen."

"Gee, Wally, where have we heard that before?"

"Keep it up, Beav, and I won't tell you anything." Fuentes continued. "His alibis are solid for Spalding — the night she disappeared, the night she was killed — there's no way he could have done her."

"Shit."

"Thought you'd feel that way. I've done my homework, Jimmy. What about your assignment? Amsterdam?"

"Talked to the head of their homicide division. Seems there was a young Dutch miss who reported an attempt on her life in May, when our killer seemed to be away on holiday. Jordan Bailey was, in fact, in Amsterdam at that time. I checked with the airlines."

"And?"

"And the girl is alive, probably because our man wasn't on his home turf and wouldn't be as prepared or as comfortable in strange territory. The girl, Klara deVries, reported meeting a man, an American, at a bar near the Leidesplein. They had a few drinks and went to her apartment for a few more. She claims, once there, the guy began acting strangely, asking her for a guided tour of her apartment, checking closets, looking out the windows. She thought he was casing the joint and planning to rob her. Just as she was about to ask him to leave, he turned shy, sat down and gave her some story about having not been with many women, blah, blah, blah. You know, the endearing routine."

"She didn't buy it?"

"Oh, she bought it all right. Thought he was really sweet. Then she started to feel dizzy and wished she hadn't had so much to drink."

"Could be your ordinary Yankee tourist rapist, no?"

"No. She's woozy, sits down on the couch, and he sits beside her, real close. Things are heating up, and she's finding him really sexy. Then he describes the things he's going to do to her, and she hopes she doesn't pass out and miss the whole thing. Now her eyes are crossing and she sees double, but she's aware enough to notice he's caressing her, not with his hands, but with a knife."

"Shit."

"Double shit. The knife had a white ceramic blade."

"And she's alive to tell about it?"

"She was smart enough to know that if she screamed, he could slice her throat open. She pretended to be turned on by the sight of the knife, claimed he was the type of guy who knew what women really wanted. She thinks this took him by surprise, and she picked the right moment to kick over a lamp. When he turned in the direction of the crash, she jumped up from the couch. There was a lot of commotion after that, but the authorities gather she just started flinging stuff all over the place, making as much noise as she could. Neighbours pounded on the door, and the guy bolted out."

"A white ceramic blade," Fuentes repeated. "So our guy was in Amsterdam."

"Yeah," Kearns said. "Only one problem."

"What's that?"

"The guy looks nothing like Jordan Bailey. Here," Kearns said, "take a look for yourself." He flipped open a red file folder and handed two pages to Fuentes. "Courtesy of our friends in the Netherlands."

Fuentes stared at the computer-manufactured image of Klara deVries's description of her attacker. The accompanying page listed physical characteristics as deVries remembered them.

"Not Bailey," Fuentes said.

"Not even close."

"So, unless Bailey is a master of disguise or is working with a partner, he's off the hook."

"Maybe," Kearns said. "Or maybe one ceramic knife on Dutch soil does not a conclusion make."

"Jimmy, this page states that Klara deVries was given doses of warfarin, both in her drinks at the Leidesplein bar and again at her apartment; the last drink was also laced with barbiturates. Lab tests confirmed it. DeVries met our man all right, and Bailey he ain't. Need I remind you Anscombe couldn't link him to knowing Patricia Mowatt?"

"I don't know, Manny. Those health clubs have dozens of instructors. Not everybody can see everything that goes on. And what if Bailey *is* a master of disguise?"

The debate was interrupted by the jangle of the telephone. Kearns grabbed for it. "Make it good news," he said. Then, "Send her up."

The last time Natalie Gorman's younger sister had come to Kearns's office, she'd worn a thin cotton dress, her gaunt body fragile as a stick of driftwood. Now an oversized wool sweater swallowed her up. The sleeves hung to her bony knuckles. Black tights accentuated skeletal legs.

"Lieutenant Kearns," she spoke, her voice shaky. "Have you seen this evening's paper?"

"Kearns rose to his feet and rolled a swivel chair into position near Fuentes. "Please, Ms. Gorman, sit down. You remember Inspector Fuentes?"

Stefanie nodded politely, though clearly she couldn't recall their brief meeting. Kearns wheeled his own chair around from behind the desk, not wanting the barrier of furniture between them.

This girl needs a pot roast dinner, Kearns thought. Extra gravy. How was it possible she'd gotten thinner? Her cheekbones jutted through parchment skin. Kearns knew he was witnessing a case of passive suicide. Stefanie Gorman was killing herself with grief.

"What's this about tonight's paper?" Kearns asked, his voice gentle as if any amount of volume would shatter her.

"Look," she said. "Here."

Kearns shifted his gaze from Stefanie's deep-set eyes to where she was pointing, at a grainy picture in the *Chronicle*. "I'll be damned," Kearns said. "So Phillip Rossner's finally been reeled in. Remember him, Manny, from that magazine article about the city's most eligible bachelors?" The photo showed a distinguished gentleman, proud head held high. A woman identified as Nora Prescott had her arm linked through his, her expression unreadable.

"I remember. We teased you about not being in the article."

Kearns was taken aback by Stefanie's audible sigh of frustration. He cleared his throat, shot Fuentes a warning look and said, "Sorry, Ms. Gorman. How is it we can help you?"

"The picture," she said, clearly exasperated. "Look. *There.*" She jabbed her index finger on Nora Prescott's lapel. Fuentes leaned over for an upside-down look. "The brooch. The one I told you about. It's Natalie's."

Fuentes relaxed in his chair. Kearns knew what he was thinking. There's almost no such thing as one-of-a-kind these days. Anything — jewellery, art, money — could be copied, the knock-offs getting better all the time. He told Stefanie so.

"No," she repeated, her annoyance plain. "You don't understand. Our grandpa was a jeweller. He made the pin for our grandma Nettie. And this brooch," she pointed again, "is Natalie's. How'd this woman get it? Who is she?"

Kearns slammed his fist on the desk. Stefanie Gorman gasped. Even Fuentes's eyes widened. "Shit!" Kearns shouted. "Quadruple shit!" He sprang to his feet.

Fuentes stood, and so did Stefanie. Kearns paused long enough to glance at the bewildered expressions on their faces, then said, "I apologize for being so abrupt, Ms. Gorman. If this is Natalie's brooch, your family will have it back. Soon."

Fuentes cupped Stefanie's elbow and began leading her away. She stopped, and turned to face Kearns again. "Lieutenant Kearns," she said, "that man in the picture. Did he kill my sister?"

"It's too soon to speculate," Kearns replied, trying too late to collect himself. "We'll be in touch."

The two were scarcely three desk lengths away when Kearns lunged toward his filing cabinet. By the time Fuentes returned, Kearns had the phone book out and was scribbling frantically on a piece of paper.

"What the hell was that all about?" Fuentes asked, coming around the desk.

"I'll bet you anything that this woman in the photo has been receiving gifts from our killer."

"Phillip Rossner's the killer?"

"Not bloody likely. But tonight's a great night to pay a social call and offer my congratulations on the impending nuptials."

Kearns grabbed his topcoat just as the telephone rang. He was nearly out of his office when he heard Fuentes's voice.

"Jimmy? You ought to take this one. It's Father Daniel Fortescue. From the School of the Good Shepherd."

41

Ginny Rizzuto climbed up Beth's front steps and rang the doorbell. Through the door's grillwork, she could see Samson the tabby staring at her. Ginny checked her watch, tapped her foot, then rang the bell again. When that brought no results, she pounded on the door, sending the cat running for cover.

"Come on, will ya, Beth?" she hollered. "Supper's gonna get cold."

She pressed her ear to the door but heard nothing. She tried the bell again.

The door opened wide. "Give a girl a break, Gin," Beth said, catching her breath. "I can't run down the steps in these heels."

"Trick or treat!" Ginny hollered as she spun around. "It's La Rizzuto. Best piece of tail in town!"

Ginny stood on the porch, clad in a leopard costume. Beth rolled her eyes and hustled her friend inside.

Ginny didn't get trick or treaters at her apartment, so it had become tradition for her to help Beth shell out goodies to the children who paraded the Marina's streets looking for a free sugar high. Beth put Ginny's share of chocolate bars in a huge stainless steel bowl on the sideboard in the entry hall.

"You look great, as always," Ginny told her. "It's just not fair."

Clad in a snug black dress, black stilettos, a crisp white apron and starched cap, Beth thought she had done a reasonable job with her upstairs maid outfit. "What's in the bag?"

Ginny was carrying a large, grease-spattered paper bag, stapled at the top. "Seafood. "Let's chow down. It won't be long before the little beggars are out in full force."

They entered the living room. Samson, perched on a stack of mail on Beth's desk, stared quizzically at Ginny's furry costume. "Now what do you suppose he's looking at. Hey, new chair?"

Beth nodded. "New old chair. Jordan refinished it and gave it to me the other night. Isn't it gorgeous?"

Ginny stepped closer for a full inspection of the oak pressback rocker. "Whew. He must be crazy about you. All these fiddly grooves and spindles would have driven me nuts. So you two are still hot and heavy?"

"More like lukewarm," Beth replied as she led Ginny into the kitchen. "We've agreed to take things a little slower. Big date Saturday night, though. Jordan says he's got something special planned."

"Something special, huh? Sounds like a night of Hide the Genoa Salami."

Beth ignored the comment, set the cartons on the centre work island, and hoisted herself onto a stool, her black dress riding thigh high. Ginny's idea of seafood consisted of two portions of battered cod and a soggy clump of French fries.

"Hey Beth, we should've gone to the Exotic Erotic Ball," Ginny announced. "We'd have had a blast."

"Forget it, Gin. Once was enough."

Four years ago, Beth had caved in to Ginny's pleas and accompanied her to what was once known as the Hookers' Ball. Ginny, in her leopard costume, assailed anyone who would listen with an endless stream of pussy jokes. Beth, clad as a Stone Age Wilma Flintstone, got several requests to get male revellers' rocks off. Being housebound with Ginny was much safer.

"Heard anything from Brad?" she asked Ginny.

"Brad from the party? Uh-uh."

"You okay with that?"

"Hell yes," Ginny replied, her supper disappearing quickly. "Two warm bodies collided for a while and that was great, but the guy's just not my type." She shovelled in another mouthful. "Isn't this fish the best?"

Beth wondered where the Ginny she knew had disappeared to, the Ginny who would surrender every detail of her sexual escapades.

With the arrival of dusk, the doorbell rang, and Beth and Ginny headed into the living room just as Samson made a hasty scramble up the stairs, scattering Beth's mail on the carpet.

After shelling out goodies to a dinosaur and a prisoner dragging a ball and chain, Beth and Ginny closed the door and surveyed the damage caused by the cat's flight for peace and quiet. "Good," Beth said, stooping to retrieve her mail. "Here's my bank statement. Maybe now I'll find out why I'm short of cash this month."

She ripped open the envelope. Fourth in the pile of cancelled cheques was one in the amount of $550, made out to the Van Moppes Diamant factory in Amsterdam. "What on earth?"

"What's wrong?" Ginny asked.

"I asked Anne to check into some diamond earrings for me."

Ginny peered over Beth's shoulder. "Did Anne stiff you?"

"She wouldn't. My guess is that I should be the owner of a pair of diamond studs."

"Congratulations."

"Not so fast. I cleared out Anne's things. Looked in every purse. There weren't any earrings. So — where are they?"

Beth and Ginny returned to the kitchen, but Beth hardly touched her meal, this new connection to Anne deeply disturbing. She recognized her former roommate's handwriting on the cheque, her distinctive backhand filling in the date and particulars. Beth caught Ginny's look and cut into the cod. The inside of her fish was jiggly and grey, a closer resemblance to the human brain than anything she wanted to eat. She tried stabbing a french fry. Six others stuck to it. Beth pushed the carton aside. Grease smudged the countertop. Luckily Beth was spared the explanation regarding her lack of appetite. The doorbell rang again.

This Halloween, Scott Street was evenly populated with adults and children, the grownups trying to get into the spirit of the festivities. A life-sized package of Marlboros and Elvis Presley waited on the side walk while Tweety Bird and a Ninja Turtle held out shopping bags. In spite of the costumes, this Halloween was different, the merriment contrived. No child was unaccompanied, not with the Spiderman still on the prowl.

There was a brief lull at eight o'clock, and Ginny was hungry. "You make the popcorn," she said, "and I'll get the Scrabble board."

The air popper sent kernels flying everywhere. Beth tried to judge the trajectory of the popcorn, sliding the bowl along the countertop with each volley. Suddenly Ginny was in the kitchen, pulling the plug from its socket.

"Ginny, what are you doing?"

"I thought I heard something outside."

"Of course you did, Gin. It's Halloween. Ther —"

"No," Ginny insisted. "Something weird. Come into the living room."

From the direction of Beth's front door, came a low moan, then a scraping, like claws against wood. Beth flung the door wide.

Before her loomed a monster, a hideous gargoyle, its pitted face lolling on top of stooped shoulders. Shreds of sinewy muscle hung from tattered clothing. A bony taloned hand reached toward her, grazing the side of her neck. She gasped.

The creature laughed.

"Tim O'Malley, are you out of your mind?" Beth swatted at his arm. A piece of torn muscle flopped onto the porch.

"Wet pink Kleenex," Tim said proudly. "Helps to have a friend who works for Warner Brothers. And that joke store on Chestnut has great masks." He bent to retrieve the chunk of his arm. "Off to a party. Think I'll win a prize?"

"Oh, you're a prizewinner, all right," Beth said, feeling her heartbeat return to normal. "But don't be surprised if your dance card doesn't get filled up. Handsome you're not."

"Say, you're in costume," Tim said, giving her legs an appraising stare, "how about coming with me? We'd make quite a pair."

"Threesome you mean," Ginny announced, emerging from her hiding place around the corner.

"Sorry, Tim," Beth said. "This cat's in line ahead of you."

Tim shrugged his shoulders and limped, Quasimodo-style down Beth's stairs toward his driveway.

There were a few stragglers between eight-thirty and nine — a ballerina, two ghosts, and Mickey Mouse, and a young boy in his mother's bathrobe and curlers. Beth and Ginny took turns answering the door, then went once more to the window.

"Looks as though that will be the last of them," Beth said and started to pull her wood shutters across the expanse of glass.

"Wait," Ginny said, grabbing her arm. "Look over there. That guy."

"So?"

"It's Elvis. What's he doing out there?"

"Waiting for his child, what else?"

"I don't think so. He was on the street earlier, don't you remember? With the Tweety Bird gang."

Beth thought for a moment. "Standing with the package of cigarettes — you're right. Oh, never mind. He's leaving now."

The man clad as the king of rock and roll headed down the street toward the Bay.

Tim O'Malley's van was still parked next door. Odd he hadn't left yet, then Beth reasoned he must have taken a cab. She closed the shutters, then walked to the entry hall and clicked off the light switch that operated the coach lanterns on either side of her garage door. She and Ginny traded in their costumes for more comfortable sweats, then settled cross-legged on the living room carpet. They were well into their second Scrabble game when the doorbell rang again.

"Damn," Beth said, struggled to her feet and shook off the cramp in her legs. "It's almost ten o'clock. Don't these kids know that no outside lights means it's all over? Hang in there, Gin. I've got a triple word score in the works."

Three swashbuckling pirates stood on her porch, who, judging from their size, couldn't have been more than eleven years old.

"A bit late, isn't it, guys?" Beth said when she opened the door.

The middle boy grinned. "We just live up the block. We're on our way home." All three had pillowcases loaded with candy.

"Looks like a profitable night," Beth said, adding several chocolate bars to their collection.

The boy on the right, the tallest of the buccaneers, held out an envelope. "Is this yours? It was lying right here on the mat."

Beth took the envelope from his hand. She noticed her name neatly typed on the front and felt the tightness of a frown at the corners of her mouth. "Straight home now, guys. I'll watch you from the window to make sure you're okay."

"'Night," they chorused.

Beth peered through the slats in her living room shutters until the boys rounded the corner at Bay Street, then returned to her place on the carpet.

"Guess I spoke too soon, Gin," she said, setting the envelope down on the Scrabble board.

"Left it on your porch?" Ginny said, incredulous. "While we were sitting here, not fifteen feet away? Guy's got balls of iron. Want me to open it?"

Beth shook her head, inhaled deeply and tore open the envelope. "No," she whispered, feeling a sob catch in her throat.

Ginny took the paper from her. "Jesus, Mary, and Joseph."

It was a drawing, done in pen and ink, showing a detailed aerial view of a woman, lying naked and bound to something rectangular. The woman had long dark hair. Her mouth was open wide in a silent scream, her eyes reflecting terror as she looked down at a vertical slash that split her body between the breasts. The entire page was covered with spiky concentric circles, joined by other lines radiating outward.

A spider's web.

42

F ATHER DANIEL FORTESCUE'S PHONE CALL, coming as it did on
the heels of Stefanie Gorman's visit was more than any homicide lieutenant could hope for. The priest also promised to fax Kearns a copy of a
yearbook photo. As Kearns sped along Van Ness, he offered a silent thank
you for this latest twist of fate and impeccable timing. Finally, a break. He
wished he could thank God for the gift of a logical brain or hyper-
intuition that had given him his first important connection to the killer,
but it was timing. No more, no less, and he couldn't take the credit.

He didn't like to imagine the what-ifs, like what if Stefanie Gorman
hadn't read today's *Chronicle*, or what if Father Daniel had gone against his
instincts and not called.

Outside Phillip Rossner's house on Russian Hill, a handful of disappointed trick-or-treaters were shouting obscenities at whoever wasn't coming
to the door. The ground floor of the palatial home was cloaked in darkness,
though a pale yellow lamplight glowed from a second-storey window.

Kearns parked the car, turned his wheels toward the curb and applied
the emergency brake. Knowing that ringing the bell would get him
nowhere, Kearns pulled his phone book from beneath the passenger seat,
activated his car phone, and punched in Rossner's number. He wondered if
the influential moneyman was home. Kearns recalled the many news articles he'd read about Rossner's workaholism and decided he'd probably be

out. Kearns hadn't time to prepare his approach, what strategy he would use to acquire the information he needed from Nora, but he knew Rossner's presence would alter the tone of the discussion. The last thing he needed was Nora telling a pocketful of lies to preserve an image in front of her fiancé.

Nora answered on the fourth ring. "Hello?"

"Mrs. Prescott? This is Lieutenant Jim Kearns." He thought he heard a brief gasp, but he couldn't be sure. "Homicide," he added for extra measure. "I'm parked outside your house —" She'd like the sound of that, Kearns thought, having already sized up Nora's type from the haughty, triumphant look she wore in the engagement photo. "— and I know you're not answering your door. On a crazy night like this, I don't blame you, but I have a few questions to ask you."

The woman sounded flustered. "What's this about, Sergeant — Kearns was it?"

He winced at the incorrect title. "I'd rather discuss this in person, if you don't mind."

If Nora minded she didn't say, because Kearns didn't give her a chance. He'd already hung up.

Quickly, he strode across the street, his presence breaking up the gang of youths and silencing their limited vocabulary. A light came on in Rossner's ground-floor foyer.

The home's front door, a carved oaken masterpiece with bevelled glass, had been soaped and egged, bits of crumbled shell still sticking to the goo. Serves 'em right, Kearns thought, wondering why the well-to-do couldn't be bothered to cough up a couple of Snickers bars for some fun-loving kids once a year.

"This is most unusual, I must say," Nora announced when she opened the door. Kearns produced the necessary identification, which Nora made a grand show of examining. If she noticed the vandalism of the front door, she gave no indication.

Though it was nearly ten o'clock Nora still wore makeup, and her ash-blonde hair was twisted into a classic style that Kearns guessed must have taken at least a half hour in front of the mirror. Her lounging outfit was nicer than Mary's best dress. Maybe this was how the rich lived, but to Kearns, this gal needed too much upkeep.

"I can't imagine what you have to speak to me about," Nora was in the midst of saying when Kearns brushed past her and entered the house.

Nora's heels clicked on the marble floor behind him then grew silent as she stepped on dense, richly patterned carpet. Kearns would have given anything to turn around and catch the expression on her face. Instead, he eyed the room, scouting for a decent piece of furniture to sit on. He settled quickly on one of a pair of down-filled sofas, the sturdiest-looking seating in a room full of spindly antiques. Kearns had no use for rooms like this, such vast spaces that looked decorated but never lived in.

"Mr. Rossner not in this evening?"

"He's dining with a client," Nora replied as she perched on the edge of a fragile-looking needlepoint armchair.

Kearns tried to adopt what he hoped was a cheery expression, then said, "I saw your engagement photograph in the *Chronicle*. Congratulations are in order."

"Why, thank you," Nora responded. "Phillip is a wonderful man."

"Actually, it's about that newspaper photograph that I'm here."

"But I don't understand. You said you were involved with a homicide, Sergeant."

"Lieutenant," he corrected. Kearns produced a copy of the photograph from his pants pocket and pointed at Natalie Gorman's brooch. "This article of jewellery," he said. "Where did you get it?"

A crimson flush crept up from the neckline of Nora's fancy outfit and spread across her cheeks. "Phillip bought it for me, of course," she answered quickly. "Why do you ask?"

"Really? How long ago?"

"Oh my goodness, I don't remember," she said, shoving a wristwatch that seemed too big for her up her sleeve. "Phillip is always giving me gifts, and thoughtful man that he is, he doesn't wait for special occasions. I honestly don't recall when I received that pin."

Kearns let the subject drop. "I don't suppose you've got any coffee around here? It's been a long day, and I could sure use some caffeine."

For a moment, Kearns saw Nora's lips purse in exasperation, but she recovered quickly and said, "I can make you some tea."

"Tea would be nice," he replied. He could hardly wait for her to leave. Like a common thief, he began a sweep of the room, carefully sliding open drawers, not sure what he was looking for, but feeling certain that somewhere in this house, along with Gorman's brooch, were other trophies.

Seven steps put him in front of the fireplace, a massive stone structure with ornate carvings of fruit cascading from fluted urns. A small, tourist-quality Delft urn perched on the mantelpiece looked oddly out of sync with the decor of the room.

The autumn nights had been cool, but not cool enough to warrant the substantial pile of ash that had collected in the grate. Kearns guessed that Nora had used the fireplace for another reason. He crouched, picked up a brass poker, and slid it across the mess. Several swishes later, he had his answer.

Too soon, Nora returned, carrying an antique silver service on a matching tray. "Great fireplace," Kearns said, rising to his feet. He brushed his sooty hand on his dark socks and replaced the poker. "You don't get workmanship like that these days."

"You do, but it costs five times as much." Nora said tightly, setting the tray on the cherry butler's table in front of the sofa. "Do you like your tea strong?"

Kearns shook his head. "Hot water with a little colour. Better pour it now." He sat down and used his fingers instead of the fancy silver tongs to drop two sugar cubes into his tea. "Much appreciated."

The handle of his china teacup was so curlicued that Kearns couldn't get his finger through it. He watched Nora, again seated opposite and managing hers nicely. He pinched his cup's handle so tightly he thought he'd break it for sure. At length, he felt comfortable enough to raise the stupid thing to his mouth. The room was oppressively silent. Nora Prescott wasn't going to mention the brooch again, that was for sure, nor was she pressing him for the reason for his visit. To Kearns, the red flags were flying.

"Tell me, Nora," he said, deliberately emphasizing her name, "do you donate any used clothing to charities?"

"Why Sergeant," she stammered, "what an odd question. Why do you ask?"

"Because I wondered why, instead of allowing someone else the benefit of your unwanted possessions, you chose instead to burn an article of clothing in that lovely fireplace over there."

"I beg your pardon? What on earth —"

But it was no use. Kearns pulled the remnants of a pink zipper from his pocket and set it on the silver tray. He looked first at her eyes, the pupils dilated, then at Nora's teacup, which she quickly set in its saucer to stop it from shaking.

Gotcha.

She swallowed. "You found that in my fireplace?"

"I did indeed. And I suspect that when I take it to our forensic team, they'll be able to match it with the *late* Patricia Mowatt's track pants. Now perhaps you'll tell me when you received a pink jacket."

"Jacket? I don't know anything about a jacket. Nor do I have any idea how that got into our fireplace." She pointed at the zipper as though it were a dead rodent, her gesture exaggerated, her tone of voice beyond flabbergasted.

She was a shitty actress. Beneath the pompous façade she was squirming, and Kearns had to admit he was enjoying it. If he had the luxury of time, he would have dragged this out.

Instead, he sprang to his feet and increased both momentum and volume. "Your fiancé did *not* buy you that brooch and you *do* know how that zipper got into that fireplace. The brooch was sent to you, along with a pink jogger's jacket and several other items. That vase, for instance." Kearns motioned toward the mantel. "It looks out of place in this room. And I suspect that wristwatch that doesn't quite fit you. How long have you known, Mrs. Prescott? How long were you planning to keep this to yourself?"

"I don't understand," she said weakly.

"Look," Kearns said, taking a step closer to her, "I'm not gonna play this ping-pong game with you. You're gonna tell me all about your son, William Prescott, and I strongly suggest you get right to it." He dropped his voice to a hiss. "You probably want this discussion concluded and me outta here by the time your meal ticket comes home."

43

"DAMN," BETH SAID, SETTING THE phone down. "Jim isn't home, and he's not at work either." She closed her address book and returned it to the centre desk drawer. "I hate bothering him. He's got so much on his plate, but he'd want to know about this note. And this one is so much worse than the others." She took another look at the drawing and shuddered. "It's like she's watching her own autopsy."

"Could be worse, Beth. At least the artist gave you a nice set of boobs."

"Go ahead, make light of this, Gin. I'd like to hear your snappy lines if that envelope were addressed to you." Beth paused to allow the words to sink in.

"You're right," Ginny replied, somewhat chastened. "It is creepy. Is Kearns sure the Spiderman's not the one sending these notes?"

Beth nodded. "Says it's not the killer's M.O."

"M.O.? I love cop talk."

Beth groaned. "This guy, whoever he is, is just playing on everyone's fear of the Spiderman, hoping to shake me up. And he's doing a great job."

"I've got the willies myself. Tell you what," Ginny said, patting the carpet, "let's finish this game. Looks like I might finally win one. You can try Kearns's number in half an hour. Nothing we can do in the meantime."

Beth settled onto the carpet. Samson reappeared and draped himself across Beth's feet. Two turns later, Beth reversed Ginny's luck and jumped ahead thirty points.

"Did you hear that?" Ginny whispered.

"Not again, Ginny. Cut it out."

"Musician's ears are never wrong. There was a creak, then metal against metal. Is your front door locked?"

"Yes, and the alarm's set. Stop worrying. You'll drive us both crazy." She checked her watch. "I'm going to try Jim's number again."

"And I'm going to see about that noise. I know what I heard." Ginny grunted as she stood up. "Damn. My foot's asleep. Come on, Samson. Let's investigate."

Ginny headed toward the front door, with Samson, to Beth's amazement, in pursuit. Beth had just located Jim Kearns's home number for the second time when she heard Ginny cry out.

"Oh shit! Beth, quick!"

Beth hurried to where Ginny stood in the entry hall, flattened against a wall, and followed the direction of Ginny's frightened stare.

Crawling across Beth's mint green broadloom were at least a dozen huge, brown spiders.

"Do something, Beth!" Ginny wailed. "I hate those things!"

Beth glanced at her stocking feet, then reached for the nearest weapon. She flung the remaining chocolate bars from the stainless steel bowl, then brought the bowl down on the carpet. Each swing was accompanied by a sickening crunch.

When she was done, Beth counted. "Fourteen spiders. My God."

"Correction," Ginny said, still rooted to the spot. "Fifteen. Look."

Samson had one of the creatures in his mouth.

"Ginny — rubber gloves and a plastic bag."

Ginny raced into the kitchen.

Samson, quite pleased with himself, dropped his treasure at Beth's feet. It was still alive. One more crash of the bowl killed the spider and sent the cat scurrying upstairs.

"Must have been your mail slot," Ginny said, returning with gloves, bags, plus paper towels and a bottle of club soda. "The noise I heard. That's where they got in."

"Thanks," Beth said as she cleaned spider guts from the rug. "You've been a big help."

"I'll show you help. Come on. Grab a jacket. Wanna bet that whoever did this is still out there? Probably laughed his ass off when we started screaming."

Minutes later, the two were outside, looking in either direction along Scott Street, though neither knew what or who they were looking for. A block away, on the corner of Scott and Beach, half a dozen teenagers were leaving a house party. They stood in a circle on the sidewalk, and as Beth and Ginny drew closer, they could see a seventh person in the middle.

"Hang back, Gin," Beth said, grabbing her friend by the arm. "I've had enough excitement for one night. Breaking up a swarming isn't on my agenda."

"No, Beth, they're joking. Listen."

"Thank you, thank you very much," one of the youths said.

"Please let me be your teddy bear," sang another.

Everyone laughed.

Beth broke into a run, Ginny following.

"Hey, you!" Ginny hollered. "Elvis Aron Presley!"

Hearing the voice, the man looked over the shoulder of one of the teenagers. When he saw the two women bearing down upon him, he broke through the group and sprinted toward the Bay.

Beth noticed he had a limp and knew they'd catch him.

"Beth, what's going on?"

Bobby Chandler was one of the teens, dressed as a clown.

"Bobby," Beth cried out, racing past, "help us get this guy!"

The boy kicked off gargantuan red plastic shoes and joined in the chase. Even in sock feet, Bobby soon overtook Ginny, then Beth, and was closing in quickly on Elvis.

At Marina Boulevard, the man turned left and headed toward the Yacht Harbor. Beth watched as Bobby Chandler made a flying leap at his target. The man thudded to the pavement.

"Get off me, you little bastard!"

Beth and Ginny helped Bobby with the struggle and, between the three of them, managed to get the man to turn over. The rest of the teens had now reached the scene, eager to witness the action.

Beth squeezed between two teens. "I'll be damned."

"That's him!" Bobby shrieked. "That's the guy! Hey Beth, why are we chasing your boyfriend?"

"My boyfriend? What are you talking about?"

"This is the older guy I was asking about. He's been around your house a lot these past few weeks. Didn't think he was your type, but Tim O'Malley told me to mind my own business."

Rex McKenna spat blood. He'd bitten his tongue when he hit the ground. "Shut up, you little twerp." He peeled off fake sideburns.

One of the teenagers used her cell phone to call 911.

Beth stared at Rex, her feelings a mixture of revulsion and relief. "The notes and the spiders were from you? Why?"

Rex McKenna spat again and answered simply, "Fuck off, bitch."

44

WHATEVER PRICEY COSMETICS NORA PRESCOTT had so skill-fully applied seemed to crack along with her veneer of gentility at the mention of her son's name. She slumped in the delicate chair, then, as if realizing how uncomfortable it was, she moved to the sofa opposite Kearns, her tiny frame cocooned by the down-filled cushions.

"William was always difficult," Nora said when she had composed her-self. "Even his birth was difficult. Three days in labour, can you imagine? I prayed for death, you know, the pain was so terrible, then finally William was born. No mother loved a baby more."

Love? Until moments ago, there had been so many layers of frost cov-ering the woman, an ice pick couldn't have penetrated. Now she was talk-ing about love. Kearns wondered how Nora would define the word.

It was clear to Kearns that Nora Prescott didn't have a friend to call her own. With him here, ready to listen, Nora would spill her guts. He could already see her relieved expression, the tracing of lines around her eyes and mouth softening.

He pressed on. "And William's father?"

Nora smiled slightly. "The age-old story. I was eighteen. William's father didn't want anything to do with me or his son. Prescott is my maid-en name. I never saw the need to pretend."

"You never took the surnames of any of your husbands?"

"No. I didn't expect my marriages to last. There seemed no point bouncing from name to name."

Marriage to Kearns was a sacrament, not some kind of hobby that could just be discarded when it got boring.

Nora seemed to read his thoughts. "You don't understand," she sighed.

"I'd like to try. Help me out."

"William, even from an early age, was a very demanding child. Very possessive. I had to hold him in my lap constantly, when I was on the phone, watching television, reading the paper. I had to lock the bathroom door for privacy."

Was William Prescott more demanding than any other kid, or was he simply reaching out for a cold-hearted mother's affections? Kearns wondered.

"Three times I brought orphaned kittens home, hoping William would eventually transfer some of his affections to his pets, learn to give rather than take."

"Didn't work?"

"None of the kittens stayed with us long. They ran away."

"Cats are funny creatures," Kearns said. "Maybe William would have been better off with a dog."

"It wouldn't have mattered." Nora sighed. "It was me he wanted. All the time. He even hated it when I went to work, but I finally managed to secure a secretarial position. William threw tantrums every morning."

"What did his teachers say?"

"William was a bully from kindergarten on. I was forever calling in sick to work so I could run to the school and deal with some catastrophe he had caused on the playground."

"Didn't he make friends with kids his own age?"

"There were boys who used to come over to play, but after a few visits, they never came back. Attracting playmates came easily to William. Keeping them as friends, however, was a different story.

"My absences from work were becoming chronic and finally, my boss questioned me. I told him everything about William, and he was wonderful, even offering to act as a surrogate parent to my son."

"Kind of an unselfish thing for a boss to do. This man wasn't single, by any chance?"

Nora pursed her lips. "Yes, Gregory was single and fond of me. Our times together were the sanest of my life. We took William everywhere, and he seemed happy." She paused. "As long as Gregory maintained a respectable physical distance from me."

"You couldn't demonstrate affection as a couple?"

"Not with William around. No hand holding, no hugging or kissing. William always found a way to come between us."

"So William had trouble seeing Mommy as a romantic, sensual woman," Kearns said. "You and this Gregory trod gently until the boy could cope."

"It all sounds quite reasonable, doesn't it? I didn't realize until much later how I was being manipulated by my own son."

"What went wrong?"

Nora heaved a sigh. "You have no idea how painful this is. I'd buried these memories ..."

Kearns bit his lip. He didn't give a shit about this woman's alleged pain. This woman had only memories to bury. What about the Mowatts, the Gormans, the families who had to bury precious loved ones? Swallowing his anger, he said, "Please, Mrs. Prescott."

"The three of us had spent the day at Candlestick Park, then we had supper in Chinatown. William had eaten like a horse all day. Not surprisingly, he was exhausted and complaining of a stomach ache, so at home he went straight to bed.

"It was a gorgeous summer night, and Gregory and I were alone so seldom —"

Kearns held up his hand. "You don't have to paint me a picture. One thing led to another —"

"Afterward, we drifted off to sleep. I awoke hours later. There was a crackling noise. The bedskirt around us was ablaze. Gregory and I were frantic, screaming and swatting at the flames with pillows, running to the bathroom for water. We put out the fire ourselves."

"You're not saying —"

"Gregory left, and I went into William's room. He was feigning sleep, as if anyone could sleep with all the racket we'd been making. I saw my son's eyelids flutter, then he opened his eyes and gave me that sleepy, helpless look that children have first thing in the morning. I can still remember him saying 'Mommy, I don't feel so good. Will you sleep in my bed?'"

"You think William set the fire?"

"Sergeant Kearns, when that little boy rolled over in bed to cuddle, I knew. It was his hands. They smelled like butane."

45

H E HAD BEEN PUMPED FOR days, running on nervous energy and caffeine. Even without the pots of coffee, he would have stayed wide-awake, wired on his fantasies of Beth, imagining what he would do and say when they were together. He played the details repeatedly in his mind until he got the scenario perfect. She would be different from the others. She was no dummy. She wouldn't resort to the feminine tactics the others had tried. Beth Wells would use her brains, try to outwit him, which would make their time together so interesting. He would feel her power, rob her of it slowly, watch it drain from her as it flowed toward him.

He had all his gear ready. And of course, the superwarfarin. He was careful when he purchased it, driving to Pasadena, Sacramento, Mendocino, altering his appearance, using the same line about his pesky rat problem. Superwarfarin, a long-acting anticoagulant, was invented for use on rats that resisted the ordinary strength of warfarin. It was one hundred times more powerful. Combined with his other goodies, the drug turned human blood the consistency of red wine. One slice along the radial artery and blood shot out like Old Faithful, pulsating with the rhythm of the heartbeat. The other cuts, the round arc forming the P and the X across the stem, were strictly decorative.

Each of the women had exsanguinated quickly. The model had taken the longest. He'd found oral contraceptives in her purse and knew birth control pills antagonized the action of blood thinners. But they'd all lain there, pleading, getting weaker, some watching the blood spurt from their wrists, others looking away.

He'd done his research. Probably knew as much about serial killers as that ass Kearns. The aura phase, the trolling phase, the wooing phase. Ted Bundy had been adept at that, with his plaster cast and helpless victim routine. But Bundy wasn't worthy of the publicity he'd received. The bludgeoning — a sign of a man out of control. Where was the art in that?

He thought about Beth Wells again and decided not to make the Chi Rho symbol this time. Though the Christograms had served him well, they were getting old. Nothing like a change in method to keep the juices flowing and the cops guessing.

One thing that damn school had instilled in him was a love of reading. Books, like his fantasies, could transport him at a moment's notice. He didn't particularly care what he read; there was something to be learned on every page. He recalled reading somewhere about methods of torture, fascinated by the death from one thousand cuts.

A medical textbook he happened upon highlighted an interesting case. An infant had accidentally received a high dosage of warfarin, a powerful anticoagulant, through an umbilical catheter. The baby, in spite of emergency treatment, bled through the umbilical stump and intravenous punctures.

The crazy 90s had been chock full of displaced Californians trying to figure out who they were, running from therapist to therapist, embracing every fad and mania in order to soothe their dispirited souls. Each decade had its share of quacks, healers and weirdoes, and the new millennium would be no different. Reflexology, biofeedback, aromatherapy, all designed to slow the hectic pace, to transport a person to another, better place. He could do that at will. He didn't need anyone prodding the soles of his feet to get him to relax. His methods suited him just fine.

He wondered about the tension in Beth Wells's life, how running a successful business must take its toll on her well-being. Once, he had followed her to a massage therapist's on Fillmore, sat in his car imagining her being rubbed and oiled, the knots worked out of her shoulders and neck. Still, there was a better way to relieve stress, headache, the ills of everyday living, and he knew it would be effective on Beth Wells.

Acupuncture.

46

KEARNS SHOOK HIS HEAD, NOT only in disbelief but also to make sure there were still a few brain cells functioning inside his thick skull. William Prescott was now responsible for the deaths of six women, and he had begun his career early, setting his mother's bedroom afire. He wondered if Nora actually believed that her son's three kittens had run away.

"At the time of the fire, how old was William?"

Nora poured more tea and added milk and sugar to her cup. Kearns was ready to throttle the woman, infuriated with her calm demeanour and her apparent desire to pace the conversation at tortoise speed. She clearly was not going to upset herself or go into hysterics. Just as he was ready to rip the teaspoon from the woman's hand, Nora replied, "William was eight."

Kearns fought to remain expressionless though his insides churned. He wished Nora's teapot was full of scotch. "You didn't report the fire, I take it." He already knew the answer.

"I decided to send William to parochial school," she replied. "A week later, he was enrolled at the School of the Good Shepherd. I believed the all-male environment and the strict regimentation would be good for him."

Who was she kidding? This woman had no interest in what would be good for her son or anyone else for that matter. Her priorities revolved in a tiny orbit, with her as the axis. Knowing her son was a killer, she had calmly burned his latest trophy and was prepared to sacrifice human life so she could remain — what? A member of respectable society?

Kearns had long ago declared a moratorium on the endless debate among his task force about whether serial killers were born or created. He had seen too many homicide cops get hot under the collar and damn near come to blows over a discussion that had no resolution. Now, after listening to Nora Prescott and watching her conduct her cozy tea party in the midst of discussing murder, Kearns realized that this woman had not only spawned evil but also casually excused it. William Prescott, for whatever recessive gene he might possess, had been created by another kind of monster, a woman who cast off men like yesterday's underwear, a woman who treated disaster as a trifling inconvenience.

Nora's silence was William's ticket to carte blanche murder.

Within days, William Prescott would capture another victim, and Nora would have let it happen.

He forced a civil tone. "What became of your boss?"

"Gregory took pity on me, of course. He kindly paid William's tuition, called it a loan, but we both knew I could never repay him. Relationships can't survive on kindness and pity, and soon it became uncomfortable seeing Gregory at the office every day. I quit my job, found another through one of Gregory's business associates —"

"Husband number one?"

Nora nodded. "William's tuition was not inexpensive, and a secretary's salary didn't stretch far —"

Kearns held up his hand. "Wait a minute. Parochial school isn't Harvard. In those days, what would it have cost to keep William at the school, a few thousand a year?"

"I made several —" she cleared her throat "— charitable donations to the school. Later on, William needed other things, a car, clothes —"

Then Kearns saw it. "You paid the school off. To keep your son there. They were going to kick him out, weren't they?"

"Several times. Father Francis Xavier called almost monthly to report some mischief or other. He said William was undisciplined, unrepentent, a bad influence on the others."

"But with a handsome cheque now and then, the staff could overlook William's behaviour. What kind of trouble was he in?"

"They told me William smuggled liquor into the residence. Pornographic literature, drugs. The priests were at their wits' end. I knew the feeling."

"I can understand that those offenses might seem serious, Mrs. Prescott, particularly to members of the clergy. I'm a Catholic myself, but detentions, withdrawal of privileges, getting booted off a sports team — the teachers at the school would have had some kind of leverage, something they could hold over your son's head."

"They tried all those things. Nothing seemed to have any effect. It was, as Father Francis told me, as though William was laughing at them."

"And counselling?"

Nora waved away the notion. "Completely useless. He had a few sessions with a young priest. They amounted to nothing. The psych. ed. reports stated that William had potential, was highly intelligent but often distracted."

Father Daniel's words? Kearns wondered.

"I told the school officials to do what they had to do," Nora continued, "but begged them to keep William there. I was afraid of him, you see. I suppose I've always been afraid of him."

It was not lost on Kearns that Nora continually shifted the conversation away from William and neatly onto herself. He would ride this conversation out and be the listener she so obviously needed. Eventually, he'd get to where he wanted to go. "Mrs. Prescott, Father Daniel Fortescue telephoned me this evening. He told me about Father Francis's death, and the death of another priest, Father Anthony Benedetto. There had been a fire at the school. A dog was hung. Did anyone from the school ever contact you about these things, express any suspicions about your son?"

"No," she said. "I read about the priests' deaths in the paper, and the fire was reported in the monthly bulletin the school sent to the parents. But no one called me."

He wasn't surprised. What good would it have done? Nora had washed her hands of her son, figuring that money not only talked, but also kept people quiet, too.

"Mrs. Prescott, there's no point in my being subtle. You're engaged to Phillip Rossner, a very wealthy man. Your son must be how old — in his mid-thirties? Earning his own living. Why the marriage to Rossner?"

Nora Prescott looked around the room as though the answer should be obvious, then heaved a resigned sigh. "Phillip is an ass, of course. A ridiculous, silly ass. But what does it matter? I give him what he wants, and he gives me what I want. I still support my son financially, Sergeant Kearns. I'm sure he has some kind of job, though what, I don't know. But I pay him, and pay him well, to stay away from me. And there was one other condition."

"What was that?"

"He had to change his name. I wanted nothing to do with him."

Kearns had come to the moment he'd been waiting for since he arrived at Russian Hill nearly an hour ago. "Mrs. Prescott, what is your son's name now, and where is he?"

She looked about to reach for the teapot again, then withdrew her hand, placing it calmly in her lap. She looked at Kearns. "I haven't the vaguest idea."

He wondered if Nora would look this unruffled if he took the silk sash from around her waist and choked her with it. "You pay him," he stated, his voice carefully modulated. "Where do you send the cheques?"

"I give him cash. When he asks for it. William writes to me, a different postmark each time, and encloses typewritten instructions specifying where I should leave the money. It's all a game to him. Once, he made me leave it in a dark alley between two strip clubs in the Tenderloin. Can you imagine? Another time, it was at a gas station in the desert, in the men's washroom. I've sent money to post office boxes in Europe, flown to Denver ... All these years and he's still tormenting me. Then the gifts started." She lowered her gaze. "I'm his prisoner, just like I've always been."

That did it. The sight of Nora Prescott cowering on her fancy sofa in her fancy clothes, making like she was the true victim ignited Kearns's fuse. He sprang to his feet and snatched the pink zipper from the silver tray, the charred toggle a pathetic remnant of Patricia Mowatt's too-brief life. He thrust it toward the woman. "Six young women have been slaughtered in your place, and you think you're the victim?" He spat the words. "Well, here's a news flash for you. One, you're gonna bring me every gift sonny boy has ever sent you, and two, you'd better start searching your memory for anything, and I mean anything, that will help me find him."

The trophies materialized quickly, the Cartier watch the last item to drop into Kearns's hands.

"I don't know where my son is, Sergeant," Nora repeated, her manner indignant once again. "I can't even tell you what he looks like now."

"No photos?"

Her look seemed to suggest that Kearns had lost his mind, and for the third time, he wanted to strangle her.

Kearns needed to get the hell out, to find a place where he could breathe clean air. He knew the longest, hottest shower wouldn't cleanse his pores of the infestation he'd been exposed to here in this elegant parlour. His parting shot as he opened the heavy front door gave him a modicum of satisfaction. "Lady, with the trouble you're in, the very least you can do is start addressing me as *Lieutenant* Kearns."

47

SINCE KEARNS'S LAST VISIT, THE Irish pub had undergone a minor facelift. Gleaming brass sconces and deep green-black textured wallpaper gave the place an aura of gentlemanly sophistication. The three-man band had just finished a set and were stepping down from the stage. The bar was as well stocked as ever, and Kearns was glad they hadn't done away with the row of wooden booths that lined one wall. He slid into the one nearest the bar and gave his order to a redheaded waitress who had Killarney written all over her.

He unzipped his windbreaker and remembered all the times he had sat here, as though being among the convivial Irish and listening to some toe-tapping tunes could somehow lift the shroud of depression.

Kearns glanced at his watch, punched in Fuentes's home number on his cellular phone, apologized to a sleepy Rosa, then called the Night Investigations Unit. Fuentes was still at work.

"Manny," he said when he got hold of him, "tonight I met the mother of the devil himself, and I wish I could say I was exaggerating."

"Well, I hope she told you where Satan's lair is, because CLETS has turned up zip on William Prescott."

Kearns had pinned little hope on the California Law Enforcement Tracking System.

"All I've got for my trouble is a stiff neck and eyes that feel like they've been through a sandstorm," Fuentes complained.

"He changed his name, Manny."

"To what?"

"She doesn't know."

"You're kidding."

"I'm not. And if our man's got a driver's license or passport, they're bogus. That's why CLETS isn't picking up a new name in the query."

"Dammit," Fuentes said. "Didn't that woman give you anything we can use?"

Kearns shook his head. "Next to Nora Prescott, Rita Bailey is Mother of the Year." He told Fuentes about his discussion with Nora.

"All I got was one shitty yearbook photograph, courtesy of Father Daniel Fortescue. Ninth grade. Bastard's standing in the back row, his head half hidden by the guy in front of him. Don't suppose the Prescott woman had anything more recent?"

"Nope. Nora Prescott isn't what you'd call the sentimental type. No childhood photos, no old report cards. Hell, it's like she never had a son. I bet none of the poor saps she married had a clue about William's existence. The invisible kid. He's sure making a name for himself now." Kearns signalled for the waitress. "And all those times Nora's dropped money off somewhere, she's never clapped eyes on her son, though she felt he must have been watching her. Big help, huh? At least I got the brooch back." Kearns pointed to his empty glass, and the redhead nodded, returning quickly with another drink.

"Recover any other trophies?"

"You bet. First thing tomorrow, I send Anscombe and Bauer back to the families to identify the belongings."

"So," Fuentes said, "let me get this straight. Prescott's our man, except he isn't Prescott anymore. He could be anybody, living anywhere."

"You're just trying to cheer me up."

"Speaking of which, it hasn't been all dull compu-biz here tonight. Your friend Beth Wells's secret adversary's been picked up."

Kearns listened as Fuentes gave him the lowdown on Rex McKenna. "Thank Christ," Kearns said when he was done. "Beth's too nice to be a victim of that kind of bullshit."

The musicians returned and immediately launched into "Black Velvet Band." Drunker patrons sang along.

"Hey," Fuentes said, "are you where I think you are?"

"*Sí.*"

"Jimmy, there'd better be soda water in your glass."

Close enough, Kearns thought as he put the cell phone back in his pocket. The waitress brought a third ginger ale. Kearns glanced at the bottles of Glenlivet, Johnny Walker, and a ten-year-old Glenfiddich lined up behind the bar like Broadway hookers waiting for a customer. Trays full of draught sailed by. Kearns could have easily grabbed a frosted mug of Smithwicks, but he didn't. He felt like shit, deserved a drink, for the love of Mike, but instead, he had walked headlong into his personal nest of vipers and ordered ginger ale instead. As if he was strong enough to be put to any kind of test right now, he thought, then realized he had passed with honours. Still, he was too pissed off and too exhausted to congratulate himself.

He checked his watch again. Ten after midnight, but he knew that if Beth had the kind of night Fuentes had described, she would still be wide awake. At least there was some good news, and Kearns wanted a piece of it. He reactivated his phone and punched in Beth's number.

She answered on the second ring. Kearns could hear her telling her cat to get off the desk.

"Can't sleep either, huh?" he said. "I'm not surprised. I heard about your adventure tonight."

"Too bad you missed the action. You'd have loved it."

He was glad to hear the note of amusement in her voice. "You must be relieved."

"I still cringe at how it must have looked, Jim — a bunch of costumed idiots chasing Elvis down the street. To be honest, I'm more confused than relieved. What was Rex thinking, scaring me like that?"

"He resented your success, for one thing," Kearns told her. "The two guys who brought him in said he spilled his guts for hours. They felt like Dr. Joyce Brothers."

"What does my success have to do with him?"

"McKenna's lived in the city all his life, spent years cold calling, pounding the pavement and taking people to lunch, schmoozing for clients. You sail in from Quaintsville, Arkansas, build a clientele through word-of-mouth, now your customers come to you —"

"Hey, wait a minute. It wasn't that simple."

"You and I know that, but that's not how McKenna sees it."

"Jim, there are plenty of successful entrepreneurs in this city. Why was I the lucky one?"

"Because you were in his face. See? From his upstairs window, McKenna watched people flock to your store all day long. *He* paid *you* rent. You're almost half his age, a pretty clear reminder of what he could never be. He's declaring bankruptcy, you know."

"So he tormented me with hate mail and put spiders in my house? Jim —"

He read her mind. "No, he's not the Spiderman. God, I hate that name. The guys third-degreed him until he nearly passed out, but McKenna's not our guy. He had alibis up the you-know-what. Wife keeps him on a pretty short leash. McKenna's got lots of the symptoms of a killer, but not the disease."

"Symptoms? What do you mean?"

"He's a bona fide misogynist, just like our killer. Heavily into violent porn. Helluva fantasy life. Plus, get this. He's a battered husband."

"Rex? Battered? Jim, have you seen his wife?"

"No, but let me guess. Barely scrapes five feet."

"Rex towers over Ida. It can't be."

"Beth, it's typical. Lots of these little gals take a frying pan to their husband's kneecaps. The men never retaliate, first out of fear that they'll kill their wives because of the sheer size difference. Later, they're too embarrassed to do anything about it. Who's McKenna gonna tell?"

"So that's why he has a limp? Unbelievable."

"Listen, Beth. At least this is off your plate now. You can relax."

After he hung up, Kearns felt only a kernel of relief. Beth would sleep better now, even if he didn't.

He still had the rest of the women in the city to worry about.

48

FRIDAY MORNING'S SKY WAS BATTLESHIP grey, and the weather report promised a weekend of pouring rain. Beth clicked off her car radio. The threat of rain would not ruin her anticipation of tomorrow night's date with Jordan. As she drove through Pacific Heights toward Sacramento Street, she mentally reviewed her schedule for the next day. It would be tight. Her part-timer, Lorna, was leaving today on a junket to Vegas, her first weekend off in six months. Tomorrow Beth would be running the store alone, as she had done the first two years she'd owned it. She would barely have time to hurry home and get ready. Jordan was picking her up at 7:00.

She still didn't know what he had planned, but he told her to wear something sexy. If the meteorologists were right about the rain, Beth would wear her hair up. Her velvet dress was back from the cleaners, and she'd bought a black lace teddy from Victoria's Secret.

Dammit, she muttered, looking at her wrist. She wasn't wearing her Medic-Alert bracelet. This was the second time this week she'd forgotten it. Beth glanced at her watch, knowing full well that she was already running late. In her mind, she could see the bracelet clearly, sitting by the soap dish on her bathroom counter.

The day ran smoothly at Personal Touch. The Stantons called to say the sectional sofa Beth helped them select had just been delivered, and they were now happily ensconced in their new Tiburon condo, admiring their view of the Bay in comfort.

Lorna was sporting a short hairdo and a new outfit; she was so excited about her Vegas weekend that Beth let her leave a half hour early, wishing her luck at the roulette wheel.

Beth was at the back of the store when she heard the door slam. She checked her watch. 4:55. Dammit. She had neglected to flip the sign in her window to CLOSED; now she'd have to deal with a last-minute browser. Horace Furwell often showed up on Fridays, the onset of a weekend sparking bordello memories. Well, if she could chase Rex McKenna down the street, she could easily deal with Horace Furwell.

But her visitor wasn't Furwell. Standing in the middle of her showroom was Brad Peterson.

"Beth? I hope you haven't forgotten our appointment. When I didn't hear from you, I thought I'd better drop by."

Beth went to her desk and traced a finger down her day planner. "Brad, forgive me. There must be some misunderstanding. I don't have you written down."

"Oh," he said with a trace of embarrassment. "This is awkward. I was sure I saw you write it down, Beth."

Beth's black shoulder bag was slung over the back of her desk chair. "Hang on a sec, Brad," she said and pulled a small datebook from her purse. Brad's name was faintly scribbled in pencil with no time shown. Then she remembered.

"Brad, you're right," she said. "Your name's in my other book, but I didn't think we'd settled on anything definite. Actually, I thought you were just making polite conversation. You know, showing an interest in design because I was dating your friend."

"No, I was serious, Beth. I plan to go south over Christmas, so I thought if we started working up some ideas ...? I'd reschedule, but Ingrid and I are leaving for Europe on Monday. She's finishing her photo essay on bridges."

Beth remembered the photographs, and the sleekness of Brad's home. Working with him would be a pleasant change. It had been awhile since she had done a contemporary design.

"Have you got your floor plans with you?" she asked.

"No, Beth. Sorry. They're back at the house with a slew of magazines."

Beth glanced out at the window. The rain had already begun to fall, and she was bone-tired. The last thing she wanted was to drive to Muir Beach.

"Brad, I know you must be eager, but tonight is just —"

"We can both go in my car. All you have to do is sit back and listen to the stereo. We'll spend an hour, two at the most, then I'll bring you back."

"Brad, I can't ask you to drive —"

"No, listen. It's not a problem. I'm coming back to the city later tonight anyway. I've got a nine o'clock date with my lady."

She smiled. Of course Brad had a date. And energy to spare. A quick mental calculation had her back at the store to pick up her car shortly after nine, showered and under the covers by ten. Samson had received an extra helping of dry food this morning, so the cat shouldn't have anything to complain about. "You've got a deal, Brad," she said. "I warn you, though. If you keep me later than eight-thirty, my price goes up."

She heard his warm laughter. "I can handle it," he said.

49

"THIS," KEARNS SAID, HOLDING UP an enlarged copy of one of the Good Shepherd's yearbook photos, "is the face of our killer."

A collective groan went up from the task force. They congregated around Kearns who was leaning against the door to his office. Some craned their necks for a better look.

"Christ, L.T. How old is that thing?"

"My grandmother can take a better picture than that, and she's got Parkinson's."

Kearns waited until the grumbling died down, then he continued. "And this is what he might look like now." The department's sketch artist had pulled out all the stops on her talent, working to produce an illustration of what the person in the photographs could resemble today. Kearns didn't know how she did it, the photographs sent by Father Daniel being so poor, but there were all kinds of skills in the world, and he was grateful for Nancy's. When Kearns compared the sketch artist's version of Prescott with the computer image he had received from Amsterdam's homicide unit showing Klara deVries's attacker, there were definite similarities.

The paper Kearns was now holding up for his task force showed a man with prominent cheekbones, a high forehead, and close-set eyes. The hair had been updated, Nancy having given the killer a short, spiky cut. "His name is, or should I say *was*, William Prescott. And maybe, just maybe, if we schlep these around to enough places, someone will recognize this guy. He's gotta be somebody's dentist or mechanic."

"Magnin's is still open," said Bauer, pointing to the clock. "I've got time to get over there and see if Lydia Price's co-workers have seen this guy."

Kearns nodded, handed Bauer copies of both the photo and the sketch and watched him head out the door.

Anscombe spoke next. "Why don't I go back to the Bay Club? Maybe this Prescott creep met Mowatt there. Besides, I don't mind being around sweaty male bodies pumping iron on a Friday night." She flashed a broad grin, but Kearns knew Anscombe was all business.

For several minutes, the room buzzed with who would go where, then the place emptied. Kearns was left to observe Fuentes, drumming his fingers on the back of Weems's chair. "You think they'll come up empty, don't you, Jimmy."

Kearns shrugged his shoulders. "We've got to do something. If we could only find out where this bastard meets the women."

"I don't know what we've missed," Fuentes said, his fingers picking up speed. "These women didn't hang out at the same restaurants and clubs. They had different hobbies, different hairdressers, different doctors. They didn't vacation in the same places."

"Yeah, I know. We've done all this before. We may know who he is, but we don't have a clue where to look. Say, Manny? Can you knock off the Gene Krupa routine? It's driving me bats."

Fuentes stopped drumming and reached into the pocket of his sports jacket. After unwrapping a stick of Trident and popping it into his mouth, he said, "I tell you, this guy's no spider. He's a chameleon. It's like he can adapt to any place, any woman, and be anything he wants."

"But why would someone like Anne Spalding hook up with him? That's what I can't figure out. Beth said Anne was on the run, that her ex-husband beat the crap out of her. Wouldn't she be wary of men?"

"Jimmy, you and I have seen enough domestic blow-ups to know that certain folks just keep going back to the kind of person who'll do them the most harm. Maybe Spalding was one of those. Or maybe she just liked having a man in her life, for better or worse, as they say."

"I'd agree with you," Kearns answered, "only I think Anne's wounds were too fresh. According to Beth, Anne went nowhere. So where in hell would she be so relaxed that she'd forget all that had happened to her?"

"After a drink or two, you know what can happen to both memories and inhibitions."

"I don't picture this woman propped on a barstool somewhere, allowing some guy to pick her up. It just doesn't fit what Beth's told me about her."

"Newly single, renting a room in a house — maybe our killer flashed some cash around Spalding. That could appeal to someone trying to make ends meet."

Kearns considered that and tried to conjure an image of a shy Anne Spalding being smooth-talked into a situation that eventually cost her her life. "Possible, I guess. Yet somehow —"

"Look, Jimmy. We could drive ourselves nuts speculating like this. Anne Spalding isn't here to explain, so we'd better hope some of our fine young inspectors turn up something with that picture. I'll go show the updated photo to Nora Prescott. Maybe she can help us figure out if it's accurate."

"Why not? Like I said, we've got to do something." He turned toward his office.

Scarce minutes later, Kearns looked up from his desk to see Fuentes standing in his office doorway, chomping his Trident like mad. "You're not gonna believe this," Fuentes said. "Nora Prescott is no longer residing on Russian Hill."

"What?"

"I just spoke to Phillip Rossner. His precious fiancée has flown the coop."

"You're not telling me —"

"Of course I am. Rossner has no idea where Nora Prescott is."

Kearns's heart sank to the soles of his shoes. "Great," he said. "Not only do we not have the killer, now we don't even have his mother. That's just fucking great."

50

B RAD PETERSEN'S BLACK BMW 750 clung to the curves of Route I as if magnetized to the slick pavement. Though he was exceeding the speed limit, he appeared confident and relaxed behind the wheel.

Beth stifled a yawn and wondered why she had let Brad talk her into this drive. So what if he had to fly to Europe? She had worked under tighter deadlines before. Even if this meeting had waited another two weeks, she could have still designed a fantastic look in time for Christmas in the Caribbean. Had Brad not told her about his nine o'clock date, Beth wouldn't have come at all. At least this way, she knew the appointment wouldn't drag on.

Beth reached over to turn down the volume on the radio. This was a working visit, and she needed to learn more about Brad and his decorating plans. It was important that Beth's customers feel their rooms weren't merely decorated, but that they became an extension of their personalities.

"At the risk of sounding like a computer date," she began, "tell me what you do in your spare time, Brad. It'll help me get a handle on what's important to you."

"I spend most of it with Ingrid. Just can't get enough of her. She's taken me on a couple of shoots. We've waited as long as eight hours in one spot for the perfect lighting conditions."

"She must be incredibly disciplined." Beth recalled Brad's immaculate house, his silver picture frames precisely lined up. Ingrid sounded perfect for him. Then why did he sleep with Ginny?

"You'd know something about discipline yourself, running your own business. Set a goal, accomplish it, set another goal. Isn't that how it goes?"

"You're right," Beth replied, thinking of her self-imposed late hours. "Ginny thinks I'm nuts." She watched Brad's face for some reaction to Ginny's name. There was none.

"Watching Ingrid in action, I've come to think that photography is like being a peeping Tom," he said. "Crouch behind a bush long enough and you're bound to get a shot of something worthwhile."

"I've never thought of it that way," she admitted, then pressed on. "Anything else you can tell me about yourself? I know you play squash and racquetball, you throw a great party —"

"Love to cook. Great way to wind down."

"I noticed your collection of videos, too."

He nodded. "There's nothing like the old stuff, is there? *Breakfast at Tiffany's, Around the World in Eighty Days* ... not that I'm a couch potato. I do a little volunteer work at a senior citizens' home. I figure I'll be old some-day, and I might need someone to look after me."

This was a side of Brad she wouldn't have guessed existed. "The peo-ple you help must give you some interesting perspectives on life."

"You bet. They've got some great stories. They just need somebody to listen, that's all. Maybe read them the newspaper if their eyesight's failing."

Beth nodded. Brad was right. Volunteer work involved just a little time, and it meant so much. How many of her New Year's resolutions involved the promise of donating a few hours a week to some cause or group? Too many to count.

"I like to keep busy," he continued. "Plan to get into snorkelling in the Caribbean, a little windsurfing. Marriage and a family aren't far off either."

To Beth, Brad appeared to thrive as a single. "I'm sure I'm not the only one who has difficulty picturing you in slippered feet, eating tuna casserole, and helping kids with homework."

He smiled. "Nothing would please me more. Of course, the tuna casserole would have to be exceptional." He let out a chuckle. "I've been lucky, Beth. Done more than my share of globe-trotting, lived the good life, but now it's time for some stability."

"With Ingrid."

He nodded. "Popped the question last month. I was over the moon when she said yes. Ingrid will be a great mom, too." He flashed a proud smile. "What about you, Beth? Any plans to settle down? Have kids?"

"Jordan and I are taking things one day at a time. But I suspect I was handed a biological pocket watch instead of the whole clock. I don't day-dream about Fisher Price toys and trips to the zoo."

Brad didn't respond, and Beth was glad. This was getting too personal.

It wasn't long before the BMW made the turn at the Pelican Inn and headed uphill to Brad's beach house.

The floor plans for Brad's condo were laid out on his dining room table. There were detailed scale drawings with an acetate overlay showing the location of electrical sockets and overhead lighting. Beth studied the plans while Brad excused himself to the kitchen. Behind her, Beth could hear cupboard doors closing. The microwave beeped.

When he returned, Brad set a mug of mulled cider, heavily scented with cloves and allspice at her elbow, along with a small plate of assorted appetizers. "You must be famished," he said, edging the plate toward her. A cocktail napkin bore the saying: Good Friends Last a Lifetime. "I feel guilty bringing you all the way out here on a Friday night, during the supper hour, no less. And I bet you didn't have lunch." He sat opposite Beth.

"You're right," Beth admitted and stabbed a meatball with a toothpick. The sauce was spicy, zestier than ordinary barbecue flavor, with an under-taste of something she couldn't put her finger on. "Delicious, Brad. What's in these?"

"Outerbridges Sherry Pepper Sauce. Made in Bermuda. Everything else is less exotic, I'm afraid. *Chez* Brad's kitchen."

"You made all this yourself?" Beth looked at the array of appetizers.

He nodded. "Told you I like to cook."

At once Beth wondered whether she'd been foolhardy in coming out to Muir Beach in Brad's car. Was this all some ruse to seduce her? At his party,

Brad had women falling all over him. Did he expect Beth to do likewise? Clients had hit on Beth before and she had handled the situation with aplomb, she thought. Both she and Lorna had their stories about male clients who had stood too close, tried to get them to drink, wanted them to admire the view from their bedrooms. Usually, the design team went together after hours to homes where they knew women didn't reside. It was a pact she and Lorna had. But Lorna was in Vegas, and Beth was here alone. The last thing she needed was an awkward situation with Jordan's friend.

"Aren't you going to eat something?" she asked him.

"I'll just steal one of these," he replied. He reached across the table and plucked a phyllo triangle from the plate and popped it into his mouth whole. "I'm saving myself for the thin crust pizza at the Postrio bar." He patted his flat stomach. "What do you say we get down to business?"

She was relieved Brad appeared to be concerned with the design project and nothing else, and she mentally cursed her apprehension. This man was Jordan's friend. Plus he had a date later. With his fiancée. Beth checked her watch. 6:15.

"It's fairly spacious, as you can see," Brad said, interrupting her thoughts and shifting the layout closer to her. "What do you think? Can you make this my dream home away from home?"

"If I can't, no one can," she said and smiled. "Give me another moment to walk through this, okay?" She flipped back the acetate overlay and studied the plan. As she did so, she drained her mug of cider and helped herself to several more hors d'oeuvres. Brad seemed content to wait. He thumbed through a stack of decorator magazines, dog-eared a few pages, and bit into a sausage roll.

"Some lovely features, Brad," she told him, though there was really nothing exceptional about it. Then again, a camper's tent would be paradise in the Caribbean. "I'm sure we can turn this into your perfect getaway."

"Like you said, if anyone can, you can. And I meant what I said at the party. You and Jordan will have to fly down for a week or two. The four of us can do some sailing, explore the local restaurant scene. St. Bart's has some fantastic French restaurants."

"That sounds nice, Brad." Beth didn't want to encourage more than a business relationship, though she felt better that Brad had mentioned Jordan, as well as his own fiancée.

Beth continued to examine the floor plan, feeling the good quality bond paper between her fingers. The condo association had assembled a typical package. There were sheets indicating square footage and layouts of the various models, along with a list of amenities contained in the members-only athletic centre. All had been inserted into a slick forest green folder. Odd that the name of the complex hadn't been printed on the front cover.

She could hear Brad mumbling something about colour schemes, aqua or perhaps pale peach, bleached wood, an aversion to rattan furniture. Though Beth felt herself nodding, she was unable to focus on what he was saying. His words seemed to run together. She sat up straight and tried to open her eyes wide.

"Beth, are you all right?"

She should be, she thought. She had taken her medication this morning, had recently gone for her checkup, and this didn't feel like the flu. "Teach me for skipping lunch." Her words were slush.

"What can I get you?" he asked, his face full of concern. "How about some strong coffee?"

"Anything cold," she gasped. "Sorry, Brad. I'll be all right in a minute."

Brad hurried to the kitchen, and Beth forced herself to concentrate on the condo layout. It would be a breeze to decorate. It was so similar to the Stanton's new place in Tiburon, only with one less bedroom and the plan reversed. Even printed on the same kind of paper.

"Brad," Beth said as he returned to the dining room carrying a tall glass of orange juice, "where did you say your condo was?"

"St. Barts. Wait till you go there. You'll love it."

Her mouth turned to rubber, and though she willed her hand to reach for the juice, it wouldn't co-operate. It hung at her side like some sleeping invertebrate. As her eyelids entombed her in darkness, she remembered that at his party, Brad had told her that his condo was in St. Croix.

51

A T 10:30 ON SATURDAY MORNING, Horace Furwell paced the side-walk in front of Personal Touch Interiors. For the fifth time since he'd arrived, he jiggled the door handle and rechecked the business hours posted there.

Tues.–Sat.: 9:00–5:00
Thurs.: 9:00–9:00

He tapped his watch, then put his wrist to his ear. Still ticking.

Two smartly dressed women came by and mimicked what Furwell had done. One of them pressed her face to the store's display window and peered inside, muttered a few unintelligible words to her companion, then both walked away.

Furwell didn't see much point in waiting either. Must be some family emergency. These things did happen.

Ginny Rizzuto's 11 a.m. student cancelled his violin lesson. A bad flu was going around. Her noon-hour pupil had succumbed to the bug as well, so Ginny had time to kill until her next lesson at 2:00.

She telephoned Beth, had planned to pick up deli takeout and drop by the store, but to her surprise, Beth's answering machine came on. That could mean only one thing: Beth was so swamped with customers that she couldn't come to the phone. The thought of a crowded store made Ginny change her mind about going. Beth wouldn't have time to eat, nor would there be much chance for a visit. Instead, Ginny left a cheery message on Beth's machine, rammed a pile of dirty clothes into a green garbage bag, and headed to the laundromat to scout for cute guys.

At 2:00, Rex McKenna came to clean out his office. He originally intended to come after hours so he wouldn't have to see that bitch downstairs, but Ida had invited the neighbours by for an evening of canasta, so he wouldn't get another opportunity. He was starting a new job Monday, selling tools in Ida's cousin's hardware store, so he was in no position to argue with his wife. Bad enough that Ida would spend the next several months reminding him of how lucky he was that she was bailing him out. Again.

Drawing near his doorway, Rex was relieved to discover he didn't have to sidestep that designer bitch after all. She wasn't there. Whole damn store was locked tight as a chastity belt. This had to be a first. In the five years since Rex had been renting the upstairs, Ms. Yuppie Lifestyle hadn't been sick a day.

He stepped over a bouquet of fresh white roses that lay in front of her shop door. As he negotiated the narrow flight of stairs, with three empty cardboard boxes bouncing against his hips, he felt a smile spread across his face. Maybe the bitch was bankrupt, too. It would serve her right. A dark store on a Saturday afternoon was like the writing on the wall.

This called for a cigar.

Through partially blurred vision Beth could make out whiter-than-white surroundings and what appeared to be a wall of multi-paned windows about three feet to her left. It reminded her of a hospital, the room she'd been in when she was four years old. She'd had her tonsils out. Her mother was there when she awoke, knowing Beth would be frightened, coming to in a strange bed. There'd been ice cream.

She swallowed and wished she had ice cream now. Her saliva tasted awful, like salty water, and even in her half-stupor, the taste alarmed her. She blinked hard once, then again.

When her vision cleared, she realized she wasn't in a hospital at all. This was one big nondescript room with steel support posts rising at intervals from the grey cement floor to the wood-beamed ceiling. She craned her neck for a better view but found her movement limited. There was nothing wrong with her eyesight now. Her wrists and ankles were bound with packaging tape, fastening her to some kind of portable table, like the one her masseur used. She was not gagged, and she was naked.

Now that she could see, she wished she couldn't. For what she had mistaken for a large window beside her was, in reality, a series of photographs, arranged in perfect symmetry, each one equidistant from the next. There were thirty pictures in all, six columns across, five photos down, filled with the most horrific images she had ever seen. Fear and cold made her shiver, the vulnerability of her nakedness shaming her into closing her eyes. Was Rex responsible for this? Why couldn't she remember?

She squeezed her eyes shut and tried to budge her restraints, to no avail. Not only was she firmly bound, but she felt dizzy, weak, as though she'd been walking in the desert for days without water. Or was dying of starvation. Her breath quickened. She had to get out of here.

Beth opened her eyes and forced herself to take inventory of her surroundings. A solitary black metal chair sat on the floor near her right knee. Just beyond her feet, a television and VCR perched on a tall stand. An extension ladder leaned up against the far corner and beside it, a two-tiered trolley held an assortment of paraphernalia too far away for Beth to distinguish. Nearer, on the wall to her right, metal brackets supported shelves lined with various manuals. There were cones that Beth recognized as reflector bowls. A pegboard beneath held scissors, tape, a ruler and set square. Lighting stands, flood lamps, and umbrella reflectors were scattered randomly about the room. The wall straight ahead was grey.

A photographer's studio.

Her gaze returned to the gruesome wall beside her, its secrets drawing her in like a cobra's stare.

The horror seemed to escalate as she looked from left to right, and when her gaze paused at the fourth row of photographs, she froze. There was a naked Anne Spalding, her mouth wide, a cavern of mute screams. The photograph was taken in this room, Anne supine on the table that now held Beth prisoner. The camera had captured a stream of blood shooting from Anne's wrist, making an impossibly high arc in the air. The bottom picture showed Anne, eyes closed, mouth closed.

The photographs were eight-by-ten-inch massacres, bloody diaries of lives ended too soon, arranged in horrifying sequence from top to bottom: captured, bleeding, dying, dying, dead. Anne Spalding, Natalie Gorman, Patricia Mowatt on the extreme left.

To the left of Patricia Mowatt's row was a bare expanse of wall, room for more photographs. Again Beth shivered and swallowed, tasting salt. She, too, would be immortalized in this gallery, her final moments a part of this montage of torture and pain.

She had been such a fool. The pristine white of this dungeon, the perfect symmetry of the photo gallery, the chrome frames.

Not Rex McKenna. Brad Petersen. She remembered now and shuddered with dread at how easily she accompanied him, how calmly and smoothly he had spoken about his fiancée, how he'd wanted to settle down and raise a family.

From somewhere behind the wall she was facing, Beth heard footsteps. Fear, on centipede feet, skittered up her back. The door in front of her opened, and he was in the room.

"Well," the Spiderman said, smiling broadly, "finally awake? You slept right through Saturday morning cartoons."

52

JORDAN BAILEY WAS WHISTLING, AND he was no whistler. He hummed along with the radio once in awhile, sang off-key in the shower, but whistling had never been one of his skills, and this was no tune anyone could recognize. All he needed was a corsage, and he'd feel like an overgrown kid on prom night. His car had been washed and vacuumed this morning, his shoes were polished, and the slacks to his dark suit had knife creases. His hair didn't need combing, his tie didn't need straightening. He was ready.

Beth should have received the roses early this afternoon. The thought of tonight's fresh start rejuvenated him, to the point that he was in his car and driving to the Marina a half-hour early. He had waited long enough to see her.

Beth's cat was sitting on the living room windowsill when Jordan pulled into the driveway. He shut off the Mazda's engine and climbed the front steps two at a time. He was whistling again.

Four rings of the doorbell brought a response from Samson, who was now on the other side of the door, peering curiously at Jordan through the grillwork. Jordan felt the first pangs of unease when, after two more rings, Beth still didn't answer. He was early, he knew, yet if she was soaking in the tub, there'd been enough time for her to throw on a robe and come downstairs.

He pounded on the door and rang the bell again, put his ear to the glass, but all was quiet. 6:35. Was Beth still at work? He knew she had been on her own today, her assistant off on some gambling holiday. Perhaps she was still closing up or had a big sale in the works and couldn't break away. No matter, he thought. Their dinner reservations were for eight o'clock, and even if Beth didn't have time to change, she'd look fantastic anyway. Meanwhile, he would just wait in the car. She'd be along any minute.

He returned to his car, moved the driver's seat back, and waited. At quarter to seven, just as he was ashamed to admit his eyes had closed, there was a tapping at his window. It was a gawky teenager wearing Levis, a Henley shirt, and a Giants' cap on backward. Jordan clicked his key in the ignition and lowered the automatic window.

The boy stooped and looked inside the car. "You waiting for Beth?"

"Yes," Jordan answered. "Looks like she's put in a full day today. You must be Bobby Chandler. Beth's told me a lot about you."

"Call me Bob. She has?"

Jordan nodded and smiled.

"You Beth's boyfriend?"

"I'm Beth's hungry boyfriend. We're supposed to go out for dinner tonight. I wonder what's keeping her?"

Bobby shrugged his shoulders. "Wasn't around last night either. I kind of pop around to check on things. Figured she must have been out late last night celebrating Elvis's arrest."

"I beg your pardon?"

Bobby looked pleased to know something about Beth's life that Jordan hadn't yet been privy to. "Some jerk's been writing Beth creepy letters. Turns out to be the guy who rents the office over Beth's store, Rex. Dressed as Elvis on Halloween and tried to scare Beth. I helped catch him." Bobby's thumb jabbed his own chest.

But for Beth, Fridays were "cocoon nights" — bath, book, and bed by nine o'clock. Still, if her ordeal with the letters was over and the loony had been caught, Beth just might want to kick up her heels a little.

"What time were you out here last night, Bob?"

The boy thought for a moment. "I went out at 8:30. There was a party up on Pierce — lots of kids from school. I came back this way a little after one. Beth still wasn't home."

"How do you know?" Jordan asked. "She was probably asleep. The lights would've been out."

"Nope. I'm pretty familiar with Beth's routine," Bobby said emphatically. "Her living room light was on. She keeps it on a timer until she gets home."

"Maybe she just forgot to turn it off."

"She wouldn't do that," Bobby said impatiently. "Besides," Bobby glanced away, "her car wasn't in the garage."

"Tell you what, Bob. I'm going to make a run past the store. Make sure Beth hasn't had a flat tire or anything."

"Want me to come?"

Jordan shook his head, turned the key in the ignition, and shifted into reverse. "You wait here," he called to Bobby as he backed the car out of the driveway. "If Beth gets here before I do, tell her I'll be right back."

As Jordan pulled away, he noticed the expression on Bobby Chandler's face. The boy was visibly delighted to be involved in yet another intrigue, particularly since it concerned Beth.

To Jordan, this particular intrigue held no thrill, and his worry tripled upon his arrival at Personal Touch. The roses he ordered had been delivered and lay untouched across the store's doorstep, still surrounded by transparent wrap, the blooms beginning to wilt.

What the hell was going on here?

A cursory glance through the shop window was no help. There didn't seem to be anything out of place. The door was locked. He raced around to the back of the building. Beth's car was still there, but she wasn't inside it, nor could he see any sign of her when he peered through the barred windows at the rear of the store. He hurried back to his car, grabbed his cellular phone, and punched in Beth's home number. The phone rang seven, eight, nine times. Still no answer. Moments later, Jordan was heading back to the Marina, cursing every stop sign and every pedestrian who forced his foot off the gas pedal. He racked his brain wondering where she could be. Did this have something to do with that McKenna character? There'd been a pervert, too, some old fart Beth had been trying to stroke off her client list.

No. Beth wouldn't be caught alone with either of those losers. She was smarter than that, and more cautious. Car trouble. That had to be it. She had grabbed a cab and was probably just getting home now. She would apologize for her lateness, and he would find out he'd worried for nothing. Hair appointment, some last minute detail — why assume anything sinister?

Bobby Chandler was pacing the sidewalk and playing his sentinel role to the hilt when Jordan's car screeched to a stop in the driveway. The squeal of tires brought Bobby over to the car.

"Anything?"

"No sign of her there," Jordan said, and checked the digital clock on the dash. 8:00.

"Maybe Beth was running late and went straight to the restaurant."

There was an instant flash of hope, then Jordan said, "She couldn't have. She didn't know where we were going."

Bobby was on a roll now, sensing Jordan was a captive audience. He let fly a host of what-ifs, from the ridiculous to the incredibly stupid. Beth could be on a bender in some bar, abducted by aliens and used for medical experiments —

"Listen, *Bobby*," Jordan cut in.

"Maybe she just stood you up," the boy added smugly.

Jordan shot him a look, and Bobby's smile vanished.

He needed time to think, and Bobby's yammering wasn't helping.

Jordan signalled the end of the conversation by raising the window, then he reached for his phone once more. He struggled to recall Ginny's last name, knew there was a baseball connection, then remembered Rizzuto. He listened to Ginny's suggestive answering machine message four times. At 8:30, he remembered his reservation and called the Hotel Vintage Court. Masa, the hotel's restaurant, had already given away his table.

He checked his rear-view mirror constantly, as though by looking, he could make Beth's Audi magically materialize in the driveway. Every set of headlights that came up Scott Street brought him to attention.

At 9:00, he got through to Ginny, who hadn't heard from Beth and was as worried as Jordan.

By 9:30, with no hospitals reporting any recent admissions matching Beth's description, Jordan knew she was in trouble.

53

HER FINGERS AND TOES WERE freezing. Goosebumps rose on her naked flesh. Her nipples were taut, her abdomen distended. She needed to urinate.

The Spiderman drew closer. Beth jerked her head to the left and squeezed her eyes shut, as though the action would make it all go away, make him go away.

"Time to face reality," Brad said, his voice eerily calm and controlled. "I've chosen you. The least you can do is look at me, get to know me a little better. That's what you wanted, right? It's what everyone wants. To find out what makes a guy like me tick."

Slowly Beth turned her head toward the voice, opened her eyes, and examined the face of the man looming over her. He was clean-shaven and smelled faintly of cologne. His complexion was unmarred by scars or moles. A hint of a smile revealed even, perfect teeth. Dark brows and eyelashes framed his blue eyes, making them brighter, bigger, more hypnotic.

He seemed oblivious to her nakedness; his gaze did not travel the length of her body the way Rex McKenna's often had. She almost wished it would — lechery, however abominable, was at least understandable. But Brad appeared to look beyond her, to a netherworld created for him, a place where his evil took shape and festered. She could not surrender to hysteria, would not allow him to smell the fear he craved.

"I have no interest in you whatsoever," she said, surprised at the sound of her own voice. It was alarmingly normal, as though the agonizing horror that squirmed along her flesh belonged to someone else. Another Beth Wells. "How long have I been asleep?"

"It's 10:00 Saturday night."

"I've been out for over twenty-four hours?" She should be with Jordan now, all dressed up, perhaps finishing dessert. A huge lump lodged in her throat. She couldn't think about that now. Jordan didn't know where she was. He couldn't save her.

"You've obviously never used sedatives," Brad said, then dragged the chair closer to the table and sat down. "They kept you under longer than I had planned."

"The appetizers."

Beth remembered the pharmacopoeia under Brad's bathroom sink, over-the-counter drugs she had assumed Brad purchased to alleviate stress. The chloral hydrate in the sedatives, the acetaminophen, the Pepto-Bismol, all would aggravate her regular dose of warfarin. What had he given her? Again she looked down at her skin, her knees freckled with rash, her ankles bloated. Her blood was running like tap water and would soon gush to her brain or stomach, the destination of her impending hemorrhage nothing more than a crapshoot. The awful taste in her mouth. She was already dying.

She lay perfectly still, knowing her blood coursed through her body according to Brad's schedule. She had to gain the upper hand. Somehow. Even if she was powerless to move, unable to escape, she would do whatever she could to give herself some kind of upper hand. She had been a victim before. She didn't like the way it felt at age seventeen, and she was damned if she was going to allow it now. She intended to spoil this photo shoot, shatter some illusions, if only to achieve some final sense of victory.

"Are you going to carve me, like the others?"

"*Carve*. Such a savage, primitive verb. No, I'm not going to carve you. You're not like the others. I knew that immediately. You didn't even scream when you woke up. The others did."

Beth knew she couldn't scream. Didn't dare. Her larynx or trachea could hemorrhage. She would be screaming herself to death.

She kept her voice low, barely above a whisper. "What good would it do?"

"Precisely. Good girl."

This wasn't a fair fight. Beth watched him rise to his feet and start preparing the camera.

Right now, the only weapon she had, and a flimsy one it was, was time. Victims had used it in fact and fiction and Beth knew Brad would recognize any stall tactic for exactly what it was. She didn't care. She had to try.

She watched Brad climb to the top of the ladder, a camera slung over his shoulder.

"There isn't any fiancée, is there?"

He shook his head.

"But that picture beside your bed, in the silver frame —"

"My first," he responded calmly. "Her name may have been Ingrid. I don't remember. She posed happily for that photo. Right before she passed out."

"But you were with Ginny. Why not her?" she asked.

"Who?"

"Ginny Rizzuto. My friend. At your party."

"I danced with your friend. Big deal."

"You slept with her. She told me you were terrific in bed." Beth couldn't believe this conversation, a dialogue that sounded like a couple arguing on a morning talk show.

He erupted in laughter, a full-bellied guffaw that echoed in the cavernous room. "I can assure you," he managed between gasps, "I didn't sleep with your friend. On a first date? What kind of guy do you think I am?" he said with mock indignance.

"Ginny said —"

"Your friend lied." The camera's flash winked obscenely. "How nasty of her."

Of course she did. Ginny, who wanted so badly to be loved, who was always out to prove something, had lied about Brad. To save face. To show

Beth that a man who looked like Brad could actually want her. And because Ginny said she'd been with him, Beth thought it would be fine to come all the way to Muir Beach with him. Alone.

Damn you, Ginny.

"Your Caribbean condo?"

"A product of my imagination."

"Even you have to admit your story about volunteer work with seniors was a bit over the top."

Brad looked disappointed. "That, actually, is true." He paused, waiting for Beth to assimilate this bizarre information, to wonder how this gentleman killer, this butcher, could spend time performing acts of kindness for old people while randomly destroying youth, then he said, "I get some of my best drugs from seniors' medicine cabinets. Can't always be buying rat poison from the garden centres. Someone might remember my face. Retirement apartments are a warfarin paradise. All the old folks are on blood thinners, and you know how forgetful seniors can be, always misplacing things."

Duping the aged to procure drugs so he could watch women bleed to death.

"Lots of women at the party were attracted to you," Beth said, not knowing where this would take her, aware only that she had to keep talking. "Why, Brad? Why this way?"

"Such a common question. Very disappointing to hear it from you. I was sure you'd come up with something original."

He couldn't tire of her. Not yet. Beth struggled for the right thing to say.

He spared her the effort. "Could be my dysfunctional family," he shrugged, in answer to her question. "Abusive mother, alcoholic father, the usual. Or maybe it was the time I fell from the jungle gym and hit my head."

Beth lay there, not knowing how to react. Was it sympathy he wanted? Understanding? She took the therapist's approach, blinked, and waited for him to continue.

"How about impotence? A classic motive. Can't get off without hurting someone. There are guys like that. Or maybe some lousy LSD experience in high school left me unhinged. There's quite a list to choose from.

Pick one. It could be any of them, or maybe a combination of two or more. More than likely though —"

He stopped, held his breath, then stated simply, "— they're all bullshit." He smiled, not a cruel leering smile, but a matter-of-fact good old buddy smile, which made it all worse. "Really had you going there, didn't I?"

"Yes," Beth answered, "you really did."

He was still winning, still master of his game, but there was something else. Since awakening in the basement, Beth noticed a change in Brad, not just in his eyes, but in his speech. She recalled how he spoke to her last evening, both in his car and once they'd arrived at the house; she remembered, too, how Brad had worked the room at his party. He called everyone by name, used names often. A smooth public relations move.

Down here, he hadn't used her name once. Ginny, too, had been referred to as "your friend," and Natalie Gorman was "the model." In this cellar, Brad's victims stopped being people. Could she change that, get Brad to see her as a human being, or was he already too immersed in his ritual for it to do any good?

"Why the nudity, Brad?" she asked. "This isn't about sex, so why take off my clothes? Are you trying to compare me physically to Natalie Gorman? Or Anne Spalding? Is that it? Does Beth Wells measure up?"

Brad heaved a sigh and slowly rose to his feet. He looked bored again, and for a moment, Beth thought he would ignore her question and walk away. With a sudden movement, he was over her, his mouth close to her breast. "Tell me, how do you feel when you're naked? Do you feel liberated, comfortable?"

She felt the heat from his breath, and tightened every muscle until she ached. "You know I don't."

He brought his face up close to hers. "Exactly. Besides, you're a much better photographic subject without your clothes. And worth a lot more money to a discriminating clientele."

He turned away then, and walked toward the door ahead. Just before he went through, he turned to face her again. His cold whisper sliced the air. "And now, I've got something for you."

He opened the door and disappeared.

54

J IM KEARNS DRAINED HIS FOURTH mug of coffee and was debating pouring a fifth when he looked up and realized he wasn't the only guy in town without a date for Saturday night.

The Kid, Ted Weems, threaded his way through the labyrinth of desks and approached Kearns's office shaking his head. "You're too popular for your own good, L.T."

"Tell me something I don't know." Kearns had read about himself in this morning's paper, his bad reviews rivalling a B-movie actor's. "What's wrong now?"

"Look at all these messages." Weems patted his blazer then pulled several bits of paper from the inside pocket. "I hope I'm never this famous."

"You mean infamous," Kearns said, glancing at the messages. The captain had called; so had the mayor. "Jesus. I've only been gone an hour."

On Kearns's desk were three cardboard containers of Chinese food. After a week of meals consisting mainly of chocolate bars, coffee and lukewarm Cup-A-Soup, Kearns had decided to treat himself. He would reacquaint himself with vegetables and actually sit down to eat for a change. Despite his good intentions and Henry Ng's promise that his Peking duck was "focking amazing," the food had barely been sampled.

"Kid," Kearns said, "I can understand me being here eating food from a box, but you? You should be out on the town with some hot young thing.

I thought you had tonight off. What gives?"

Weems ran a hand over his close-cropped hair. "My hot young thing dumped me, L.T. Last night. Go figure, huh? Nice guy like me?"

"Hey, Kid, that's rough."

"Yeah, I thought we had something special, but I guess it was only me who thought so. Anyway, being busy helps, so I may as well stick around here. This case is getting under my skin. Bet you feel that way sometimes too, huh L.T.?"

"Quite a few times, Kid," Kearns answered, a hint of sadness creeping into his voice. "That's why I don't have a date tonight either."

Jordan didn't know what else he could do. He struggled to think of some other way to get to Kearns and convince him that Beth was missing. He hadn't been able to make contact by telephone, and it was clear the cop he'd spoken to was both overworked and preoccupied.

The young inspector had tried not to be condescending. "Lieutenant Kearns is out of his office at the moment."

"But Beth's his friend. He'd want to know."

"I'll give him the information as soon as he gets back. Still, your girl-friend hasn't been gone that long ..."

Jordan could see the look in the man's eyes, a mixture of pity and frustration. "You don't know her," he tried to explain, but already he could see the cop losing patience. Jordan scribbled his name and phone number on a slip of paper. "Give this to Lieutenant Kearns and tell him what I said. Please."

He watched the cop shove the paper into his pants' pocket.

As Jordan steered his car toward home, he felt Beth's safety slip further from his control.

"Hey, I hope everything works out and your girl shows up soon," the young inspector had said. "You seem like a decent guy."

Decent was the last thing Jordan felt like. He wanted to smash windows, run through Beth's store, her house, fling open drawers, search closets, turn over furniture, look for any clue that might tell him where she was. He wanted to scream her name.

When he arrived home and locked his door, he did exactly that.

55

BLEEDING TO DEATH.

Beth wondered how long it would take. Her physician had never told her, and why would he? Beth was always careful, took her medication faithfully, refrained from contact sports, ate the proper food. Neither she nor her doctor would assume the worst. But the worst had happened, and so Beth thought about dying.

The cut would sting, maybe burn a little, then what? Would she just fall asleep, peacefully, like some 1940s movie heroine, or would she struggle for breath, choke on her own bloody vomit . . .

The need to urinate had disappeared. Her back ached, and there was pain in her joints that had nothing to do with her physical confinement. When she glanced down, she saw that her flesh was tinged yellow. Her symptoms were worsening.

So what? She was going to die anyway. If she could control nothing else, at least she could be master of her own fate. She would do it to herself before he could do it to her.

The massage table was lightweight, perhaps on wheels like the one in her masseur's office. She could probably topple the table by rocking from side to side until it flipped over. The fall might kill her.

She jerked her neck upward and jackknifed her body, her ribcage straining against the heavy tape beneath her breasts. She rocked laterally, slapping

CATHY VASAS-BROWN

left shoulder, then right, against the vinyl of the massage table. It didn't budge.

He had bolted it to the floor.

Weary and aching, she collapsed. She would not be able to kill herself by falling.

She placed her tongue between her molars and began to press. Would it hurt, she wondered, when her teeth clamped down hard on her own flesh? Only for a moment, she rationalized, and by then, she would be past caring. She hoped that when the time came, she would have enough strength left to spit a mouthful of her own blood in Brad's face.

All at once, she hated herself. She had spent her entire life running, fleeing her hometown to escape memories of a con man, jumping from date to meaningless date. Now, faced with the malevolence of Brad Petersen, she was opting for escape again, planning her own death. She hadn't bothered to consider the alternative of living.

She remained a prisoner, held to a table by yards of tape. Grappling with her bonds guaranteed a hemorrhage. If she was to survive, she couldn't risk the tiniest bruise. There was only one solution. Brad had to free her.

He came back into the room carrying a stack of videos. "Since you're going to be here awhile, I thought you would appreciate some entertainment. No fair me having all the fun." He set the cassettes on the table beside her left hip. "I've got quite an assortment. What kind of movies do you like?"

Beth had prepared herself to appear fearless in the face of any cruelty he would inflict, but she could not have foreseen this. She didn't know how to respond.

"Please," he said, his voice adopting a maddening lilt, "you're the guest. Are you a dance fan? I've got *Top Hat.*"

This couldn't be happening. No one knew how the Spiderman's victims spent their final days, but watching an Astaire classic? It had to be a ruse, something designed to keep her off-balance. But why? Until he cut her loose, she wasn't going anywhere.

Brad removed a video cassette from the pile and set the rest on the floor. Beth watched as Brad wheeled the television set closer, then turned his chair to face the screen.

"There. All set? Good. Now just lie there and enjoy the show."

The cassette disappeared into the slot.

56

F RED ASTAIRE DID NOT DANCE in the Spiderman's version of *Top Hat*. Beth watched the events unfold on screen with revulsion as another dancer, Carole Van Horne, pleaded for her life. The woman had undergone a metamorphosis in the video, whimpering quietly at first, then hurling obscenity after obscenity at her captor. Near the end, she was reduced to garbled begging and proclamations of dreams not yet realized. She recited the names of people who loved her. Carole's final line was a gut-wrenching scream as she watched a fountain of blood spurt from her wrist.

Brad played his role without flinching, his face on screen the same as it was now — detached, bored, as though he had entered some kind of fugue state. The films no longer satisfied his hunger, Beth knew. He needed the real thing, and more often.

Beth lay paralyzed, encircled by tentacles of fear. Carole's scream made her own heart race. In spite of the relentless clamour in her head, she harnessed her emotions and forced slow, even breaths from her lungs.

On screen, Carole Van Horne died, and Beth did not turn away.

Brad cast a curious glance in her direction but said nothing. He pressed his thumb on the remote, and the film rewound. The entire video had lasted only fifteen minutes. How long had dying seemed to Carole?

Beth waited for the whirring of the machine to stop, then in a voice completely foreign, she said, "It must be frustrating for you, Brad, able only to be in one place at a time."

He arched an eyebrow. "What do you mean?"

"Well, you need to be near the women at the time of their deaths, which necessitates mounting the video camera on a tripod. I'm no film expert, but it seems that in order to capture the true essence of what's happening, some variety would be in order. Close-ups, different angles, I don't know. As it stands, the film is — well, flat. You fare much better as a still photographer."

"That is my specialty, of course," he replied nonplussed. "Still, maybe another film might be more to your liking."

Calmly, she said, "Let me look at the titles again."

She caught a flicker of surprise in his eyes.

Brad retrieved the videos from the floor and held the stack over her. One of his knuckles grazed her breast. She quelled a shudder and raised her head off the table. There were a dozen videos, all neatly labelled. The Spiderman was being held accountable for six murders in San Francisco. This collection was proof the police were just scratching the surface. Who knew how many murders he was actually responsible for?

Beth examined the titles. *An American in Paris. Funeral in Berlin. Jewel of the Nile.* Robert Altman's *Prêt à Porter.* Kathy Smith's *Low-Impact Aerobics.*

"Third from the bottom," Beth said.

She steeled herself for more real-life horror, knowing she was using others' tragedies to buy herself precious time. Still, the films removed the Spiderman's focus from her. More importantly, her reaction to the events on screen, or apparent lack of one, had thrown Brad a curve ball. The films were meant to shock, to frighten, and she'd given him none of it. Some instinct told her this shift in equilibrium was important.

Where had her instincts been the night of the party, when Brad had spoken to her, when he had stood too close, his smile too friendly? He had been a predator that night, searching for his next victim. The discomfort she'd felt at his proximity was the first ripple of fear, but she hadn't recognized it.

She had to pay attention now. Every nuance of Brad's actions, every phrase uttered on screen might provide her with the clue she needed to pull the rug out from under him.

The VCR inhaled the cassette. Seconds later, Beth choked back a sob. Too late, she realized the significance of the film's title. *Around the World in Eighty Days*, now humming in the machine, depicted the final hours of Anne Spalding.

57

WHEN KEARNS REMOVED HIS GRINDING fists from his fatigue-scorched eyes, he saw Inspector Anscombe coming toward him, her face jubilant.

"We got another bingo, L.T.," she said, perching herself on the edge of the desk. "The watch. It's Lydia Price's."

The Cartier, the one trophy Nora Prescott had been reluctant to part with. He damn near had to pry it off her arm.

During the week, Kearns had sent Sharon, with all her people skills, out to the victims' families, on what he was calling a trophy match, a who-owned-what mission. The Prices were the last family Anscombe contacted, Lydia's parents having felt the need to get away to their cabin in Tahoe for a few days. Anscombe's blue eyes, intensified by tinted contact lenses, sparkled with triumph. She appeared to be waiting for her pat on the back.

"Helluva job," Kearns managed to say, trying to muster some sincerity past the tennis-ball lump in his throat.

"The Prices didn't recognize the guy in the picture though. But we're a little closer," Anscombe said. "At least, we have an idea who he is now, right?"

Kearns nodded. The tennis ball had worked its way down Kearns's esophagus and was now lodged in his upper abdomen. En route, it had become encased in lead. He winced, his physical agony now matching his mental exhaustion.

"Sharon, you don't need much sleep, true?"

Anscombe grinned. "What do you want me to do?"

"Check all the major hotels in town, starting with the most expensive. It's time to find Nora Prescott and bring her back in for questioning. She's got to have some clue to where her son is. Use some of those persuasive people skills of yours."

The grin widened. "My pleasure. "I'll grind the shit out of her."

"Good," Kearns replied. "It's time her life got fucked up a little."

Anscombe turned to leave, then paused. Over her shoulder, she said, "Say, L.T., you did get back to that friend of yours who was talking to Weems, didn't you?

Kearns looked blank.

"You did get that message?"

58

A S THOUGH SHE WAS SISKEL to his Ebert, Brad asked her opinion of the film.

The lullaby quiet of his voice crawled over his skin. She wanted to claw at his eyes, make them run like rivers, do to him what he'd done to the others. She wanted to shatter the tomb of silence he created, yank the photos from his gallery of death, drive shards of glass through his perfect skin.

She realized then, that there were two monsters in the room.

Beth paused, made it appear she was gathering her thoughts to form an educated reply. She swallowed bile and forced the tortured image of Anne Spalding from her mind.

When Beth was certain she could respond without her voice betraying her emotions, she said, "I maintain your best work is done with a 35mm, not a video camera. That shot there, for instance" — she pointed to the photograph of her former roommate, really six overlapping Annes, one after the other, blood flowing from six slashed wrists — "there's no comparison between the artistic merit of that photograph versus the video. How was that done?"

"I used a multi-faceted lens," Brad explained with a measure of pride. "I worried the effect might be too gimmicky, but I think it came out rather well. Of course, I wouldn't ever use the same technique twice. Special lenses and filters are no substitute for imagination."

"I think that's why the stills are better than the videos," Beth told him. "The viewer can wonder 'why all the blood? Why is this happening?' The fear is more real when the imagination is allowed to run amok. The videos, on the other hand, reveal too much. There's no mystery, no room for the viewer's own intelligence."

Brad, the *artiste*, seemed to appreciate this insight. "You're right, of course. However, the market is more lucrative for video. Sometimes we creative types have to forego craft for finance."

"You don't seem to be suffering in that department. Your home, your car, all this equipment —"

"I'm an only child," Brad said. "My mother dotes on me."

Beth gulped. From the moment she'd awakened in Brad's basement, she had objectified him as much as he had her. He was the shadowy figure from all childhood nightmares. Now he was speaking about a mother. He was a member of someone's family. A chill coursed through her.

Brad laughed. "You're wondering about my mother, how she can love someone like me, what she really sees when she looks at me."

"No, I —"

"She's always known about me," he stated matter-of-factly. "Oh, she tried to close her eyes to who I was, tried to make me invisible, but I think she realizes now she can never escape. Just like you."

Beth forced the last sentence to some dark recess in her mind. *Keep the focus away from you*, her internal voice warned. "She knows about —"

"The women? She does now. Mother's been so generous, this grateful son feels compelled to shower her with tokens of affection." The scorn in his voice was unmistakable.

The souvenirs. The articles Kearns told her were taken from the victims. Given to Brad's mother.

Beth saw the anger in Brad's eyes and knew this was forbidden territory. She couldn't risk tipping his emotional scale in that direction. Not yet.

Better to stroke his ego, she thought, and cast her glance toward another one of Brad's framed photos. "How did you manage that shot?"

He followed her gaze toward an artsy picture of one of his victims. The camera must have been positioned somewhere behind the table. The woman's head dangled over the edge, her breasts thrust desperately upward, her heart still beating beneath. Her naked skin was covered with images of multi-hued bottles of nail polish. The esthetician. Monica Turner.

"I took a slide of a nail polish display in a department store, then projected the slide onto her skin, keeping the background black so the images wouldn't appear anywhere else."

As best as she could, Beth glanced around the room. "I don't see a slide projector. Or any of your lenses. Do you keep them back there?" She directed her gaze toward the door on the opposite wall.

Brad nodded. "In the darkroom."

Where there might be a way out. Or a weapon. She had to get in there, but she couldn't appear too eager. "All that equipment must cost a fortune. I really don't know much about photography —"

"And I'm sure you don't give a damn." Though his voice carried the kindergarten singsong lilt, it had taken on an edge. "This chat has been fun, a pleasant change from the usual snivelling and pleading, but you don't think this glibness will change anything, do you?"

What was left of her heart plunged into the abyss, and with it her last flimsy vestige of hope. Had she really believed she could pull this off, when at least a dozen others had failed?

At length she said, "No, Brad. I know I'm going to die here. You control when that will happen. But I refuse to worsen my situation by expending my remaining energy on bursts of hysteria." She remembered Carole Van Horne, the obscene ravings of a woman gone mad with fear.

He shot her a curious look. "This is either an Oscar-winning performance, or you're an ice woman."

"Neither," she answered. "But the Desiderata works for me. 'Lord, grant me the serenity to accept the things I cannot change —"

"Philosophy bores me," he cut in. "Especially the trite kind that's printed on posters and bookmarks." He looked at his watch and yawned.

Beth held her tongue. Whatever avenue she chose still moved her closer to the end. She had been here a little over one day, and already Brad was tiring of her, his boredom escalating too quickly. Her effort to be different from his other victims had been for nothing. Much as Brad claimed to disdain hysteria, he had probably been amused by it, perhaps empowered by it. Nothing Beth did now would make any difference. Perhaps she *should* accept what she couldn't change. She was going to die. And soon. Her nose was bleeding.

Brad produced a stark white handkerchief from his pants' pocket and dabbed at her nose. Then his thumb and forefinger pinched her nostrils together and she couldn't breathe. She jerked her head upward, opened her mouth and gasped, swallowing gulps of precious air. Blood escaped down her throat, and she coughed. Brad pulled his hand away. The bleeding slowed, a trickle oozing down her upper lip. He wiped the area clean. "There, there. It's all right. All better."

Then suddenly, as though nothing life-threatening had occurred, he asked, "How about another film? I could show you my latest release. That aerobics instructor was down here the night of my party. The night you and I met. You can faintly hear the music in the background."

Patricia Mowatt. Held captive in this tomb while upstairs scores of partygoers ate, drank, and danced. She would have heard their laughter, felt the rhythm of their celebration. Ginny, Jordan, Beth, and nearly a hundred others. And not one had saved her.

"I'd rather see your darkroom," she replied.

He leaned closer. "Why this obsession with what's behind the door?"

"No obsession. Just curiosity. For one, my neck is getting stiff. For another, I'm as vain as they come. If you're going to take my picture, I think I should have some say about how I'd like to be portrayed."

She had no idea where that had come from. She only knew that remaining confined to this table spelled hopelessness.

He appeared surprised by her statement. A victim's participation in her own death — a team effort — maybe this was the new experience Brad craved. A fresh twist to what seemed to be a tiresome ritual.

"I'll think about it," he said nonchalantly, then rose to his feet and strode across the room. The wooden door closed with a thunk.

59

T HE KID'S COMPLEXION LOOKED LIKE it had been doused with bleach. Ted Weems struggled for composure, but despite his discomfort, Kearns wasn't done with him.

"Goddammit, Kid. What the hell happened?"

"The message was in my pants' pocket, L.T. I guess I forgot about it."

"Jesus. Women's bodies all over the place, my friend is missing, and you forgot. Explain how a conversation like that could slip your mind."

"I don't know, L.T. I screwed up. I wasn't thinking straight. But your friend hasn't been gone that long."

Kearns bit his lip. He hadn't bothered to close his office door and some of the cops in the next room were doing their best not to appear to be listening. For everyone's benefit, Kearns raised his voice another notch. "Look, Kid. This is a major fuck-up. When you walk into this building, you leave your personal problems outside the door."

"Yes, L.T. Sorry, L.T."

"You'll be sorrier if my friend doesn't turn up. Bet your last dollar on it. Now get out of here so I can find out what the hell is going on."

Weems spun around and made a clumsy exit, smashing his hip against the door jamb.

"Goddammit," Kearns muttered after Weems had gone.

Kearns's midnight call to Jordan Bailey nearly gave the poor bastard a coronary.

"Beth!"

"No, Bailey, it's Lieutenant Kearns."

"Have you found her? Where is she?"

The panic in Bailey's voice made his own heart quicken. "Take it easy. What the hell happened?"

"I went to pick her up at seven. She never showed. And I sent flowers. To her store. They're still in the doorway, wrapped up. Beth never opened for business this morning, Lieutenant."

Kearns didn't like the sound of that. Saturday was Beth's busiest day. "Let's rule out a few things before we go jumping the gun. Family emergency?"

"No. Ginny called Beth's parents. Everything's fine at their end."

"We're not dealing with anything like a lover's spat, are we?"

"So she leaves her car at the store? Come on, Lieutenant. You know Beth. She'd call someone."

If she could. The pilot was right. Something wasn't adding up.

"Get some sleep, Bailey. I'll see what I can do."

"Just find her, Lieutenant. Please."

The second Bailey had hung up, Kearns vaulted into action. Two members of his team were dispatched to check out Beth's house in the Marina; another pair combed the coffee shops along Chestnut Street.

Kearns drove to Beth's store, worry gnawing at his insides. It could be nothing, he tried to tell himself. A sick friend, he imagined. There could be a dozen logical explanations, yet Kearns couldn't ignore the shooting pains in his stomach, nor could he get the voice of Jordan Bailey out of his mind. Days ago, Kearns had been prepared to hate him and was ready to arrest the guy if he so much as crossed his eyes. But tonight, hearing the emotion in his voice that was barely concealed by a slight cough, Kearns was drawn into an allegiance with the pilot.

At Personal Touch, Kearns shone his flashlight through the storefront window, though nothing within the showroom appeared suspicious. The white roses were where Bailey said they were, just inside the doorway, untouched.

The sight of Beth's Audi, the only vehicle in the rear lot, sent a wave of sadness through him for reasons he couldn't quite explain. The beam of his flashlight revealed what Bailey had already told him — the car was empty, and though he flattened his palm against the hood, he knew what he would discover. The engine was cold.

Kearns went to his car, grabbed a tire iron, and punched the Audi's trunk lock, just in case. He let out a relieved sigh when the trunk hinged open, revealing nothing more than a gym bag and a folded beach chair.

Two windows flanked the store's service entrance, both shielded by wrought iron cages. Kearns jammed his flashlight between the bars of each window, but there was no sign of Beth at the back of the store either. The door's lock hadn't been tampered with.

The tire iron was put to use a second time, and Kearns entered the store, but the flashlight revealed what he already knew — Beth wasn't there.

Five years ago, when Mary was threatening to walk, Kearns made a bargain with God — no more booze, he promised. Just let me keep my wife. He'd lost out big on that one. Luckily, he hadn't burned any religious bridges. Perhaps he could still strike another deal, although he wondered what he had left to trade to ensure Beth's safe return.

Anything, he suddenly realized. I'll give you anything, sweet Jesus. Just bring Beth back.

He checked his watch. 1:30. He called the station, saying he needed two officers to take his place at Beth's store in case she returned for her car. He asked Anscombe to look up Rex McKenna and find out what he knew, and no, he didn't give a shit what time it was.

Anscombe told Kearns that Jordan Bailey had called his office twice.

"There's nothing here, Bailey," Kearns said after he dialed the pilot's number. The man was a basket case. "It pretty much looks like she locked up on Friday night and someone picked her up after work. You call me if you hear from her, and I'll do the same." Then he added, "I'm sorry."

"Me too, Lieutenant. Me too."

In spite of mobilizing half his task force to search for Beth, he felt useless. His friend needed help, and he knew it, marrow-deep. Kearns was barely conscious of traffic signs or other vehicles as he steered through the quiet streets, his vision clouded by the recurring image of a dozen wilted roses.

60

With brad gone from the room, Beth expected to feel relief. Instead, she felt worse. She would never know what he was thinking, yet while he was with her, she could monitor his facial expressions, gauge his reactions to her spoken words, and perhaps learn something that might save her. Left on his own, she knew how dangerous Brad was.

It was pointless to worry about it. Second-guessing every word she uttered was a waste of energy and time, and her body was telling her she didn't have much left of either. Her stomach was beginning to cramp. She contracted her sphincter, knowing that bloody diarrhea would be the next indignity. She gazed at her left wrist, the one Brad said he wouldn't carve. It appeared yellower now, with a faint white band where her watch had been.

Minutes, or perhaps hours later, Brad appeared in the doorway to his darkroom. He had changed his clothes. His white shirt looked crisply starched. He was clean-shaven, and a trace of his citrusy aftershave wafted across the room. This was all part of the torture, Beth knew, a physical reminder that Brad's life would go on, that he, in this freshly groomed state, was superior while she grew more pathetic, more hopeless.

Brad hesitated on the threshold, then came over to her carrying a glass of orange juice and a pair of handcuffs. "Tit for tat," he said, and set the juice glass on the table between her thighs.

Beth tensed her muscles, the proximity of his hand to her vulva evoking a new set of fears.

"You drink this, and I'll give you the grand tour."

She knew what was in the glass. It wouldn't poison her if she drank it, but it would kill her just the same. "I'm not very thirsty right now," she answered, the tremor in her voice revealing the fear she had tried so hard to control.

Gently, Brad lay the handcuffs across her bare abdomen, the bracelets arranged in perfect symmetry on either side of her navel. From the back pocket of his trousers, he produced a knife, its pure white blade glinting obscenely in the light of the flood lamp. He let it hover over her, caressed it with his gaze, then moved it slowly in the air, watching the light play off its surface.

In one swift move, it was against her throat. "We can get this over with right now," he whispered. "Is that what you want?"

"I thought you said I was different," she babbled, the press of the blade insistent at her neck. "You said you wouldn't cut me."

He shrugged. "This wouldn't be the first time something hadn't gone according to plan. I could just start here —" the tip of the knife pressed at the base of her throat "— and work my way down to here —" He traced a line between her breasts, continued downward past the handcuffs until the knife poised above her pubic hair. "I'd hide your body, too. Your family wouldn't know what had become of you. Your beloved Jordan would be heartsick, maybe spend years searching for you, waiting for you to come home. The police wouldn't have a clue that you'd ever met their Spiderman."

Please, she thought. Let this be quick. If she had to die, she didn't want to see it coming. One swift plunge of that white blade, and it would be over. She closed her eyes.

His breath was close to her face now. Time stretched until she felt herself strain toward the knife, each minute she was alive becoming not the gift she had hoped for, but excruciating agony. But the blade didn't enter her, and she couldn't sense where it was. There was only his breath, crawling over her like an army of ants, and the damnable smell of his cologne.

She opened her eyes and glanced at her body. The knife hadn't pierced her skin.

Brad held it over her abdomen and playfully flicked the blade with his thumb. He grinned. "You want to die now, don't you," he crooned. "You're like a little bird that's flown against a window. You can't move, and being alive is torture."

"You said I was different," she cried out, the last trace of composure gone from her voice.

A derisive laugh escaped from his mouth, and he shrugged again. "There's plenty more where you came from. Now, did you say you were thirsty?" He removed the glass from its resting place between her legs and lay the knife in its place.

When Brad raised the glass to her lips, she drank. Though she tried to swallow slowly, the liquid flowed down her throat. She clamped her lips against the glass, hoping some of the juice would dribble from the corners of her mouth. Brad's free hand reached for the knife.

In the end, she drained the contents of the glass, expecting the mixture to taste foul, bitter, to give some indication of the damage it was meant to do. It tasted like orange juice.

"I'll show you how different you are," he announced and turned toward the two-tiered trolley in the corner. Seconds later, he wheeled the trolley beside the table, then held his right palm outstretched. On it rested a small box.

"Straight pins," she whispered. "No."

He nodded, and explained the inevitable. "You'll be my human sieve. My fountain of blood." He placed the box on her belly.

Her last shred of strength evaporated, and the tears came, flowing freely from the corners of her eyes, dripping into her ears. "Please." She heard herself whimper, "No." She hated herself but couldn't stop.

Brad scooped up a camera from the trolley and took her picture. Then a dozen more. He moved around the table, capturing her suffering from every conceivable angle.

She lashed her head from side to side, trying to avoid the sickening flash. "Please," she sobbed. He zoomed in close, clicked off three more shots. "Brad, I don't want to die."

"There, there," he trilled. "Not time yet. I promised you a tour, remember?" He produced a pristine white handkerchief from his pants pocket and dabbed at her eyes. His touch was gentle, almost paternal, as he wiped her temples, the surface of her ears, the flesh of her cheeks.

"Before we go," he said, leaning closer, "tell me what you were doing at the Good Shepherd in Ventura."

"You followed me?"

He smiled, then folded the handkerchief into a perfect square and returned it to his pocket.

Her mind raced for an answer, but whatever drugs he had given her had made it sluggish. "I was checking you out," she said. "I was attracted to you at the party, but when I spoke to one of your former teachers, he said you were bad news. Nothing could be proven, but he warned me to stay away from you anyway."

"Really?" he said with a hint of a sneer.

Beth kept going. "And I told Lieutenant Kearns about you, that you fit the profile of the man the police are looking for."

Brad examined her face, studying her like a laboratory specimen. She held her breath as he drew closer. His lips touched her ear. "You're the worst liar I've ever met."

"No, I —"

He shook his head. "There's an art to lying, you know. If you interject enough truth into your story, that's when lies become believable. You're nowhere near mastering the craft. My former teachers have never heard of Brad Petersen. You really went to my alma mater to check out your boyfriend, am I right? Yes, of course you did, especially after I happened to mention a certain flight attendant he used to date."

He played me, Beth thought, from the moment he met me. And I was fool enough to let him.

"Good old Jordan. I remember him from school, you know. Helluva basketball player in those days. I admired that about him. Of course, being a few years older, he never gave me the time of day. Mind you, the tables have turned now, haven't they? Your Jordan just can't seem to hang on to a girlfriend. And his squash game is mediocre." He stared deep into her eyes and added, "Just doesn't have the killer instinct."

She felt one of the handcuffs encircle her left wrist, then Brad attached the other bracelet to his own wrist. He reached down and knifed through the tape binding her feet, freed the bonds across her hips, then her chest and arms. He allowed her to swing her legs around and slip down from the table. She wobbled unsteadily, the cement floor cold on her bare feet. Her nose was bleeding again.

"Come into my parlour," the Spiderman said.

61

BY 2:00 A.M. ON MONDAY, Jordan was past the point of questioning his own sanity, aware that much earlier, he had crossed over the threshold into the realm of madness.

He removed his shoes, his feet swollen from having paced the kitchen tiles for the better part of Sunday, and brewed a second pot of coffee. He was still wearing the same T-shirt and track pants he had on yesterday. He didn't dare shower, wouldn't risk the sound of running water drowning out the phone's ring. His normally clean-shaven face was itchy with razor stubble, and there were spots on both cheeks he had scratched bloody.

He poured a mug of coffee and watched it get cold.

He had known such impotence only once before. The memory of standing in his mother's bedroom doorway, in his best clothes, watching her earning her living in her naked glory paralleled how he felt now, paralyzed by the fear of what he had learned and powerless to change it.

Machines were easy, a 747 to him nothing more complicated than a car. It was people he had trouble with, and it had been much easier to bury his emotions where they couldn't find him, couldn't hurt him.

Beth had changed all that. The two of them, wounded by their past, had found peace in each other, and more quickly than he thought possible. Being with Beth was both exhilarating and calming, and he felt liberated by her, unaware until he'd met her that he required liberation.

He had to find her. He called Kearns's work number and discovered the lieutenant was still there. Jolted by caffeine and desperation, he bolted up the stairs, grabbed a hooded sweatshirt, then threw on a pale yellow windbreaker. The brunette on the weather channel was predicting rain. In less than an hour, Jordan had Ginny replacing him by his kitchen telephone, and he was on his way downtown.

The lieutenant was reorganizing his desk, shuffling file folders from one pile to another. Jordan looked at his pressed shirt, the smooth skin, and felt a pang of empathy. Though Kearns had gone through the motions of freshening up, there was a defeated look in the man's eyes that a shower and a change of clothes would not mask.

Kearns looked up. "You couldn't sleep either?"

"No sign of her?" Jordan asked.

Kearns shook his head. "Nothing." He motioned to a vacant chair. "Coffee?"

"No thanks. I'm already fuelled for lift-off," Jordan said. "We've got to do something."

"Listen," Kearns said, "I have my crew looking everywhere, but they've turned up squat. And Bailey, I've got leads to follow up on. I've still got to find this lunatic before Sondra Devereaux, the mayor, and the rest of the city lynches me. More importantly, I just can't look at another corpse."

"That's why Beth's absence has me crazy. What if the Spiderman has her? Are you any closer to finding the killer?"

Kearns snorted. "Well, we know it isn't you. You had my vote for a while. Any idea how closely you fit the profile?"

"Look at this face, lieutenant," he tried to joke, the sound of his voice hollow. "Is this the face of a killer?"

"No, and this guy doesn't look like one either," Kearns replied, shoving a photocopied sheet across the desk, "but he's probably our man anyway. Face of an angel, if only we could find him."

Jordan took the paper and stared at the photograph. It was a copy of a picture taken nearly twenty years ago, judging from the hairstyle. The blazer with its trademark crest and piped lapels drew Jordan's gaze closer. "This is the Spiderman? This guy went to the same school as me."

"See what I mean about the profile? Don't suppose you recognize him?"

Jordan shook his head. "I didn't mix much during my school days. Kept my nose in the books. Played basketball because of my height, but this guy wasn't on the team, I know that. Wasn't in any of my classes either. What's his name?"

"William Prescott. Ring a bell?"

Jordan paused for a moment, feeling a slight niggling thought. He tried to concentrate. "No," he said at last. "I thought there might be something, but it's no good forcing it. If there's something for me to remember, it'll come. But I'm not much for memories of that time. I never even bought the yearbook."

"That picture came courtesy of Father Daniel Fortescue. Here's the only other picture we have of the guy."

Jordan took the sheet. It was a blown-up copy of a sports page from the Good Shepherd's yearbook, a messy collage of geometric cutouts showing various athletes in action. Jordan was able to pick out one of himself going for a lay-up shot, though due to the enlargement process, some of the details had become blurred. "Father Daniel sent you pictures? Why?"

"When I have an hour, I'll tell you."

The photo of William Prescott had been circled with red felt-tip pen. It showed a taut, muscular body, angled mid-air, rigid right arm extended, a badminton racquet poised to make a tough return. The face was locked in a grimace of athletic effort. An alarm went off in Jordan's head.

"Let me see that other picture again." His gaze travelled the short distance between the two photos, but it was the one of the badminton player that nagged at him. Jordan examined the teeth, the nose, the slant of the forehead, stared at the picture until his vision blurred.

He rearranged the papers on Kearns's desk, located three unimportant scraps and lay them on top of the graduation photo, one above the boy's forehead, the other two over his ears. The hair was completely covered.

"Oh, Jesus. No. It can't be."

Kearns vaulted to the other side of his desk. He looked at the photographs, then at Jordan. "Can't be what?"

"The hair's dark in these pictures. That's what threw me off, but dammit, I know that face. It's Brad Petersen."

"Who the hell is Brad Petersen?"

"He's a guy I play squash with a couple of times a month. It's the face in the badminton picture that I recognize. Brad doesn't play to lose. I'm almost sure it's him."

Kearns looked at the picture again. "Almost? You nearly give me a coronary for *almost?*"

"Hey, take it easy. People change. I don't look like the goofy kid in this basketball photo either."

Suddenly, Jordan knew there wasn't time to think. He sprang from the chair and grabbed Kearns by the sleeve. "Come on!"

"What the hell — Bailey!"

Jordan was already sprinting for the door. He hollered over his shoulder. "Do you want to meet the guy in the picture or not?"

He was halfway down the aisle between rows of desks when Kearns caught him by the hood of his sweatshirt. "Hold up a minute!"

"Sit," Kearns ordered, rolling a chair toward the pilot. Bailey remained standing. Kearns perched on a nearby desk. "Tell me what just happened here."

"Anne Spalding. She met Brad. And now she's dead. And Beth —" His breath came in quick gasps. "We can't stand around talking. We've got to get her out of there!"

Kearns shook his head in confusion. "Fill in some missing pieces, Bailey. How did Anne meet Brad?"

"A party." Jordan paced the floor between the arcade of desks. He told Kearns about the parties hosted by the members of the fitness club. "Anne and I stopped seeing each other shortly after she met Brad at the party I hosted. And when I took Beth out to Brad's place, he pretended to be all over her friend Ginny. But I watched him. It was Beth he was staring at." A sickening realization dawned. "I led them both straight to him. Anne and now Beth. Brad's hair is blond now. But his eyelashes and eyebrows are dark. It's one of the things Anne noticed right away."

"Dyes his hair?"

"I don't know. Probably. But while we're standing around —"

"Hold on a minute," Kearns replied, stepping closer. "You're not going anywhere except home. I'll go check out this Petersen character. Give me his address."

Jordan scrawled the information on the scrap of paper that Kearns shoved at him. "But it's hard to find. I'm coming with you."

"The hell you are." Kearns's strong hands gripped his shoulders. "I don't climb into the cockpit with you, do I? Go home. Wait by the phone. I'll call you as soon as I know something."

Jordan was about to argue, but Kearns was inches from his face, his fingers digging into flesh. "Go home," he repeated.

62

THE SPIDERMAN'S INNER SANCTUM WAS a well-equipped, well-ventilated laboratory, its L-shaped countertop loaded with an assortment of beakers, trays, tongs and funnels. A portable projection screen leaned against a corner. Beside it, Beth's clothes hung from a chrome coat rack, her shoes and purse arranged symmetrically on the floor. There was a sink, and a paper towel dispenser was affixed to the wall above it. Everything in its place.

Brad had several shelves mounted on metal brackets over the counter-top, three of which contained identical ring-binder photo albums arranged vertically, each with a dated label along its spine. Victims' catalogues. The one closest to Beth was dated: November, 2000.

Brad conducted the tour of his darkroom like the proud owner of a greenhouse full of rare orchids. He pointed to his photo enlarger, developing tanks, a print trimmer, but Beth's gaze remained fixed on two items lying on the counter near a timer: a pair of scissors and an X-Acto knife. Brad noticed them too and used his free hand to whisk them into a drawer, all without a pause in his seminar.

She had been too slow, and it had cost her. It would be impossible for her to open the drawer without his knowing. The other knife, the one with the white blade, was in Brad's left rear pants pocket. To get to it, she would have to swing around, position herself back to back with him and pull the knife from his pocket before he grabbed it. It couldn't be done. He would use it on her first. She had to think of something else.

Blood from her nose trickled down her chin. Tear-shaped droplets landed on her bare chest. With the fingers of her right hand, she pinched her nostrils to stanch the flow.

"I thought you were interested in my hobby," Brad said sulkily, "but you haven't said much since we came in here. After all the trouble I've gone to."

"You're right," she said, thinking quickly. "I wanted to know how you did some of your special effects, you know, like on the photographs in the other room."

He led her to a section of countertop at the extreme end of the L and slid open a drawer. The inside was compartmentalized like a woman's jewellery box, each labelled cubicle containing a protective case. He showed her what he called a multi-image filter, its glass surface cut to resemble large facets on a gemstone. Then there was a split-field close-up lens, starburst filters, defraction filters, over a dozen colour filters, and a fog filter.

But while it was clear Brad enjoyed talking about himself, Beth was running out of time. She pinched her nostrils constantly, but her nose was no longer merely dripping. Blood flowed steady and warm down her upper lip, and she lapped at it with her tongue as though the act of swallowing it would delay her exsanguination.

On a shelf above the drawer of filters lay several lens attachments. Some were small but there were a few huge cylinders — zoom lenses, Beth guessed. Because of their weight, the photographer would need a tripod to hold the camera steady. She kept her eye on the largest one. While Brad droned on about sandwiching slides to produce a composite picture, Beth stole glances at him through her peripheral vision. She studied his profile, calculated the swing arc from her right hand to his nose and hoped her aim would be true.

"Why do you need so many lens attachments?" she asked him. "There are at least fifteen on this shelf."

"Photographers like to experiment. There's always some gadget on the market that might give a fresh approach to an overused subject."

Like dead women. Beth reached toward the smallest lens. "Tell me about this one."

While Brad explained the uses of the lens she had selected, Beth turned it over in her hand, then held it up to her eye and peered through. She did not replace the lens on the shelf; instead, she put it in front of her on the counter and asked about another lens midway along the shelf. For a moment, it appeared Brad would take the small lens and put it in its rightful spot, but to Beth's relief, he began to lecture about the benefits of the second lens Beth had chosen.

"I think I'm beginning to understand a little more about photography, though I can't possibly imagine anyone lugging this thing around. It must weigh a ton." She grabbed hold of the biggest lens, tilted it toward her eye and took a look. She feigned disgust at its heft and put it down, nudging it slightly further away from the other two, but still within reach.

Brad was still too much in the present, too wary of her and her questions. She had to find a way to induce that fugue state, the one she'd seen in the videos right before he had cut his victims. When he became truly lost in his fantasy, caught up in the exhilaration of whatever it was that drove him to kill, his reaction time would be slowed. It might be only a micro-second, but it was all she had.

She turned to face him. "Tell me about the first person you killed."

63

KEARNS THOUGHT HE HAD PUT on a reasonable performance for
Bailey, his apparent calmness serving to get the pilot the hell home.
In truth, Kearns didn't feel the slightest bit calm. He was strung tight, and
for the first time since the disappearance of the first victim, Carole Van
Horne, his cop's nose had picked up the scent of a killer.

Van Horne had been found on Route I, the road Petersen would take
to get from his place in Muir Beach to the city.

I made him change his name, Nora Prescott had said.

Kearns applied more pressure to the gas pedal and watched the
speedometer needle respond. If Petersen was Prescott, and if he had Beth,
Kearns had little time. As much as he wanted to bring the bastard in himself, he knew he needed backup. Muir Beach was out of SFPD jurisdiction.
Kearns reached for his cell phone. The Marin County sheriff let Kearns
know that patrol officers were on the way.

The Crown Victoria screeched to a standstill in the double driveway.
Kearns bolted from the car and ran through the mist to ring the doorbell.

Fuentes greeted him wearing a T-shirt, boxer shorts, and a scowl. This
time, Rosalie didn't bother to conceal her anger. "Four thirty in the morning! Goddamn it, Manuel! Maybe he should move in here, and I should
move out!" Kearns heard a door slam upstairs, then a child's voice.
"Mommy, what's wrong?"

"There," Fuentes said. "Satisfied? Wasn't enough for your marriage to fall apart, now you come here to screw up mine?"

Kearns flapped his hands. "We've got no time for this. Grab some pants. We're going spider hunting."

"What?"

"Trust me, Manny."

Fuentes massaged a worried brow, then cast a fleeting glance upstairs. "Give me two minutes."

Kearns waited in the hallway, heard more harsh words from overhead, remembering too well the clash of job with home. Mary, like Rosa Fuentes, had despised the late-night phone calls, the absolute urgency of an immediate response, her second-fiddle status. In the beginning, she had tolerated the weeks and months of tension when he worked on a case, and the boredom after it was solved. But Mary elected not to follow her husband into his dark corner. Her reason for leaving had been summed up in one sentence: she wanted to laugh again.

Minutes later, Fuentes descended the stairs, now clad in khakis and a wool sweater. He refused to get into Kearns's car. "How much sleep have you had in the past week? Five, six hours max? I'll drive. We'll take my car. I've got a full tank of gas."

The two men headed out the door, Fuentes careful not to let the wind slam it shut. Kearns took one look at the four-year-old Taurus, complete with a pair of beaded seat covers, and groaned. "That thing's an embarrassment." A peeling "Mom's taxi" decal adorned the rear window, put there by one of the Fuentes brood during an unsupervised moment. Kearns groaned again but climbed in anyway.

Route I north was slick with fresh falling rain, and Mom's taxi didn't appreciate it. Every curve in the road was accompanied by a plaintive squeal.

"Dammit, Manny," Kearns hissed. "Can't this crate go any faster?"

"This is a fine car." Fuentes patted the dashboard and applied the brake. Another squeal. "It's the tires that are shit. Besides, I'm not about to get us both killed. What if this turns out to be some wild goose ch —"

"Might not be so wild." Kearns filled Fuentes in on his conversation with Jordan Bailey.

"So that's what this is about? Your girlfriend's missing?"

"Yeah, Beth's missing," he replied, his annoyance plain. "But is that the only thing you've heard? Bailey saw the photo of Prescott. He's almost sure it's this Petersen guy."

"Wait a minute," Fuentes said, removing his gaze from the road to shoot Kearns a look. "We're out in the wee hours. It's pissing down rain. All because of an 'almost sure?'"

"I know, I know." The tires met the gravel shoulder. "Keep your eyes on the road, would ya?"

Fuentes worked the wheel, and the car regained traction.

"Petersen and Bailey belong to a health club. Young clientele. Real emphasis on the social. The members take turns throwing parties. Theme nights. Getting-to-know-you things. Invite an Out-of-Towner. Bring Your Cousin. All guests have to come in threes. So even if there's a couple, it's the third person that does the mixing, but it doesn't have that swinging singles sleaziness about it. It seems like a safe way to meet people."

"And you think he does his trolling there? How many people at one of these shindigs?"

"Hundred — Bailey's ballpark figure. Just think about it. A smorgasbord of unattached women parading around, and Petersen gets to play the sheik. The guy doesn't have to hit one bus station, bar, or university campus. He can hunt right in someone's living room. He window shops, selects his victim, throws a little charm her way, maybe gets her phone number. Or he learns enough about her through small talk that he can familiarize himself with her routine. Then he accidentally shows up somewhere he knows that she'll be. 'Hey, I remember you. Party out at so-and-so's.' Could go something like that."

Fuentes increased the speed on his wipers. "Yeah," he nodded, "it could. But we don't know that it does."

"What better way for the killer to relieve his post-murder depression than to go to a party, gear up for his next ritual?"

"Shee-it!" Kearns hollered. "Watch it!"

A fat raccoon waddled across the lane. Instinctively, Fuentes's foot hit the brake. He clutched the wheel as the car went into a skid. "Mother of

God," he intoned and released his foot from the brake. Again the car found traction, and both men exhaled simultaneously. From the passenger mirror, Kearns saw the raccoon continue across the road and vanish into a ditch.

Fuentes squinted through the rain-streaked windshield, then said, "Maybe you better get on the blower and call the Marin County SO for backup. This is no time for heroics."

Kearns nodded. "Already done. With any luck, they should get there ahead of this bucket and have the bastard cuffed by the time we arrive. But just in case, could you speed it up a little, Manny?"

Fuentes manoeuvred a sharp curve in the road. His face nearly touched the steering wheel as his whole body leaned into the curve. When the pavement straightened, he relaxed his shoulders a little and said, "Worst-case scenario. Petersen is the Spiderman. He's got your friend. We know the killer keeps the women alive for nearly a week. Beth Wells hasn't been missing for that long. She's still okay."

"That's where you're wrong," Kearns told him. "Beth has an artificial heart valve. She already takes blood thinners. If that bastard has given her anything beyond her required dosage, she could already be a dead woman. So for God's sake, Manny, *now* will you show me what this fucking car can do?"

64

"You've been outsmarting the police for years, haven't you?" The Spiderman smiled. Beth looked for evil in the expression, some trace of a sneer, but found none. Brad's smile radiated warmth. "I've been killing since I was thirteen," he told her. "Animals don't count, do they?"

Beth hadn't expected this. She felt sick, wanted to vomit but choked it back. She couldn't afford to lose more fluid. She needed whatever strength she had left.

She swallowed, controlled her intake of air and tried to guess what reaction he would want. "Thirteen? You must have been extremely smart even then."

"Don't be so transparent. The others tried to flatter me too, you know."

She tried to ignore the skittering of fear up her spine. "I'm not trying to flatter you. I'm just amazed that you could keep something like murder a secret. Most young people boast about their misdeeds. Certainly most aren't bright enough to cover all their tracks. How did you do it?"

"The police focused on the older boys, ones who'd already had trouble with the law. They weren't going to centre their investigation around a thirteen-year-old altar server whose mother made generous contributions to the school."

"Thirteen," Beth repeated. "You must have been filled with anger."

He related a tale of a mother who cared more about buying cosmetics than providing her son with a hot meal, how she had let him lie at the bottom of the cellar steps while she entertained a male companion. "I had fallen," he said, an edge of bitterness in his voice, "and I could hear her tell the guy I was just doing it for attention. She actually told the bastard I was her nephew. By the time she sent me away to school, I was determined to make something of myself. I wasn't going to be invisible to her anymore."

He spoke about two elderly priests and the abuse he had suffered at their hands. As his thoughts drifted, he turned his body toward the counter, leaning on it for support. Beth cast nervous glances at the zoom lens, then at Brad's profile, mentally adjusted the angle of the swing arc to compensate for his new posture. She needed to see his eyes. Just one glimpse at his face would tell her how deeply entrenched he was in his story. Standing shoulder to shoulder, she couldn't tell. "The old bastard was dying in the hospital," Brad was saying. "The shock of the fire was too much for him. Still, I wished he hadn't gone quite so peacefully. I was determined that Anthony would kick off with more of a bang." There was a curious high-pitched giggle. "I drugged the Communion wine. And the decanter of sherry in his room. Anthony always had a nip or two before saying Mass. By the time the police got there, I had wiped my fingerprints from the decanter and was joining in with the commotion. Everyone was nuts, running around screaming about how Anthony had hurled himself off the bell tower. No one even noticed me. It was all so easy."

Beth detected the singsong lilt in his voice, the same one she'd heard when she had awakened in Brad's basement two days ago. She thought then that he was crooning to mock her. Now she realized he was comforting himself, the way children rock themselves or suck their thumbs.

"We all saw him standing up there, his vestments flapping. He looked like some clumsy stupid bird. I didn't know he would die then. It worked out better than I ever dreamed. Do you have any idea what it sounds like when someone's head hits the pave —"

Beth swung the heavy lens in a horizontal line through the air and smashed it against the bridge of his nose. Brad's left hand came up, touched blood. He let out a brief whimper of pain — or was it surprise? Beth didn't wait for another. She struck again, this time coming up low and hitting the point of his nose. There was a sickening crunch and blood spurted from his nostrils onto her chest, mingling with her own. A third swing, then a fourth. She lost count after that, only knowing she needed to knock him out and wouldn't stop until she had.

When Brad slumped onto the cement floor, Beth was dragged down with him, the pressure from the pull on her handcuffs causing her to cry out. Lying naked on top of him filled her with a new revulsion. She half-expected him to open his eyes and grin at her. How badly had she hurt him? Carefully, she rolled off him, wondering how much time she had before he regained consciousness. She used her free hand to probe his pockets for the key to the handcuffs. His front pockets were empty. Frantic, she reached behind him, jammed her hand between his buttocks and the cold cement floor and wrestled the knife from his back pocket. She set the knife on the floor beside her, away from Brad. He wouldn't realize she had it, and if he came to, she knew she would kill him, plunge the blade deep into whatever part of him she could aim at. But she wouldn't use it unless she had to. Beth continued to probe his pockets for the key to the cuffs.

The damn key could be anywhere. She clawed at his starched shirt, buttons popping as she tore it open. Resting on the Spiderman's nearly hairless chest was a Chi Rho medallion, exactly like Jordan's. It seemed to mock her from where it lay. Filled with rage and frustration, she yanked the chain until it broke, then she flung the necklace across the room.

The labyrinth of storage containers, drawers, and cupboards that surrounded her were all potential hiding places for her key to freedom. Or it could be up in the house. Wherever it was didn't matter. Beth's body told her there wasn't time to search. Her stomach heaved, and she rolled toward Brad and vomited, the bright red froth spattering Brad's chest. She tasted salt and heaved again.

When her insides ceased their spasm, she squeezed the thumb of her left hand against her baby finger, hoping that, after little nourishment and some fluid loss, she could make her hand small enough to fit through the handcuff. The metal bracelet got as far as the padded muscle beneath her thumb and stayed there. A small bruise formed around the first knuckle bone. She relaxed her hand and remembered the knife.

With the tip of the knife's blade, Beth poked carefully at the keyhole. One slip would be fatal. The handcuffs held fast. She saw nothing in the room strong enough to smash against the metal bonds. The photo cropper, X-Acto knife, and scissors were as useless to her as the ceramic knife.

There was only one thing she could do. She had to get out of this dungeon. There was no telephone here, and no one could help her if they couldn't see her. Her only hope was outside and that meant dragging Brad with her.

He was shorter than Beth by almost four inches, but he was a solid mass of athletic muscle and Beth, in her weakened state, knew she couldn't possibly get him to his feet. She clamped the knife between her teeth, used her free right hand to grasp at Brad's belt and struggled to pull him. The stickiness of her own vomit felt cold against her bare skin. The pressure of Brad's weight against the handcuff bracelet made Beth cry painfully between teeth clamped on the knife blade. A bruise was already forming on her wrist.

She hazarded a glance at his face, inches from hers. Her cry hadn't awakened him, but when she tried to adjust her grip and raise herself to a standing position, her knees buckled and they both toppled to the floor. The ceramic knife flew from her mouth, then Brad's body hit the cement, breaking the impact of Beth's fall. She heard his head smack against the concrete. There was no danger of Brad regaining consciousness any time soon.

Beth caught her breath, kneeled on the floor, straddling Brad, carefully planted her feet where her knees had been, and rose to a jackknife position, her crotch over the Spiderman's face. The handcuffed wrist couldn't withstand further injury. The bruise was an angry purple now, so her free arm would have to do all the work. Reaching down, Beth picked up the knife and clenched it between her teeth once more, and began to drag Brad across the floor. When she reached the door to the darkroom, she stopped to rest, but only for a split second. Vision in her right eye was cloudy, and she knew the eye had hemorrhaged. She released her grip on the Spiderman and reached up to where her clothes hung from the metal stand. She tugged her blouse from its hanger and shoved it into the space between the hand-cuff and her wrist. The flimsy silk would be a small buffer for her bruised skin, but she had to hurry. It was a long way to the outside, and the trek might kill her, but she was determined not to die here in this horrible place. Gritting her teeth against the knife blade, she tugged at Brad with both hands and staggered to the next door.

The distance across the room, a room she'd traversed easily not so long ago, seemed to lengthen with each painful step. When she finally reached the door, she could barely see, and felt a tug of fear. What if the door was locked?

The knob turned easily in her hand. Of course Brad hadn't expected her to escape, nor did he, in his deluded mind, ever think anyone would discover the truth about him and come to search his lair. The door opened, and Beth felt the rush of fresh air hit her body.

Through blurred vision, Beth could make out a glimmer of light, a pale grey rectangle overhead, and to reach it, she had six, no — seven steps to climb, with a load that grew heavier with each breath. Her whole being screamed out for rest. She could just curl up here, in the doorway to the Spiderman's prison. She could die a peaceful death. In minutes, overcome by exhaustion, she would fall asleep, and her body would continue to hem-orrhage. There would be no violent spasms, no pain. The Spiderman would be denied his grand finale. Brad would awaken to find her already dead, and paradoxically, she would triumph. There was some dignity to that. Others had not been as fortunate.

But the light overhead continued to beckon, and Beth adjusted the blouse around her injured wrist, bit down hard on the knife blade, and began to climb the stairs.

65

KEARNS AND FUENTES COULD HAVE parked in Petersen's driveway. They could have knocked on his door, introduced themselves, asked some routine questions. They could have listened to Petersen's lies. They could have waited for the backup from Marin, which, because of an overturned truck blocking the road, had yet to arrive. Instead, Kearns made Fuentes steer the Taurus in the direction of the deserted beach, his cop's sixth sense guiding him toward an ambush from the rear.

His intuitive nose had led him astray before, his antagonism toward Jordan Bailey way off the mark. If Kearns was wrong now and Sondra Devereaux got wind of it, she would bust a gut laughing, right before she crucified him. He patted his jacket, felt for his cell phone and his revolver, and got out of the car.

The predawn sky was the colour of mercury. By the time Fuentes stepped around the car to join Kearns, he was soaked. Both men moved across the sand toward the homes, an assortment of beachy architectural styles at the top of a steep grade.

"Which one is Petersen's?" Fuentes shouted above the storm.

"Fourth one up the hill," Kearns hollered back and pointed, remembering the description Bailey had given him. "Redwood deck and all the windows. Let's go."

Kearns broke into a run, with Fuentes keeping pace right behind. Beneath Petersen's deck, there was a flicker of movement. Kearns wiped his eyes with a soggy sleeve. "What the hell was that?"

Fuentes squinted, the rain pelting against his face. "Where? I didn't see anything."

Kearns gestured frantically. "Near the deck! Something moved up there! Come on!"

Fuentes pulled his gun, but Kearns, recognizing the pale yellow jacket, grabbed his arm. "Wait! It's Bailey!"

The two men raced across the wet sand and scrambled up the hillside. The rain had turned the slope into freshly poured concrete. Their shoes formed dents in the sand as they dug their toes in for a firm hold. When they finally reached the top, neither was prepared for the gruesome sight awaiting them.

Beth lay sprawled face down on the ground, the last of her strength expended on raising her head in hopes of making herself more visible to someone, anyone. The sight of her nude body shackled to a fully clothed Brad Petersen filled Kearns with unbelievable loathing. He grabbed his phone from his pocket and called for a chopper as he watched Jordan Bailey wrap his windbreaker around Beth.

It seemed eons until the helicopter arrived. In the distance, Kearns heard the mournful wail of sirens, then the muffled stampede of the back-up units swarming the place, the sound of his own bargain with God drowning out the surrounding din.

Let her be all right, and I'll do whatever you ask.

Bailey covered Beth's body with his own, shielding her from the driving wind and rain. Beth was aware of nothing. She was unconscious.

Kearns was cold to the bone, his earlier numbness now surpassed by a full body shudder. Despite the fleece-lined tracksuit one of the rookies had found him, and the strong hot coffee he'd forced himself to drink, Kearns was certain he would never be warm again. He spotted Jordan Bailey at the end of the hospital corridor not looking much better. Four empty Styrofoam cups sat on the table next to him.

"Had to report to the captain," Kearns said. "I got back here as soon as I could. How's she doing?"

Jordan rose to his feet. Kearns saw the effort it took, put a hand on the pilot's shoulder and guided him back onto the seat. Kearns dragged another chair from its perfectly aligned row and sat across from him.

"Still critical," Jordan told him. "They're giving her fresh frozen plasma. The doctors are trying to bring her prothrombin level back to normal, but even if they do, it'll be at least two weeks before we'll know if she's over the worst of it."

"Son of a bitch." Kearns didn't know what the hell a prothrombin level was, but it didn't take a Ph.D. to know that Beth was in bad shape. When they had come upon her naked and cuffed to her captor, Beth's skin had been a perverse patchwork of hues. There were bruises the colour of African violets, blood-red eyes, muddy rust-coloured blotches across her chest, upper lip and chin, and a horrible yellow cast to the parts of her not covered in sand, gravel, and grass.

Kearns had nearly lost his mind in the rescue helicopter, could barely restrain himself in his seat. He felt only a microbe of relief when the sight of the large "H" of the hospital helipad appeared just beyond the windshield.

Only once during the ride did Beth open her eyes, and above the thwacking of the copter's rotor, she uttered one word.

"Who's Kay?" Kearns now asked, remembering.

"Not who," Jordan answered. "What. *Vitamin* K. It's the primary agent used to clot blood."

Kearns nodded. "I'll never forget those red eyes. Her wrist looked pretty bad, too."

"Imagine her dragging that sicko, the condition she was in."

"She needed to get outside. She had no way of knowing we were coming for her."

"Doctor said the handcuffs had a lot of scratches on them," Jordan told Kearns. "Looks like she tried to break free. Where was the damn key?"

"In the bastard's shoe."

Jordan buried his face in his hands. "Shit."

Kearns clamped a supportive hand on Bailey's shoulder. "You gonna tell her Petersen was already dead?"

The Spiderman, Kearns had told the ravenous press, had died when the cartilage from his nose was rammed upward into his brain. The city had its hero. Now all she had to do was pull through.

66

J IM KEARNS GAVE HIS PANTS a generous tug. In the six weeks since
Brad Petersen's death, Kearns had shrunk a belt size. He was battling
chronic fatigue, his sense of desolation nearly equal to those bleak months
following his divorce. The adrenaline bursts and the mental challenge of
the Spiderman investigation were replaced by a kind of post-crime depression. A return to the same-old-same-old. Kearns imagined Brad Petersen/
William Prescott bottoming out like this on a month-by-month basis.

When he neared Beth's home, he noticed changes there, too. There was
no Christmas wreath on the door, no coloured lights strung on potted
conifers. After being ushered inside, Kearns was struck by the same sense
of abandonment. Unread mail littered the top of the desk. Miscellaneous
shoes piled up near the door. Purses hung from doorknobs. Still, the air
bore the aroma of a simmering *coq au vin*, a dish Beth had promised to cook
for him and one he'd looked forward to all day.

She greeted him with a smile, and he wrapped her in a bear hug, sum-
moning every effort to keep his mood light. Kearns presented her with a
bag of shortbread cookies from his neighbourhood bakery. "Pardon the
look of the place," she said. "I just got home."

"Really?" Kearns inhaled deeply. "Then who's —"

Jordan Bailey emerged from the kitchen with a tray bearing three mugs of
spiced eggnog. "Hi, Jim. Hope you don't mind me playing chef this evening."

"Not if it tastes as good as it smells."

They sat in the living room, Jordan and Beth close together on the loveseat, and Kearns on a chair opposite. Samson wrapped himself possessively around Beth's ankle.

"It's Monday," Kearns said. "Don't tell me you went in to work?"

Beth shook her head. "I've started volunteering. At Sanctuary."

Sanctuary was a safe haven for battered women. The Victorian house, with its rusty iron fence and peeling paint buried itself among others like itself in Haight-Ashbury, the shelter's system of passwords, padlocks, and alarms a grim reminder that there were potential killers everywhere.

"I think it will be good for me, Jim," Beth said. "My adversary is dead. So many others still exist."

Kearns gave her a smile of encouragement, and the three quietly toasted the season.

"You'll never guess who volunteers at the shelter with me."

He shrugged and took a long swallow of eggnog. "I give up. Who?"

"Sondra Devereaux."

"Well I'll be damned. Every time I try to hate her, something like this happens." He set his mug on the table.

They spoke about Ginny Rizzuto, who had sent flowers and phoned daily. Beth had finally agreed to have lunch with her on Friday. "I suppose I'll have to forgive her," Beth acknowledged. "But she's got some changing to do, that's for sure. If you'll excuse me, I'll go check on dinner." Beth rose, gave Samson a gentle nudge, and both cat and owner headed toward the kitchen.

Once she had gone, Kearns quietly asked, "Is she all right?"

Jordan nodded. "Most days are pretty good, but she's had a few rough nights." He spoke of Beth's troubled sleep, when unbidden images would loom up to haunt her, images of a handsome man hovering over her, his deep blue eyes impaling her with their gaze until the eyes became four, then six, then eight. Then he wasn't a man anymore, but a slavering, grotesque spider. The horrid sensation of mandibles twitching near her face invariably awakened her screaming. "On those nights," Jordan said, "we pop a comedy into the VCR and stay up until dawn."

Kearns knew all about bad dreams and those dreadful hours before sunrise that should be tranquil but often were not. "The dreams will go away in time," he said, avoiding Bailey's gaze.

"You sound skeptical. She's doing just fine, Jim. Really."

"Of course she is. She's got you." He paused, felt his cheeks warm, then said, "I never did thank you. I should have."

"What for?"

"If you hadn't come back to the station and identified Brad in that picture, Beth might not be with us. She's pretty special."

"I know," Jordan said. "I'm glad you two are friends. And you know I had to go out to Brad's house. I was the fool who introduced her to him in the first place."

Kearns hung his head. Seated across from him was a man he'd originally thought to be too pretty to be anything but a lightweight; now he knew Bailey had real guts. He reached into his trouser pocket, took out a small velvet box and flipped open the lid. "You think Beth is strong enough to deal with this?"

Beth re-entered the room carrying a large bowl of salad. Samson followed close at her heels. She looked at Kearns's hand, then set the bowl on the dining room table and stepped toward him. "What's that?"

Inside the box was a pair of diamond stud earrings.

"Oh, no," she gasped. "Not the ones Anne bought."

Kearns cut her off. "You sure as hell paid for them."

"What do I do with them? I can't w —" Her voice caught.

Kearns snapped the lid shut and handed the box to Jordan. "Shove 'em in a drawer someplace. Maybe someday you'll be able to see them as just a nice pair of earrings."

Jordan rose to his feet and planted a tender kiss on Beth's forehead. "You don't have to decide anything right now, Beth. Why don't we eat? Jim could use a few pounds."

Over dinner, the conversation was superficial. They traded commentary about what had made the evening papers—the newest shock-rock group, the crime rate as Christmas approached, a recent political scandal.

It wasn't until Kearns was preparing to leave that Beth mentioned the earrings again. "I'm going to sell them," she announced calmly. "The women at Sanctuary can use the money. I think Anne would be pleased, don't you?"